TALES FROM

THE
ROGUES'
GALLERY

TALES FROM
THE ROGUES' GALLERY

A Guided Tour by
PETER HAINING

WARNER BOOKS

A *Warner* Book

First published in Great Britain
by Little, Brown and Company in 1994
This edition published by Warner Books in 1995

A CIP catalogue record for this book
is available from the British Library.

ISBN 0 7515 1318 0

Printed in England by Clays Ltd, St Ives plc

Warner Books
A Division of
Little, Brown and Company (UK)
Brettenham House
Lancaster Place
London WC2E 7EN

For
Pete and Beverley Francis
— with whom we've spent many
a roguish evening

Contents

Introduction

Some years ago there was a rumour that Madame Tussaud's were offering a reward of £5,000 to anyone who was brave enough to spend a night alone in the Chamber of Horrors. It was said that only one person had ever done so: a policeman who indulged a little too freely in the liquid refreshment at a reception to mark the opening of the original Chamber under the Marylebone Road, and he was discovered there flat out the following morning. It was the alcohol and certainly nothing which occurred during the night – it was said – that had ensured his oblivion to any horrors seen . . . or imagined.

Of course the offer was only a rumour, but I don't suppose for a moment that I was the only small boy who had heard the story and, believing it to be true, discussed with some friends the possibility of braving the terrors of that cellar full of waxworks at Madame Tussaud's. Nor do I imagine I would have been the only one not quite brave enough to put my name forward if it *had* been true!

The thought of a visit to the Chamber of Horrors has always been enough to give anyone, regardless of age or sex, a little shiver of anticipation. I have certainly enjoyed all my visits: studying those displays of figures and pictures of some of the most infamous creatures of evil and their wretched victims. Today, of course, the Chamber of Horrors has competition from the London Dungeon and similar establishments in York and Edinburgh, all of them bearing witness to our delight at being half scared to death by coming into close proximity to the most notorious men and women from the past, albeit that they are only made of wax and hair and, sometimes, the clothes the famous originals wore.

In fact, wandering amongst these waxworks gave me the idea for this collection. The seed began to grow as I looked at the kitchen where Christie had hidden the corpse of one of his victims, then took shape as I passed the bathroom where one of George Joseph Smith's brides lay gasping for air below the surface of her bath, and flowered when I stopped to stare at Crippen with his mistress Ethel le Neve so incongruously disguised as a boy. How could my imagination also remain unmoved at the sight of Burke and Hare manhandling one of their corpses, or the shadow of Jack the Ripper across the mutilated remains of Catherine Eddowes while nearby Mary Kelly leant on her doorway waiting to become the killer's last victim? Each of them studies in infamy – and the raw material from which, I have discovered, great short stories of crime and horror have been woven.

In the intervening years, my interest in mystery fiction as a whole – from murder to the supernatural – has introduced me to a variety of stories featuring these rogues and villains. I found the first few examples when my interest was young (as I was, too), but since then many more have come to my attention, and the best of them now form the collection herein. I would not claim it to be a labour of love, rather a gruesome one, which at the same time has enabled me to bring together within the covers of one volume some of the most respected names in crime and fantasy fiction.

The Chamber of Horrors is now just 110 years old – its doors were first opened in 1884 – but the scope of the exhibits there cover a much wider period of history, as indeed do the contents of this book. From Nero to Crippen, Cesare Borgia to Reginald Christie and from the body snatchers to the serial killers, the collection ranges through almost two thousand years. Not forgetting, of course, that ageless patron of villainy, Satan himself.

The contributions are divided into two sections: firstly, tales about the rogues themselves; and, secondly, stories of the continuing influence their crimes have had on society. Great evil transcends time, it has been said, and the reader will soon discover that the authors are in full agreement.

Apparently, the late Brian Johnston also once had the idea of broadcasting all night from the Chamber of Horrors in the hope of hearing or seeing the ghost of the Grey Lady who supposedly haunts the building. In the end, he settled for transmitting from 6 p.m. until just before midnight when, having experienced nothing untoward, he beat a thankful retreat to the bright lights of Baker Street. I would also not recommend sitting up with the rogues in this gallery a moment after the witching hour . . .

PETER HAINING, December 1993

Section One

THE ROLL OF INFAMY

Down, Satan!

CLIVE BARKER

The Devil, as mankind's archetypal villain throughout all of recorded history – the tempter who offers worldly possessions in return for souls – needs no introduction. He has been portrayed in tales and illustrations since time immemorial and continues to fascinate writers of horror stories right through to the present day. Clive Barker, the author of this first story, also requires very little to be said about him. Since his stunning debut with the six-volume Books of Blood *(1984–5) he has proved himself a master of the genre and a favourite with readers through out the world. His interest in the Devil has been evident since that first collection – as well as his Faustian novel,* The Damnation Game, *published in 1985 – and emerges here again in 'Down, Satan!'. What may at first seem like one more story in the time-honoured tradition on the 'Pact With The Devil' theme, very quickly becomes something far more ingenious and sinister . . .*

CIRCUMSTANCES HAD MADE Gregorius rich beyond all calculation. He owned fleets and palaces; stallions; cities. Indeed he owned so much that to those who were finally charged with enumerating his possessions – when the events of this story reached their monstrous conclusion – it sometimes seemed it might be quicker to list the items Gregorius did *not* own.

Rich he was, but far from happy. He had been raised a Catholic, and in his early years – before his dizzying rise to fortune – he'd found succor in his faith. But he'd neglected it, and it was only at the age of fifty-five, with the world at his feet, that he woke one night and found himself Godless.

It was a bitter blow, but he immediately took steps to make good his loss. He went to Rome and spoke with the Supreme Pontiff; he prayed night and day; he founded seminaries and leper colonies. God, however, declined to show so much as His toenail. Gregorius, it seemed, was forsaken.

Almost despairing, he took it into his head that he could only win his way back into the arms of his Maker if he put his soul into the direst jeopardy. The notion had some merit. Suppose, he thought, I could contrive a meeting with Satan, the Archfiend. Seeing me *in extremis*, would not God be obliged to step in and deliver me back into the fold?

It was a fine plot, but how was he to realize it? The Devil did not just come at a call, even for a tycoon such as Gregorius, and his researches soon proved that all the traditional methods of summoning the Lord of Vermin – the defiling of the Blessed Sacrament, the sacrificing of babes – were no more effective than his good works had been at provoking Yahweh. It was only after a year of deliberation that he finally fell upon his master plan. He would arrange to have built a hell on earth – a modern inferno so monstrous that the Tempter would be tempted, and come to roost there like a cuckoo in a usurped nest.

He searched high and low for an architect and found, languishing in a madhouse outside Florence, a man called Leopardo, whose plans for Mussolini's palaces had a lunatic grandeur that suited Gregorius's project perfectly. Leopardo was taken from his cell – a fetid, wretched old man – and given his dreams again. His genius for the prodigious had not deserted him.

In order to fuel his invention the great libraries of the world were scoured for descriptions of hells both secular and metaphysical. Museum vaults were ransacked for forbidden images of martyrdom. No stone was left unturned if it was suspected something perverse was concealed beneath.

The finished designs owed something to de Sade and to Dante, and something more to Freud and Krafft Ebing, but there was also much there that no mind had conceived of before, or at least ever dared set to paper.

A site in North Africa was chosen, and work on Gregorius's New Hell began. Everything about the project broke the records. Its foundations were vaster, its walls thicker, its plumbing more elaborate than any edifice hitherto attempted. Gregorius watched its slow construction with an enthusiasm he had not tasted since his first years as an empire builder. Needless to say, he was widely thought to have lost his mind. Friends he had known for years refused to associate with him. Several of his companies collapsed when investors took fright at reports of his insanity. He didn't care. His plan could not fail. The Devil would be bound to come, if only out of curiosity to see this leviathan built in his name, and when he did, Gregorius would be waiting.

The work took four years and the better part of Gregorius's fortune. The finished building was the size of half a dozen cathedrals and boasted every facility the Angel of the Pit could desire. Fires burned behind its walls, so that to walk in many of its corridors was almost unendurable agony. The rooms off those corridors were fitted with every imaginable device of persecution – the needle, the rack, the dark – that the genius of Satan's torturers be given fair employ. There were ovens large enough to cremate families; pools deep enough to drown generations. The New Hell was an atrocity waiting to happen; a celebration of inhumanity that only lacked its first cause.

The builders withdrew, and thankfully. It was rumored among them that Satan had long been watching over the construction of his pleasure dome. Some even claimed to have glimpsed him on the deeper levels, where the chill was so profound it froze the piss in your bladder. There was some evidence to support the belief in supernatural presences converging on the building as it neared completion, not least the cruel death of Leopardo, who had either thrown himself or – the superstitious argued – been pitched *through* his sixth-story hotel window. He was buried with due extravagance.

So now, alone in hell, Gregorius waited.

He did not have to wait long. He had been there a day, no more, when he heard noises from the lower depths. Anticipation brimming, he went in search of their source, but found only the roiling of excrement baths and the rattling of ovens. He returned to his suite of chambers on the ninth level and waited. The noises came again; again he went in search of their source; again he came away disappointed.

The disturbances did not abate, however. In the days that followed scarcely ten minutes would pass without his hearing some sound of occupancy. The Prince of Darkness was here, Gregorius could have no doubt of it, but he was keeping to the shadows. Gregorius was content to play along. It was the Devil's party, after all. His to play whatever game he chose. But during the long and often lonely months that followed, Gregorius wearied of this hide-and-seek and began to demand that Satan show himself. His voice rang unanswered down the deserted corridors, however, until his throat was bruised with shouting. Thereafter he went about his searches stealthily, hoping to catch his tenant unawares. But the Apostate Angel always flitted away before Gregorius could step within sight of him.

They would play a waiting game, it seemed, he and Satan, chasing each other's tails through ice and fire and ice again. Gregorius told himself to be patient. The Devil had come, hadn't he? Wasn't that his fingerprint on the door handle? His turd on the stairs? Sooner or later the Fiend would show his face, and Gregorius would spit on it.

The world outside went on its way, and Gregorius was consigned to the company of other recluses who had been ruined by wealth. His Folly, as it was known, was not entirely without visitors, however. There were a few who had loved him too much to forget him – a few, also, who had profited by him and hoped to turn his madness to their further profit – who dared the gates of the New Hell. These visitors made the journey without announcing their intentions, fearing the disapproval of their friends. The investigations into their subsequent disappearance never reached as far as North Africa.

And in his folly Gregorius still chased the Serpent, and the Serpent still eluded him, leaving only more and more terrible signs of his occupancy as the months went by.

It was the wife of one of the missing visitors who finally discovered the truth and alerted the authorities. Gregorius's Folly was put under surveillance, and finally – some three years after its completion – a quartet of officers braved the threshold.

Without maintenance the Folly had begun to deteriorate badly. The lights had failed on many of the levels, its walls had cooled, its pitch pits solidified. But as the officers advanced through the gloomy vaults in search of Gregorius they came upon ample evidence that despite its decrepit condition the New Hell was in good working order. There were bodies in the ovens, their faces wide and black. There were human remains seated and strung up in many of the rooms, gouged and pricked and slit to death.

Their terror grew with every door they pressed open, every new abomination their fevered eyes fell upon.

Two of the four who crossed the threshold never reached the chamber at its center. Terror overtook them on their way and they fled. Only to be waylaid on some choked passageway and added to the hundreds who had perished in the Folly since Satan had taken residence.

Of the pair who finally unearthed the perpetrator, only one had courage enough to tell his story, though the scenes he faced there in the Folly's heart were almost too terrible to bear relating.

There was no sign of Satan, of course. There was only Gregorius. The master builder, finding no one to inhabit the house he had sweated over, had occupied it himself. He had with him a few disciples whom he'd mustered over the years. They, like him, seemed unremarkable creatures. But there was not a torture device in the building they had not made thorough and merciless use of.

Gregorius did not resist. Indeed he seemed pleased to have a platform from which to boast of his butcheries. Then, and later at his trial, he spoke freely of his ambition and his appetite; and of how much *more* blood he would spill if they would only set him free to do so. Enough to drown all belief and its delusions, he swore. And still he would not be satisfied. For God was rotting in paradise, and Satan in the abyss, and who was to stop him?

He was much reviled during the trial, and later in the asylum where under some suspicious circumstances, he died barely two months later. The Vatican expunged all report of him from its records. The seminaries founded in his unholy name were dissolved.

But there were those, even among the cardinals, who could not put his unrepentant malice out of their heads, and – in the privacy of their doubt – wondered if he had not succeeded in his strategy. If, in giving up all hope of angels – fallen or otherwise – he had not become one himself.

Or all that earth could bear of such phenomena.

A Story of Don Juan

V. S. PRITCHETT

Don Juan has been described as 'one of the worst lechers and scoundrels in Rennaisance Spain'. Certainly the enduring legend about this rogue has been such as to make him the subject of innumerable works of art and literature – including stories and poems by Molière, Byron, Balzac, Robert Browning and George Bernard Shaw – as well as Mozart's famous opera, Don Giovanni. *Scholars have devoted a great deal of research to the origins of the Don Juan legend, a popular theory claiming that he was based on a certain Don Juan Tenorio of Seville who – like the 'hero' of the legend – is said to have seduced a girl and killed her father when he protested. According to tradition, the callous Don then invited a statue of the father to a feast – and when the man of stone actually arrived, the libertine found himself seized and dragged off to Hell. V. S. Pritchett is one of the leading English novelists and short story writers of this century and has an enviable reputation for bringing to life unusual characters through his use of dialogue and description. This skill has rarely been better employed than in the following tale of Don Juan in which even his fabled powers of seduction seem destined to fail . . .*

IT IS SAID that on one night of his life Don Juan slept alone, though I think the point has been disputed. Returning to Seville in the spring he was held up, some hours' ride from the city, by the floods of the Quadalquiver, a river as dirty as an old lion after the rains, and was obliged to stay at the finca of the Quintero family. The doorway, the walls, the windows of the house were hung with the black and violet draperies of mourning when he arrived there. God rest her soul (the peasants said), the lady of the house was dead. She had been dead a year. The young Quintero was a widower. Nevertheless Quintero took him in and even smiled to see a gallant spattered and drooping in the rain like a sodden cockerel. There was malice in that smile, for Quintero was mad with loneliness and grief; the man who had possessed and discarded all women, was received by a man demented because he had lost only one.

'My house is yours,' said Quintero, speaking the formula. There was bewilderment in his eyes; those who grieve do not find the world and its people either real or believable. Irony inflects the voices of mourners, and there was malice, too, in Quintero's further greetings; for grief appears to put one at an advantage, the advantage (in Quintero's case) being the macabre one that he could receive Juan now without that fear, that terror which Juan brought to the husbands of Seville. It was perfect, Quintero thought, that for once in his life Juan should have arrived at an empty house.

There was not even (as Juan quickly ascertained) a maid, for Quintero was served only by a manservant, being unable any longer to bear the sight of women. This servant dried Don Juan's clothes and in an hour or two brought in a bad dinner, food which stamped up and down in the stomach like people waiting for a coach in the cold. Quintero was torturing his body as well as his mind, and as the familiar pains arrived they agonized him and set him off about his wife. Grief had also made Quintero an actor. His eyes had that hollow, taper-haunted dusk of the theatre as he spoke of the beautiful girl. He dwelled upon their courtship, on details of her beauty and temperament, and how he had rushed her from the church to the marriage bed like a man racing a tray of diamonds through the streets into the safety of a bank vault. The presence of Don Juan turned every man into an artist when he was telling his own love story – one had to tantalize and surpass the great seducer – and Quintero, rolling it all off in the grand manner, could not resist telling that his bride had died on her marriage night.

'Man!' cried Don Juan. He started straight off on stories of his own. But Quintero hardly listened; he had returned to the state of exhaustion and emptiness which is natural to grief. As Juan talked the madman followed his own thoughts like an actor preparing and mumbling the next entrance; and the thought he had had when Juan had first appeared at his door returned to him: that Juan must be a monster to make a man feel triumphant that his own wife was dead. Half-listening, and indigestion aiding, Quintero felt within himself the total hatred of all the husbands of Seville for this diabolical man. And as Quintero brooded upon this it occurred to him that it was probably not a chance that he had it in his power to effect the most curious revenge on behalf of the husbands of Seville.

The decision was made. The wine being finished Quintero called for his manservant and gave orders to change Don Juan's room.

'For,' said Quintero drily, 'his Excellency's visit is an honour and I cannot allow one who has slept in the most delicately scented rooms in Spain to pass the night in a chamber which stinks to heaven of goat.'

'The closed room?' said the manservant, astonished that the room which still held the great dynastic marriage bed and which had not been used more than half-a-dozen times by his master since the lady's death – and then only at the full moon when his frenzy was worst – was to be given to a stranger.

Yet to this room Quintero led his guest and there parted from him with eyes so sparkling with ill-intention that Juan, who was sensitive to this kind of point, understood perfectly that the cat was being let into the cage only because the bird had long ago flown out. The humiliation was unpleasant. Juan saw the night stretching before him like a desert.

What a bed to lie in: so wide, so unutterably vacant, so malignantly inopportune! Juan took off his clothes, snuffed the lamp wick. He lay down conscious that on either side of him lay wastes of sheet, draughty and uninhabited except by the nomadic bug. A desert. To move an arm one inch to the side, to push out a leg, however cautiously, was to enter desolation. For miles and miles the foot might probe, the fingers or the knee explore a friendless Antarctica. Yet to lie rigid and still was to have a foretaste of the grave. And here, too, he was frustrated; for though the wine kept him yawning, that awful food romped in his stomach, jolting him back from the edge of sleep the moment he got there.

There is an art in sleeping alone in a double bed but, naturally, this art was unknown to Juan; he had to learn it. The difficulty is easily solved. If you cannot sleep on one side of the bed, you move over and try the other. Two hours or more must have passed before this occurred to Juan. Sullen-headed he advanced into the desert and the night air lying chill between the sheets flapped, and made him shiver. He stretched out his arm and crawled towards the opposite pillow. Mother of God, the coldness, the more than virgin frigidity of linen! Juan put down his head and, drawing up his knees, he shivered. Soon, he supposed, he would be warm again, but in the meantime, ice could not have been colder. It was unbelievable.

10

Ice was the word for that pillow and those sheets. Ice. Was he ill? Had the rain chilled him that his teeth must chatter like this and his legs tremble? Far from getting warmer he found the cold growing. Now it was on his forehead and his cheeks, like arms of ice on his body, like legs of ice upon his legs. Suddenly in superstition he got up on his hands and stared down at the pillow in the darkness, threw back the bed-clothes and looked down upon the sheet; his breath was hot, yet blowing against his cheeks was a breath colder than the grave, his shoulders and body were hot, yet limbs of snow were drawing him down; and just as he would have shouted his appalled suspicion, lips like wet ice unfolded upon his own and he sank down to a kiss, unmistakably a kiss, which froze him like a winter.

In his own room Quintero lay listening. His mad eyes were exalted and his ears were waiting. He was waiting for the scream of horror. He knew the apparition. There would be a scream, a tumble, hands fighting for the light, fists knocking at the door. And Quintero had locked the door. But when no scream came, Quintero lay talking to himself, remembering the night the apparition had first come to him and had made him speechless and left him choked and stiff. It would be even better if there were no scream! Quintero lay awake through the night building castle after castle of triumphant revenge and receiving, as he did so, the ovations of the husbands of Seville. 'The stallion is gelded!' At an early hour Quintero unlocked the door and waited downstairs impatiently. He was a wreck after a night like that.

Juan came down at last. He was (Quintero observed) pale. Or was he pale?

'Did you sleep well?' Quintero asked furtively.

'Very well,' Juan replied.

'I do not sleep well in strange beds myself,' Quintero insinuated. Juan smiled and replied that he was more used to strange beds than his own. Quintero scowled.

'I reproach myself: the bed was large,' he said. But the large, Juan said, were necessarily as familiar to him as the strange. Quintero bit his nails. Some noise had been heard in the night – something like a scream, a disturbance. The manservant had noticed it also. Juan answered him that disturbances in the night had indeed bothered him at the beginning of his career, but now he took them in his stride.

Quintero dug his nails into the palms of his hands. He brought out the trump.

'I am afraid,' Quintero said, 'it was a cold bed. You must have *frozen.*'

'I am never cold for long,' Juan said, and, unconsciously anticipating the manner of a poem that was to be written in his memory two centuries later, declaimed: 'The blood of Don Juan is hot, for the sun is the blood of Don Juan'.

Quintero watched. His eyes jumped like flies to every movement of his guest. He watched him drink his coffee. He watched him tighten the stirrups of his horse. He watched Juan vault into the saddle. Don Juan was humming and when he went off was singing, was singing in that intolerable tenor of his which was like a cock crow in the olive groves.

Quintero went into the house and rubbed his unshaven chin. Then he went out again to the road where the figure of Don Juan was now only a small smoke of dust between the eucalyptus trees. Quintero went up to the room where Juan had slept and stared at it with accusations and suspicions. He called the manservant.

'I shall sleep here to-night,' Quintero said.

The manservant answered carefully. Quintero was mad again and the moon was still only in its first quarter. The man watched his master during the day looking towards Seville. It was too warm after the rains, the country steamed like a laundry.

And then, when the night came, Quintero laughed at his doubts. He went up to the room and as he undressed he thought of the assurance of those ice-cold lips, those icicle fingers and those icy arms. She had not come last night; oh what fidelity! To think, he would say in his remorse to the ghost, that malice had so disordered him that he had been base and credulous enough to use the dead for a trick.

Tears were in his eyes as he lay down and for some time he dared not turn on his side and stretch out his hand to touch what, in his disorder, he had been willing to betray. He loathed his heart. He craved — yet how could he hope for it now? — the miracle of recognition and forgiveness. It was this craving which moved him at last. His hands went out. And they were met.

The hands, the arms, the lips moved out of their invisibility and soundlessness towards him. They touched him, they clasped him,

12

they drew him down, but – what was this? He gave a shout, he fought to get away, kicked out and swore; and so the manservant found him wrestling with the sheets, striking out with fists and knees, roaring that he was in hell. Those hands, those lips, those limbs, he screamed, were *burning* him. They were of ice no more. They were of fire.

The Philosophers' Stone

AUGUST DERLETH

No name is writ larger in the history of poison and poisoners than the infamous Borgia family of fifteenth-century Italy. Cesare Borgia, the illegitimate son of Pope Alexander VI who was made a cardinal by his father at the age of 17, turned his evil nature and ingenuity towards overthrowing a number of the Italian city-republics and soon seemed hell-bent on establishing his own kingdom. Poison was one of his favourite means for ridding himself of enemies, although in 1503 he very nearly died of the same potion that killed his father. His end came rather more prosaically four years later in the seige of Viana. His sister, Lucrezia, was also enmeshed in the same web of plotting and murder and their names are frequently linked by history. Cesare Borgia's crimes and vices have particularly fascinated generations of authors like August Derleth, the American horror writer and anthologist, who in this next story sparingly recreates one of the more fiendish episodes from his evil life.

THE LACKEY AT the window inclined his head toward Messer Orsini, who sat fidgeting nervously at the high oaken table near the center of the room.

'The three come, Excellency.'

Messer, the Duke Ercola di Orsini, turned and rose, and walked swiftly to the window. The lackey pulled aside the heavy, velvet hangings. Three men were walking on the drawbridge of his castle. The duke made a sign; the hangings dropped.

'It is well. Admit them at once to this room.'

The lackey departed. Messer Orsini meditatively donned a mask, then seated himself to await the three. He had not long to wait.

The three came into the room, bowing servilely. 'You have brought it?' came from the masked Orsini.

'We have, Messer.'

'Let me see it.'

14

One of the three men drew a long glass phial from his doublet. In the bottom of the glass gleamed a jewel. Messer Orsini repressed an exclamation.

'The philosophers' stone, as you commanded, Messer.'

'Of what portent is the scroll above the stone?'

'It is a formula of death, Messer.'

The Duke di Orsini threw a pouch of gold upon the table. One of the three seized it. The duke spoke again.

'There is to be no word of this in outer circles.'

'It shall be as you say, Messer. Our instructions were to warn you not to open the phial before the hour of midnight; seven glasses of sand hence.'

'They shall be obeyed. But carry back this warning: If the stone is not true, you die in company with your master.'

'We are at your command, at your mercy, if the stone fails to perform its duty.'

The curtains swished behind the three. At once Messer Orsini struck a gong. A lackey appeared.

'Seize and bind the three men who are leaving my abode. Cast them into the dungeons until further word from me is received.'

The lackey disappeared. As if summoned by magic another came to take his place.

'Messer, a runner from Rome awaits your pleasure.'

'From Rome?'

'Yes, Excellency.'

'Bring him to me.'

The lackey departed as silently as he had come. In a trice the runner stood before the Duke di Orsini. He bowed low. With a quick motion he opened an amulet about his neck and drew from it a piece of folded paper, which he threw to the table before him. The duke grasped it and read:

> *Be armed; prepare to attack the Bull.*
> *Your cousin.*

At once the duke struck his gong, and as before, a lackey appeared.

'Ring the alarum bell.'

The lackey vanished, and the duke turned again to the messenger.

'You come from His Eminence?'

15

'Yes, Excellency.'

'You are acquainted with the content of this message?'

'No, Excellency. I was told to read it only in case of attack.'

'You are from my cousin's household?'

'Yes, Highness.'

'It is well; you may go. Tonight you shall be housed with me; tomorrow you join my army.'

A lackey conducted the runner from the room. From outside came the insistent pealing of the alarum bell, and the clatter of arms; the duke's soldiers were assembling. Messer Orsini rose and moved across the room to the terrace; he stepped onto the balcony and addressed his men-at-arms.

'It is by command of His Eminence, the Cardinal Orsini, coupled with that of His Eminence, the Cardinal della Rovere, that you are to remain constantly in arms in preparation for an attack upon the Borgia, who moves now through this country. An attempt will be made in Rome tonight to poison the Borgia usurper on the papal throne. The men of our ally, the Duke di Colonna, are in readiness; the Milanese Sforzas have declared themselves neutral. As usual, the Doge of Venice remains neutral until such time as he sees who will win the victory; then he will ally himself to the victorious standard. The Florentine de Medicis are willing to aid us, but not openly; all negotiations must be in secret. They are by no means in favor of our cause, but they live in constant fear of the Borgia Bull.'

As one man the soldiers inclined their heads. The duke stepped back into the room and pulled the curtains across the window. Meditatively he turned the hour-glass. He sat down at his table and regarded the phial containing the philosophers' stone.

For a long time he sat there. A lackey came and lit the candles in their sconces, and withdrew again, leaving the duke alone. At length the Duke di Orsini drew from a panel in the table a map of the surrounding country, and began to sketch the passage of Cesare Borgia's troops. He wondered how his cousin's envoy had managed to get through the Borgia's lines. He saw clearly that the envoy would have had to come through the enemy's lines to reach him. But abruptly he dismissed the question and turned his attention to the attack he would make on the morrow.

The last grains of sand of the eleventh hour dribbled into a heap as Messer Orsini rose from the table with the phial in his hand. He moved quickly beneath a sconce of candles, the better to see the precious stone, upon which the light glittered and sparkled. Almost feverishly he broke the end of the phial. He drew out the scroll, then turned the phial upside down to catch the jewel with the palm of his outstretched hand.

But though the jewel slid down the polished surface of the glass, it never reached the hand of the Duke Ercola di Orsini. For suddenly came a sharp pop, as if a glass bubble had been broken, and immediately afterward a thin film of white dust rose like a vapor to the nostrils of the duke.

For a moment he stared in amazement at his dust-laden palm. Then he tore at the scroll, madly, as if in a frenzy. He opened it and read. His face twisted into an expression of horrible fear. He made as if to step forward. Two steps he went, then fell flat on his face, the opened scroll beneath his palm. He twitched convulsively and lay still.

The candles gleamed on the writing on the scroll, while from without came the sharp cries of a surprized army. The scroll read:

With the compliments of Cesare Borgia!

The Proof

J. C. MOORE

The name of Matthew Hopkins has become synonymous with witch-hunting and the use of superstition and gossip to put innocent people – in the main simple-minded old women – to death in the cause of religion. The Suffolk-born lawyer who became known as 'The Witch Finder General' lived during particularly superstitious times in the seventeenth century and earned his evil reputation when, between 1645 and 1646, 'he sent to the gallows more witches than all the other witch hunters of England have hung in the 160 years during which the persecution flourished in England,' according to historian Wallace Notestein. The number he put to death has never been accurately estimated, but it certainly ran into several hundreds throughout the Eastern counties. Although the exact cause of Hopkins's own death is also surrounded by mystery, rumour has it that he was ducked by outraged villagers in a river in the very same manner that he had treated many of his suspects, and died as a result of this exposure late in 1646. In 'The Proof', J. C. Moore turns back the pages of history to provide a chilling insight into just one of Hopkins' cases of 'exposing' a witch . . .

THE TWO MEN who watched her took turn and turn about. Towards evening the tall scowling one came back, and the short fat one who had yawned on the hard bench for two or three hours got up respectfully. 'Nothing has entered,' he said. Just then a bee buzzed at the open window, and the scowling man, whom she knew as Matthew Hopkins, strode swiftly across the room to examine it. The other followed him, and together they watched the bee intently until it flew away.

'Only a bumble,' said the short fat man.

'Nevertheless I have known them take the form of insects,' said Mr. Hopkins. He added sharply: 'You have to keep your wits about you in this business.'

'Yes, sir.'

'Birds and animals are more usual,' Mr. Hopkins went on. He quoted some Latin which she did not understand, and she guessed that the short man, although he tried to look very wise, didn't understand it either. Mr. Hopkins, however, translated for his benefit. 'Owls and bats and cats are especially favoured, but insects are not unheard of, by any means. Night moths and chafers for instance. And even slugs.'

'Yes, sir.'

'Even slugs,' repeated Mr. Hopkins darkly. 'So remember to keep your eyes open always. You may go now: I will watch. Dusk is their favourite hour.' He sat down on the bench and stared with his pale wild eyes towards the window.

Now at last she began to understand what they were about. At first she had been so bewildered and frightened that she thought they had tied her cross-legged to the stool as part of her punishment. Sooner or later, surely, they would let her go and she would creep back to her cottage and shut the door against the gossiping neighbours and try to forget the shame and the indignities which had been put upon her. But now she realised that this new ordeal was merely a continuation of the trial: they were waiting and watching for her Familiar Spirit, or something of the kind, to come through the window. Well, they could wait for that till Domesday; for she was no witch, and despite her weariness and her cramp and the pain of the cords which bound her so tightly she still had enough assurance and confidence left to be angry.

'You can wait till Domesday,' she said aloud. But the scowling man with the pale eyes took no notice, he did not even shift his stare from the window, and her own words sounded strange in the quiet room. She bit her lip, wishing she had not spoken.

It was best, she told herself, to keep silent; for they twisted your own words against you, as she had discovered that morning when they took her before the magistrate and accused her of things which she had never imagined or dreamed of. She had answered with spirit, and Mr. Hopkins had said with a conventional shrug of his shoulders: 'You see, sir, how the Devil puts these pert replies into the woman's mouth?'

'Confine your answers to yes and no,' said the magistrate; and Mr. Hopkins began to cross-examine her again.

'Were you or were you not in love with the young man called Reuben Taylor?'

'Yes,' she said at last. It was no use denying it, the whole

19

neighbourhood had known it. Alas, she had worn her heart upon her sleeve!

'And did not his mother oppose the match?'

'Yes.'

'And did you or did you not, on his mother's doorstep, in the hearing of several god-fearing and respectable persons put a curse upon his mother, because she would not let you go in to see him when he lay dying?'

'It wasn't a curse! I knew he was ill, and within the house I could hear him calling for me, and – and I was so distressed I didn't know what I said.'

Mr. Hopkins pounced on her like some swift beast.

'*So you knew he was ill?*'

'Everybody knew.'

'Yes or no,' said Mr. Hopkins.

'Yes.'

'And then he died?' said Mr. Hopkins.

She bowed her head. It was two years ago, and the world had been empty ever since, yet she had never cried until now. She did not easily cry. But suddenly tears came and she hid her face, so that she scarcely heard the things which Mr. Hopkins was saying to the magistrate nor troubled to deny the meaningless questions he put to her: Was she aware that Mother Taylor's dun cow had died on the first of March 1644 of an unaccountable milk fever? Did she not know that the pied cow had died on the 15th of the same affliction? And the roan cow on the 2nd April? 'Oh, what do I care about cows!' she cried, with all the grief and loneliness of twenty-four months lapping about her. 'The milk, sir,' went on Mr. Hopkins inexorably, 'is said to have curdled in their udders, which thereupon mortified.'

At last the magistrate said:

'I find a *prima facie* case. Mr. Hopkins, you may proceed with your examination.'

They took her then to another room in the Town Hall, but the crowd followed and clamoured at the door so loudly that Mr. Hopkins had to let them in; and at least a dozen people were pressing about her when the short fat man suddenly pinioned her arms behind her back and Mr. Hopkins lifted her skirt and pressed a pin into her thigh. She scarcely felt the prick, for she was faint with terror and shame. 'Ho, ho, a presentable witch,' said a coarse voice in the crowd. 'She bleeds, she bleeds,' said somebody else, and Mr. Hopkins let her skirt fall. 'The Devil has many artifices,' he said. 'It is therefore proper to decide these matters not upon one fallible test, but upon many.' He began to make much of a small wart which she had on her wrist, and a mole on her forearm. She could scarcely bear the touch of his questioning fingers on her skin, and she cried out in protest:

'I have had it since childhood.'

'Aye, aye,' scowled Mr. Hopkins, 'maybe your Master put it as a mark upon ye, as a shepherd burns a brand upon his sheep. We will proceed nevertheless to a further experiment.' It was then that they bound her to the stool in the middle of the room, opened the window, and drove out the inquisitive crowd. The Watching began.

The light from the sinking sun now came slanting through the narrow window in a thin beam which fell between her and her watcher. Somehow it reminded her of a flaming sword, and made her think of angels, from which thought she drew comfort for a while, for surely God would not let them find her guilty of these things which she had never done? So she prayed, but silently, lest Mr. Hopkins should hear her and think she prayed to the Devil and not to God. 'Make them let me go,' she said, and repeated it again and again, so that soon she almost persuaded herself that when night came they would untie the cords and allow her to scurry back to her cottage just up the lane. For a few moments her faith was so strong that she shut her eyes and actually saw herself unlatching the green door and going inside among all her friendly and familiar things, the spinning-wheel in the corner, the kettle on the hob, the brown milk-jug on the table. And Tibb would be crying for her milk, for it was past supper-time, Tibb, whose eyes grew as round and as luminous as moons in the rushlight, Tibb jumping on to her shoulder and rubbing a soft head against her face.

The thought of Tibb's purring welcome gave her comfort, for during the last two lonely years she had lavished all her pent-up love on the small black cat. At least Tibb would not shun her as the neighbours had shunned her to-day, when she was being led through the streets and had called out in vain for someone to come and testify on her behalf. They had turned away, and some of them had mocked her; inquisitive heads peering out of windows had been swiftly withdrawn. Once she had heard, or thought she had heard, a blood-chilling cry of 'Burn her! Burn her!' She had never felt so alone as she did then, knowing that the only one who would have spoken for her lay in the churchyard at the top of the hill. So now in her loneliness and misery her thoughts turned to the black cat, and behind her shut eyelids she saw Tibb playing the absurd game which they played together every evening, when she would crook her fingers in front of the light so that a shadow fell upon the wall, now of a bird with flapping wings, now of a rabbit with twitching ears. Then Tibb with arched back and hackles raised would mince before the shadows adding to them the tantalising reflection of her own tail; to and fro, to and fro, prancing, leaping, scrabbling up the wall in pursuit of the uncatchable phantom, her lunar eyes ablaze with the weird pale light that was neither yellow nor green. And so the game went on, until both were tired and they went up the creaking stairs to bed.

Perhaps she dozed, in spite of her cramped position and the cruel cords; for surely she dreamed that she was in bed, and safe, and felt in her dreams the pressure of Tibb's small body stirring at her feet. But suddenly a queer sound, a dry crackling flutter, startled her and made her open her eyes. The beam from the window was much paler now, it was no longer like a flaming sword, but the specks of dust still danced in it and through it, as through a piece of thin gauze, she saw her watcher crouch as if he were about to spring. At the same moment a moving shadow fell across the beam, there was a swish of wings, and Mr. Hopkins leapt towards the window. His leap was all the more terrifying because she did not know the reason for it; she screamed, and then the beam was clear once more and she saw the bat for a second as it fluttered away against the pale evening sky. Mr. Hopkins went slowly back to the bench and resumed his watching.

She did not close her eyes again, but sat taut and upright, straining against the cords, with all her nerves a-tingle. For the first time she fully understood her danger. Her assurance ebbed away from her. It was true enough that she was no witch and possessed no Familiar Spirit, – ah, but *what if something did enter the room while they watched her*? What if the bat had blundered in? Or even the bee?

She prayed again, but with less confidence: 'Please God, don't let anything come in.' Panic came nearer with the gathering darkness, for the beam from the window had faded altogether and the darkness crouched in all the four corners of the room like the blurred figure of Mr. Hopkins crouched on his bench: like him, it waited to spring. The smallest sound made her pounding heart beat faster – even the ping of a mosquito, which Mr. Hopkins scowled upon as if he suspected that

22

even such an atomy might conceal the Devil. Outside, the barn owl which lived in the apple-tree half-way down the lane began his evening hunting, and because she was still young, and had sharp ears, she could hear what Mr. Hopkins couldn't – the slate-pencil squeaking of the bats as they hawked for flies. She remembered what Mr. Hopkins had said to the short fat man who seemed to be his assistant: 'Owls and bats and cats are especially favoured.'

And cats! Her heart thumped again as she remembered Tibb. By now, surely, Tibb would be hungry and crying for her supper, stalking about the cottage and down the garden-path, only a hundred yards away, looking for her mistress who had never failed to feed her before. What if Tibb—? But no, that was impossible, dogs would follow a person – to the ends of the earth, it was said – but cats were different, their strange unfathomable little minds were centred upon a hearth, like lonely spinsters they worshipped household gods. So she reasoned, and was able to calm herself a little. Tibb would not seek her, nor in any case know where to find her. As for the bats and the owls, they were creatures of the sky, why should she imagine that they might blunder into a room, – and through this particular window, of all the windows in the town?

Nothing would come in, she told herself. In the morning they would let her go.

And then she heard the cat mewing. She didn't know which came first – the very faint, distant mewing, or the recollection that she had screamed when the bat's shadow fell across the sunbeam. But as soon as she heard that tiny cry, half-way between a mew and a chirrup, she recognised it as the answer which Tibb always gave when she called her, and she realised that Tibb had heard her screams.

Mr. Hopkins, motionless on the bench, made no sign; and even when the mewing came nearer he did not stir. Perhaps even now Tibb would fail to find her and would go back to the cottage up the lane. She strove to quieten her breathing, and held it until the blood surged and thundered in her ears. When at last she was compelled to let it go, it came in short choking gasps, so loud that Mr. Hopkins turned his head to stare at her.

She saw him stiffen. '*Ah,*' he said 'The Devil begins to manifest himself.'

There was a sound so slight that it might have been the stirring of the evening wind and suddenly she saw Tibb on the windowsill, framed against the pale square of sky. For a second Tibb paused there, ears pricked, hackles raised, tail curved over the arched back; and then with a little chirrup Tibb jumped and the duck-egg-blue square was empty again, the cat was on her lap purring and rubbing its head against her, and she was tugging frantically against the cords which bit into her wrists, perhaps to stroke it, perhaps to push it away.

Mr. Hopkins did not leap this time. He rose very slowly from the bench and came towards her. Almost wearily, without triumph and without surprise. '*Probatum est*,' he said. 'It is proved.'

The Unnamable

H. P. LOVECRAFT

America also had its ferocious witch hunters who brought to punishment many innocent men and women accused of trafficking with the devil. Of these, Cotton Mather, a Boston minister, remains the best known for his involvement in the infamous Salem Witch Trials of 1692 which have been featured in dozens of books, plays and even films. Mather was the author of a treatise, Wonders of the Invisible World *(1693) an 'account of the sufferings brought upon the country by witchcraft' which helped foster the popular delusions about it and fanned the hysteria which took hold of the country during the closing years of the seventeenth century and into the first two decades of the next. Though he believed himself a God-fearing man, Mather became a fanatic in his cause and through his relentless pursuit of suspects has been regarded ever since his death in 1728 as typifying the prejudices and limitations of his time. H. P. Lovecraft, one of the half-dozen most famous writers of horror fiction, also grew up in New England and was familiar with the story of Cotton Mather and the witch trials. He used this knowledge as the basis for one of his eeriest short stories, 'The Unnamable', written in 1924.*

WE WERE SITTING on a dilapidated seventeenth-century tomb in the late afternoon of an autumn day at the old burying ground in Arkham, and speculating about the unnamable. Looking toward the giant willow in the cemetery, whose trunk had nearly engulfed an ancient, illegible slab, I had made a fantastic remark about the spectral and unmentionable nourishment which the colossal roots must be sucking from that hoary, charnel earth; when my friend chided me for such nonsense and told me that since no interments had occurred there for over a century, nothing could possibly exist to nourish the tree in other than an ordinary manner. Besides, he added, my constant talk about 'unnamable' and 'unmentionable' things was a very puerile device, quite in keeping with my lowly standing as an author. I was too fond of ending my stories with sights or sounds which paralyzed my heroes' faculties and left them without courage, words, or associations to tell what they had experienced. We know things, he said, only through our five senses or our religious intuitions; wherefore it is quite impossible to refer to any object or spectacle which cannot be clearly depicted by the solid definitions of fact or the correct doctrines of theology – preferably those of the Congregationalists, with whatever modifications tradition and Sir Arthur Conan Doyle may supply.

With this friend, Joel Manton, I had often languidly disputed. He was principal of the East High School, born and bred in Boston and sharing New England's self-satisfied deafness to the delicate overtones of life. It was his view that only our normal, objective experiences possess any esthetic significance, and that it is the province of the artist not so much to rouse strong emotion by action, ecstasy, and astonishment, as to maintain a placid interest and appreciation by accurate, detailed transcripts of everyday affairs. Especially did he object to my pre-occupation with the mystical and the unexplained; for although believing in the supernatural much more fully than I, he would not admit that it is sufficiently commonplace for literary treatment. That a mind can find its greatest pleasure in escapes from the daily treadmill, and in original and dramatic re-combinations of images usually thrown by habit and fatigue into the hackneyed patterns of actual existence, was something virtually incredible to his clear, practical, and logical intellect. With him all things and feelings had fixed dimensions, properties, causes, and effects; and although he vaguely knew that the mind sometimes holds visions and sensations of far less geometrical, classifiable, and workable nature, he believed himself justified in drawing an arbitrary line and ruling out of court all that cannot be experienced and understood by the average citizen. Besides, he was almost sure that nothing can be really 'unnamable.' It didn't sound sensible to him.

Though I well realized the futility of imaginative and metaphysical arguments against the complacency of an orthodox sun-dweller, something in the scene of this afternoon colloquy moved me to more than usual contentiousness. The crumbling slate slabs, the patriarchal trees, and the centuried gambrel roofs of the witch-haunted old town that stretched around, all combined to rouse my spirit in defense of my work; and I was soon carrying my thrusts into the enemy's own country. It was not, indeed, difficult to begin a counter-attack, for I knew that Joel Manton actually half clung to many old-wives' superstitions which sophisticated people had long outgrown; beliefs in the appearance of dying persons at distant places, and in the impressions left by old faces on the windows through which they had gazed all their lives. To credit these whisperings of rural grandmothers, I now insisted, argued a faith in the existence of spectral substances on the earth apart from and subsequent to their material counterparts. It argued a capability of believing in phenomena beyond all normal notions; for if a dead man can transmit his visible or tangible image half across the world, or down the stretch of the centuries, how can it be absurd to suppose that deserted houses are full of queer sentient things, or that old graveyards teem with the terrible, unbodied intelligence of generations? And since spirit, in order to cause all the manifestations attributed to it, cannot be limited by any of the laws of matter; why is it extravagant to imagine psychically living dead things in shapes — or absences of shapes — which must for human spectators be utterly and appallingly 'unnamable'? 'Common sense' in reflecting on these subjects, I assured my friend with some warmth, is merely a stupid absence of imagination and mental flexibility.

Twilight had now approached, but neither of us felt any wish to cease speaking. Manton seemed unimpressed by my arguments, and eager to refute them, having that confidence in his own opinions which had doubtless caused his success as a teacher; whilst I was too sure of my ground to fear defeat. The dusk fell, and lights faintly gleamed in some of the distant windows, but we did not move. Our seat on the tomb was very comfortable, and I knew that my prosaic friend would not mind the cavernous rift in the ancient, root-disturbed brickwork close behind us, or the utter blackness of the spot brought by the intervention of a tottering, deserted seventeenth-century house between us and the nearest lighted road. There in the dark, upon that riven tomb by the deserted house, we talked on about the 'unnamable,' and after my friend had finished his scoffing I told him of the awful evidence behind the story at which he had scoffed the most.

My tale had been called *The Attic Window*, and appeared in the January, 1922, issue of *Whispers*. In a good many places, especially the South and the Pacific coast, they took the magazines off the stands at the complaints of silly milksops; but New England didn't get the thrill and merely shrugged its shoulders at my extravagance. The thing, it was averred, was biologically impossible to start with; merely another of those crazy country mutterings which Cotton Mather had been gullible enough to dump into his chaotic *Magnalia Christi Americana*, and so poorly authenticated that even he had not ventured to name the locality where the horror occurred. And as to the way I amplified the bare jotting of the old mystic – that was quite impossible, and characteristic of a flighty and notional scribbler! Mather had indeed told of the thing as being born, but nobody but a cheap sensationalist would think of having it grow up, look into people's windows at night, and be hidden in the attic of a house, in flesh and in spirit, till someone saw it at the window centuries later and couldn't describe what it was that turned his hair gray. All this was flagrant trashiness, and my friend Manton was not slow to insist on that fact. Then I told him what I had found in an old diary kept between 1706 and 1723, unearthed among family papers not a mile from where we were sitting; that, and the certain reality of the scars on my ancestor's chest and back which the diary described. I told him, too, of the fears of others in that region, and how they were whispered down for generations; and how no mythical madness came to the boy who in 1793 entered an abandoned house to examine certain traces suspected to be there.

It had been an eldritch thing – no wonder sensitive students shudder at the Puritan age in Massachusetts. So little is known of what went on beneath the surface – so little, yet such a ghastly festering as it bubbles up putrescently in occasional ghoulish glimpses. The witchcraft terror is a horrible ray of light on what was stewing in men's crushed brains, but even that is a trifle. There was no beauty: no freedom – we can see that from the architectural and household remains, and the poisonous sermons of the cramped divines. And inside that rusted iron straitjacket lurked gibbering hideousness, perversion, and diabolism. Here, truly, was the apotheosis of the unnamable.

Cotton Mather, in that demoniac sixth book which no one should read after dark, minced no words as he flung forth his anathema. Stern as a Jewish prophet, and laconically unamazed as none since his day could be, he told of the beast that had brought forth what was more than beast but less than man – the thing with the blemished eye – and of the screaming drunken wretch that they hanged for having such an eye. This much he baldly told, yet without a hint of what came after. Perhaps he did not know, or perhaps he knew and did not dare to tell. Others knew, but did not dare to tell – there is no public hint of why they whispered about the lock on the door to the attic stairs in the house of a childless, broken, embittered old man who had put up a blank slate slab by an avoided grave, although one may trace enough evasive legends to curdle the thinnest blood.

It is all in that ancestral diary I found; all the hushed innuendoes and furtive tales of things with a blemished eye seen at windows in the night or in deserted meadows near the woods. Something had caught my ancestor on a dark valley road, leaving him with marks of horns on his chest and of apelike claws on his back; and when they looked for prints in the trampled dust they found the mixed marks of split hooves and vaguely anthropoid paws. Once a post-rider said he saw an old man chasing and calling to a frightful loping, nameless thing on Meadow Hill in the thinly moonlit hours before dawn, and many believed him. Certainly, there was strange talk one night in 1710 when the childless, broken old man was buried in the crypt behind his own house in sight of the blank slate slab. They never unlocked that attic door, but left the whole house as it was, dreaded and deserted. When noises came from it, they whispered and shivered; and hoped that the lock on that attic door was strong. Then they stopped hoping when the horror occurred at the parsonage, leaving not a soul alive or in one piece. With the years the legends take on a spectral character – I suppose the thing, if it was a living thing, must have died. The memory had lingered hideously – all the more hideous because it was so secret.

During this narration my friend Manton had become very silent, and I saw that my words had impressed him. He did not laugh as I paused, but asked quite seriously about the boy who went mad in 1793, and who had presumably been the hero of my fiction. I told him why the boy had gone to that shunned, deserted house, and remarked that he ought to be interested, since he believed that windows retained latent images of those who had sat at them. The boy had gone to look at the windows of that horrible attic, because of tales of things seen behind them, and had come back screaming maniacally.

Manton remained thoughtful as I said this, but gradually reverted to his analytical mood. He granted for the sake of argument that some unnatural monster had really existed, but reminded me that even the most morbid perversion of nature need not be *unnamable* or scientifically indescribable. I admired his clearness and persistence, and added some further revelations I had collected among the old people. Those later spectral legends, I made plain, related to monstrous apparitions more frightful than anything organic could be; apparitions of gigantic bestial forms sometimes visible and sometimes only tangible, which floated about on moonless nights and haunted the old house, the crypt behind it, and the grave where a sapling had sprouted beside an illegible slab. Whether or not such apparitions had ever gored or smothered people to death, as told in uncorroborated traditions, they had produced a strong and consistent impression; and were yet darkly feared by very aged natives, though largely forgotten by the last two generations – perhaps dying for lack of being thought about. Moreover, so far as esthetic theory was involved, if the psychic emanations of human creatures be grotesque distortions, what coherent representation could express or portray so gibbous and infamous a nebulosity as the specter of a malign, chaotic perversion, itself a morbid blasphemy against nature? Molded by the dead brain of a hybrid nightmare, would not such a vaporous terror constitute in all loathsome truth the exquisitely, the shriekingly *unnamable*?

The hour must now have grown very late. A singularly noiseless bat brushed by me, and I believe it touched Manton also, for although I could not see him I felt him raise his arm. Presently he spoke.

'But is that house with the attic window still standing and deserted?'

'Yes,' I answered. 'I have seen it.'

'And did you find anything there – in the attic or anywhere else?'

'There were some bones up under the eaves. They may have been what that boy saw – if he was sensitive he wouldn't have needed anything in the window-glass to unhinge him. If they all came from the same object it must have been an hysterical, delirious monstrosity. It would have been blasphemous to leave such bones in the world, so I went back with a sack and took them to the tomb behind the house. There was an opening where I could dump them in. Don't think I was a fool – you ought to have seen that skull. It had four-inch horns, but a face and jaw something like yours and mine.'

At last I could feel a real shiver run through Manton, who had moved very near. But his curiosity was undeterred.

'And what about the window-panes?'

'They were all gone. One window had lost its entire frame, and in all the others there was not a trace of glass in the little diamond apertures. They were that kind – the old lattice windows that went out of use before 1700. I don't believe they've had any glass for a hundred years or more – maybe the boy broke 'em if he got that far; the legend doesn't say.'

Manton was reflecting again.

'I'd like to see that house, Carter. Where is it? Glass or no glass, I must explore it a little. And the tomb where you put those bones, and the other grave without an inscription – the whole thing must be a bit terrible.'

'You did see it – until it got dark.'

My friend was more wrought upon than I had suspected, for at this touch of harmless theatricalism he started neurotically away from me and actually cried out with a sort of gulping gasp which released a strain of previous repression. It was an odd cry, and all the more terrible because it was answered. For as it was still echoing, I heard a creaking sound through the pitchy blackness, and knew that a lattice window was opening in that accursed old house beside us. And because all the other frames were long since fallen, I knew that it was the grisly glassless frame of that demoniac attic window.

Then came a noxious rush of noisome, frigid air from that same dreaded direction, followed by a piercing shriek just beside me on that shocking rifted tomb of man and monster. In another instant I was knocked from my gruesome bench by the devilish threshing of some unseen entity of titanic size but undetermined nature; knocked sprawling on the root-clutched mold of that abhorrent graveyard, while from the tomb came such a stifled uproar of gasping and whirring that my fancy peopled the rayless gloom with Miltonic legions of the mis-shapen damned. There was a vortex of withering, ice-cold wind, and then the rattle of loose bricks and plaster; but I had mercifully fainted before I could learn what it meant.

Manton, though smaller than I, is more resilient; for we opened our eyes at almost the same instant, despite his greater injuries. Our couches were side by side, and we knew in a few seconds that we were in St. Mary's Hospital. Attendants were grouped about in tense curiosity, eager to aid our memory by telling us how we came there, and we soon heard of the farmer who had found us at noon in a lonely field beyond Meadow Hill, a mile from the old burying ground, on a spot where an ancient slaughterhouse is reputed to have stood. Manton had two malignant wounds in the chest, and some less severe cuts or goug-ings in the back. I was not so seriously hurt, but was covered with welts and contusions of the most bewildering character, including the print of a split hoof. It was plain that Manton knew more than I, but he told nothing to the puzzled and interested physicians till he had learned what our injuries were. Then he said we were the victims of a vicious

31

bull – though the animal was a difficult thing to place and account for.

After the doctors and nurses had left, I whispered an awe struck question:

'Good God, Manton, but *what was it*? Those scars – *was it like that?*'

And I was too dazed to exult when he whispered back a thing I had half expected—

'No – it wasn't that way at all. It was everywhere – a gelatin – a slime – yet it had shapes, a thousand shapes of horror beyond all memory. There were eyes – and a blemish. It was the pit – the maelstrom – the ultimate abomination. Carter, it was the *unnamable!*'

Martin's Close

M. R. JAMES

*In the ranks of the judiciary, no name is more reviled than that of
Chief Justice George Jeffreys, known variously as 'Infamous Jeffreys'
and 'Bloody Jeffreys', and notorious for his brutality. Born at Acton,
near Wrexham, and called to the bar in 1668, he rose rapidly in the
legal profession, mainly through intriguing to earn royal favour. He
was actively involved in many political trials, and after being made
Chief Justice of the King's Bench in 1683 established his notoriety
with the 'judicial murder' of Algernon Sidney. Among his other trials
at which he showed himself a willing tool of King James were those of
Titus Oates and Richard Baxter, as well as the followers of the Duke
of Monmouth whom he judged at what became known as the 'Bloody
Assizes'. There he was responsible for executing 320 rebels and had
hundreds more flogged, imprisoned or transported. In 1685 the King
created him Lord Chancellor, but when the monarch was forced to flee
the country, Jeffreys tried to follow suit. He was, however, caught at
Wapping disguised as a sailor and sent to the Tower of London to save
him from the mob. He died there in April 1689. 'Bloody Jeffreys'
story has fascinated historians and novelists alike ever since, none
more so than M. R. James, England's greatest ghost story writer,
who features him in the supernatural events which occurred at
'Martin's Close' . . .*

SOME FEW YEARS back I was staying with the rector of a parish in the
West, where the society to which I belong owns property. I was to go
over some of this land: and, on the first morning of my visit, soon after
breakfast, the estate carpenter and general handy-man, John Hill, was
announced as in readiness to accompany us. The rector asked which
part of the parish we were to visit that morning. The estate map was
produced, and when we had showed him our round, he put his finger
on a particular spot. 'Don't forget,' he said, 'to ask John Hill about
Martin's Close when you get there. I should like to hear what he tells

you.' 'What ought he to tell us?' I said. 'I haven't the slightest idea,' said the rector, 'or, if that is not exactly true, it will do till lunch-time.' And here he was called away.

We set out; John Hill is not a man to withhold such information as he possesses on any point, and you may gather from him much that is of interest about the people of the place and their talk. An unfamiliar word, or one that he thinks ought to be unfamiliar to you, he will usually spell – as c-o-b cob, and the like. It is not, however, relevant to my purpose to record his conversation before the moment when we reached Martin's Close. The bit of land is noticeable, for it is one of the smallest enclosures you are likely to see – a very few square yards, hedged in with quickset on all sides, and without any gate or gap leading into it. You might take it for a small cottage garden long deserted, but that it lies away from the village and bears no trace of cultivation. It is at no great distance from the road, and is part of what is there called a moor, in other words, a rough upland pasture cut up into largish fields.

'Why is this little bit hedged off so?' I asked, and John Hill (whose answer I cannot represent as perfectly as I should like) was not at fault. 'That's what we call Martin's Close, sir: 'tes a curious thing 'bout that bit of land, sir: goes by the name of Martin's Close, sir. M-a-r-t-i-n Martin. Beg pardon, sir, did Rector tell you to make inquiry of me 'bout that, sir?' 'Yes, he did.' 'Ah, I thought so much, sir. I was tell'n Rector 'bout that last week, and he was very much interested. It 'pears there's a murderer buried there, sir, by the name of Martin. Old Mr. Samuel Saunders, that formerly lived yurr at what we call Southtown, sir, he had a long tale 'bout that, sir: terrible murder done 'pon a young woman, sir. Cut her throat and cast her in the water down yurr.' 'Was he hung for it?' 'Yes, sir, he was hung just up yurr on the roadway, by what I've 'eard, on the Holy Innocents' Day, many 'undred years ago, by the man that went by the name of the bloody judge: terrible red and bloody, I've 'eard.' 'Was his name Jefferies, do you think?' 'Might be possible 'twas – Jefferies – J-e-f – Jefferies. I reckon 'twas, and the tale I've 'eard many times from Mr. Saunders, – how this young man Martin – George Martin – was troubled before his crule action come to light by the young woman's sperit.' 'How was that, do you know?' 'No, sir, I don't exactly know how 'twas with it: but by what I've 'eard he was fairly tormented: and rightly tu. Old Mr. Saunders, he told a history regarding a cupboard down yurr in the New Inn. According to what he related, this young woman's sperit come out of this cupboard: but I don't racollact the matter.'

This was the sum of John Hill's information. We passed on, and in due time I reported what I had heard to the Rector. He was able to show me from the parish account-books that a gibbet had been paid for in 1684, and a grave dug in the following year, both for the benefit of George Martin; but he was unable to suggest any one in the parish, Saunders being now gone, who was likely to throw any further light on the story.

Naturally, upon my return to the neighbourhood of libraries, I made search in the more obvious places. The trial seemed to be nowhere reported. A newspaper of the time, and one or more newsletters, however, had some short notices, from which I learnt that, on the ground of local prejudice against the prisoner (he was described as a young gentleman of a good estate), the venue had been moved from Exeter to London; that Jefferies had been the judge, and death the sentence, and that there had been some 'singular passages' in the evidence. Nothing further transpired till September of this year. A friend who knew me to be interested in Jefferies then sent me a leaf torn out of a secondhand bookseller's catalogue with the entry: JEFFERIES, JUDGE: *Interesting old MS. trial for murder*, and so forth, from which I gathered, to my delight, that I could become possessed, for a very few shillings, of what seemed to be a verbatim report, in shorthand, of the Martin trial. I telegraphed for the manuscript and got it. It was a thin bound volume, provided with a title written in longhand by some one in the eighteenth century, who had also added this note: 'My father, who took these notes in court, told me that the prisoner's friends had made interest with Judge Jefferies that no report should be put out: he had intended doing this himself when times were better, and had shew'd it to the Revd. Mr. Glanvil, who incourag'd his design very warmly, but death surpriz'd them both before it could be brought to an accomplishment.'

The initials W. G. are appended; I am advised that the original reporter may have been T. Gurney, who appears in that capacity in more than one State trial.

This was all that I could read for myself. After no long delay I heard of some one who was capable of deciphering the shorthand of the seventeenth century, and a little time ago the type-written copy of the

35

whole manuscript was laid before me. The portions which I shall communicate here help to fill in the very imperfect outline which subsists in the memories of John Hill and, I suppose, one or two others who live on the scene of the events.

The report begins with a species of preface, the general effect of which is that the copy is not that actually taken in court, though it is a true copy in regard of the notes of what was said; but that the writer has added to it some 'remarkable passages' that took place during the trial, and has made this present fair copy of the whole, intending at some favourable time to publish it; but has not put it into longhand, lest it should fall into the possession of unauthorised persons, and he or his family be deprived of the profit. The report then begins:—

This case came on to be tried on Wednesday, the 19th of November, between our sovereign lord the King, and George Martin Esquire, of (I take leave to omit some of the place-names), at a sessions of oyer and terminer and gaol delivery, at the Old Bailey, and the prisoner, being in Newgate, was brought to the bar.

Clerk of the Crown. George Martin, hold up thy hand (which he did).

Then the indictment was read, which set forth that the prisoner 'not having the fear of God before his eyes, but being moved and seduced by the instigation of the devil, upon the 15th day of May, in the 36th year of our sovereign lord King Charles the Second, with force and arms in the parish aforesaid, in and upon Ann Clark, spinster, of the same place, in the peace of God and of our said sovereign lord the King then and there being, feloniously, wilfully, and of your malice afore-thought did make an assault and with a certain knife value a penny the throat of the said Ann Clark then and there did cut, of the which wound the said Ann Clark then and there did die, and the body of the said Ann Clark did cast into a certain pond of water situate in the same parish (with more that is not material to our purpose) against the peace of our sovereign lord the King, his crown and dignity.'

Then the prisoner prayed a copy of the indictment.

L.C.J (Sir George Jefferies). What is this? Sure you know that is never allowed. Besides, here is a plain indictment as ever I heard; you have nothing to do but to plead to it.

Pris. My lord, I apprehend there may be matter of law arising out of the indictment, and I would humbly beg the court to assign me to counsel to consider of it. Besides, my lord, I believe it was done in another case: copy of the indictment was allowed.

L.C.J. What case was that?

Pris. Truly, my lord, I have been kept close prisoner ever since I came up from Exeter Castle, and no one allowed to come at me and no one to advise with.

L.C.J. But I say, what was that case you allege?

Pris. My lord, I cannot tell your lordship precisely the name of the case, but it is in my mind that there was such an one, and I would humbly desire—

L.C.J. All this is nothing. Name your case, and we will tell you whether there be any matter for you in it. God forbid but you should have anything that may be allowed you by law: but this is against law, and we must keep the course of the court.

Att. Gen. (Sir Robert Sawyer). My lord, we pray for the King that he may be asked to plead.

Cl. of Ct. Are you guilty of the murder whereof you stand indicted, or not guilty?

Pris. My lord, I would humbly offer this to the court. If I plead now, shall I have an opportunity after to except against the indictment?

L.C.J. Yes, yes, that comes after verdict: that will be saved to you, and counsel assigned if there be matter of law: but that which you have now to do is to plead.

Then after some little parleying with the court (which seemed strange upon such a plain indictment) the prisoner pleaded *Not Guilty*.

Cl. of Ct. Culprit. How wilt thou be tried?

Pris. By God and my country.

Cl. of Ct. God send thee a good deliverance.

L.C.J. Why, how is this? Here has been a great to-do that you should not be tried at Exeter by your country, but be brought here to London, and now you ask to be tried by your country. Must we send you to Exeter again?

Pris. My lord, I understood it was the form.

L.C.J. So it is, man: we spoke only in the way of pleasantness. Well, go on and swear the jury.

So they were sworn. I omit the names. There was no challenging on the prisoner's part, for, as he said, he did not know any of the persons called. Thereupon the prisoner asked for the use of pen, ink, and paper, to which the L.C.J. replied: 'Ay, ay, in God's name let him have it.' Then the usual charge was delivered to the jury, and the case opened by the junior counsel for the King, Mr. Dolben.

The Attorney-General followed:—

May it please your lordship, and you gentlemen of the jury, I am of counsel for the King against the prisoner at the bar. You have heard that he stands indicted for a murder done upon the person of a young girl. Such crimes as this you may perhaps reckon not to be uncommon, and, indeed, in these times, I am sorry to say it, there is scarce any fact so barbarous and unnatural but what we may hear almost daily instances of it. But I must confess that in this murder that is charged upon the prisoner there are some particular features that mark it out to be such as I hope has but seldom if ever been perpetrated upon English ground. For as we shall make it appear, the person murdered was a poor country girl (whereas the prisoner is a gentleman of a proper estate) and, besides that, was one to whom Providence had not given the full use of her intellects, but was what is termed among us commonly an innocent or natural: such an one, therefore, as one would have supposed a gentleman of the prisoner's quality more likely to overlook, or, if he did notice her, to be moved to compassion for her unhappy condition, than to lift up his hand against her in the very horrid and barbarous manner which we shall show you he used.

Now to begin at the beginning and open the matter to you orderly: About Christmas of last year, that is the year 1683, this gentleman, Mr. Martin, having newly come back into his own country from the University of Cambridge, some of his neighbours, to show him what civility they could (for his family is one that stands in very good repute all over that country) entertained him here and there at their Christmas merrymakings, so that he was constantly riding to and fro, from one house to another, and sometimes, when the place of his destination was distant, or for other reason, as the unsafeness of the roads, he would be constrained to lie the night at an inn. In this way it happened that he came, a day or two after the Christmas, to the place where this young girl lived with her parents, and put up at the inn there, called the New Inn, which is, as I am informed, a house of good repute. Here was some dancing going on among the people of the place, and Ann Clark had been brought in, it seems, by her elder sister to look on; but being, as I have said, of weak understanding, and, besides that, very uncomely in her appearance, it was not likely she should take much part in the merriment; and accordingly was but standing by in a corner of the room. The prisoner at the bar, seeing her, one must suppose by way of a jest, asked her would she dance with him. And in spite of what her sister and others could say to prevent it and to dissuade her—

L.C.J. Come, Mr. Attorney, we are not set here to listen to tales of Christmas parties in taverns. I would not interrupt you, but sure you have more weighty matters than this. You will be telling us next what tune they danced to.

Att. My lord, I would not take up the time of the court with what is not material: but we reckon it to be material to show how this unlikely acquaintance begun: and as for the tune, I believe, indeed, our evidence will show that even that hath a bearing on the matter in hand.

L.C.J. Go on, go on, in God's name: but give us nothing that is impertinent.

Att. Indeed, my lord, I will keep to my matter. But, gentlemen, having now shown you, as I think, enough of this first meeting between the murdered person and the prisoner, I will shorten my tale so far as to say that from then on there were frequent meetings of the two: for the young woman was greatly tickled with having got hold (as she conceived it) of so likely a sweetheart, and he being once a week at least in the habit of passing through the street where she lived, she would be always on the watch for him; and it seems they had a signal arranged: he should whistle the tune that was played at the tavern: it is a tune, as I am informed, well known in that country, and has a burden, '*Madam, will you walk, will you talk with me?*'

L.C.J. Ay, I remember it in my own country, in Shropshire. It runs somehow thus, doth it not? [Here his lordship whistled a part of a tune, which was very observable, and seemed below the dignity of the court. And it appears he felt it so himself; for he said]: But this is by the mark, and I doubt it is the first time we have had dance-tunes in this court. The most part of the dancing we give occasion for is done at Tyburn. [Looking at the prisoner, who appeared very much disordered.] You said the tune was material to your case, Mr. Attorney, and upon my life I think Mr. Martin agrees with you. What ails you, man? staring like a player that sees a ghost!

Pris. My lord, I was amazed at hearing such trivial, foolish things as they bring against me.

L.C.J. Well, well, it lies upon Mr. Attorney to show whether they be trivial or not: but I must say, if he has nothing worse than this he has said, you have no great cause to be in amaze. Doth it not lie something deeper? But go on, Mr. Attorney.

Att. My lord and gentlemen — all that I have said so far you may indeed very reasonably reckon as having an appearance of triviality. And, to be sure, had the matter gone no further than the humouring of a poor silly girl by a young gentleman of quality, it had been very well. But to proceed. We shall make it appear that after three or four weeks the prisoner became contracted to a young gentlewoman of that country, one suitable every way to his own condition, and such an arrangement was on foot that seemed to promise him a happy and a reputable living. But within no very long time it seems that this young gentlewoman, hearing of the jest that was going about that countryside with regard to the prisoner and Ann Clark, conceived that it was not only an unworthy carriage on the part of her lover, but a derogation to herself that he should suffer his name to be sport for tavern company: and so without more ado she, with the consent of her parents, signified to the prisoner that the match between them was at an end. We shall show you that upon the receipt of this intelligence the prisoner was greatly enraged against Ann Clark as being the cause of his misfortune, (though indeed there was nobody answerable for it but himself,) and that he made use of many outrageous expressions and threatenings against her, and subsequently upon meeting with her both abused her and struck at her with his whip: but she, being but a poor innocent, could not be persuaded to desist from her attachment to him, but would often run after him testifying with gestures and broken words the affection she had to him: until she was become, as he said, the very plague of his life. Yet, being that affairs in which he was now engaged necessarily took him by the house in which she lived, he could not (as I am willing to believe he would otherwise have done) avoid meeting with her from time to time. We shall further show you that this was the posture of things up to the 15th day of May in this present year. Upon that day the prisoner comes riding through the village, as of custom, and met with the young woman: but in place of passing her by, as he had lately done, he stopped, and said some words to her with which she appeared wonderfully pleased, and so left her; and after that day she was nowhere to be found, not withstanding a strict search was made for her. The next time of the prisoner's passing through the place, her relations inquired of him whether he should know anything of her whereabouts; which he totally denied. They expressed to him their fears lest her weak intellects should have been upset by the attention he had showed her, and so she might have committed some rash act against her own life, calling him to witness the same time how often they had beseeched him to desist from taking notice of her, as fearing trouble might come of it: but this, too, he easily laughed away. But in spite of this light behaviour, it was noticeable in him that about this time his carriage and demeanour changed, and it was said of him that he seemed a troubled man. And here I come to a passage to which I should not dare to ask your attention, but that it appears to me to be founded in truth, and is supported by testimony deserving of credit. And, gentlemen, to my judgment it doth afford a great instance of God's revenge against murder, and that He will require the blood of the innocent.

[Here Mr. Attorney made a pause, and shifted with his papers: and it was thought remarkable by me and others, because he was a man not easily dashed.]

L.C.J. Well, Mr. Attorney, what is your instance?
Att. My lord, it is a strange one, and the truth is that, of all the cases I have been concerned in, I cannot call to mind the like of it. But to be short, gentlemen, we shall bring you testimony that Ann Clark was seen after this 15th of May, and that, at such time as she was so seen, it was impossible she could have been a living person.

[Here the people made a hum, and a good deal of laughter, and the Court called for silence, and when it was made]—

L.C.J. Why, Mr. Attorney, you might save up this tale for a week; it will

41

be Christmas by that time, and you can frighten your cook-maids with it [at which the people laughed again, and the prisoner also, as it seemed]. God, man, what are you prating of – ghosts and Christmas jigs and tavern company – and here is a man's life at stake! (To the prisoner): And you, sir, I would have you know there is not so much occasion for you to make merry neither. You were not brought here for that, and if I know Mr. Attorney, he has more in his brief than he has shown yet. Go on, Mr. Attorney. I need not, mayhap, have spoken so sharply, but you must confess your course is something unusual.

Att. Nobody knows it better than I, my lord: but I shall bring it to an end with a round turn. I shall show you, gentlemen, that Ann Clark's body was found in the month of June, in a pond of water, with the throat cut: that a knife belonging to the prisoner was found in the same water: that he made efforts to recover the said knife from the water: that the coroner's quest brought in a verdict against the prisoner at the bar, and that therefore he should by course have been tried at Exeter: but that, suit being made on his behalf, on account that an impartial jury could not be found to try him in his own country, he hath had that singular favour shown him that he should be tried here in London. And so we will proceed to call our evidence.

Then the facts of the acquaintance between the prisoner and Ann Clark were proved, and also the coroner's inquest. I pass over this portion of the trial, for it offers nothing of special interest.

Sarah Arscott was next called and sworn.

Att. What is your occupation?

S. I keep the New Inn at —.

Att. Do you know the prisoner at the bar?

S. Yes: he was often at our house since he come first at Christmas of last year.

Att. Did you know Ann Clark?

S. Yes, very well.

Att. Pray, what manner of person was she in her appearance?

S. She was a very short thick-made woman: I do not know what else you would have me say.

Att. Was she comely?

S. No, not by no manner of means: she was very uncomely, poor child! She had a great face and hanging chops and a very bad colour like a puddock.

L.C.J. What is that, mistress? What say you she was like?

S. My lord, I ask pardon; I heard Esquire Martin say she looked like a puddock in the face; and so she did.

L.C.J. Did you that? Can you interpret her, Mr. Attorney?

Att. My lord, I apprehend it is the country word for a toad.

L.C.J. Oh, a hop-toad! Ay, go on.

Att. Will you give an account to the jury of what passed between you and the prisoner at the bar in May last?

S. Sir, it was this. It was about nine o'clock the evening after that Ann did not come home, and I was about my work in the house; there was no company there only Thomas Snell, and it was foul weather. Esquire Martin came in and called for some drink, and I, by way of pleasantry, I said to him, ''Squire, have you been looking after your sweetheart?' and he flew out at me in a passion and desired I would not use such expressions. I was amazed at that, because we were accustomed to joke with him about her.

L.C.J. Who, her?

S. Ann Clark, my lord. And we had not heard the news of his being contracted to a young gentlewoman elsewhere, or I am sure I should have used better manners. So I said nothing, but being I was a little put out, I begun singing, to myself as it were, the song they danced to the first time they met, for I thought it would prick him. It was the same that he was used to sing when he come down the street; I have heard it very often: *'Madam, will you walk, will you talk with me?'* And it fell out that I needed something that was in the kitchen. So I went out to get it, and all the time I went on singing, something louder and more bold-like. And as I was there all of a sudden I thought I heard some one answering outside the house, but I could not be sure because of the wind blowing so high. So then I stopped singing, and now I heard it plain, saying, *'Yes, sir, I will walk, I will talk with you,'* and I knew the voice for Ann Clark's voice.

Att. How did you know it to be her voice?

S. It was impossible I could be mistaken. She had a dreadful voice, a kind of a squalling voice, in particular if she tried to sing. And there was nobody in the village that could counterfeit it, for they often tried. So, hearing that, I was glad, because we were all in an anxiety to know what was gone with her: for though she was a natural, she had a good disposition and was very tractable: and says I to myself, 'What, child! are you returned, then?' and I ran into the front room, and said to Squire Martin as I passed by, 'Squire, here is your sweet-heart back again: shall I call her in?' and with that I went to open the door; but Squire Martin he caught hold of me, and it seemed to me he was out of his wits, or near upon. 'Hold, woman,' says he, 'in God's name!' and I know not what else: he was all of a shake. Then I was angry, and said I, 'What! are you not glad that poor child is found?' and I called to Thomas Snell and said, 'If the Squire will not let me, do you open the door and call her in.' So Thomas Snell went and opened the door, and the wind setting that way blew in and overset the two candles that was all we had lighted: and Esquire Martin fell away from holding me; I think he fell down on the floor, but we were wholly in the dark, and it was a minute or two before I got a light again: and while I was feeling for the fire-box, I am not certain but I heard some one step 'cross the floor, and I am sure I heard the door of the great cupboard that stands in the room open and shut to. Then, when I had a light again, I see Esquire Martin on the settle, all white and sweaty as if he had swounded away, and his arms hanging down; and I was going to help him; but just then it caught my eye that there was something like a bit of a dress shut into the cupboard door, and it came to my mind I had heard that door shut. So I thought it might be some person had run in when the light was quenched, and was hiding in the cupboard. So I went up closer and looked: and there was a bit of a black stuff cloak, and just below it an edge of a brown stuff dress, both sticking out of the shut of the door: and both of them was low down, as if the person that had them on might be crouched down inside.

Att. What did you take it to be?

S. I took it to be a woman's dress.

Att. Could you make any guess whom it belonged to? Did you know any one who wore such a dress?

S. It was a common stuff, by what I could see. I have seen many women wearing such a stuff in our parish.

Att. Was it like Ann Clark's dress?

S. She used to wear just such a dress: but I could not say on my oath it was hers.

Att. Did you observe anything else about it?

S. I did notice that it looked very wet: but it was foul weather outside.

L.C.J. Did you feel of it, mistress?

S. No, my lord, I did not like to touch it.

L.C.J. Not like? Why that? Are you so nice that you scruple to feel of a wet dress?

S. Indeed, my lord, I cannot very well tell why: only it had a nasty ugly look about it.

L.C.J. Well, go on.

S. Then I called again to Thomas Snell, and bid him come to me and catch any one that come out when I should open the cupboard door, 'for,' says I, 'there is some one hiding within, and I would know what she wants.' And with that Squire Martin gave a sort of a cry or a shout and ran out of the house into the dark, and I felt the cupboard door pushed out against me while I held it, and Thomas Snell helped me: but for all we pressed to keep it shut as hard as we could, it was forced out against us, and we had to fall back.

L.C.J. And pray what came out – a mouse?

S. No, my lord, it was greater than a mouse, but I could not see what it was: it fleeted very swift over the floor and out at the door.

L.C.J. But come; what did it look like? Was it a person?

S. My lord, I cannot tell what it was, but it ran very low, and it was of a dark colour. We were both daunted by it, Thomas Snell and I, but we made all the haste we could after it to the door that stood open. And we looked out, but it was dark and we could see nothing.

L.C.J. Was there no tracks of it on the floor? What floor have you there?

S. It is a flagged floor and sanded, my lord, and there was an appearance of a wet track on the floor, but we could make nothing of it, neither Thomas Snell nor me, and besides, as I said, it was a foul night.

L.C.J. Well, for my part, I see not – though to be sure it is an odd tale she tells – what you would do with this evidence.

Att. My lord, we bring it to show the suspicious carriage of the prisoner immediately after the disappearance of the murdered person: and we ask the jury's consideration of that; and also to the matter of the voice heard without the house.

Then the prisoner asked some questions not very material, and Thomas Snell was next called, who gave evidence to the same effect as Mrs. Arscott, and added the following:—

Att. Did anything pass between you and the prisoner during the time Mrs. Arscott was out of the room?

Th. I had a piece of twist in my pocket.

Att. Twist of what?

Th. Twist of tobacco, sir, and I felt a disposition to take a pipe of tobacco. So I found a pipe on the chimney-piece, and being it was twist, and in regard of me having by an oversight left my knife at my house, and me not having over many teeth to pluck at it, as your lordship or any one else may have a view by their own eyesight—

L.C.J. What is the man talking about? Come to the matter, fellow! Do you think we sit here to look at your teeth?

Th. No, my lord, nor I would not you should do, God forbid! I know your honours have better employment, and better teeth, I would not wonder.

L.C.J. Good God, what a man is this! Yes, I *have* better teeth, and that you shall find if you keep not to the purpose.

Th. I humbly ask pardon, my lord, but so it was. And I took upon me, thinking no harm, to ask Squire Martin to lend me his knife to cut my tobacco. And he felt first of one pocket and then of another and it was not there at all. And says I, 'What! have you lost your knife, Squire?' And up he gets and feels again and he sat down, and such a groan as he gave, 'Good God!' he says, 'I must have left it there.' 'But,' says I, 'Squire, by all appearance it is *not* there. Did you set a value on it,' says I, 'you might have it cried.' But he sat there and put his head between his hands and seemed to take no notice to what I said. And then it was Mistress Arscott come tracking back out of the kitchen place.

Asked if he heard the voice singing outside the house, he said 'No,' but the door into the kitchen was shut, and there was a high wind: but says that no one could mistake Ann Clark's voice.

Then a boy, William Reddaway, about thirteen years of age, was called, and by the usual questions, put by the Lord Chief Justice, it was ascertained that he knew the nature of an oath. And so he was sworn. His evidence referred to a time about a week later.

Att. Now, child, don't be frighted: there is no one here will hurt you if you speak the truth.

L.C.J. Ay, if he speak the truth. But remember, child, thou art in the presence of the great God of heaven and earth, that hath the keys of hell, and of us that are the king's officers, and have the keys of Newgate; and remember, too, there is a man's life in question; and if thou tellest a lie, and by that means he comes to an ill end, thou art no better than his murderer; and so speak the truth.

Att. Tell the jury what you know, and speak out. Where were you on the evening of the 23rd of May last?

L.C.J. Why, what does such a boy as this know of days. Can you mark the day, boy?

W. Yes, my lord, it was the day before our feast, and I was to spend sixpence there, and that falls a month before Midsummer Day.

One of the Jury. My lord, we cannot hear what he says.

L.C.J. He says he remembers the day because it was the day before the feast they had there, and he had sixpence to lay out. Set him up on the table there. Well, child, and where wast thou then?

W. Keeping cows on the moor, my lord.

But, the boy using the country speech, my lord could not well apprehend him, and so asked if there was any one that could interpret him, and it was answered the parson of the parish was there, and he was accordingly sworn and so the evidence given. The boy said—

'I was on the moor about six o'clock, and sitting behind a bush of furze near a pond of water: and the prisoner came very cautiously and looking about him, having something like a long pole in his hand, and stopped a good while as if he would be listening, and then began to feel in the water with the pole: and I being very near the water – not above five yards – heard as if the pole struck up against something that made a wallowing sound, and the prisoner dropped the pole and threw himself on the ground, and rolled himself about very strangely with his hands to his ears, and so after a while got up and went creeping away.'

Asked if he had had any communication with the prisoner, 'Yes, a day or two before, the prisoner, hearing I was used to be on the moor, he asked me if I had seen a knife laying about, and said he would give sixpence to find it. And I said I had not seen any such thing, but I would ask about. Then he said he would give me sixpence to say nothing, and so he did.

L.C.J. And was that the sixpence you were to lay out at the feast?
W. Yes, if you please, my lord.

Asked if he had observed anything particular as to the pond of water, he said, 'No, except that it begun to have a very ill smell and the cows would not drink of it for some days before.'

Asked if he had ever seen the prisoner and Ann Clark in company together, he began to cry very much, and it was a long time before they could get him to speak intelligibly. At last the parson of the parish, Mr. Matthews, got him to be quiet, and the question being put to him again, he said he had seen Ann Clark waiting on the moor for the prisoner at some way off, several times since last Christmas.

Att. Did you see her close, so as to be sure it was she?
W. Yes, quite sure.
L.C.J. How quite sure, child?
W. Because she would stand and jump up and down and clap her arms like a goose (which he called by some country name: but the parson explained it to be a goose). And then she was of such a shape that it could not be no one else.
Att. What was the last time that you so saw her?

Then the witness began to cry again and clung very much to Mr. Matthews, who bid him not be frightened. And so at last he told this story: that on the day before their feast (being the same evening that he had before spoken of) after the prisoner had gone away, it being then twilight and he very desirous to get home, but afraid for the present to stir from where he was lest the prisoner should see him, remained some few minutes behind the bush, looking on the pond, and saw something dark come up out of the water at the edge of the pond furthest away from him, and so up the bank. And when it got to the top where he could see it plain against the sky, it stood up and flapped the arms up and down, and then run off very swiftly in the same direction the prisoner had taken: and being asked very strictly who he took it to be, he said upon his oath that it could be nobody but Ann Clark.

Thereafter his master was called, and gave evidence that the boy had come home very late that evening and been chided for it, and that he seemed very much amazed, but could give no account of the reason.

Att. My lord, we have done with our evidence for the King.

Then the Lord Chief Justice called upon the prisoner to make his defence; which he did, though at no great length, and in a very halting way, saying that he hoped the jury would not go about to take his life on the evidence of a parcel of country people and children that would believe any idle tale; and that he had been very much prejudiced in his trial; at which the L.C.J. interrupted him, saying that he had had singular favour shown to him in having his trial removed from Exeter, which the prisoner acknowledging, said that he meant rather that since he was brought to London there had not been care taken to keep him secured from interruption and disturbance. Upon which the L.C.J. ordered the Marshal to be called, and questioned him about the safe keeping of the prisoner, but could find nothing: except the Marshal said that he had been informed by the underkeeper that they had seen a person outside his door or going up the stairs to it: but there was no possibility the person should have got in. And it being inquired further what sort of person this might be, the Marshal could not speak to it save by hearsay, which was not allowed. And the prisoner, being asked if this was what he meant, said no, he knew nothing of that, but it was very hard that a man should not be suffered to be at quiet when his life stood on it. But it was observed he was very hasty in his denial. And so he said no more, and called no witnesses. Whereupon the Attorney-General spoke to the jury. [A full report of what he said is given, and, if time allowed, I would extract that portion in which he dwells on the alleged appearance of the murdered person: he quotes some authorities of ancient date, as St. Augustine *de cura pro mortuis gerenda* (a favourite book of reference with the old writers on the supernatural) and also cites some cases which may be seen in Glanvil's, but more conveniently in Mr. Lang's books. He does not, however, tell us more of those cases than is to be found in print.]

The Lord Chief Justice then summed up the evidence for the jury. His speech, again, contains nothing that I find worth copying out: but he was naturally impressed with the singular character of the evidence, saying that he had never heard such given in his experience; but that there was nothing in law to set it aside, and that the jury must consider whether they believed these witnesses or not.

And the jury after a very short consultation brought the prisoner in Guilty.

So he was asked whether he had anything to say in arrest of judgment, and pleaded that his name was spelt wrong in the indictment, being Martin with an I, whereas it should be with a Y. But this was overruled as not material, Mr. Attorney saying, moreover, that he could bring evidence to show that the prisoner by times wrote it as it was laid in the indictment. And, the prisoner having nothing further to offer, sentence of death was passed upon him, and that he should be hanged in chains upon a gibbet near the place where the fact was committed, and that execution should take place upon the 28th December next ensuing, being Innocents' Day.

Thereafter the prisoner being to all appearance in a state of desperation, made shift to ask the L.C.J. that his relations might be allowed to come to him during the short time he had to live.

L.C.J. Ay, with all my heart, so it be in the presence of the keeper; and Ann Clark may come to you as well, for what I care.

At which the prisoner broke out and cried to his lordship not to use such words to him, and his lordship very angrily told him he deserved no tenderness at any man's hands for a cowardly butcherly murderer that had not the stomach to take the reward of his deeds: 'and I hope to God,' said he, 'that she *will* be with you by day and by night till an end is made of you.' Then the prisoner was removed, and, so far as I saw, he was in a swound, and the court broke up.

I cannot refrain from observing that the prisoner during all the time of the trial seemed to be more uneasy than is commonly the case even in capital causes: that, for example, he was looking narrowly among the people and often turning round very sharply, as if some person might be at his ear. It was also very noticeable at this trial what a silence the people kept, and further (though this might not be otherwise than natural in that season of the year), what a darkness and obscurity there was in the court room, lights being brought in not long after two o'clock in the day, and yet no fog in the town.

★

It was not without interest that I heard lately from some young men who had been giving a concert in the village I speak of, that a very cold reception was accorded to the song which has been mentioned in this narrative: '*Madam, will you walk?*' It came out in some talk they had next morning with some of the local people that that song was regarded with an invincible repugnance – it was not so, they believed, at North Tawton – but here it was reckoned to be unlucky. However, why that view was taken no one had the shadow of an idea.

The Cold-Blooded Tigress
of London

ANTHONY SHAFFER

Catherine Hayes is the first person in British criminal history to have disposed of the body of her victim – her husband – by dismembering the corpse. The case in 1725 has been described as 'one of the most gruesome crimes on record' as well for bringing the perpetrator to an end that was as gruesome as her felony. The story of Catherine Hayes began with the discovery of a human head, progressed through Mrs Hayes's simulated grief when the head was identified as that of her 'poor husband', and then finally brought to light a story of jealousy, intrigue and cold-blooded murder that shocked the whole of eighteenth-century England. The trial also caught the interest of Anthony Shaffer, a former London barrister and mystery novelist as well as the author of the classic play, Sleuth (1970). This drama about a mystery writer who toys diabolically with his wife's lover, has been a sensational success in both London and Broadway where one critic called it, 'The best mystery play ever written'. It has also been brilliantly filmed, too, of course, with Laurence Olivier as the writer and Michael Caine as the lover. In 'The Cold-Blooded Tigress of London', which Anthony wrote some twenty years earlier, he is also dealing with an equally cunning and manipulative criminal, but this time it is a woman . . .

ON THE MORNING of March 2nd, 1726, a London watchman called Robinson saw the head of a man lying on the mud at Home Ferry Wharf, Westminster. It was covered with blood and filth, and bloated slightly with sea-water. Near by was a bucket, empty except for some hairs floating in a little blood in the bottom. By the order of the London magistrates the head was washed, its hair was combed, and it was paraded on the top of a pole in the City in the hope that someone would recognize it, or that alternatively the guilty party would come to view his handiwork out of curiosity and would behave in such a manner as to give himself away. Orders were also given for a narrow watch to be kept on all coaches making for the outskirts of London, as it was thought that an attempt would be made to dispose of the rest of the corpse. So began an investigation which led to the uncovery of one of the most bestially cold-blooded murders London has ever known.

The gruesome story really starts in a little Warwickshire village in 1690 with the birth of a girl who was christened Catherine. Contemporary reports speak of her as being a turbulent, ill-natured, vexatious person and a constant trial to her parents.

The next we hear of her is when she is only fifteen. Tired of the narrow, dull life of the village, she joined up with some army officers and lived with them for a while. Inevitably she was seduced and abandoned by them. It was while she was in this novelettish situation that she met Mrs. Hayes, who took pity on her and employed her as a maid.

John Hayes, the eldest son of the house, fell in love with her and, knowing that his father would never give his consent, a secret marriage was arranged. Pretending that he had to buy some tools he went to Worcester, where he was joined by Catherine, and they were duly married. Unfortunately, on the day of the wedding Catherine met up with the officers who had seduced her and learning of the marriage, they determined to play a trick on Hayes. Waiting until nightfall, until the very moment, in fact, when he was climbing into his marriage bed, they burst into the room, pretending to be members of a press gang, and marched the unfortunate bridegroom off under close arrest to await the arrival of his regiment.

All plans for keeping the marriage secret had now to be abandoned. The father's help was invoked; he came to Worcester, and exposed the officers for the tricksters they were. He was naturally furious at the marriage, but faced with a *fait accompli* there was little he could do but give his blessing and help his son to set up in his trade of carpenter.

A little later, however, Catherine, always anxious for the exciting life, persuaded her husband to join the army, and he was posted to the Isle of Wight. After a few months of this, the father's aid was once more sought, and for the sum of £60 he procured his son's discharge.

It was at this point that Hayes senior, foreseeing the seeds of possible future tragedy in the difference between the son's sober, sedate, almost prim, nature and his wife's erratic, passionate discontent, advised a separation. But John Hayes would not hear of this, and at his wife's instigation they moved to London.

The London of 1719 was not a difficult place to make money for a man of enterprise and spirit. Starting by selling sea-coal and chandleryware in the Tottenham Court Road, John Hayes prospered fairly swiftly, and before long he had changed his business to money lending and farming, and his address to Tyburn Road (now Oxford Street).

But the private life of the couple was not going so smoothly. Already the ugly story had started to take its course. Catherine Hayes, though extolling the virtues of her husband to the people who knew him for the peaceable character that he was, made a habit of telling strangers that her husband was a mean, vicious brute and that 'it would mean no more to kill him than a mad dog.'

Her resolution to kill him was strengthened by an unfortunate incident. Hayes hit her as a result of the neighbours telling him of Catherine's debauched carryings-on when he was away from London on business. They had moved again, this time to the house of a Mr. Whizzard, and had taken in two lodgers – Mr. Billings, a tailor, and Thomas Wood, a neighbour's son in the country who had come to London to avoid the press gang and whom Hayes very kindly invited to stay with them.

Catherine Hayes now loathed her husband with an insensate and evergrowing fury. She hated his meanness, his dullness, his propriety. She wanted, above all things, to be rid of him.

Billings seemed not unwilling to oblige her, but Wood was a more difficult conspirator. Having been taken in and treated with every kindness by John Hayes, he was naturally reluctant to butcher him in cold blood to suit the tantrums of his wife. But Catherine Hayes was a clever woman and a convincing liar. She made use of her husband's occasional blasphemies to convince Wood's religious nature that he was no better than a beast. She also persuaded Wood to believe that Hayes had murdered a man in the country, and had also killed his two children by her, and had buried one under an apple-tree and the other under a pear-tree. As a last argument, she told Wood that when her husband died she would inherit £1,500, which was his for the asking. Needless to say, all this was pure fiction, but it was enough to sway Wood. Billings, the other lodger, was already convinced. All that was wanted now was the opportunity.

They did not have to wait long. The date was March 1st, 1726. The victim himself gave his murderers their chance. He was boasting that at one time it was quite customary for himself and a friend to drink at a sitting as much wine as came to a guinea. Billings thereupon bet him that he could not drink six bottles of Mountain Ale straight off, the loser to pay for it. This, it should be noted, was a gallon and a half. Hayes rose to the bait; the wager was agreed and the liquor was ordered from a local tavern.

That night they all sat down to watch him, Mrs. Hayes being careful to supply her two accomplices with enough beer to ensure they didn't shrink from their foul purpose when their victim was sufficiently insensible to offer no resistance. The macabre procedure of toasting him and cheering him went on until he had finished the six bottles, whereupon Catherine sent out for another bottle just to make sure.

At last he rose unsteadily and, making his way next door, fell on his bed in a stupor. The time had come. Seizing a coal-hatchet, Billings followed the unlucky man into his room and smashed it down on his head, fracturing the skull. In his agony he drummed loudly on the wooden floor. A neighbour, Mrs. Springate, came to enquire what was up, but Catherine Hayes faced her out with the story that her husband had been drinking with friends, but that they were just on the point of leaving.

Apparently satisfied, Mrs. Springate left, whereupon Wood finished off the job with two more blows.

Now came the job of disposing of the body. Mrs. Hayes proposed cutting off the head so that recognition of the corpse would be impossible. The others agreed, and so she fetched a pail and a candle, and they entered the bedroom. Billings held the head whilst Wood severed it from the trunk with his clasp-knife. Catherine herself held the pail to catch the head and to see that no blood fell on the floor. She then poured the blood down the sink and washed it away with hot water. In spite of her efforts, however, traces were later found both in the sink and on the floorboards.

Now standing, scared of the slightest noise, in the flaring candle-light, the three of them debated what to do with the head. Catherine Hayes was for boiling it until the flesh parted from the bones, but Billings and Wood thought it would take too much time and advised throwing it into the Thames, where it would sink.

The two men gained their point, and with the head in the pail concealed under Billings's coat they crept down the stairs. Suddenly the door on the landing above opened. Mrs. Springate had heard them. Holding a candle above her head, she peered down the dusty stairs. 'What's the matter?' she called. In a voice which she struggled to keep controlled, Mrs. Hayes replied that her husband was going out on a long journey. There then followed an elaborately pantomimed leave-taking with many injunctions to hurry back soon. The door above closed.

The gates at Whitehall were closed, and so the head was eventually flung over into the Thames at Westminster, where it was found the next morning by a watchman and later displayed on a pole for recognition purposes.

The evening of March 2nd found the three murderers intent on disposing of the body. Catherine Hayes wanted to put it in a box and bury it, but the one she had bought for the purpose proved to be too small. They therefore hacked off the arms and legs. However, the box was still too small, and this necessitated cutting off the thighs and packing the parts one on top of the other. Later that night the plan was changed, and the mangled portions were taken in a blanket by Billings and Wood and dumped in a pond near Marylebone.

The head was a great source of interest in London, and by March 4th a few people claimed to have recognized it. There were Mr. Bennett, apprentice to the King's organ builder, who thought he recognized it as the head of John Hayes. He called on Catherine to tell of his discovery, but she persuaded him that her husband was still alive and kicking. There was a journeyman tailor called Patrick, who worked in the same establishment as Billings in Monmouth Street and who thought he recognized Hayes and told as much to his master. The master asked Billings, who claimed to have left Hayes in bed that morning.

On March 6th a surgeon named Westbrook put the head in a glass of spirits in order to prevent putrefaction. More and more people came to see it.

Aware that her plan had gone astray, Catherine Hayes moved from her lodgings and went to live with a certain Mr. Jones, a distiller. At this point she started collecting all the debts owed to her husband in order to pay Wood and Billings. She also was paying Mrs. Springate's rent and had taken her with her.

John Hayes's disappearance could not go unexplained for ever, and with interest growing in the identity of the head recovered from the Dock at Westminster, Catherine had to invent a story.

A Mr. Ashby was the first person to enquire directly for Mr. Hayes, and to him Catherine told a curious story. Her husband had killed a man, she explained, as a result of a quarrel. He had come to an amicable arrangement with the widow to pay her £15 per annum, but, unable to afford this arrangement and fearful of being exposed, he had fled to Portugal.

Mr. Ashby was not fully convinced by this story, and repeated it to Mr. Longmore, a cousin of the deceased. He went to see Mrs. Hayes, not revealing that he had seen Mr. Ashby, in order to see if the two stories tallied. In point of fact, she did tell him the same story, but substituted Hertfordshire for Portugal as the place where her husband had fled to. In this interview, however, she made three mistakes. Firstly she told Mr. Longmore that her husband had travelled with four pistols for self-protection. This was a thing no one would ever have done for fear of being taken for a highwayman.

Secondly, on his mentioning this, she claimed that he had in fact once been arrested as a highwayman, but had been released on the evidence of one man. In reality two witnesses were always necessary to procure such a release.

Thirdly, she got Mrs. Springate to back her up to the effect that her husband was a cruel and vicious man. This Longmore knew to be untrue, and set him and Ashby thinking that Hayes must have been murdered. The finding of the mutilated corpse by a Mr. Huddle and his servant out walking prompted them to go and have a further look at the preserved head. This time they were certain.

Horrified by their discovery, they called on Mr. Eaton, who was a lifeguard, and recited their evidence. Eaton, in his turn, sent to Justice Lambert, who immediately issued a warrant for the arrest of Wood, Billings, Mrs. Hayes and Mrs. Springate.

Billings and Catherine Hayes were taken together in circumstances which looked suspiciously as if they were sleeping together. This was all the more unpleasant, as Mrs. Hayes later claimed he was her natural son by one of the officers who had originally seduced her. This, however, is open to much doubt.

Mrs. Springate was sent to the Gate House, but was later released, as all confessions absolved her from any complicity. Billings was taken to New Prison and Mrs. Hayes to Bridewell; as was Wood, who was caught later, on the following Sunday, at the Green Dragon at King Street.

Catherine's first request was to see the head of her husband. On seeing it she cried out, 'Oh, it is my dear husband,' and had the surgeon take it out of the preserving bottle so that she could kiss and fondle it. She asked for a lock of his hair, but Westbrook answered, 'I fear you have too much of his blood already.'

On March 27th Wood confessed, and on the next day Billings made a similar confession. Catherine Hayes, on the other hand, pleaded not guilty, and went to trial. Her own story that she was not with Wood and Billings when they did the murder but was sitting in the shop downstairs, and that she heard blows but did not cry out for fear of being killed herself, carried no weight against the combined testimony of her accomplices, and of Joseph Mercer and Mary Springate. (Mercer had visited her in prison and she had told him about the murder.)

Wood and Billings were sentenced to be hanged, and then to be exposed on gibbets. Catherine Hayes herself was sentenced to be burnt, the usual penalty for petty treason.

Wood, perhaps the most to be pitied of all, died in prison of a fever two days after being sentenced. Catherine tried to take poison, but a fellow prisoner broke the phial and the attempt was unsuccessful.

On the morning of May 9th, 1726, Billings, along with eight others, was taken to Tyburn, and there, after a short respite for private prayer, was despatched. Catherine Hayes was drawn on a sledge to where a pyre of faggots and light brushwood had been prepared. A chain was fastened round her waist to the stake, and a rope was tied round her neck and the end held by the executioner. This was done to all prisoners so that they might be strangled, out of mercy, when the flames reached their waists, rather than be left to a lingering death.

Unfortunately on this occasion the flames burnt the hands of the executioner so that he had to let go of the rope prematurely, and the poor woman was seen moving around in the flames for a long time, trying to push the blazing branches away from her and shrieking convulsively under the nightmare torment. It took three hours for her body to be reduced to ashes.

The Body-Snatcher

ROBERT LOUIS STEVENSON

The trade of body-snatching to provide corpses for unscrupulous surgeons and medical students is another blot on British history. These resurrectionists — or 'Sack-'em-up-men' as they were known — frequently proved to be as ready to kill people as dig up corpses. But none have earned the same notoriety as William Burke and William Hare who together gave rise to one of the most celebrated cases of mass murder in the early years of the nineteenth century. The two men fell into their murdering ways almost by accident while living in Edinburgh and discovered the trade in dead bodies. During the year 1828 the pair killed and delivered to medical men who 'asked no questions' at least sixteen bodies, and probably a good many more. They were arrested when their greed led them to kill a couple of people whose disappearances were sure to be reported. William Hare at once turned King's Evidence and was allowed to walk free, while Burke paid the penalty for their grisly crimes and went to the gallows in January 1829. Here again this story has attracted the attention of a number of writers, the first of them being Robert Louis Stevenson who was born in Edinburgh in 1854 when body-snatching in general was still well-remembered by older residents — and the story of Burke and Hare in particular. He used the events as the basis for 'The Body-Snatcher' which was first published in the Pall Mall Christmas Extra *of 1884 and has since been acclaimed as one of his finest stories as well as being brilliantly filmed with Boris Karloff and Bela Lugosi.*

EVERY NIGHT IN the year, four of us sat in the small parlour of the *George* at Debenham — the undertaker, and the landlord, and Fettes, and myself. Sometimes there would be more; but blow high, blow low, come rain or snow or frost we four would be each planted in his own particular arm-chair. Fettes was an old drunken Scotsman, a man of education obviously, and a man of some property, since he lived in idleness. He had come to Debenham years ago, while still young, and by a mere continuance of living had grown to be an adopted towns-man. His blue camlet cloak was a local antiquity, like the church-spire. His place in the parlour at the *George,* his absence from church, his old, crapulous, disreputable vices, were all things of course in Debenham. He had some vague Radical opinions and some fleeting infidelities, which he would now and again set forth and emphasise with tottering slaps upon the table. He drank rum – five glasses regularly every evening; and for the greater portion of his nightly visit to the *George* sat, with his glass in his right hand, in a state of melancholy alcoholic saturation. We called him the Doctor, for he was supposed to have some special knowledge of medicine, and had been known, upon a pinch, to set a fracture or reduce a dislocation; but, beyond these slight particulars, we had no knowledge of his character and antecedents.

One dark winter night – it had struck nine some time before the landlord joined us – there was a sick man in the *George,* a great neigh-bouring proprietor suddenly struck down with apoplexy on his way to Parliament; and the great man's still greater London doctor had been telegraphed to his bedside. It was the first time that such a thing had happened in Debenham, for the railway was but newly open, and we were all proportionately moved by the occurrence.

'He's come,' said the landlord, after he had filled and lighted his pipe.

'He?' said I. 'Who?— not the doctor?'

'Himself,' replied our host.

'What is his name?'

'Dr. Macfarlane,' said the landlord.

Fettes was far through his third tumbler, stupidly fuddled, now nod-ding over, now staring mazily around him; but at the last word he seemed to awaken, and repeated the name 'Macfarlane' twice, quietly enough the first time, but with sudden emotion at the second.

'Yes,' said the landlord, 'that's his name, Doctor Wolfe Macfarlane.'

Fettes became instantly sober; his eyes awoke, his voice became clear, loud, and steady, his language forcible and earnest. We were all startled by the transformation, as if a man had risen from the dead.

'I beg your pardon,' he said, 'I am afraid I have not been paying much attention to your talk. Who is this Wolfe Macfarlane?' And then, when he had heard the landlord out, 'It cannot be, it cannot be,' he added; 'and yet I would like well to see him face to face.'

'Do you know him, Doctor?' asked the undertaker, with a gasp.

'God forbid!' was the reply. 'And yet the name is a strange one; it were too much to fancy two. Tell me, landlord, is he old?'

'Well,' said the host, 'he's not a young man, to be sure, and his hair is white; but he looks younger than you.'

'He is older, though; years older. But,' with a slap upon the table, 'it's the rum you see in my face — rum and sin. This man, perhaps, may have an easy conscience and a good digestion. Conscience! Hear me speak. You would think I was some good, old, decent Christian, would you not? But no, not I; I never canted. Voltaire might have canted if he'd stood in my shoes; but the brains' — with a rattling fillip on his bald head — 'the brains were clear and active, and I saw and made no deductions.'

'If you know this doctor,' I ventured to remark, after a somewhat awful pause, 'I should gather that you do not share the landlord's good opinion.'

Fettes paid no regard to me.

'Yes,' he said, with sudden decision, 'I must see him face to face.'

There was another pause, and then a door was closed rather sharply on the first floor, and a step was heard upon the stair.

'That's the doctor,' cried the landlord. 'Look sharp, and you can catch him.'

It was but two steps from the small parlour to the door of the old *George* inn; the wide oak staircase landed almost in the street; there was room for a Turkey rug and nothing more between the threshold and the last round of the descent; but this little space was every evening brilliantly lit up, not only by the light upon the stair and the great signal-lamp below the sign, but by the warm radiance of the bar-room window. The *George* thus brightly advertised itself to passers-by in the cold street. Fettes walked steadily to the spot, and we, who were hanging behind, beheld the two men meet, as one of them had phrased it, face to face. Dr. Macfarlane was alert and vigorous. His white hair set off his pale and placid, although energetic, countenance. He was richly dressed in the finest of broadcloth and the whitest of linen, with a great gold watchchain, and studs and spectacles of the same precious material. He wore a broad-folded tie, white and speckled with lilac, and he carried on his arm a comfortable driving-coat of fur. There was no doubt but he became his years, breathing, as he did, of wealth and consideration; and it was a surprising contrast to see our parlour sot — bald, dirty, pimpled, and

61

robed in his old camlet cloak – confront him at the bottom of the stairs.

'Macfarlane!' he said somewhat loudly, more like a herald than a friend.

The great doctor pulled up short on the fourth step, as though the familiarity of the address surprised and somewhat shocked his dignity.

'Toddy Macfarlane!' repeated Fettes.

The London man almost staggered. He stared for the swiftest of seconds at the man before him, glanced behind him with a sort of scare, and then in a startled whisper, 'Fettes!' he said, 'you!'

'Ay,' said the other, 'me! Did you think I was dead too? We are not so easy shut of our acquaintance.'

'Hush, hush!' exclaimed the doctor. 'Hush, hush! this meeting is so unexpected – I can see you are unmanned. I hardly knew you, I confess, at first; but I am overjoyed – overjoyed to have this opportunity. For the present it must be how-d'ye-do and good-bye in one, for my fly is waiting, and I must not fail the train; but you shall – let me see – yes – you shall give me your address, and you can count on early news of me. We must do something for you, Fettes. I fear you are out at elbows; but we must see to that for auld lang syne, as once we sang at suppers.'

'Money!' cried Fettes; 'money from you! The money that I had from you is lying where I cast it in the rain.'

Dr. Macfarlane had talked himself into some measure of superiority and confidence, but the uncommon energy of this refusal cast him back into his first confusion.

A horrible, ugly look came and went across his almost venerable countenance. 'My dear fellow,' he said, 'be it as you please; my last thought is to offend you. I would intrude on none. I will leave you my address, however—'

'I do not wish it – I do not wish to know the roof that shelters you,' interrupted the other. 'I heard your name; I feared it might be you; I wished to know if, after all, there were a God; I know now that there is none. Begone!'

He still stood in the middle of the rug, between the stair and the doorway; and the great London physician, in order to escape, would be forced to step to one side. It was plain that he hesitated before the thought of this humiliation. White as he was, there was a dangerous glitter in his spectacles; but while he still paused uncertain, he became aware that the driver of his fly was peering in from the street at this unusual scene and caught a glimpse at the same time of our little body from the parlour, huddled by the corner of the bar. The presence of so many witnesses decided him at once to flee. He crouched together, brushing on the wainscot, and made a dart like a serpent, striking for the door. But his tribulation was not yet entirely at an end, for even as he was passing Fettes clutched him by the arm and these words came in a whisper, and yet painfully distinct, 'Have you seen it again?'

The great rich London doctor cried out aloud with a sharp, throttling cry; he dashed his questioner across the open space, and, with his hands over his head, fled out of the door like a detected thief. Before it had occurred to one of us to make a movement, the fly was already rattling toward the station. The scene was over like a dream, but the dream had left proofs and traces of its passage. Next day the servant found the fine gold spectacles broken on the threshold, and that very night we were all standing breathless by the bar-room window, and Fettes at our side, sober, pale, and resolute in look.

'God protect us Mr. Fettes!' said the landlord, coming first into possession of his customary senses. 'What in the universe is all this? These are strange things you have been saying.'

Fettes turned toward us; he looked us each in succession in the face. 'See if you can hold your tongues,' said he. 'That man Macfarlane is not safe to cross; those that have done so already have repented it too late.'

And then, without so much as finishing his third glass, far less waiting for the other two, he bade us good-bye and went forth, under the lamp of the hotel, into the black night.

We three turned to our places in the parlour, with the big red fire and four clear candles; and as we recapitulated what had passed the first chill of our surprise soon changed into a glow of curiosity. We sat late; it was the latest session I have known in the old *George*. Each man, before we parted, had his theory that he was bound to prove; and none of us had any nearer business in this world than to track out the past of our condemned companion, and surprise the secret that he shared with the great London doctor. It is no great boast, but I believe I was a better hand at worming out a story than either of my fellows at the *George*; and perhaps there is now no other man alive who could narrate to you the following foul and unnatural events.

In his young days Fettes studied medicine in the schools of

63

Edinburgh. He had talent of a kind, the talent that picks up swiftly what it hears and readily retails it for its own. He worked little at home; but he was civil, attentive, and intelligent in the presence of his masters. They soon picked him out as a lad who listened closely and remembered well; nay, strange as it seemed to me when I first heard it, he was in those days well favoured, and pleased by his exterior. There was, at that period, a certain extramural teacher of anatomy, whom I shall here designate by the letter K. His name was subsequently too well known. The man who bore it skulked through the streets of Edinburgh in disguise, while the mob that applauded at the execution of Burke called loudly for the blood of his employer. But Mr. K——— was then at the top of his vogue; he enjoyed a popularity due partly to his own talent and address, partly to the incapacity of his rival, the university professor. The students, at least, swore by his name, and Fettes believed himself, and was believed by others, to have laid the foundations of success when he had acquired the favour of this meteorically famous man. Mr. K——— was a *bon vivant* as well as an accomplished teacher; he liked a sly allusion no less than a careful preparation. In both capacities Fettes enjoyed and deserved his notice, and by the second year of his attendance he held the half-regular position of second demonstrator or sub-assistant in his class.

In this capacity, the charge of the theatre and lecture-room devolved in particular upon his shoulders. He had to answer for the cleanliness of the premises and the conduct of the other students, and it was a part of his duty to supply, receive, and divide the various subjects. It was with a view to this last – at that time very delicate – affair that he was lodged by Mr. K——— in the same wynd, and at last in the same building, with the dissecting-rooms. Here, after a night of turbulent pleasures, his hand still tottering, his sight still misty and confused, he would be called out of bed in the black hours before the winter dawn by the unclean and desperate interlopers who supplied the table. He would open the door to these men, since infamous throughout the land. He would help them with their tragic burthen, pay them their sordid price, and remain alone, when they were gone, with the unfriendly relics of humanity. From such a scene he would return to snatch another hour or two of slumber, to repair the abuses of the night, and refresh himself for the labours of the day.

Few lads could have been more insensible to the impression of a life thus passed among the ensigns of mortality. His mind was closed against all general considerations. He was incapable of interest in the fate and fortunes of another, the slave of his own desires and low ambitions. Cold, light, and selfish in the last resort, he had that modicum of prudence, miscalled morality, which keeps a man from inconvenient drunkenness or punishable theft. He coveted, besides, a measure of consideration from his masters and his fellow-pupils, and he had no desire to fail conspicuously in the external parts of life. Thus he made it his pleasure to gain some distinction in his studies, and day after day rendered unimpeachable eye-service to his employer, Mr. K——. For his day of work he indemnified himself by nights of roaring, blackguardly enjoyment; and when that balance had been struck, the organ that he called his conscience declared itself content.

The supply of subjects was a continual trouble to him as well as to his master. In that large and busy class, the raw material of the anatomists kept perpetually running out; and the business thus rendered necessary was not only unpleasant in itself, but threatened dangerous consequences to all who were concerned. It was the policy of Mr. K—— to ask no questions in his dealings with the trade. 'They bring the body, and we pay the price,' he used to say, dwelling on the alliteration – '*quid pro quo.*' And, again, and somewhat profanely, 'Ask no questions,' he would tell his assistants, 'for conscience' sake.' There was no understanding that the subjects were provided by the crime of murder. Had that idea been broached to him in words, he would have recoiled in horror; but the lightness of his speech upon so grave a matter was, in itself, an offence against good manners, and a temptation to the men with whom he dealt. Fettes, for instance, had often remarked to himself upon the singular freshness of the bodies. He had been struck again and again by the hang-dog, abominable looks of the ruffians who came to him before the dawn; and, putting things together clearly in his private thoughts, he perhaps attributed a meaning too immoral and too categorical to the unguarded counsels of his master. He understood his duty, in short, to have three branches: to take what was brought, to pay the price, and to avert the eye from any evidence of crime.

One November morning this policy of silence was put sharply to the test. He had been awake all night with a racking toothache – pacing his room like a caged beast or throwing himself in fury on his bed – and had fallen at last into that profound, uneasy slumber that so often follows on a night of pain, when he was awakened by the third or fourth angry repetition of the concerted signal. There was a thin, bright moonshine: it was bitter cold, windy, and frosty; the town had not yet awakened, but an indefinable stir already preluded the noise and business of the day. The ghouls had come later than usual, and they seemed more than usually eager to be gone. Fettes, sick with sleep, lighted them upstairs. He heard their grumbling Irish voices through a dream; and as they stripped the sack from their sad merchandise he leaned dozing, with his shoulder propped against the wall; he had to shake himself to find the men their money. As he did so his eyes lighted on the dead face. He started; he took two steps nearer, with the candle raised.

'God Almighty!' he cried. 'That is Jane Galbraith!'

The men answered nothing, but they shuffled nearer the door.

'I know her, I tell you,' he continued. 'She was alive and hearty yesterday. It's impossible she can be dead; it's impossible you should have got this body fairly.'

'Sure, sir, you're mistaken entirely,' said one of the men.

But the other looked Fettes darkly in the eyes, and demanded the money on the spot.

It was impossible to misconceive the threat or to exaggerate the danger. The lad's heart failed him. He stammered some excuse, counted out the sum, and saw his hateful visitors depart. No sooner were they gone than he hastened to confirm his doubts. By a dozen unquestionable marks he identified the girl he had jested with the day before. He saw, with horror, marks upon her body that might well betoken violence. A panic seized him, and he took refuge in his room. There he reflected at length over the discovery that he had made; considered soberly the bearing of Mr. K——'s instructions and the danger to himself of interference in so serious a business, and at last, in sore perplexity, determined to wait for the advice of his immediate superior, the class assistant.

This was a young doctor, Wolfe Macfarlane, a high favourite among all the reckless students, clever, dissipated, and unscrupulous to the last degree. He had travelled and studied abroad. His manners were agreeable and a little forward. He was an authority on the stage, skilful on the ice or the links with skate or golf-club; he dressed with nice audacity, and, to put the finishing touch upon his glory, he kept a gig and a strong trotting horse. With Fettes he was on terms of intimacy; indeed their relative positions called for some community of life; and when

66

subjects were scarce the pair would drive far into the country in Macfarlane's gig, visit and desecrate some lonely graveyard, and return before dawn with their booty to the door of the dissecting-room.

On that particular morning Macfarlane arrived somewhat earlier than his wont. Fettes heard him, and met him on the stairs, told him his story, and showed him the cause of his alarm. Macfarlane examined the marks on her body.

'Yes,' he said with a nod, 'it looks fishy.'

'Well, what should I do?' asked Fettes.

'Do?' repeated the other. 'Do you want to do anything? Least said soonest mended, I should say.'

'Someone else might recognize her,' objected Fettes. 'She was as well known as the Castle Rock.'

'We'll hope not,' said Macfarlane, 'and if anybody does – well, you didn't, don't you see, and there's an end. The fact is, this has been going on too long. Stir up the mud, and you'll get K—— into the most unholy trouble; you'll be in a shocking box yourself. So will I, if you come to that. I should like to know how any one of us would look, or what the devil we should have to say for ourselves, in any Christian witness-box. For me, you know there's one thing certain – that, practically speaking, all our subjects have been murdered.'

'Macfarlane!' cried Fettes.

'Come now!' sneered the other. 'As if you hadn't suspected it yourself!'

'Suspecting is one thing—'

'And proof another. Yes, I know; and I'm as sorry as you are this should have come here,' tapping the body with his cane. 'The next best thing for me is not to recognize it; and,' he added coolly, 'I don't. You may, if you please. I don't dictate, but I think a man of the world would do as I do; and I may add, I fancy that is what K—— would look for at our hands. The question is, Why did he choose us two for his assistants? And I answer, because he didn't want old wives.'

This was the tone of all others to affect the mind of a lad like Fettes. He agreed to imitate Macfarlane. The body of the unfortunate girl was duly dissected, and no one remarked or appeared to recognize her.

One afternoon, when his day's work was over, Fettes dropped into a popular tavern and found Macfarlane sitting with a stranger. This was a small man, very pale and dark, with coal-black eyes. The cut of his features gave a promise of intellect and refinement which was but feebly realized in his, manners for he proved, upon a nearer acquaintance, coarse, vulgar, and stupid. He exercised, however, a very remarkable control over Macfarlane; issued orders like the Great Bashaw; became inflamed at the least discussion or delay, and commented rudely on the servility with which he was obeyed. This most offensive person took a fancy to Fettes on the spot, plied him with drinks, and honoured him with unusual confidences on his past career. If a tenth part of what he confessed were true, he was a very loathsome rogue; and the lad's vanity was tickled by the attention of so experienced a man.

'I'm a pretty bad fellow myself,' the stranger remarked, 'but Macfarlane is the boy – Toddy Macfarlane I call him. Toddy, order your friend another glass.' Or it might be, 'Toddy, you jump up and shut the door.' 'Toddy hates me,' he said again. 'Oh, yes, Toddy, you do!'

'Don't you call me that confounded name,' growled Macfarlane.

'Hear him! Did you ever see the lads play knife? He would like to do that all over my body,' remarked the stranger.

'We medicals have a better way than that,' said Fettes. 'When we dislike a dead friend of ours, we dissect him.'

Macfarlane looked up sharply, as though this jest was scarcely to his mind.

The afternoon passed. Gray, for that was the stranger's name, invited Fettes to join them at dinner, ordered a feast so sumptuous that the tavern was thrown in commotion, and when all was done commanded Macfarlane to settle the bill. It was late before they separated; the man Gray was incapably drunk. Macfarlane, sobered by his fury, chewed the cud of the money he had been forced to squander and the slights he had been obliged to swallow. Fettes, with various liquors singing in his head, returned home with devious footsteps and a mind entirely in abeyance. Next day Macfarlane was absent from the class, and Fettes smiled to himself as he imagined him still squiring the intolerable Gray from tavern to tavern. As soon as the hour of liberty had struck he posted from place to place in quest of his last night's companions. He could find them, however, nowhere; so returned early to his rooms, went early to bed, and slept the sleep of the just.

At four in the morning he was awakened by the well-known signal. Descending to the door, he was filled with astonishment to find Macfarlane with his gig, and in the gig one of those long and ghastly packages with which he was so well acquainted.

'What?' he cried. 'Have you been out alone? How did you manage?'

But Macfarlane silenced him roughly, bidding him turn to business. When they had got the body upstairs and laid it on the table, Macfarlane made at first as if he were going away. Then he paused and seemed to hesitate; and then, 'You had better look at the face,' said he, in tones of some constraint. 'You had better,' he repeated, as Fettes only stared at him in wonder.

'But where, and how, and when did you come by it?' cried the other.

'Look at the face,' was the only answer.

Fettes was staggered; strange doubts assailed him. He looked from the young doctor to the body, and then back again. At last, with a start, he did as he was bidden. He had almost expected the sight that met his eyes, and yet the shock was cruel. To see, fixed in the rigidity of death and naked on that coarse layer of sack-cloth, the man whom he had left well-clad and full of meat and sin upon the threshold of a tavern, awoke, even in the thoughtless Fettes, some of the terror of the conscience. It was a *cras tibi* which re-echoed in his soul, that two whom he had known should have come to lie upon these icy tables. Yet these were only secondary thoughts. His first concern regarded Wolfe. Unprepared for a challenge so momentous, he knew not how to look his comrade in the face. He durst not meet his eye, and he had neither words nor voice at his command.

It was Macfarlane himself who made the first advance. He came up quietly behind and laid his hand gently but firmly on the other's shoulder.

'Richardson,' said he, 'may have the head.'

Now Richardson was a student who had long been anxious for that portion of the human subject to dissect. There was no answer, and the murderer resumed: 'Talking of business, you must pay me; your accounts, you see, must tally.'

Fettes found a voice, the ghost of his own: 'Pay you!' he cried. 'Pay you for that?'

'Why, yes, of course you must. By all means and on every possible account, you must,' returned the other. 'I dare not give it for nothing, you dare not take it for nothing; it would compromise us both. This is another case like Jane Galbraith's. The more things are wrong the more we must act as if all were right. Where does old K—— keep his money?'

'There,' answered Fettes hoarsely, pointing to a cupboard in the corner.

'Give me the key, then,' said the other, calmly, holding out his hand. There was an instant's hesitation and the die was cast. Macfarlane could not suppress a nervous twitch, the infinitesimal mark of an immense relief, as he felt the key between his fingers. He opened the cupboard, brought out pen and ink and a paper-book that stood in one compartment and separated from the funds in a drawer a sum suitable to the occasion.

'Now, look here,' he said, 'there is the payment made – first proof of your good faith: first step to your security. You have now to clinch it by a second. Enter the payment in your book, and then you for your part may defy the devil.'

The next few seconds were for Fettes an agony of thought; but in balancing his terrors it was the most immediate that triumphed. Any future difficulty seemed almost welcome if he could avoid a present quarrel with Macfarlane. He set down the candle which he had been carrying all the time, and with a steady hand entered the date, the nature, and the amount of the transaction.

'And now,' said Macfarlane, 'it's only fair that you should pocket the lucre. I've had my share already. By-the-by, when a man of the world falls into a bit of luck, has a few shillings extra in his pocket – I'm ashamed to speak of it, but there's a rule of conduct in the case. No treating, no purchase of expensive class-books, no squaring of old debts; borrow, don't lend.'

'Macfarlane,' began Fettes, still somewhat hoarsely, 'I have put my neck in a halter to oblige you.'

'To oblige me?' cried Wolfe. 'Oh, come! You did, as near as I can see the matter, what you downright had to do in self-defence. Suppose I got into trouble, where would you be? This second little matter flows clearly from the first. Mr. Gray is the continuation of Miss Galbraith. You can't begin and then stop. If you begin, you must keep on beginning; that's the truth. No rest for the wicked.'

A horrible sense of blackness and the treachery of fate seized hold upon the soul of the unhappy student.

'My God!' he cried, 'but what have I done? and when did I begin? To be made a class assistant – in the name of reason, where's the harm in that? Service wanted the position; Service might have got it. Would he have been where *I* am now?'

'My dear fellow,' said Macfarlane, 'what a boy you are! What harm *has* come to you? What harm *can* come to you if you hold your tongue? Why, man, do you know what this life is? There are two squads of us – the lions and the lambs. If you're a lamb, you'll come to lie upon these tables like Gray or Jane Galbraith; if you're a lion, you'll live and drive a horse like me, like K——, like all the world with any wit or courage. You're staggered at the first. But look at K——! My dear fellow, you're clever, you have pluck. I like you, and K—— likes you. You were born to lead the hunt; and I tell you, on my honour and my experience of life, three days from now you'll laugh at all these scarecrows like a high-school boy at a farce.'

And with that Macfarlane took his departure and drove off up the wynd in his gig to get under cover before daylight. Fettes was thus left alone with his regrets. He saw the miserable peril in which he stood involved. He saw, with inexpressible dismay, that there was no limit to his weakness, and that, from concession to concession, he had fallen from the arbiter of Macfarlane's destiny to his paid and helpless accomplice. He would have given the world to have been a little braver at the time, but it did not occur to him that he might still be brave. The secret of Jane Galbraith and the cursed entry in the day-book closed his mouth.

Hours passed; the class began to arrive; the members of the unhappy Gray were dealt out to one and to another, and received without remark. Richardson was made happy with the head; and before the hour of freedom rang Fettes trembled with exultation to perceive how far they had already gone toward safety.

For two days he continued to watch, with increasing joy, the dreadful process of disguise.

On the third day Macfarlane made his appearance. He had been ill, he said, but he made up for lost time by the energy with which he directed the students. To Richardson in particular he extended the most valuable assistance and advice, and that student, encouraged by the praise of the demonstrator, burned high with ambitious hopes, and saw the medal already in his grasp.

Before the week was out Macfarlane's prophecy had been fulfilled. Fettes had outlived his terrors and had forgotten his baseness. He began to plume himself upon his courage, and had so arranged the story in his mind that he could look back on these events with an unhealthy pride. Of his accomplice he saw but little. They met, of course, in the

71

business of the class; they received their orders together from Mr. K——
——. At times they had a word or two in private, and Macfarlane was
from first to last particularly kind and jovial. But it was plain that he
avoided any reference to their common secret; and even when Fettes
whispered to him that he had cast in his lot with the lions and forsworn
the lambs, he only signed to him smilingly to hold his peace.

At length an occasion arose which threw the pair once more into a
closer union. Mr. K—— was again short of subjects; pupils were eager,
and it was a part of this teacher's pretensions to be always well supplied.
At the same time there came the news of a burial in the rustic graveyard of Glencorse. Time has little changed the place in question. It
stood then, as now, upon a crossroad, out of call of human habitations,
and buried fathom deep in the foliage of six cedar trees. The cries of
the sheep upon the neighbouring hills, the streamlets upon either
hand, one loudly singing among pebbles, the other dripping furtively
from pond to pond, the stir of the wind in mountainous old flowering
chestnuts, and once in seven days the voice of the bell and the old
tunes of the precentor, were the only sounds that disturbed the silence
around the rural church. The Resurrection Man – to use a by-name of
the period – was not to be deterred by any of the sanctities of customary piety. It was part of his trade to despise and desecrate the scroll
and trumpet of old tombs, the paths worn by the feet of worshippers
and mourners, and the offerings and the inscriptions of bereaved affection. To rustic neighbourhoods, where love is more than commonly
tenacious, and where some bonds of blood or fellowship unite the
entire society of a parish, the body-snatcher, far from being repelled by
natural respect, was attracted by the ease and safety of the task. To bodies that had been laid in earth, in joyful expectation of a far different
awakening, there came that hasty, lamp-lit, terror-haunted resurrection
of the spade and mattock. The coffin was forced, the cerements torn,
and the melancholy relics, clad in sackcloth, after being rattled for
hours on moonless by-ways, were at length exposed to uttermost
indignities before a class of gaping boys.

Somewhat as two vultures may swoop upon a dying lamb, Fettes
and Macfarlane were to be let loose upon a grave in that green and
quiet resting-place. The wife of a farmer, a woman who had lived for
sixty years, and been known for nothing but good butter and a godly
conversation, was to be rooted from her grave at midnight and carried,
dead and naked, to that far-away city that she had always honoured

72

with her Sunday best; the place beside her family was to be empty till the crack of doom; her innocent and almost venerable members to be exposed to that last curiosity of the anatomist.

Late one afternoon the pair set forth, well wrapped in cloaks and furnished with a formidable bottle. It rained without remission – a cold, dense, lashing rain. Now and again there blew a puff of wind, but these sheets of falling water kept it down. Bottle and all, it was a sad and silent drive as far as Penicuik, where they were to spend the evening. They stopped once, to hide their implements in a thick bush not far from the churchyard, and once again at the Fisher's Tryst, to have a toast before the kitchen fire and vary their nips of whisky with a glass of ale. When they reached their journey's end the gig was housed, the horse was fed and comforted, and the two young doctors in a private room sat down to the best dinner and the best wine the house afforded. The lights, the fire, the beating rain upon the window, the cold, incongruous work that lay before them, added zest to their enjoyment of the meal. With every glass their cordiality increased. Soon Macfarlane handed a little pile of gold to his companion.

'A compliment,' he said. 'Between friends these little d——d accommodations ought to fly like pipe-lights.'

Fettes pocketed the money, and applauded the sentiment to the echo. 'You are a philosopher,' he cried. 'I was an ass till I knew you. You and K—— between you, by the Lord Harry! but you'll make a man of me.'

'Of course we shall,' applauded Macfarlane. 'A man? I tell you, it required a man to back me up the other morning. There are some big, brawling, forty-year-old cowards who would have turned sick at the look of the d——d thing; but not you – you kept your head. I watched you.'

'Well, and why not?' Fettes thus vaunted himself. 'It was no affair of mine. There was nothing to gain on the one side but disturbance, and on the other I could count on your gratitude, don't you see?' And he slapped his pocket till the gold pieces rang.

Macfarlane somehow felt a certain touch of alarm at these unpleasant words. He may have regretted that he had taught his young companion so successfully, but he had no time to interfere for the other noisily continued in this boastful strain:

'The great thing is not to be afraid. Now, between you and me, I don't want to hang – that's practical; but for all cant Macfarlane, I was

73

born with a contempt. Hell, God, Devil, right, wrong, sin, crime, and all the old gallery of curiosities – they may frighten boys, but men of the world, like you and me, despise them. Here's to the memory of Gray!'

It was by this time growing somewhat late. The gig, according to order, was brought round to the door with both lamps brightly shining, and the young men had to pay their bill and take the road. They announced that they were bound for Peebles, and drove in that direction till they were clear of the last houses of the town, then extinguishing the lamps, returned upon their course, and followed a by-road toward Glencorse. There was no sound but that of their own passage, and the incessant, strident pouring of the rain. It was pitch dark; here and there a white gate or a white stone in the wall guided them for a short space across the night, but for the most part it was at a foot pace, and almost groping that they picked their way through that resonant blackness to their solemn and isolated destination. In the sunken woods that traverse the neighbourhood of the burying-ground the last glimmer failed them, and it became necessary to kindle a match and reillumine one of the lanterns of the gig. Thus, under the dripping trees, and environed by huge and moving shadows, they reached the scene of their unhallowed labours.

They were both experienced in such affairs, and powerful with the spade; and they had scarce been twenty minutes at their task before they were rewarded by a dull rattle on the coffin lid. At the same moment Macfarlane, having hurt his hand upon a stone, flung it carelessly above his head. The grave, in which they now stood almost to the shoulders, was close to the edge of the plateau of the graveyard; and the gig lamp had been propped, the better to illuminate their labours, against a tree, and on the immediate verge of the steep bank descending to the stream. Chance had taken a sure aim with the stone. Then came a clang of broken glass; night fell upon them; sounds alternately dull and ringing announced the bounding of the lantern down the bank, and its occasional collision with the trees. A stone or two, which it had dislodged in its descent, rattled behind it into the profundities of the glen; and then silence, like night, resumed its sway; and they might bend their hearing to its utmost pitch, but naught was to be heard except the rain, now marching to the wind, now steadily falling over miles of open country.

They were so nearly at an end of their abhorred task that they judged it wisest to complete it in the dark. The coffin was exhumed and broken open; the body inserted in the dripping sack and carried between them to the gig; one mounted to keep it in its place, and the other, taking the horse by the mouth, groped along by wall and bush until they reached the wider road by the Fisher's Tryst. Here was a faint, diffused radiancy, which they hailed like daylight; by that they pushed the horse to a good pace and began to rattle along merrily in the direction of the town.

They had both been wetted to the skin during their operations, and now, as the gig jumped among the deep ruts, the thing that stood propped between them fell now upon one and now upon the other. At every repetition of the horrid contact each instinctively repelled it with greater haste; and the process, natural although it was, began to tell upon the nerves of the companions. Macfarlane made some ill-favoured jest about the farmer's wife, but it came hollowly from his lips, and was allowed to drop in silence. Still their unnatural burthen bumped from side to side; and now the head would be laid, as if in confidence, upon their shoulders, and now the drenching sackcloth would flap icily about their faces. A creeping chill began to possess the soul of Fettes. He peered at the bundle, and it seemed somehow larger than at first. All over the country-side, and from every degree of distance, the farm dogs accompanied their passage with tragic ululations; and it grew and grew upon his mind that some unnatural miracle had been accomplished, that some nameless change had befallen the dead body, and that it was in fear of their unholy burden that the dogs were howling.

'For God's sake,' said he, making a great effort to arrive at speech, 'for God's sake, let's have a light!'

Seemingly Macfarlane was affected in the same direction; for though he made no reply, he stopped the horse, passed the reins to his companion, got down, and proceeded to kindle the remaining lamp. They had by that time got no farther than the cross-road down to Auchendinny. The rain still poured as though the deluge were returning, and it was no easy matter to make a light in such a world of wet and darkness. When at last the flickering blue flame had been transferred to the wick and began to expand and clarify and shed a wide circle of misty brightness round the gig, it became possible for the two young men to see each other and the thing they had along with them. The rain had moulded the rough sacking to the outlines of the body

75

underneath; the head was distinct from the trunk, the shoulders plainly modelled; something at once spectral and human riveted their eyes upon the ghastly comrade of their drive.

For some time Macfarlane stood motionless, holding up the lamp. A nameless dread was swathed, like a wet sheet, about the body, and tightened the white skin upon the face of Fettes; a fear that was meaningless, a horror of what could not be, kept mounting to his brain. Another beat of the watch, and he had spoken. But his comrade forestalled him.

'That is not a woman,' said Macfarlane, in a hushed voice.

'It was a woman when we put her in,' whispered Fettes.

'Hold that lamp,' said the other. 'I must see her face.' And as Fettes took the lamp his companion untied the fastening of the sack and drew down the cover from the head. The light fell very clear upon the dark, well-moulded features and smooth-shaven cheek of a too familiar countenance, often beheld in dreams of both of these young men. A wild yell rang up into the night; each leaped from his own side into the roadway; the lamp fell, broke, and was extinguished; and the horse, terrified by this unusual commotion, bounded and went off toward Edinburgh at a gallop, bearing along with it, sole occupant of the gig, the body of the dead and long-dissected Gray.

The Black Cabinet

JOHN DICKSON CARR

The nature of this next item is such that I cannot mention the name of the central character without giving away the denoument of the story. Suffice it to say that it features a notorious killer whose name ranks high on the list of American infamy. There is, however, no secret about the fact that the American author John Dickson Carr has frequently dipped into real stories of crime and murder for the plots of his books — an interest he inherited from his father who was a lawyer specialising in criminal cases and also served for a term as a Member of Congress. Among John's best novels of this kind are The Murder of Sir Edmund Godfrey *(1936),* The Bride of Newgate *(1950),* The Devil in Velvet *(1951) and* Papa La-Bas *(1968); whilst among his innumerable short stories, 'The Black Cabinet', written in 1951, is an outstanding example of the same. The author is deservedly highly regarded for his ingenuity in conceiving and explaining 'impossible crime' stories, and though his themes can be macabre the clues are always fairly presented to the reader. In Britain he is remembered with affection as the creator of the famous radio series 'Appointment with Fear', in which Valentine Dyall starred as the sepulchural-voice narrator 'The Man in Black'. Only one word of warning before reading this story — do not be tempted to turn to the last page or you will spoil one of the most stunning surprises in the whole book!*

As the Emperor's closed carriage swung towards the private entrance at the Opera, with the gentlemen's carriages ahead and the white horses of the Imperial Guard clattering behind, three bombs were thrown from the direction of the Opera steps.

And, only a minute before, a small nine-year-old girl in the crowd had been almost mutinous.

She was too grown-up, Nina thought, to be lifted up in *maman's* arms as though she were four years old or even six. True, the fusty-smelling coats and tall hats of the men, even the bonnets and crinolines of the women, made so high a black hedge that Nina could see little except the gas-jets illuminating the façade of the Opera and the bright lamps of the Parisian street. But it was warm down here: warm, at least, for a night in mid-January of 1858.

Then up Nina went, on the arm of *maman*. Already they could hear in the distance the measured applause – the slow, steady, clap-clap of hands, as at a play – and a ragged cheer as the procession approached.

But Nina did not even know what it was, or why they were here.

'Mother, I —' she began in French.

Maman's bonnet, lined with ruffles, was so long-sided that Nina could not see her mother's face until it was turned round. Then *maman's* dark Italian eyes, always so kindly, took on a glassy bulging glare of hatred and triumph as she pressed her lips against Nina's long curls; bright brown curls, like the hair of Nina's American father.

'Look well!' whispered the handsome Signora Maddelena Bennett, in the Italian language. 'At last you will see the death of the devil.'

And Nina understood. She too hated, as she had been taught to hate, without knowing why. She had been schooled not to sob or tremble. Yet tears welled up in her eyes, because Nina was sick with fear. In one of those carriages must be Napoleon the Third, Emperor of the French.

Clop-clop, clop-clop moved the horses; slowly, but ever nearer the carpet of white sand spread in front and at the side of the Opera. Then, suddenly, Signora Bennett's whole expression changed. She had never dreamed that the murderers – Orsini and his conspirators – would hold their hands so long, or might throw bombs from the very side or steps of the Opera itself.

'No!' she shrieked aloud.

Holding the child closely, Signora Bennett flung the side of her fur pelisse over Nina's head and dropped down into the half-frozen mud among the spectators. Just as she fell, a black object flew over the heads of the crowd, high-sailing against gas-lamps.

Through a crack between the fur pelisse and *maman's* fashionable deep-bosomed gown with the steel buttons, Nina saw the edge of a white flash. Though they were protected, the first explosion seemed to crush rather than crash, driving steel needles through her eardrums. There were two more explosions, at seconds' intervals. But the street went dark at the first crash, blinding the gas-lamps, setting the air a-sing with flying glass from lamps or windows. Nina's scream was lost amid other screams.

Afterwards the small girl felt little or nothing.

A curtain of nightmare, now called shock, wrapped soothingly round Nina's mind and nerves. She looked without surprise, or with very little surprise, at anything she saw. Though her mother, also unhurt, still crouched and breathed heavily, Nina stood up on shaky legs.

Most of the black hedge of tall shiny hats had fallen away. It lay motionless, or tried to crawl across bloodied white sand. And, as Nina turned sideways, she saw the Emperor's state-coach near the foot of the steps.

'Sire! Sire!' she heard military voices shouting, amid other shouts. And, above it, the bellow of a military-policeman: 'Sire!'

The great closed carriage was at a standstill. Stabbed with blast and steel-splinters and needles of glass, it had toppled partly towards Nina but remained intact except for its windows. Also, by some miracle, one great gold-bound carriage-lantern was still burning on this side.

Before the officers of the Emperor's bodyguard could reach the handle of the coach-door, the door opened. There emerged a stately-looking man, plump rather than stout, who jumped to the coach-step and thence to the ground.

The carriage-lamp gleamed on gold epaulets against a blue coat, and white trousers. His (apparently) steady hand was just putting back on his head the over-decorated cocked hat he wore fore-and-aft. Nina knew, if only from pictures, that he was the Emperor. Though he might be sallow-faced and growing puffy under the eyes, yet between his heavy black moustaches and fox-brush of imperial beard there appeared the edge of a cool smile.

'He is not hurt, the Emperor! Louis Napoleon is unhurt!'

'Long live the Emperor!'

Gravely the sallow-faced man handed down from the carriage a pretty, bad-tempered lady, her countenance as white as her long pearl ear-rings; she must be the Empress Eugénie. Officers, their uniform-coats torn and their faces slashed, whipped out sabres in salute.

'Long live the Empress!'

'And the Emperor! And the Emperor!'

A thick, low rattle of drums ran urgently along the line. Foot-soldiers, dark silhouettes, flowed across and stood up at present-arms, so that the Emperor might not see fallen men with half faces or women carrying bomb-splinters where they might have carried children. Round that wrecked carriage, with its two dead horses, lay one hundred and fifty persons, dead or wounded.

The Emperor smiled broadly, concealing agitation.

For the first time genuine hatred, a hatred of what she saw for herself, entered into Nina Bennett and never left her. It made her small body squirm, choking back her voice. It may have been due partly to the teaching of her mother's friends of Young Italy, of the Carbonari, who derisively called Napoleon the Third 'the sick parrot' when they did not call him devil. But now it was Nina's own hatred.

She could not have explained what had happened, even now. Though she had heard something of bombs, she did not even think of bombs — or of the men who had thrown them. Nina felt only that a white lightning-bolt had struck down beside her, hurting, *hurting* these people and perhaps even making them die as her own father had died a year ago in Naples.

Yet the yellow-faced Emperor, with his black moustache and imperial, had taken no scathe. He stood there and (to Nina) smiled hatefully and hatefully. He had caused this. It was his fault. His!

Instinctively, amid the reek and the drum-beating, Nina cried out in English: the language her father had taught her, and which she spoke far better than French or even Italian.

'Sick parrot!' the small lungs screeched, the words lost. 'Devil! Usurper!'

And then her mother enfolded her, feeling over her for wounds and whispering furiously.

'Be silent, my child!' she whispered. 'Not another word, I tell thee!'

Gathering up Nina under her fur pelisse, and adding indignity to hysteria, *maman* fought and butted her way out of the crowd with such fury that suspicious eyes turned. Up in front of them loomed a military-policeman, his immense cocked hat worn side-ways.

'The child!' cried Signora Bennett, clutching Nina with true stage-effect, and tragically raised dark eyes to a dark muffled sky. 'The child,' she lied, 'is injured!'

'Pass, madame,' gruffly. 'Regret.'

Though the distance was not great, it took them almost an hour in the crowds to reach their fine furnished lodgings in the rue de Rivoli. There waited Aunt Maria, also Italian and *maman's* maid-companion, fiercely twisting the point of a knife into a rosewood table as Aunt Maria awaited news. Afterwards Nina could remember little except a bumping of portmanteaux and a horrible seasickness.

For Signora Bennett, Nina and Aunt Maria left Paris next day. They had long been safe in England when two of the bomb-assassins – Orsini and Pieri – dropped on the plank and looked out through the everlasting window of the guillotine.

II

And that had been just over ten years ago.

So reflected Miss Nina Bennett, at the very mature age of nineteen, on the warm evening early in July, 1868, which was the third evening after her return to Paris. Nobody could have denied that she was beautiful. But all those years in England had made her even more reserved than the English, with a horror of elaborate gestures like those of her late mother.

Though the sky was still bright over the Place de la Concorde, Nina Bennett had told Aunt Maria to close the heavy striped curtains on the windows. Aunt Maria was very fat now. She had a faint moustache of vertical hairs, like a tiny portcullis between nose and mouth. As she waddled over to scrape shut the curtains, and waddled back to her chair, wrath exuded from her like a bad perfume.

Nina sat at the dressing-table before a mirror edged in gold-leaf. Two gas-jets, one in the wall on either side of the mirror, sent up yellow flames in flattish glass dishes. They shone on Nina's pink-and-white complexion, her dark blue eyes, her bright brown hair parted in the middle and drawn across the ears to a soft, heavy pad along the nape of the neck. The evening gown of that year was cut just an inch and a half below each shoulder, curving down in lace across the breast; and Nina's gown was so dark a red that it seemed black except when the gas-light rippled or flashed.

Yet her intense composure gave Nina's beauty a chilly quality like marble. She sat motionless, unsmiling, her arms stretched out and hands lightly crossed on the dressing-table.

'No,' she thought, 'I am not unattractive.' The thought, or so she imagined, gave her neither pleasure nor displeasure.

At her left on the dressing-table stood a great bouquet of yellow roses in a glass vase of water. Nina Bennett had bought them herself, as a part of her plan of death. In the dressing-table drawer lay the weapon of death.

'I have no heroics,' she thought, looking at the reflection of her blue eyes. 'I do not think of myself as Joan of Arc or Charlotte Corday. Though I may be insane, I do not believe so. But I will kill this puff-ball Emperor, who still mysteriously reigns over the French. I will kill him, I will kill him. I will kill him.'

Her intensity was so great that she breathed faster, and faint color tinged her pink-and-white face. Suddenly, out of the darkling background in the mirror, she saw fat Aunt Maria, with grey-streaked hair and fish-bone moustache, writhing and flapping with anger.

Aunt Maria's hoarse, harsh voice spoke in Italian.

'Now I wonder,' sneered Aunt Maria, 'why you must close the curtains, and dare not look on the beauty of Paris?'

Nina hesitated before she replied, moistening her lips. Despite her flawless English speech and her tolerable French, she had half-forgotten her mother's Italian and must grope for it.

'You are at liberty,' she said, 'to wonder what you like.'

Again Aunt Maria slapped the chair-arms and writhed, almost in tears. Never in her life could Nina believe that these gesticulations were real, as they were, and not mere theatricalism. Intensely she disliked them.

'Out there,' panted Aunt Maria, 'is the city of light, the city of pleasure. And who made it so? It was your be-loathed Louis Napoleon and Baron Haussmann, planning their wide boulevards and their lamps and greenery. If we now have the Wood of Boulogne, it is because Louis Napoleon loves trees.'

Nina raised her brown eyebrows so slightly that they hardly seemed to move.

'Do you tell *me*,' she asked, 'the history of the sick parrot?'

The gas-jets whistled thinly, in a shadowy room with black satin wall-panels figured in gold. With a studied grace Nina Bennett rose from the dressing-table, and turned around. The monstrous crinolines of the past decade had dwindled into smaller, more manageable hoop-skirts which rustled with petticoats at each step. Glints of crimson darted along Nina's dark close-fitting gown.

'Have you forgotten, Maria?' she asked, in a passionately repressed voice. 'In these rooms, these very rooms, where we lived ten years ago?

How you took a great knife, and stabbed a dozen times into the top of a rosewood table, when you heard Orsini had failed? Can you deny it?'

'Ah, blood of the Madonna!'

'Can you deny it?'

'I was younger; I was foolish!' The harsh voice rose in pleading. 'See, now! This Emperor, in his youth, worshipped the memory of his uncle, the war-lord, the first Napoleon. The first Napoleon they exiled—'

'Yes,' agreed Nina. 'And kings crept out again to feel the sun.'

Aunt Maria was galvanized. 'That is a noble line; that is a heart-shaking line!'

'It is the late Mrs Browning's. A trifle. No matter.'

'Well! This young man (yes, yes, it is the way of all young men!) was also a republican; a lover of liberty; a member of the Carbonari itself. Once he promised us a united Italy. But he wavered, and more than a few of us tried to kill him. He wavers always; I say it! But has he not done much in these past few years, to redeem his promise? Body of Bacchus! Has he not?'

Though Nina was not tall, she stood high above Maria in the chair and looked down at her indifferently. Nina's white shoulders rose very slightly in the dark-red gown.

'Ah, God, your mother has taught you well!' She hesitated. 'And yet, when she died six months ago, it did not seem to me that you were much affected.'

'I did not weep or tear my hair, if that is what you mean.'

'Unnatural! Pah, I spit! What do you care for Italy?'

'A little, perhaps. But I am an American, as was my father before me.'

'So I have heard you say.'

'And so I mean!' Nina drew a deep breath; the gown seemed to be constricting her heart as well as her flesh. 'My father was of what they call New England, in the state of Massachusetts. His money, though my mother sneered, has kept us above poverty all these years.' Her tone changed. 'Poor Maria! Do the closed curtains stifle you?'

Whereupon Nina, with the same grace in managing her hoop-skirt, went to the left-hand window and threw back the curtains. Then she opened the curtains of the other window.

Outside, to the little wrought-iron balcony above the rue de Rivoli, was fastened a flagstaff at an oblique angle. From it floated the beloved flag, the flag of the Union, the stars-and-stripes little more than three years triumphant in bitter civil war.

'Now what patriotism,' jeered Aunt Maria, 'for a country you have never seen!'

'It is more than that,' said Nina, wanting to laugh. 'In a sense it protects us. Have you not heard . . .?'

'Speak!'

'This is our Day of Independence, the Fourth of July.'

'Mad! Mad! Mad!'

'I think not. His Majesty Napoleon the Third made a futile, stupid attempt to establish an Empire in Mexico. That did not please the States of America.' Nina lifted her exquisite hands and dropped them. 'But the traditional friendship of France and America has been renewed. This evening, less than an hour from now, your hypocritical Emperor drives in state to the Opera, for a French-American ball, with ceremonies. As his carriage crosses the Place de la Concorde into the rue Royale . . .'

Aunt Maria heaved her laundry-bag shape up out of the chair. 'Blood of the Madonna!' she screamed. 'You do not mean this madwoman's gamble for tonight?'

'Oh, but I do.' And for the first time Nina Bennett smiled.

There was a silence, while Nina stood with her back to the window, with the soft and magical sky-glow competing with these harsh-singing gas-lights. And Nina was uneasy.

She had expected Aunt Maria to stamp, to howl, even possibly to shout from the window for help. But the ageing woman only fell back into the chair, not speaking. Tears flowed out of her eyes, tears running down grotesquely past her nose and the hair-spikes of her moustache. Nina Bennett spoke sharply.

'Come, Aunt Maria. This is ridiculous! Why should you weep?'

'Because you are beautiful,' Aunt Maria said simply.

There was a silence.

'Well! I . . . I thank you, Maria. Still!—'

'Oh, your plan is good.' Aunt Maria turned her streaming eyes toward the great bouquet of yellow roses on the dressing-table, and the drawer which held the weapon. 'No doubt you will kill him, my dear. Then you will go to the guillotine, in bare feet and with a black veil over your head, because to kill the Emperor is an act of parricide. You

84

will have had no life, none! No laughter. No affection. No love of men.'

Nina's face had gone white. For some reason she retorted cruelly.

'And your own vast experience of love, dear Maria . . .?'

'That too is ridiculous, eh? Oho, that is comic; yes? This to you!' Aunt Maria made the gesture. 'For I have known love more than you think! And the good strong passion, and the heartache too. But you will not know it. You are poisoned; your veins are poisoned. If an honest lover bit your arm until the blood flowed, he would die. Ah, behold! You shrink in disgust like a cold Englishwoman!'

'No, good Maria. And Englishwomen are not cold, save perhaps in public. It is as stupid a legend as the legend that they are all fair-haired.'

'Listen!' blurted Maria, dabbing at her eyes. 'Do you know who poisoned you?'

'If you please, Maria . . .!'

'It was your own mother. Yes! Do you think she knew no man except your father? Body of Venus, she had enough lovers to fill a prison! I startled you? But, because she must dedicate you to her "cause" of murder, she would turn you against men. How long she spoke to you, when you were thirteen or fourteen, in the accursed great cold house in London! Have I not seen you rush out of the drawing-room, crimson-faced, and your sainted mother laughing secretly?'

'I . . .I have thought of love,' Nina said calmly. 'I would love well, perhaps, if I did not hate. And now, Maria, it is time to fetch my jewel-box; and set out my hat and cloak.'

Aunt Maria paid no attention. There was a wild shining of inspiration in her eyes, as though at last she had seen some way to turn this inflexible girl from a mad course. But the time was going, the time was going!

'Come, a test!' panted Aunt Maria. 'Are you in truth as poisoned as I said?'

'Did you hear my command, Maria?'

'No! Listen! You remember three nights ago, the evening of the first day we came to Paris? How we returned from our walk, and the young man you met in the courtyard? Well, I saw your eyes kindle!' Aunt Maria cackled with mirth. 'You an American? You are a Latin of the Latins! And this young man: was he French – or Italian?'

Nina Bennett grew rigid.

'You have strange fancies,' she said. 'I cannot remember this at all.'

But she did remember it. As Nina turned around briefly to look out of the long window, where a faint breeze rippled the vivid colors of the stars-and-stripes, that whole brief scene was recreated in every detail.

As the courtesy-aunt said, it had been at about this time on the evening of July second. Aunt Maria had marched beside Nina as they returned from their walk. Even in this modern age, the most emancipated American or English girl would not have gone through such tree-bewitched streets, full of summer's breath and mirrors a-wink of cafés, without a formidable chaperone. The house in which they had taken furnished lodgings was unlike most of those in the same street. It was of an older day, patterned after a nobleman's *hôtel*. Through a smaller door in high-arched wooden doors, you passed through a cool tunnel smelling of old stone, with the concierge's lodge on the right. Then you emerged into a green courtyard; it had galleries built round on three sides, and stone balustrades carved with faces. An outside staircase led up to each gallery. In the middle of the green scented turf was a dead fountain.

As Aunt Maria creaked up the staircase, Nina followed her. Vaguely Nina had noticed a young man standing a little distance away, smoking a cigar and leaning on a gold-headed stick. But she paid little attention. In both hands, if only for practice's sake, she carried a large bouquet of red roses in which was hidden a small but heavy object, and two fingers of her right hand held the chains of her reticule. Though strung-up and alert, Nina was very tired.

Perhaps that was why the accident happened. When she had gone six steps up behind Aunt Maria, Nina's reticule – a heavy, flower-painted handbag – slipped through her fingers, bounced down the steps, and landed on the lowermost one.

'Ah, so-and-so!' exclaimed Aunt Maria, and wheeled round her moustache.

There was a flick in the air as the dark-complexioned young man flung away his cigar. He had suffered some injury to his left leg. But, so deft was his use of the stick, that he scarcely seemed to limp when he made haste. In an instant he was at the foot of the staircase.

The cane was laid down. With his left hand he swept off his high glassy hat, and his right hand scooped up the reticule. His eyes strayed to Nina's ringless left hand.

'If you will permit me, mademoiselle . . .?' he said.

The man, whether French or Italian, had a fine resonant voice, fashioning each French syllable clearly. His dark hair, parted on one side, was so thick that it rose up on the other side of the parting. A heavy moustache followed the line of his delicate upper lip. His sombre dark clothes, though carelessly worn, were of fine quality.

Nina Bennett, who had turned round, looked down the stairs straight into his eyes. Nina, in a dress of dark-purple, taffeta and a boat-shaped hat with a flat plume, would have denied coldly that she was a romantic.

'But he is undeniably handsome,' she was thinking, 'and without oiliness or exaggeration. He has endured great suffering, by the whiteness of his face and the little grey in his hair. And yet his mockery of eye, as though he knew too much of women . . .!'

Abruptly Nina straightened up.

'I thank—' she began coldly; and then the worst happened.

Nina, still holding the bouquet of red roses, either by accident or nervousness jerked her left wrist against the stair-balustrade. The roses seemed to spill apart. Out of their stems leaped a derringer pistol, short of barrel but large of bore. It banged on the step, and clattered down to the lowermost one. Though it was loaded with wad, powder, and heavy ball, it did not explode; there was no percussion-cap on the firing-nipple.

Nina stood rigid with horror, like Aunt Maria. For a moment, in that shadowy green courtyard under the light of a pink sunset, it was as silent as though they stood in the Forest of Marly.

The young man looked strangely at the pistol, and suddenly jumped back as though he feared it might still go off. Then he smiled. After a swift glance at the lodge of the concierge, he dropped the reticule on top of the derringer, concealing it. He picked up both, advanced up the stairs, and gravely handed the fallen objects to Nina.

'Permit me, mademoiselle, to return your reticule and your – your protection against footpads. If I might suggest . . .'

'I thank you, monsieur. But it is not necessary to suggest.'

'Alas, I have already done so,' he said, and again looked her in the eyes. His French voice both pointed the double-meaning, yet smilingly robbed the words of offence. Pressing the brim of his hat against the black broadcloth over his heart, he bowed slightly. 'Until a re-meeting, mademoiselle!'

'Until a re—' said Nina, and stopped. She had not meant to speak at all.

Whirling round her skirts, the roses and pistol and reticule like a mortifying weight in her arms, Nina marched up the stairs after Aunt Maria.

And this was the brief scene which returned in every detail to Nina Bennett, in the dark old room with the gas-jets, during the moment when she looked out of the long window over the rue de Rivoli. She has only to concentrate, and it was gone forever. But she felt the pressure of Aunt Maria's eyes, wet and crafty, boring into her back; and anger rose again.

Turning round, Nina took four steps and stood over Aunt Maria in the chair.

'Why do you remind me of this?' Nina asked.

'Ola, then we *were* smitten!'

'Hardly.' The voice was dry. But, then Nina opened her blue eyes wide, Maria shrank back because they were maniacal and terrifying. 'Do you imagine that some sordid affair of love would keep me back from the only cause I have for living?'

'This "cause"!' sneered Aunt Maria. 'I tell you, it is a cold warming-pan for a long night, instead of a husband. Away with it! With your looks and your money: body of Bacchus, you might wed any man you chose.' Abruptly, amid her tears, the fat woman began to cackle again with laughter. 'But not the young Italian of the courtyard, poor Nina! No, no! Not that one!'

'And why not?' demanded Nina.

'Listen, my child. Pay heed to an old conspirator like me! For I have seen them all. I know the ingratiating air, the cringing approach, the mark of the almost-gentleman . . .'

'How dare you!' Nina amazed herself by crying out. Then she controlled her voice. 'You will allow me, please, to pass my own judgment on a gentleman.'

'Ola, then we were not smitten! Oh, no!' cackled Aunt Maria. Then her laughter died. 'Shall I tell you what this young man really is?'

'Well?'

'He is what the French call *a mouchard*. A police-spy.'

'You lie!' A pause. 'In any event,' Nina added casually, 'it is of no importance. Since you disobey my order to fetch my hat and cloak and jewel-box . . .'

'No, no, I will find them!' said Aunt Maria, and surged up out of the chair.

On creaking slippers she wheezed across to an immense dark wardrobe, beside the door and opposite the windows. Opening one door of the wardrobe, she plucked out a waist-length cape of rich material in stripes of silver and wine-red.

'Well!' snorted Aunt Maria, examining the cape and giving no sign of furious thought. 'You will go to kill the Emperor. I have promised not to interfere; good, I keep my promise! But it will be sad for you, hot-blood, when they arrest you – as they will, mark it! – before you have fired the shot.'

Nina's gaze had gone to the grandfather clock, near the alcove which housed the big curtained bed. The time: the time was running out. True, she still had many minutes. But there would be a crowd. She must be in place, the exact spot she had chosen, long before the Imperial procession went past.

Now the meaning of Maria's words stabbed into her brain for the first time.

'What did you say, fussbudget?'

'Enough,' muttered the fat woman darkly. 'I said enough!'

'Come, good Maria. Is this another of your childish tricks to divert me?'

'Childish!' cried Aunt Maria, now in a real temper. 'Was I your mother's companion for twenty years, or was I not? Do I know every dog'-tail of plotting, or do I not?'

'Of old and clumsy plotting, yes. But my device . . .'

'Faugh!' snorted Aunt Maria, past patience. 'How do you think Louis Napoleon keeps so quiet his bright city, his toy? Ask the Prefect of Police, M. Pietri – yes, I said Pietri, not Pieri – but above all ask M. Lagrange, the chief of the political police! They buy more spies than the sandgrains at Dieppe! By my immortal soul, Lagrange will stir up a riot for the very joy of showing how quickly he can suppress it!'

Aunt Maria shook the cape. With her own version of a haughty shrug, she reached again into the wardrobe and drew out a very wide-brimmed velvet hat of the same dark-red as Nina's gown.

'You don't believe an old woman, eh?' she taunted. 'Good! For I have finished with you. But this I swear on the Cross: you have been betrayed.'

'Lies and lies and lies! – Betrayed by whom?'

'Why, by your young man down in the courtyard.'

She was going dangerously far, to judge by Nina's eyes and breathing.

'Little stupid!' she continued to taunt. 'Did you not observe how he started and jumped, when the pistol fell at his feet? He thought there might be a bullet for *him*. Did you not see how he looked with quickness towards the lodge of the concierge, who was watching? The concierge, who feeds the police with a spoon?'

Now Aunt Maria did not actually believe one word of what she had said about the young man. In fact, three nights ago she had scarcely noticed him except as a possible moustache-twisting sinner of the boulevards. But these ideas foamed into her brain; she could not stop; she must speak faster and faster.

For it seemed to her that there was a hesitation in Nina's eyes . . .

Nina moved slowly to the side of the dressing-table, still looking steadily at the other woman. Gas-light burnished the wings of Nina's soft brown hair. With her left hand she pulled open the drawer of the dressing-table, in which the derringer pistol lay fully loaded, and with a percussion-cap resting under the light pressure of its hammer.

'What do you do?' Aunt Maria screamed out. Then, abruptly glancing at the door and holding up cape and hat as though to call for silence, she added: 'Listen!'

Outside the door, the only door in the room, was a drawing-room with a polished hardwood floor unmuffled by any carpet. There was a sound. Both women heard the soft thump of the cane as the visitor slid forward a lame leg; then silence, then again the bump of the cane. Someone was slowly but steadily approaching the bedroom door. Both women knew who it was.

'My God!' thought the staggered Aunt Maria. 'He really *is a mouchard* after all!' A fist, not loudly but firmly and with authority, knocked at the bedroom door.

Aunt Maria, terrified, backed away towards the bed-alcove and held up cape and hat as though they might shield her.

If there had ever been any uncertainty in Nina's face, it was gone now. Her cold movements were swift but unhurried. From the vase she whipped the bouquet of yellow roses, squeezing the water from the stems and wrapping them in heavy tissue-paper from the drawer.

90

Gripping the stems in her left hand, she plucked out the pistol. There was a soft click as she drew back the hammer. She made an opening in the roses, hiding the derringer so that nothing should catch in the hammer when she snatched it out.

There would still be time to reload, if she must dispose of an intruder first.

'Enter!' Nina calmly called in French. It was the language they spoke afterwards.

Their visitor, the man of the courtyard, came in and closed the door behind him. He was in full evening-dress, partly covered by his ankle-length black cloak, which yet showed his white frilled shirt-front and a carelessly tied stock. In one white-gloved hand he held his hat, in the other his gold-headed stick.

Again Nina noted the delicacy of his white, handsome face, in contrast to the heavy dark hair and moustache. Even his figure was somewhat slight, though well-made.

'For this intrusion,' he said in his fine voice, 'I deeply apologize to mademoiselle; and, understood,' bowing towards Aunt Maria, 'to madame.'

Nina's pink lips went back over fine teeth.

'Your best apology lies behind you.' She nodded towards the door.

'Unfortunately, no.' The stranger, at leisure, put down his hat and stick on a table at the left of the door. His dark eyes, with that odd life-in-death quality, grew strong with a fierce sincerity, and so did his voice. 'For I presume to have an interest in you, mademoiselle.'

'Who are you? What do you want?'

The stranger leaned his back against door, seeming to lounge rather than lean, in a devil-may-care swagger which to Nina seemed vaguely familiar.

'Let us say that I am the detective Lecoq, in the admirable police-romances of M. Gaboriau. Lecoq is a real person, remember, as was the character D'Artagnan. Well! I am Lecoq.'

Nina breathed a little faster. Her finger tightened round the trigger of the pistol.

'How did you enter by a locked front door?'

'Believe me, I have passed through more difficult doors than that. Stop!' His white-gloved hand went up to forestall her, and he smiled. 'Let us suppose (I say merely let us suppose!) that Mademoiselle Nina Bennett had intent to kill the Emperor of the French, I who speak to

91

you, I also live in this house. I can put questions to a concierge.'

'Did I not tell you?' screamed Aunt Maria, hiding her face behind the cape and hat.

Neither of them looked at her.

'To any reader of the French journals, the name of your mother is well-known. The nationality of your father,' and he nodded towards the flag outside the window, his nostrils thin and bitter, 'you too obviously display. However! If it be your intent to kill the Emperor, where would you go? Assuredly not far from here, or you would have been gone now.'

('If you must kill this sly one here,' Aunt Maria thought wildly, 'kill him now! Shoot!')

'I think,' continued the stranger, 'you have chosen the corner of the rue Royale and the rue de Rivoli. Every journal in Paris will have told you, with exactness, the route and time of the procession. It is summer; there will be an open carriage, low-built.

The Emperor, a fact well-known, sits always on the right-hand side facing forward, the Empress on the left.

'How lovely—' His strong voice shook; he checked himself. 'How innocent you will look, in your finery and jewels, chattering English and deliberately bad French, on the kerb-stone! The military, even the military-police, will only smile when you walk out slowly towards the slow-moving carriage, and speak English as you offer (is it not so?) the bouquet of roses to the Empress Eugénie of Montijo.'

('I was mad, I was mad!' mentally moaned Aunt Maria. 'Let him take the damned pistol from her now!')

'Holding the bouquet in your left hand,' he went on quietly, 'you must lean partly across His Majesty. With your right hand you will take out an old-style single-shot pistol, and fire it at the Emperor's head so closely that you cannot miss. Have I, M. Lecoq, correctly deduced your plan?'

Nina Bennett cast a swift glance at the clock.

Time, time, time! A while ago, when she had looked out of the window, far up to the right there had been a red sky over Neuilly beyond the top of the Champs Elysees.

Now the whole sky was tinged with pink amid white and pale blue. It brightened the gaslights in that black-silk panelled room, which might have been a symbol of espionage since the days of Savary and Napoleon the First.

'Are you the only one,' Nina asked levelly, 'who knows of this . . . this plan?'

'The only one, mademoiselle.'

With a steady hand Nina took the derringer from among the roses, moving aside the yellow bouquet. It is a sober fact that the young man did not even notice it.

'And now,' he said in that hypnotic voice, 'I must tell you of my interest in you. It is very easy.' He straightened up, his face whiter, and clenched his gloved fists. 'You are Venus in the body of Diana; you are Galatea not yet kissed to true life. You are . . . I will not say the most beautiful woman I have ever met; but the most maddening and stimulating.' Cynicism showed in his eyes. 'And I have known so many women.'

'How modest you are!' Nina cried furiously.

'I state a fact. But I tell you one of the reasons, my love, why I will not permit you to go from this room for at least half an hour.'

Again Nina started, almost dropping the pistol.

From the street below, and from the open spaces beyond, there were cries and shouts. She heard the confused running of feet, seeming from every direction at once, which can conjure up a Paris crowd in one finger-snap. Very faintly, in the distance, she also heard the slow *clop-clop* of many horses in procession.

According to every newspaper, the procession to the Opera would be headed by the Imperial band. The instruments of the band were clear rather than brassy; already they had begun with the swinging tune, *Partant pour la Syrie*, which was the official song of Napoleon the Third.

> *Setting out for Syria*
> *Young and brave Dunois . . .*

There was still time. Nina Bennett's hand was as steady as a statue's.

'You call yourself a detective, M. Lecoq. But you are only a police-spy. Now stand away from that door!'

'No, my dear,' smiled the other, and folded his arms lazily.

'I will count to three . . .'

'Count to five thousand; I would hear your voice. What matter if you kill me? Most people,' and his dark eyes seemed to wander out to

93

the boulevards, 'think me already dead. Put your hand in mine; let fools flourish pistols or knives.'

'One!' said Nina, and thought she meant it.

The *clop-clop* of the procession, thought still not loud, was drawing nearer. What sent a shiver through Nina's body was the tune into which the band changed, in honor of the French-American ball at the Opera. There were no words. There were only dreams and memories. Slow, sombre, the great battle-hymn rolled out.

Mine eyes have seen the glory of the coming of the Lord.
He is trampling out the vintage where the grapes of wrath are stored . . .

'In a moment,' continued the visitor, 'I will come and take that pistol from you. But first hear what I have to say.' His tone changed, fiercely, 'This political assassination is more than wrong. It changes nothing. It is the act of an idiot. I know! I tell you I know! If I could make you understand . . .'

Abruptly he paused.

He too had heard the music, clear in the hush of evening. His face darkened. Had Aunt Maria been watching, she would have seen in his eyes the same maniacal glitter as in those of Nina Bennett. And he spoke the only words which could have ended his life.

'By God!' he snarled. 'You might have been a human being, without your mother and your damned Yankee father!'

Nina pulled the trigger, firing straight for his heart at less than ten feet's distance. The percussion-cap flared into the bang of the explosion, amid heavy smoke. The stranger, flung back against the door, still stood upright and emerged through smoke.

She had missed the heart. But the pistol-ball, smashing ribs on the right of his chest, had torn open his right lung. And Nina knew now that never, never in her life, could she have fired at the Emperor unless he had first uttered some maddening insult, as this stranger had.

'I thank you, my dear,' gravely said the stranger, pressing his reddening fingers to his chest, and white-faced at his own choked breathing. 'Now be quick! Put that derringer into my hand; and I shall have time to say I did it myself.'

Then another realization struck Nina.

'You've been speaking in English!' she cried in that language. 'Ever since you said "damned Yankee." Are you English?'

'I am an American, my dear,' he answered drawing himself up and swallowing blood.

'And at least no one can call me a police spy. My name,' he added casually, 'is John Wilkes Booth.'

A Kind of Madness

ANTHONY BOUCHER

There have been an almost uncountable number of books and stories about Jack the Ripper in fact and fiction. The savage and gruesome murders that the mysterious man — or woman? — committed in the East End of London just over one hundred years ago have proved endlessly fascinating to each succeeding generation of mystery readers, and the theories about Jack's identity are many and varied. Selecting a short story about the Ripper has been by far the most difficult of any for this collection because there are simply so many good ones. In the end I plumped for 'A Kind of Madness' by the American crime writer, editor and critic, Anthony Boucher, for two reasons. Firstly, because of the author's stature in the mystery field — the annual mystery convention, the Bouchercon, is named after him — and, secondly, because his story offers a perfectly feasible solution to the identity of Jack the Ripper. It is also interesting because it contains references to a quite different murder, the infamous killing of Paris solicitor Marcel Gouffé in 1890 by Michael Eyraud and his mistress, Gabrielle Bompard, which put Eyraud on the guillotine and Bompard in gaol for 20 years. I also admit to finding irresistible the coincidence that Anthony Boucher used the pseudonym H. H. Holmes on a number of his crime stories. Holmes was the name of the Chicago mass-murder who for many years held the record for multiple killings . . .

IN 1888 LONDON was terrified, as no city has been before or since, by Jack the Ripper, who from April through November killed and dissected at least seven prostitutes, without leaving a single clue to his identity. The chain of murders snapped abruptly. After 1888 Jack never ripped again. Because on 12th July, 1889 . . .

He paused on the steps of University College, surrounded by young ladies prattling the questions that were supposed to prove they had paid careful attention to his lecture–demonstration.

The young ladies were, he knew as a biologist, human females; dissection would establish the fact beyond question. But for him womankind was divided into three classes: angels and devils and students. He had never quite forgiven the college for admitting women nine years ago. That these female creatures should irrelevantly possess the same terrible organs that were the arsenal of the devils, the same organs through which the devils could strike lethally at the angels, the very organs which he . . .

He answered the young ladies without hearing either their questions or his answers, detached himself from the bevy, and strolled towards the Euston Road.

For eight months now he had seen neither angel nor devil. The events of 1888 seemed infinitely remote, like a fever remembered after convalescence. It had indeed been a sort of fever of the brain, perhaps even – he smiled gently – a kind of madness. But after his own angel had died of that unspeakable infection which the devil had planted in him – which had affected him so lightly but had penetrated so fatally to those dread organs which render angels vulnerable to devils . . .

He observed, clinically, that he was breathing heavily and that his hand was groping in his pocket – a foolish gesture, since he had not carried the scalpel for eight months. Deliberately he slowed his pace and his breathing. The fever was spent – though surely no sane man could see anything but good in an effort to rid London of its devils.

'Pardon, m'sieur.'

The woman was young, no older than his students, but no one would mistake her for a female of University College. Even to his untutored eye her clothes spoke of elegance and chic and, in a word, Paris. Her delicate scent seemed no man-made otto but pure *essence de femme*. Her golden hair framed a piquant face, the nose slightly tilted, the upper lip a trifle full – irregular, but delightful.

'Ma'm'selle?' he replied, with courtesy and approbation.

'If m'sieur would be so kind as to help a stranger in your great city . . . I seek an establishment of baggages.'

He tried to suppress his smile, but she noticed it, and a response sparkled in her eyes. 'Do I say something improper?' she asked almost hopefully.

'Oh, no. Your phrase is quite correct. Most Englishmen, however, would say "a luggage shop".'

'Ah, *c'est ca*. "A luggage shop" – I shall remember me. I am on my first voyage to England, though I have known Englishmen at Paris. I feel like a small child in a world of adults who talk strangely. Though I know' – his gaze was resting on what the French politely call the throat – 'I am not shaped like one.'

An angel, he was thinking. Beyond doubt an angel, and a delectable one. And this innocently provocative way of speaking made her seem only the more angelic.

He took from her gloved fingers the slip of paper on which was written the address of the 'establishment of baggages'.

'You are at the wrong end of the Euston Road,' he explained. 'Permit me to hail a cab for you; it is too far to walk on such a hot day.'

'Ah, yes, this is a July of Julys, is it not? One has told me that in England it is never hot, but behold I sweat!'

He frowned.

'Oh, do I again say something beastly? But it is true: I do sweat.' Tiny moist beads outlined her all but invisible blonde moustache.

He relaxed. 'As a professor of biology I should be willing to acknowledge the fact that the human female is equipped with sweat glands, even though proper English usage would have it otherwise, Forgive me, my dear child, for frowning at your innocent impropriety.'

She hesitated, imitating his frown. Then she looked up, laughed softly, and put her small plump hand on his arm. 'As a token of forgiveness, m'sieur, you may buy me an ice before hailing my cab. My name,' she added, 'is Gaby.'

He felt infinitely refreshed. He had been wrong, he saw it now, to abstain so completely from the company of women once his fever had run its course. There was a delight, a solace, in the presence of a woman. Not a student, or a devil, but the true woman: an angel.

Gaby daintily dabbed ice and sweat from her full upper lip and rose from the table. 'M'sieur has been most courteous to the stranger within his gates. And now I must seek my luggage shop.'

'Mademoiselle Gaby—'

'Hein? Speak up, m'sieur le professeur. Is it that you wish to ask if we shall find each other again?'

'I should indeed be honoured if while you are in London—'

'Merde alors!' She winked at him, and he hoped that he had misunderstood her French. 'Do we need such fine phrases? I think we understand ourselves, no? There is a small bistro – a pub, you call it? – near my lodgings. If you wish to meet me there tomorrow evening . . .' She gave him instructions. Speechless, he noted them down.

'You will not be sorry, m'sieur. I think well you will enjoy your little tour of France after your dull English diet.'

She held his arm while he hailed a cab. He did not speak except to the cabman. She extended her ungloved hand and he automatically took it. Her fingers dabbled deftly in his palm while her pink tongue peered out for a moment between her lips. Then she was gone.

'And I thought her an angel,' he groaned.

His hand fumbled again in his empty pocket.

The shiny new extra large trunk dominated the bedroom.

Gabrielle Bompart stripped to the skin as soon as the porter had left (more pleased with her wink than with her tip) and perched on the trunk. The metal trim felt refreshingly cold against her flesh.

Michel Eyraud looked up lazily from the bed where he was sprawled. 'I never get tired of looking at you, Gaby.'

'When you are content just to look,' Gaby grinned, 'I cut your throat.'

'It's hot,' said Eyraud.

'I know, and you are an old man. You are old enough to be my father. You are a very wicked lecherous old man, but for old men it is often hot.'

Eyraud sprang off the bed, strode over to the trunk, and seized her by her naked shoulders. She laughed in his face. 'I was teasing you. It is too hot. Even for me. Go lie down and tell me about your day. You got everything?'

Eyraud waved an indolent hand at the table. A coil of rope, a block and tackle, screws, screwdriver . . .

Gaby smiled approvingly. 'And I have the trunk, such a nice big one, and this.' She reached for her handbag, drew out a red-and-white girdle. 'It goes well with my dressing gown. And it is strong.' She stretched it and tugged at it, grunting enthusiastically.

Eyraud looked from the girdle to the rope to the pulley to the top of the door leading to the sitting-room, then back to the trunk. He nodded.

Gaby stood by the full-length mirror contemplating herself. 'That

99

silly bailiff, that Gouffé. Why does he dare to think that Gaby should be interested in him? This Gaby, such as you behold her . . .' She smiled at the mirror and nodded approval.

'I met a man,' she said. 'An Englishman. Oh, so very stiff and proper. He looks like Phileas Fogg in Jules Verne's *Le Tour du Monde*. He wants me.'

'Fogg had money,' said Eyraud. 'Lots of it.'

'So does my professor . . . Michi?'

'Yes?'

Gabrielle pirouetted before the mirror. 'Am I an actress?'

'All women are actresses.'

'Michi, do not try to be clever. It is not becoming to you. Am I an actress?'

Eyraud lit a French cigarette and tossed the blue pack to Gaby. 'You're a performer, and entertainer. You have better legs than any actress in Paris. And if you made old Gouffé think you love him for his fat self . . . Yes, I guess you're an actress.'

'Then I know what I want.' Gaby's eyelids were half closed. 'Michi, I want a rehearsal.'

Eyraud looked at the trunk and the block and tackle and the red-and-white girdle. He laughed, heartily and happily.

He found her waiting for him in the pub. The blonde hair picked up the light and gave it back, to form a mocking halo around the pert devil's face.

His fingers reassured him that the scalpel was back where it belonged. He had been so foolish to call 'a fever' what was simply his natural rightful temperature. It was his mission in life to rid the world of devils. That was the simple truth. And not all devils had cockney accents and lived in Whitechapel.

'Be welcome, m'sieur le professeur.' She curtseyed with impish grace. 'You have thirst?'

'No,' he grunted.

'Ah, you mean you do not have thirst in the throat. It lies lower, hein?' She giggled, and he wondered how long she had been waiting in the pub. She laid her hand on his arm. The animal heat seared through his sleeve. 'I go upstairs. You understand, it is more chic when you do not see me make myself ready. You ascend in a dozen of minutes. It is on the first floor, at the left to the rear.'

He left the pub and waited on the street. The night was cool and the fog was beginning to settle down. On just such a night in last August . . . What was her name? He had read it later in *The Times*. Martha Tabor? Tabby? Tabbypussydevil.

He had nicked his finger on the scalpel. As he sucked the blood he heard a clock strike. He had been waiting almost half hour; where had the time gone? The devil would be impatient.

The sitting-room was dark, but subdued lamplight gleamed from the bedroom. The bed was turned down. Beside it stood a huge trunk.

The devil was wearing a white dressing-gown and a red-and white girdle that emphasized its improbably slender waist. It came towards him and stroked his face with hot fingers and touched its tongue like a branding iron to his chin and ears and at last his lips. His hands closed around its waist.

'Ouf!' gasped the devil, 'You may crush me, I assure you M'sieur. I love that. But please to spare my pretty new girdle. Perhaps if I debarrass myself of it . . .' It unclasped the girdle and the dressing-gown fell open.

His hand took a firm grip on the scalpel.

The devil moved him towards the door between the two rooms. It festooned the girdle around his neck. 'Like that,' it said gleefully. 'There – doesn't that make you a pretty red-and-white cravat?'

Hand and scalpel came out of his pocket.

And Michel Eyraud, standing in the dark sitting-room fastened the ends of the girdle to the rope running through the block and tackle and gave a powerful jerk.

The rope sprang to the ceiling, the girdle followed it, and the professor's thin neck snapped. The scalpel fell from his dead hand.

The rehearsal had been a complete success.

Just as they planned to do with the bailiff Gouffé, they stripped the body and plundered the wallet. 'Not bad,' said Eyraud. 'Do actresses get paid for rehearsing?'

'This one does,' said Gaby. And they dumped the body in the trunk.

Later the clothes would be disposed of in dustbins, the body carried by trunk to some quiet countryside where it might decompose in naked namelessness.

Gaby swore when she stepped on the scalpel. 'What the hell is this?' She picked it up. 'It's sharp. Do you suppose he was one of those

101

types who like a little blood to heighten their pleasures? I've heard of them but never met one.'

Gaby stood pondering, her dressing-gown open . . .

The first night, to the misfortune of the bailiff Gouffé, went off as smoothly as the rehearsal. But the performers reckoned without the patience and determination and génie policier of Marie-Francois Goron, Chief of the Paris Sûreté.

The upshot was, as all aficionados of true crime know, that Eyraud was guillotined, nineteen months after the rehearsal, and Gaby, who kept grinning at the jury, was sentenced to twenty years of hard labour.

When Goron was in London before the trial, he paid his usual courtesy call at Scotland Yard and chatted at length with Inspector Frederick G. Abberline.

'Had one rather like yours recently ourselves,' said Abberline. 'Naked man, broken neck, left to rot in the countryside. Haven't succeeded in identifying him yet. You were luckier there.'

'It is notorious,' Goron observed, 'that the laboratories of the French police are the best in the world.'

'We do very well, thank you,' said Abberline distantly.

'Of course.' The French visitor was all politeness: 'As you did last year in that series of Whitechapel murders.'

'I don't know if you're being sarcastic, Mr Goron, but no police force in the world could have done more than we did in the Ripper case. It was a nightmare with no possible resolution. And unless he strikes again, it's going to go down as one of the greatest unsolved cases in history. Jack the Ripper will never hang.'

'Not,' said M. Goron, 'so long as he confines his attention to the women of London.' He hurried to catch the boat train thinking of Gabrielle Bompard and feeling a certain regret that such a woman was also such a devil.

The Fall River Axe Murders

ANGELA CARTER

There are few rhymes more famous than this one which children of all ages have chanted with malicious glee for the past one hundred years:

> *Lizzie Borden took an axe*
> *And gave her mother forty whacks*
> *And when she saw what she had done*
> *She gave her father forty-one.*

Compressed into those two dozens words are virtually the entire details of this crime which was committed in 1893 by a thirty-two-year-old spinster of Fall River, Massachusetts. It merely needs to be added that she stood trial for slaying her father and stepmother in a case which is now among the most familiar in American criminal history – and was acquitted. The public opinions about Lizzie at the time ranged from those who were convinced she was guilty from the moment a freshly-cleaned axe blade was found in her home, to the others who were convinced by her performance in court – fainting fits and all – that she must be innocent. Indeed, for the rest of her life, all of which Lizzie spent in Fall River until her death in 1927, the arguments continued to rage; and have engaged the interest of historians and writers ever since. Angela Carter has written a number of award-winning fantasy novels and collections of short stories in which vampires and were-wolves have mixed with characters from fiction including Puss-in-Boots and Alice (who went through the looking glass) and real-life characters such as Mary Magdalene, Edgar Allan Poe and Lizzie Borden. Although there have certainly been other tales about the axe murderess, I venture there has never been one quite like 'The Fall River Axe Murders'.

EARLY IN THE morning of the fourth of August, 1892 in Fall River, Massachusetts.

Hot, hot, hot . . . very early in the morning, before the factory whistle, but, even at this hour, everything shimmers and quivers under the attack of white, furious sun already high in the still air.

Its inhabitants have never come to terms with these hot, humid summers – for it is the humidity more than the heat that makes them intolerable; the weather clings like a low fever you cannot shake off. The Indians who lived here first had the sense to take off their buckskins when hot weather came and sit up to their necks in ponds; not so the descendants of the industrious, self-mortifying saints who imported the Protestant ethic wholesale into a country intended for the siesta and are proud, proud! of flying in the face of nature. In most latitudes with summers like these, everything slows down, then. You stay all day in penumbra behind drawn blinds and closed shutters; you wear clothes loose enough to make your own breeze to cool yourself when you infrequently move. But the ultimate decade of the last century finds us at the high point of hard work, here; all will soon be bustle, men will go out into the furnace of the morning well wrapped up in flannel underclothes linen shirts, vests and coats and trousers of sturdy woollen cloth, and they garrotte themselves with neckties, too, they think it is so virtuous to be uncomfortable.

And today it is the middle of a heat wave; so early in the morning and the mercury has touched the middle eighties, already, and shows no sign of slowing down its headlong ascent.

As far as clothes were concerned, women only appeared to get off more lightly. On this morning, when, after breakfast and the performance of a few household duties, Lizzie Borden will murder her parents, she will, on rising, don a simple cotton frock – but, under that, went a long, starched cotton petticoat; another short, starched cotton petticoat; long drawers; woollen stockings; a chemise; and a whalebone corset that took her viscera in a stern hand and squeezed them very tightly. She also strapped a heavy linen napkin between her legs because she was menstruating.

In all these clothes, out of sorts and nauseous as she was, in this dementing heat, her belly in a vice, she will heat up a flat-iron on a stove and press handkerchiefs with the heated iron until it is time for her to go down to the cellar woodpile to collect the hatchet with which our imagination – 'Lizzie Borden with an axe' – always equips her, just as we always visualise St Catherine rolling along her wheel, the emblem of her passion.

Soon, in just as many clothes as Miss Lizzie wears, if less fine, Bridget, the servant girl, will slop kerosene on a sheet of last night's newspaper crumpled with a stick or two of kindling. When the fire settles down, she will cook breakfast; the fire will keep her suffocating company as she washes up afterwards.

In a serge suit, one look at which would be enough to bring you out in prickly heat, Old Borden will perambulate the perspiring town, truffling for money like a pig until he will return home mid-morning to keep a pressing appointment with destiny.

But nobody here is up and about, yet; it is still early morning, before the factory whistle, the perfect stillness of hot weather, a sky already white, the shadowless light of New England like blows from the eye of God, and the sea, white, and the river, white.

If we have largely forgotten the physical discomforts of the itching, oppressive garment of the past and the corrosive effects of perpetual physical discomfort on the nerves, then we have mercifully forgotten, too, the smells of the past, the domestic odours – ill-washed flesh; infrequently changed underwear; chamber-pots; slop-pails; inadequately plumbed privies; rotting food; unattended teeth; and the streets are no fresher than indoors, the omnipresent acridity of horse piss and dung, drains, sudden stench of old death from butchers' shops, the amniotic horror of the fishmonger.

You would drench your handkerchief with cologne and press it to your nose. You would splash yourself with parma violet so that the reek of fleshly decay you always carried with you was overlaid by that of the embalming parlour. You would abhor the air you breathed.

Five living creatures are asleep in a house on Second Street, Fall River. They comprise two old men and three women. The first old man owns all the women by either marriage, birth or contract. His house is narrow as a coffin and that was how he made his fortune – he used to be an undertaker but he has recently branched out in several directions and all his branches bear fruit of the most fiscally gratifying kind.

But you would never think, to look at his house, that he is a successful and a prosperous man. His house is cramped, comfortless, small and mean – 'unpretentious', you might say, if you were his sycophant – while Second Street itself saw better days some time ago. The Borden house – see 'Andrew J. Borden' in flowing script on the brass plate next to the door – stands by itself with a few scant feet of yard on either side. On the left is a stable, out of use since he sold the horse. In the back lot grow a few pear trees, laden at this season.

On this particular morning, as luck would have it, only one of the two Borden girls sleeps in their father's house. Emma Lenora, his oldest daughter, has taken herself off to nearby New Bedford for a few days, to catch the ocean breeze, and so she will escape the slaughter.

Few of their social class stay in Fall River in the sweating months of June, July and August but, then, few of their social class live on Second Street, in the low part of town where heat gathers like fog. Lizzie was invited away, too, to a summer house by the sea to join a merry band of girls but, as if on purpose to mortify her flesh, as if important business kept her in the exhausted town, as if a wicked fairy spelled her in Second Street, she did not go.

The other old man is some kind of kin of Borden's. He doesn't belong here; he is visiting, passing through, he is a chance bystander, he is irrelevant.

Write him out of the script.

Even though his presence in the doomed house is historically unimpeachable, the colouring of this domestic apocalypse must be crude and the design profoundly simplified for the maximum emblematic effect.

Write John Vinnicum Morse out of the script.

One old man and two of his women sleep in the house on Second Street.

The City Hall clock whirrs and sputters the prolegomena to the first stroke of six and Bridget's alarm clock gives a sympathetic skip and click as the minute-hand stutters on the hour; back the little hammer jerks, about to hit the bell on top of her clock, but Bridget's damp eyelids do not shudder with premonition as she lies in her sticking flannel nightgown under one thin sheet on an iron bedstead, lies on her back, as the good nuns taught her in her Irish girlhood, in case she dies during the night, to make less trouble for the undertaker. She is a good girl, on the whole, although her temper is sometimes uncertain and then she will talk back to the missus, sometimes, and will be forced to confess the sin of impatience to the priest. Overcome by heat and nausea – for everyone in the house is going to wake up sick today – she will return to this little bed later in the morning. While she snatches a few moments rest, upstairs, all hell will be let loose, downstairs.

A rosary of brown glass beads, a cardboard-backed colour print of the Virgin bought from a Portuguese shop, a flyblown photograph of her solemn mother in Donegal – these lie or are propped on the mantelpiece that, however sharp the Massachusetts winter, has never seen a lit stick. A banged tin trunk at the foot of the bed holds all Bridget's worldly goods.

There is a stiff chair beside the bed with, upon it, a candlestick, matches, the alarm clock that resounds the room with a dyadic, metallic clang, for it is a joke between Bridget and her mistress that the girl could sleep through anything, *anything*, and so she needs the alarm as well as all the factory whistles that are just about to blast off, just this very second about to blast off . . .

A splintered deal washstand holds the jug and bowl she never uses; she isn't going to lug water up to the third floor just to wipe herself down, is she? Not when there's water enough in the kitchen sink.

Old Borden sees no necessity for baths. He does not believe in total immersion. To lose his natural oils would be to rob his body.

A frameless square of mirror reflects in corrugated waves a cracked, dusty soap dish containing a quantity of black metal hairpins.

On bright rectangles of paper blinds move the beautiful shadows of the pear trees.

Although Bridget left the door open a crack in forlorn hopes of coaxing a draught into the room, all the spent heat of the previous day has packed itself tightly into her attic. A dandruff of spent whitewash flakes from the ceiling where a fly drearily whines.

The house is thickly redolent of sleep, that sweetish, clinging smell. Still, all still; in all the house nothing moves except the droning fly. Stillness on the staircase. Stillness pressing against the blinds. Stillness, mortal stillness in the room below, where Master and Mistress share the matrimonial bed.

Were the drapes open or the lamp lit, one could better observe the differences between this room and the austerity of the maid's room. Here is a carpet splashed with vigorous flowers, even if the carpet is of the cheap and cheerful variety; there are mauve, ochre and harsh cerise flowers on the wallpaper, even though the wallpaper was old when the Bordens arrived in the house. A dresser with another distorting mirror; no mirror in this house does not take your face and twist it. On the dresser, a runner embroidered with forget-me-nots; on the runner, a bone comb missing three teeth and lightly threaded with grey hairs, a hairbrush backed with ebonised wood, and a number of lace mats

107

underneath small china boxes holding safety-pins, hairnets etc. The little hairpiece that Mrs Borden attaches to her balding scalp for daytime wear is curled up like a dead squirrel. But of Borden's male occupation of this room there is no trace because he has a dressing- room of his own, through *that* door on the left . . .

What about the other door, the one next to it?

It leads to the back stairs.

And that yet other door, partially concealed behind the head of the heavy, mahogany bed?

If it were not kept securely locked, it would take you into Miss Lizzie's room.

One peculiarity of this house is the number of doors the rooms contain and, a further peculiarity, how all these doors are always locked. A house full of locked doors that open only into other rooms with other locked doors, for, upstairs and downstairs, all the rooms lead in and out of one another like a maze in a bad dream. It is a house without passages. There is no part of the house that has not been marked as some inmate's personal territory; it is a house with no shared, no common spaces between one room and the next. It is a house of privacies sealed as close as if they had been sealed with wax on a legal document.

The only way to Emma's room is through Lizzie's. There is no way out of Emma's room. It is a dead end.

The Bordens' custom of locking all the doors, inside and outside, dates from a time, a few years ago, shortly before Bridget came to work for them, when the house was burgled. A person unknown came through the side door while Borden and his wife had taken one of their rare trips out together; he had loaded her into a trap and set out for the farm they owned at Swansea to ensure his tenant was not bilking him. The girls stayed at home in their rooms, napping on their beds or repairing ripped hems or sewing loose buttons more securely or writing letters or contemplating acts of charity among the deserving poor or staring vacantly into space.

I can't imagine what else they might do.

What the girls do when they are on their own is unimaginable to me.

Emma is more mysterious by far than Lizzie, for we know much less about her. She is a blank space. She has no life. The door from her room leads only into the room of her sister.

'Girls' is, of course, a courtesy term. Emma is well into her forties,

Lizzie in her thirties, but they did not marry and so live in their father's house, where they remain in a fictive, protracted childhood.

While the master and the mistress were away and the girls asleep or otherwise occupied, some person or persons unknown tiptoed up the back stairs to the matrimonial bedroom and pocketed Mrs Borden's gold watch and chain, the coral necklace and silver bangle of her remote childhood, and a roll of dollar bills Old Borden kept under clean union suits in the third drawer of the bureau on the left. The intruder attempted to force the lock of the safe, that featureless block of black iron like a slaughtering block or an altar sitting squarely next to the bed on Old Borden's side, but it would have taken a crowbar to penetrate adequately the safe and the intruder tackled it with a pair of nail scissors that were lying handy on the dresser so *that* didn't come off.

Then the intruder pissed and shat on the cover of the Bordens' bed, knocked the clutter of this and that on the dresser to the floor, smashing everything, swept into Old Borden's dressing-room there to maliciously assault his funeral coat as it hung in the moth-balled dark of his closet with the self-same nail scissors that had been used on the safe (the nail scissors now split in two and were abandoned on the closet floor), retired to the kitchen, smashed the flour crock and the treacle crock, and then scrawled an obscenity or two on the parlour window with the cake of soap that lived beside the scullery sink.

What a mess! Lizzie stared with vague surprise at the parlour window; she heard the soft bang of the open screen door, swinging idly, although there was no breeze. What was she doing, standing clad only in her corset in the middle of the sitting-room? How had she got there? Had she crept down when she heard the screen door rattle? She did not know. She could not remember.

All that happened was: all at once here she is, in the parlour, with a cake of soap in her hand. She experienced a clearing of the senses and only then began to scream and shout.

'Help! We have been burgled! Help!'

Emma came down and comforted her, as the big sister had comforted the little one since babyhood. Emma it was who cleared from the sitting-room carpet the flour and treacle Lizzie had heedlessly tracked in from the kitchen on her bare feet in her somnambulist trance. But of the missing jewellery and dollar bills no trace could be found.

I cannot tell you what effect the burglary had on Borden. It utterly disconcerted him; he was a man stunned. It violated him, even. He was a man raped. It took away his hitherto unshakeable confidence in the integrity inherent in things.

The burglary so moved them that the family broke its habitual silence with one another in order to discuss it. They blamed it on the Portuguese, obviously, but sometimes on the Canucks. If their outrage remained constant and did not diminish with time, the focus of it varied according to their moods, although they always pointed the finger of suspicion at the strangers and newcomers who lived in the gruesome ramparts of the company housing a few squalid blocks away. They did not always suspect the dark strangers exclusively; sometimes they thought the culprit might very well have been one of the mill-hands fresh from saucy Lancashire across the ocean who committed the crime, for a slum landlord has few friends among the criminal classes.

However, the possibility of a poltergeist occurs to Mrs Borden, although she does not know the word; she knows, however, that her younger stepdaughter is a strange one and could make the plates jump out of sheer spite, if she wanted to. But the old man adores his daughter. Perhaps it is then, after the shock of the burglary, that he decides she needs a change of scene, a dose of sea air, a long voyage, for it was after the burglary he sent her on the grand tour.

After the burglary, the front door and the side door were always locked three times if one of the inhabitants of the house left it for just so much as to go into the yard and pick up a basket of fallen pears when pears were in season or if the maid went out to hang a bit of washing or Old Borden, after supper, took a piss under a tree.

From this time dated the custom of locking all the bedroom doors on the inside when one was on the inside oneself or on the outside when one was on the outside. Old Borden locked his bedroom door in the morning, when he left it, and put the key in sight of all on the kitchen shelf.

The burglary awakened Old Borden to the evanescent nature of private property. He thereafter undertook an orgy of investment. He would forthwith invest his surplus in good brick and mortar, for who can make away with an office block?

A number of leases fell in simultaneously at just this time on a certain street in the downtown area of the city and Borden snapped them up. He owned the block. He pulled it down. He planned the Borden building, an edifice of shops and offices, dark red brick, deep tan stone, with cast-iron detail, from whence, in perpetuity, he might reap a fine harvest of unsaleable rents, and this monument, like that of Ozymandias, would long survive him – and, indeed, stands still, foursquare and handsome, the Andrew Borden Building, on South Main Street.

Not bad for a fish peddler's son, eh?

For, although 'Borden' is an ancient name in New England and the Borden clan between them owned the better part of Fall River, our Borden, Old Borden, these Bordens, did not spring from a wealthy branch of the family. There were Bordens and Bordens and he was the son of a man who sold fresh fish in a wicker basket from house to house to house. Old Borden's parsimony was bred of poverty but learned to thrive best on prosperity, for thrift has a different meaning for the poor; they get no joy of it, it is stark necessity to them. Whoever heard of a penniless miser?

Morose and gaunt, this self-made man is one of few pleasures. His vocation is capital accumulation.

What is his hobby?

Why, grinding the faces of the poor.

First, Andrew Borden was an undertaker, and death, recognising an accomplice, did well by him. In the city of spindles, few made old bones; the little children who laboured in the mills died with especial frequency. When he was an undertaker, no! – it was not true he cut the feet off corpses to fit into a job lot of coffins bought cheap as Civil War surplus! That was a rumour put about by his enemies!

With the profits from his coffins, he bought up a tenement or two and made fresh profit off the living. He bought shares in the mills. Then he invested in a bank or two, so that now he makes a profit on money itself, which is the purest form of profit of all.

Foreclosures and evictions are meat and drink to him. He loves nothing better than a little usury. He is halfway on the road to his first million.

At night, to save the kerosene, he sits in lampless dark. He waters the pear trees with his urine; waste not, want not. As soon as the daily newspapers are done with, he rips them up in geometric squares and stores them in the cellar privy so that they all can wipe their arses with them. He mourns the loss of the good organic waste that flushes down the WC. He would like to charge the very cockroaches in the kitchen rent. And yet he has not grown fat on all this; the pure flame of his passion has melted off his flesh, his skin sticks to his bones out of sheer parsimony. Perhaps it is from his first profession that he has acquired his bearing, for he walks with the stately dignity of a hearse.

To watch Old Borden bearing down the street towards you was to be filled with an instinctual respect for mortality, whose gaunt ambassador he seemed to be. And it made you think, too, what a triumph over nature it was when we rose up to walk on two legs instead of four, in the first place! For he held himself upright with such ponderous assertion it was a perpetual reminder to all who witnessed his progress how it is not *natural* to be upright, that it is a triumph of will over gravity, in itself a transcendence of the spirit over matter.

His spine is like an iron rod, forged, not born, impossible to imagine that spine of Old Borden's curled up in the womb in the big C of the foetus; he walks as if his legs had joints at neither knee nor ankle so that his feet hit the trembling earth like a bailiff pounding a door.

He has a white, chin–strap beard, old–fashioned already in those days. He looks as if he'd gnawed his lips off. He is at peace with his god for he has used his talents as the Good Book says he should.

Yet do not think he has no soft spot. Like Old Lear, his heart – and, more than that, his cheque-book – is putty in his youngest daughter's hands. On his pinky – you cannot see it, it lies under the covers – he wears a gold ring, not a wedding ring but a high-school ring, a singular trinket for a fabulously misanthropic miser. His youngest daughter gave it to him when she left school and asked him to wear it, always, and so he always does, and will wear it to the grave to which she is going to send him later in the morning of this combustible day.

He sleeps fully dressed in a flannel nightshirt over his long-sleeved underwear, and a flannel nightcap, and his back is turned towards his wife of thirty years, as is hers to his.

They are Mr and Mrs Jack Spratt in person, he tall and gaunt as a hanging judge and she, such a spreading, round little doughball. He is a miser, while she, she is a glutton, a solitary eater, most innocent of vices and yet the shadow or parodic vice of his, for he would like to eat up all the world, or, failing that, since fate has not spread him a sufficiently large table for his ambitions, he is a mute, inglorious Napoleon, he does not know what he might have done because he never had the opportunity – since he has not access to the entire world, he would like to gobble up the city of Fall River. But she, well, she just gently,

112

continuously stuffs herself, doesn't she; she's always nibbling away at something, at the cud, perhaps.

Not that she gets much pleasure from it, either; no gourmet, she, forever meditating the exquisite difference between a mayonnaise sharpened with a few drops of Orleans vinegar or one pointed up with a squeeze of fresh lemon juice. No. Abby never aspired so high, nor would she ever think to do so even if she had the option; she is satisfied to stick to simple gluttony and she eschews all overtones of the sensuality of indulgence. Since she relishes not one single mouthful of the food she eats, she knows her ceaseless gluttony is no transgression.

Here they lie in bed together, living embodiments of two of the Seven Deadly Sins, but he knows his avarice is no offence because he never spends any money and she knows she is not greedy because the grub she shovels down gives her dyspepsia.

She employs an Irish cook and Bridget's rough-and-ready hand in the kitchen fulfils Abby's every criterion. Bread, meat, cabbage, potatoes – Abby was made for the heavy food that made her. Bridget merrily slaps on the table boiled dinners, boiled fish, cornmeal mush, Indian pudding, johnnycakes, cookies.

But those cookies . . . ah! there you touch on Abby's little weakness. Molasses cookies, oatmeal cookies, raisin cookies. But when she tackles a sticky brownie, oozing chocolate, then she feels a queasy sense of having gone almost too far, that sin might be just around the corner if her stomach did not immediately palpitate like a guilty conscience.

Her flannel nightdress is cut on the same lines as his nightshirt except for the limp flannel frill round the neck. She weighs two hundred pounds. She is five feet nothing tall. The bed sags on her side. It is the bed in which his first wife died.

Last night, they dosed themselves with castor oil, due to the indisposition that kept them both awake and vomiting the whole night before that; the copious results of their purges brim the chamber-pots beneath the bed. It is fit to make a sewer faint.

Back to back they lie. You could rest a sword in the space between the old man and his wife, between the old man's backbone, the only rigid thing he ever offered her, and her soft, warm, enormous bum. Their purges flailed them. Their faces show up decomposing green in the gloom of the curtained room, in which the air is too thick for flies to move.

The youngest daughter dreams behind the locked door.

Look at the sleeping beauty!

She threw back the top sheet and her window is wide open but there is no breeze, outside, this morning, to shiver deliciously the screen. Bright sun floods the blinds so that the linen-coloured light shows us how Lizzie has gone to bed as for a levée in a pretty, ruffled nightdress of starched white muslin with ribbons of pastel pink satin threaded through the eyelets of the lace, for is it not the 'naughty Nineties' everywhere but dour Fall River? Don't the gilded steamships of the Fall River Line signify all the squandered luxury of the Gilded Age within their mahogany and chandeliered interiors? But don't they sail *away* from Fall River, to where, elsewhere, it is the Belle Epoque? In New York, Paris, London, champagne corks pop, in Monte Carlo the bank is broken, women fall backwards in a crisp meringue of petticoats for fun and profit, but not in Fall River. Oh, no. So, in the immutable privacy of her bedroom, for her own delight, Lizzie puts on a rich girl's pretty nightdress, although she lives in a mean house, because she is a rich girl, too.

But she is plain.

The hem of her nightdress is rucked up above her knees because she is a restless sleeper. Her light, dry, reddish hair, crackling with static, slipping loose from the night-time plait, crisps and stutters over the square pillow at which she clutches as she sprawls on her stomach, having rested her cheek on the starched pillowcase for coolness' sake at some earlier hour.

Lizzie was not an affectionate diminutive but the name with which she had been christened. Since she would always be known as 'Lizzie', so her father reasoned, why burden her with the effete and fancy prolongation of 'Elizabeth'? A miser in everything, he even cropped off half her name before he gave it to her. So 'Lizzie' it was, stark and unadorned, and she is a motherless child, orphaned at two years old, poor thing.

Now she is two-and-thirty and yet the memory of that mother she cannot remember remains an abiding source of grief: 'If mother had lived, everything would have been different.'

How? Why? Different in what way? She wouldn't have been able to answer that, lost in a nostalgia for unknown love. Yet how could she have been loved better than by her sister, Emma, who lavished the pent-up treasures of a New England spinster's heart upon the little thing? Different, perhaps, because her natural mother, the first Mrs

Borden, subject as she was to fits of sudden, wild, inexplicable rage, might have taken the hatchet to Old Borden on her own account? But Lizzie *loves* her father. All are agreed on that. Lizzie adores the adoring father who, after her mother died, took to himself another wife.

Her bare feet twitch a little, like those of a dog dreaming of rabbits. Her sleep is thin and unsatisfying, full of vague terrors and indeterminate menaces to which she cannot put a name or form once she is awake. Sleep opens within her a disorderly house. But all she knows is, she sleeps badly, and this last, stifling night has been troubled, too, by vague nausea and the gripes of her female pain; her room is harsh with the metallic smell of menstrual blood.

Yesterday evening she slipped out of the house to visit a woman friend. Lizzie was agitated; she kept picking nervously at the shirring on the front of her dress.

'I am afraid . . . that somebody . . . will *do* something,' said Lizzie.

'Mrs Borden . . .' and here Lizzie lowered her voice and her eyes looked everywhere in the room except at Miss Russell . . . 'Mrs Borden – oh! will you ever believe? Mrs Borden thinks somebody is trying to *poison* us!'

She used to call her stepmother 'mother', as duty bade, but, after a quarrel about money after her father deeded half a slum property to her stepmother five years before, Lizzie always, with cool scrupulosity, spoke of 'Mrs Borden' when she was forced to speak of her, and called her 'Mrs Borden' to her face, too.

'Last night, Mrs Borden and poor father were so sick! I heard them, through the wall. And, as for me, I haven't felt myself all day, I have felt so strange. So very . . . strange.'

For there were those somnambulist fits. Since a child, she endured occasional 'peculiar spells', as the idiom of the place and time called odd lapses of behaviour, unexpected, involuntary trances, moments of disconnection. Those times when the mind misses a beat. Miss Russell hastened to discover an explanation within reason; she was embarrassed to mention the 'peculiar spells'. Everyone knew there was nothing odd about the Borden girls.

'Something you ate? It must have been something you have eaten. What was yesterday's supper?' solicitously queried kind Miss Russell.

'Warmed over swordfish. We had it hot for dinner though I could not take much. Then Bridget heated up the leftovers for supper but, again, for myself, I could only get down a forkful. Mrs Borden ate up the remains and scoured her plate with her bread. She smacked her lips but then was sick all night.' (Note of smugness, here.)

'Oh, Lizzie! In all this heat, this dreadful heat! Twice-cooked fish! You know how quickly fish goes off in this heat! Bridget should have known better than to give you twice-cooked fish!'

It was Lizzie's difficult time of the month, too; her friend could tell by a certain haggard, glazed look on Lizzie's face. Yet her gentility forbade her to mention that. But how could Lizzie have got it into her head that the entire household was under siege from malign forces without?

'There have been threats,' Lizzie pursued remorselessly, keeping her eyes on her nervous fingertips. 'So many people, you understand, dislike father.'

This cannot be denied. Miss Russell politely remained mute.

'Mrs Borden was so very sick she called the doctor in and Father was abusive towards the doctor and shouted at him and told him he would not pay a doctor's bills whilst we had our own good castor oil in the house. He shouted at the doctor and all the neighbours heard and I was so ashamed. There is a man, you see . . .' and here she ducked her head, while her short, pale eyelashes beat on her cheek bones . . . 'such a man, a *dark* man, with the aspect, yes, of death upon his face, Miss Russell, a dark man I've seen outside the house at odd, at unexpected hours, early in the morning, late at night, whenever I cannot sleep in this dreadful shade if I raise the blind and peep out, there I see him in the shadows of the pear trees, in the yard, a dark man . . . perhaps he puts poison in the milk, in the mornings, after the milkman fills his can. Perhaps he poisons the ice, when the iceman comes.'

'How long has he been haunting you?' asked Miss Russell, properly dismayed.

'Since . . . the burglary,' said Lizzie and suddenly looked Miss Russell full in the face with a kind of triumph. How large her eyes were; prominent, yet veiled. And her well-manicured fingers went on pecking away at the front of her dress as if she were trying to unpick the shirring.

Miss Russell knew, she just *knew*, this dark man was a figment of Lizzie's imagination. All in a rush, she lost patience with the girl; dark men standing outside her bedroom window, indeed! Yet she was kind and cast about for ways to reassure.

'But Bridget is up and about when the milkman, the iceman call and the whole street is busy and bustling, too; who would dare to put poison in either milk or ice-bucket while half of Second Street looks on? Oh, Lizzie, it is the dreadful summer, the heat, the intolerable heat that's put us all out of sorts, makes us fractious and nervous, makes us sick. So easy to imagine things in this terrible weather, that taints the food and sows worms in the mind . . . I thought you'd planned to go away, Lizzie, to the ocean. Didn't you plan to take a little holiday, by the sea? Oh, do go! Sea air would blow away these silly fancies!'

Lizzie neither nods nor shakes her head but continues to worry at her shirring. For does she not have important business in Fall River? Only that morning, had she not been down to the drug-store to try to buy some prussic acid herself? But how can she tell kind Miss Russell she is gripped by an imperious need to stay in Fall River and murder her parents?

She went to the drug-store on the corner of Main Street in order to buy prussic acid but nobody would sell it to her, so she came home empty-handed. Had all that talk of poison in the vomiting house put her in mind of poison? The autopsy will reveal no trace of poison in the stomachs of either parent. She did not try to poison them; she only had it in mind to poison them. But she had been unable to buy poison. The use of poison had been denied her; so what can she be planning, now?

'And this dark man,' she pursued to the unwilling Miss Russell, 'oh! I have seen the moon glint upon an *axe*!'

When she wakes up, she can never remember her dreams; she only remembers she slept badly.

Hers is a pleasant room of not ungenerous dimensions, seeing the house is so very small. Besides the bed and the dresser, there is a sofa and a desk; it is her bedroom and also her sitting-room and her office, too, for the desk is stacked with account books of the various charitable organisations with which she occupies her ample spare time. The Fruit and Flower Mission, under whose auspices she visits the indigent old in hospital with gifts; the Women's Christian Temperance Union, for whom she extracts signatures for petitions against the Demon Drink; Christian Endeavour, whatever that is – this is the golden age of good works and she flings herself into committees with a vengeance. What would the daughters of the rich do with themselves if the poor ceased to exist?

There is the Newsboys Thanksgiving Dinner Fund; and the

Horsetrough Association; and the Chinese Conversion Association – no class nor kind is safe from her merciless charity.

Bureau; dressing-table; closet; bed; sofa. She spends her days in this room, moving between each of these dull items of furniture in a circumscribed, undeviating, planetary round. She loves her privacy, she loves her room, she locks herself up in it all day. A shelf contains a book or two: *Heroes of the Mission Field*, *The Romance of Trade*, *What Katy did*. On the walls, framed photographs of high-school friends, sentimentally inscribed, with, tucked inside one frame, a picture postcard showing a black kitten peeking through a horseshoe. A water-colour of a Cape Cod seascape executed with poignant amateur incompetence. A monochrome photograph or two of works of art, a Della Robbia madonna and the Mona Lisa; these she bought in the Uffizi and the Louvre respectively when she went to Europe.

Europe!

For don't you remember what Katy did next? The story-book heroine took the steamship to smoky old London, to elegant, fascinating Paris, to sunny, antique Rome and Florence, the story-book heroine sees Europe reveal itself before her like an interesting series of magic-lantern slides on a gigantic screen. All is present and all unreal. The Tower of London; click. Notre Dame; click. The Sistine Chapel; click. Then the lights go out and she is in the dark again.

Of this journey she retained only the most circumspect of souvenirs, that madonna, that Mona Lisa, reproductions of objects of art consecrated by a universal approval of taste. If she came back with a bag full of memories stamped 'Never to be Forgotten', she put the bag away under the bed on which she had dreamed of the world before she set out to see it and on which, at home again, she continued to dream, the dream having been transformed not into lived experience but into memory, which is only another kind of dreaming.

Wistfully: 'When I was in Florence . . .'

But then, with pleasure, she corrects herself: 'When *we* were in Florence . . .'

Because a good deal, in fact most, of the gratification the trip gave her came from having set out from Fall River with a select group of the daughters of respectable and affluent mill-owners. Once away from Second Street, she was able to move comfortably in the segment of Fall River society to which she belonged by right of old name and new money but from which, when she was at home, her father's plentiful personal eccentricities excluded her. Sharing bedrooms, sharing state rooms, sharing berths, the girls travelled together in a genteel gaggle that bore its doom already upon it, for they were the girls who would not marry, now, and any pleasure they might have obtained from the variety and excitement of the trip was spoiled in advance by the knowledge they were eating up what might have been their own wedding-cake, using up what should have been, if they'd had any luck, their marriage settlements.

All girls pushing thirty, privileged to go out and look at the world before they resigned themselves to the thin condition of New England spinsterhood; but it was a case of look, don't touch. They knew they must not get their hands dirtied or their dresses crushed by the world, while their affectionate companionship en route had a certain steadfast, determined quality about it as they bravely made the best of the second-best.

It was a sour trip, in some ways, sour; and it was a round trip, it ended at the sour place from where it had set out. Home, again; the narrow house, the rooms all locked like those in Bluebeard's castle, and the fat, white stepmother whom nobody loves sitting in the middle of the spider web, she has not budged a single inch while Lizzie was away but she has grown fatter.

This stepmother oppressed her like a spell.

The days open their cramped spaces into other cramped spaces and old furniture and never anything to look forward to, nothing.

When Old Borden dug in his pocket to shell out for Lizzie's trip to Europe, the eye of God on the pyramid blinked to see daylight, but no extravagance is too excessive for the miser's younger daughter who is the wild card in this house and, it seems, can have anything she wants, play ducks and drakes with her father's silver dollars if it so pleases her. He pays all her dressmakers' bills on the dot and how she loves to dress up fine! She is addicted to dandyism. He gives her each week in pin-money the same as the cook gets for wages and Lizzie gives that which she does not spend on personal adornment to the deserving poor.

He would give his Lizzie anything, anything in the world that lives under the green sign of the dollar.

She would like a pet, a kitten or a puppy, she loves small animals and birds, too, poor, helpless things. She piles high the bird-table all winter. She used to keep some white pouter pigeons in the disused stable, the kind that look like shuttlecocks and go 'vroo croo', soft as a cloud.

Surviving photographs of Lizzie Borden show a face it is difficult to look at as if you knew nothing about her; coming events cast their shadow across her face, or else you see the shadows these events have cast – something terrible, something ominous in this face with its jutting, rectangular jaw and those mad eyes of the New England saints, eyes that belong to a person who does not listen to you . . . fanatic's eyes, you might say, if you knew nothing about her. If you were sorting through a box of old photographs in a junk shop and came across this particular, sepia, faded face above the choked collars of the 1890s, you might murmur when you saw her: 'Oh, what big eyes you have!' as Red Riding Hood said to the wolf, but then you might not even pause to pick her out and look at her more closely, for hers is not, in itself, a striking face.

But as soon as the face has a name, once you recognise her, when you know who she is and what it was she did, the face becomes as if of one possessed, and now it haunts you, you look at it again and again, it secretes mystery.

This woman, with her jaw of a concentration-camp attendant, and such eyes . . .

In her old age, she wore pince-nez, and truly with the years the mad light has departed from those eyes or else is deflected by her glasses – if, indeed, it *was* a mad light, in the first place, for don't we all conceal somewhere photographs of ourselves that make us look like crazed assassins? And, in those early photographs of her young womanhood, she herself does not look so much like a crazed assassin as somebody in extreme solitude, oblivious of that camera in whose direction she obscurely smiles, so that it would not surprise you to learn that she is blind.

There is a mirror on the dresser in which she sometimes looks at those times when time snaps in two and then she sees herself with blind, clairvoyant eyes, as though she were another person.

'Lizzie is not herself, today.'

At those times, those irremediable times, she could have raised her muzzle to some aching moon and howled.

At other times, she watches herself doing her hair and trying her clothes on. The distorting mirror reflects her with the queasy fidelity of water. She puts on dresses and then she takes them off. She looks at herself in her corset. She pats her hair. She measures herself with the tape-measure. She pulls the measure tight. She pats her hair. She tries

120

on a hat, a little hat, a chic little straw toque. She punctures it with a hatpin. She pulls the veil down. She pulls it up. She takes the hat off. She drives the hatpin into it with a strength she did not know she possessed.

Time goes by and nothing happens.

She traces the outlines of her face with an uncertain hand as if she were thinking of unfastening the bandages on her soul but it isn't time to do that, yet: she isn't ready to be seen, yet.

She is a girl of Sargossa calm.

She used to keep her pigeons in the loft above the disused stable and feed them grain out of the palms of her cupped hands. She liked to feel the soft scratch of their beaks. They murmured 'vroo croo' with infinite tenderness. She changed their water every day and cleaned up their leprous messes but Old Borden took a dislike to their cooing, it got on his nerves, who'd have thought he *had* any nerves but he invented some, they got on them, one afternoon he took out the hatchet from the woodpile in the cellar and chopped those pigeons' heads right off, he did.

Abby fancied the slaughtered pigeons for a pie but Bridget the servant girl put her foot down, at that: what?!? Make a pie out of Miss Lizzie's beloved turtledoves? JesusMaryandJoseph!!! she exclaimed with characteristic impetuousness, what can they be thinking of! Miss Lizzie so nervy with her funny turns and all! (The maid is the only one in the house with any sense and that's the truth of it.) Lizzie came home from the Fruit and Flower Mission for whom she had been reading a tract to an old woman in a poorhouse: 'God bless you, Miss Lizzie.' At home all was blood and feathers.

She doesn't weep, this one, it isn't her nature, she is still waters, but, when moved, she changes colour, her face flushes, it goes dark, angry, mottled red. The old man loves his daughter this side of idolatry and pays for everything she wants, but all the same he killed her pigeons when his wife wanted to gobble them up.

That is how she sees it. That is how she understands it. She cannot bear to watch her stepmother eat, now. Each bite the woman takes seems to go: 'Vroo croo.'

Old Borden cleaned off the hatchet and put it back in the cellar, next to the woodpile. The red receding from her face, Lizzie went down to inspect the instrument of destruction. She picked it up and weighed it in her hand.

That was a few weeks before, at the beginning of the spring.

Her hands and feet twitch in her sleep; the nerves and muscles of this complicated mechanism won't relax, just won't relax, she is all twang, all tension, she is taut as the strings of a wind-harp from which random currents of the air pluck out tunes that are not our tunes.

At the first stroke of the City Hall clock, the first factory hooter blares, and then, on another note, another, and another, the Metacomet Mill, the American Mill, the Mechanics Mill . . . until every mill in the entire town sings out aloud in a common anthem of summoning and the hot alleys where the factory folk live blacken with the hurrying throng: hurry! scurry! to loom, to bobbin, to spindle, to dye-shop as to places of worship, men, and women, too, and children, the streets blacken, the sky darkens as the chimneys now belch forth, the clang, bang, clatter of the mills commences.

Bridget's clock leaps and shudders on its chair, about to sound its own alarm. Their day, the Bordens' fatal day, trembles on the brink of beginning.

Outside, above, in the already burning air, see! the angel of death roosts on the roof-tree.

The Fiend

F. SCOTT FITZGERALD

The murder in June, 1895 of a young mother and her seven-year-old child at Stillwater, Minnesota, was a crime that horrified America both because of its mindless ferocity and the innocence of the victims. The swift arrest of the killer only partially appeased the public anger, and in the years which followed the 'Crenshaw Murder', as it was known, became something of a cause célèbre. It attracted a great deal of attention in the press and subsequently found its way into a number of books about great nineteenth-century American crimes. Forty years later the double murder was still a focus of interest and inspired a short story by the great jazz-age chronicler, F. Scott Fitzgerald, which has curiously never been included in the collections of his short stories. 'The Fiend' was written for Esquire *magazine in January 1935 and, aside from its intrinsic value, demonstrates Fitzgerald's interest in crime, a feature generally overlooked in his work. Apart from the elements of criminality that can be found in a number of his stories, Scott actually began work on a complete novel with murder as its central theme in 1925. The plot was about a young man of evil temperament whose father is in prison for a crime of violence and who is driven to commit the same act against his unscrupulous and domineering mother. Sadly,* The Boy Who Killed His Mother *— as the book was to be called — never got completed. It has been suggested that Fitzgerald's original inspiration for that novel may have been sparked by his interest in the Crenshaw murder — but true or not, the short story he wrote about it has, at least, survived . . .*

ON JUNE 3, 1895, on a country road near Stillwater, Minnesota, Mrs. Crenshaw Engels and her seven-year-old son, Mark, were waylaid and murdered by a fiend, under circumstances so atrocious that, fortunately, it is not necessary to set them down here.

Crenshaw Engels, the husband and father, was a photographer in Stillwater. He was 'a great reader' and considered 'a little unsafe,' for he had spoken his mind frankly about the farmer-versus-railroad struggles of the time – but no one denied that he was a devoted family man, and the catastrophe visited upon him hung over the little town for many weeks.

There was a move to lynch the perpetrator of the horror, for Minnesota did not permit the capital punishment it deserved, but the instigators were foiled by the big stone penitentiary close at hand. The cloud hung over Engels' home so that folks went there only in moods of penitence, of fear or guilt, hoping that they would be visited in compensation should their lives ever chance to trek under a black sky. The photography shop suffered also: the routine of being posed, the necessary silences and pauses in the process, permitted the client too much time to regard the prematurely aged face of Crenshaw Engels, and young high school students, married couples, mothers of babies were always glad to escape from the place into the open air.

So Crenshaw's business fell off, and he went through a time of hardship – finally liquidating the lease, the apparatus and the goodwill, and wearing out the money obtained. He sold his house for a little more than its two mortgages, went to board and took a position clerking in Radamacher's Department Store.

In the sight of his neighbours he had become a man ruined by adversity, a man *manqué*, a man emptied. But in the last opinion they were wrong – he was empty of all save one thing. His memory was long as a Jew's, and though his heart was in the grave he was sane as when his wife and son had started on their last walk that summer morning.

At the first trial he lost control and got at the Fiend, seizing him by the necktie – and had been dragged off with the tie in such a knot that the Fiend was nearly garroted.

At the second trial he cried aloud once. Afterwards he went to all the members of the State legislature in the county and handed them a bill he had written himself for the introduction of capital punishment – the bill to be retroactive on criminals condemned to life imprisonment. The bill fell through; it was on the day Crenshaw heard this that he got inside the penitentiary by a ruse and was only apprehended in time to be prevented from shooting the Fiend in his cell.

Crenshaw was given a suspended sentence, and for some months it was assumed that the agony was fading gradually from his mind. In fact, when he presented himself to the warden a year after the crime the official was sympathetic to Crenshaw's statement that he had had a change of heart, and felt he could only emerge from the valley of the shadow by forgiveness; that he wanted to help the Fiend, show him the True Path by means of good books and appeals to his buried better nature.

So, after being carefully searched, Crenshaw was permitted to sit for half an hour outside the Fiend's cell.

But had the warden suspected the truth he would not have permitted the visit – for far from forgiving, Crenshaw's plan was to wreak upon the Fiend a mental revenge to replace the physical one of which he was subducted.

When he faced the Fiend in his cell, Crenshaw felt his scalp tingle. From behind the bars a roly-poly man, who somehow made his convict's uniform resemble a business suit, a man with thick brown-rimmed glasses and the trim air of an insurance salesman, looked at him uncertainly. Feeling faint, Crenshaw sat down in the chair that had been brought for him.

'The air round you stinks!' he cried suddenly. 'This whole corridor, this whole prison.'

'I suppose it does,' admitted the Fiend. 'I notice it too.'

'You'll have time to notice it,' Crenshaw snarled. 'All your life you'll pace up and down stinking in that little cell, with everything getting blacker and blacker. And after that there'll be hell waiting for you. For all eternity you'll be shut in a little space, but in hell it'll be so small that you can't stand up or stretch out.'

'Will it now?' asked the Fiend, concerned.

'It will!' said Crenshaw. 'You'll be alone with your own vile thoughts in that little space, for ever and ever and ever and ever. You'll itch with corruption, so that you can never sleep, and you'll always be thirsty, with water just out of reach.'

'Will I now?' repeated the Fiend, even more concerned. 'I remember once—'

'All the time you'll be full of horrors.' Crenshaw interrupted. 'You'll be like a person just about to crazy but can't go crazy. All the time you'll be thinking that it's for ever and ever and ever.'

'That's bad,' said the Fiend, shaking his head gloomily. 'That's real bad.'

'Now, listen here to me,' went on Crenshaw. 'I've brought you some books you're going to read. It's arranged that you get no books, or papers except what I bring you.'

As a beginning, Crenshaw had brought half a dozen books which his vagarious curiosity had collected over as many years. They comprised a German doctor's thousand case histories of sexual abnormality – cases with no cures, no hopes, no prognoses, cases listed cold; a series of sermons by a New England divine of the Great Revival which pictured the tortures of the damned in hell; a collection of horror stories; and a volume of erotic pieces from each of which the last two pages, containing the consummations, had been torn out; and a volume of detective stories mutilated in the same manner. A tome of the Newgate calendar completed the batch. These Crenshaw handed through the bars – the Fiend took them and put them on his iron cot.

This was the first of Crenshaw's long series of fortnightly visits. Always he brought with him something sombre and menacing to say, something dark and terrible to read – save that once when the Fiend had had nothing to read for a long time be brought him four inspiringly titled books – that proved to have nothing but blank paper inside.

Another time, pretending to concede a point, he promised to bring newspapers – he brought ten copies of the yellowed journal that had reported the crime and the arrest. Sometimes he obtained medical books that showed in colour the red and blue and green ravages of leprosy and skin disease, the mounds of shattered cells, the verminous tissue and brown corrupted blood.

And there was no sewer of the publishing world from which he did not obtain records of all that was gross and vile in man.

Crenshaw could not keep this up indefinitely both because of the expense and because of the exhaustibility of such books. When five years had passed he leaned towards another form of torture. He built up false hopes in the Fiend with protests of his own change of heart and manoeuvres for a pardon, and then dashed the hopes to pieces.

Or else he pretended to have a pistol with him, or an inflammatory substance that would make the cell a raging inferno and consume the Fiend in two minutes – once he threw a dummy bottle into the cell and listened in delight to the screams as the Fiend ran back and forth waiting for the explosion.

At other times he would pretend grimly that the legislature had passed a new law which provided that the Fiend would be executed in a few hours.

A decade passed. Crenshaw was grey at forty – he was white at fifty, when the alternating routine of his fortnightly visits to the graves of his loved ones and to the penitentiary had become the only part of his life – the long days at Radamacher's were only a weary dream.

Sometimes he went and sat outside the Fiend's cell, with no word said during the half-hour he was allowed to be there. The Fiend too had grown white in twenty years. He was very respectable looking with his horn-rimmed glasses and his white hair. He seemed to have a great respect for Crenshaw, and even when the latter, in a renewal of diminishing vitality, promised him one day that on his very next visit he was going to bring a revolver and end the matter, he nodded gravely as if in agreement, said, 'I suppose so; yes, I suppose you're perfectly right,' and did not mention the matter to the guards.

On the occasion of the next visit he was waiting with his hands on the bars of the cell, looking at Crenshaw both hopefully and desperately. At certain tensions and strains death takes on, indeed, the quality of a great adventure, as any soldier can testify.

Years passed. Crenshaw was promoted to floor manager at Radamacher's – there were new generations now that did not know of his tragedy, and regarded him as an austere nonentity. He came into a little legacy, and bought new stones for the graves of his wife and son. He knew he would soon be retired, and while a third decade lapsed through the white winters, the short, sweet, smoky summers, it became more and more plain to him that the time had come to put an end to the Fiend, to avoid any mischance by which the other would survive him.

The moment he fixed upon came at the exact end of thirty years. Crenshaw had long owned the pistol with which it would be accomplished; he had fingered the shells lovingly, and calculated the lodgment of each in the Fiend's body, so that death would be sure but lingering – he studied the tales of abdominal wounds in the war news, and delighted in the agony that made victims pray to be killed.

After that, what happened to *him* did not matter.

When the day came he had no trouble in smuggling the pistol into the penitentiary. But, to his surprise, he found the Fiend scrunched up upon his cot, instead of waiting for him avidly by the bars. 'I'm sick,' the Fiend said. 'My stomach's been burning me up all morning. They gave me a physic, but now it's worse, and nobody comes.'

Crenshaw fancied momentarily that this was a premonition in the man's bowels of a bullet that would shortly ride ragged through that spot.

127

'Come up to the bars,' he said, mildly.

'I can't move.'

'Yes, you can.'

'I'm doubled up. All doubled up.'

'Come doubled up then.'

With an effort the Fiend moved himself, only to fall on his side on the cement floor. He groaned, and then lay quiet for a minute, after which, still bent in two, he began to drag himself a foot at a time toward the bars.

Suddenly Crenshaw set off at a run toward the end of the corridor.

'I want the prison doctor,' he demanded of the guard. 'That man's sick – sick, I tell you.'

'The doctor has—'

'Get him – get him now!'

The guard hesitated, but Crenshaw had become a tolerated, even privileged, person around the prison, and in a moment the guard took down his 'phone and called the infirmary.

All that afternoon Crenshaw waited in the bare area inside the gates, walking up and down with his hands behind his back. From time to time he went to the front entrance and demanded of the guard:

'Any news?'

'Nothing yet. They'll call me when there's anything.'

Late in the afternoon the Warden appeared at the door, looked about, and spotted Crenshaw. The latter, all alert, hastened over.

'He's dead,' the Warden said. 'His appendix burst. They did everything they could.'

'Dead,' Crenshaw repeated.

'I'm sorry to bring you this news. I know how—'

'It's all right,' said Crenshaw, and, licking his lips. 'So he's dead.' The Warden lit a cigarette.

'While you're here, Mr. Engels, I wonder if you can let me have that pass that was issued to you? – I can turn it in to the office. That is – I suppose you won't need it any more.'

Crenshaw took the blue card from his wallet and handed it over. The Warden shook hands with him.

'One thing more,' Crenshaw demanded as the Warden turned away, 'which is the – the window of the infirmary?'

'It's on the interior court, you can't see it from here.'

'Oh.'

When the Warden had gone Crenshaw still stood there a long time, the tears running out down his face. He could not collect his thoughts, and he began by trying to remember what day it was: Saturday – that was it, the day every other week on which he came to see the Fiend.

He would not see the Fiend two weeks from now.

In a misery of solitude and despair he muttered aloud: 'So he is dead. He has left me.' And then, with a long sigh of mingled grief and fear, 'So now at last I am alone.'

He was still saying that to himself as he passed through the outer gate. He felt the necessity of turning to the guard there and repeating it: 'Now, you see,' he muttered, 'I really am alone.'

His coat caught in the great swing of the outer door, and as the guard opened up to release it he heard a reiteration of the words:

'Now I'm alone – now I'm really alone.'

At the Fork of the Roads

ALEISTER CROWLEY

Aleister Crowley who called himself, 'The Beast 666', 'The Antichrist' and 'Father Perdurabo', and was known by the press in the years prior to his death in 1947 as 'The Wickedest Man in the World', is both the narrator and the subject of this story of twentieth-century black magic. Devil worship has a long tradition in Western history, but earned a whole new generation of followers as a result of Crowley's dabbling in the occult which included sex, perversion and drugs. Though Crowley certainly stopped short of murder, he drove some of his disciples to madness and suicide and his philosophical legacy of 'Do what thou wilt shall be the whole of the law,' continues to influence admirers today, in particular a number of poets and rock musicians who have drawn on his writings for their verses and songs. (Jimmy Page of Led Zeppelin, for example, has collected many items of Crowleyiana and owned the occultist's former house, Boleskire on the shore of Loch Ness). Several novelists have also featured Crowley, thinly-disguised, in their work — including Somerset Maugham in The Magician *and Colin Wilson in* Man Without A Shadow — *but here we have Crowley himself offering his own very special insight into the horrifying powers of Satanism . . .*

HYPATIA GAY KNOCKED timidly at the door of Count Swanoff's flat. Hers was a curious mission, to serve the envy of the long lank melancholy unwashed poet whom she loved. Will Bute was not only a poetaster but a dabbler in magic, and black jealousy of a younger man and a far finer poet gnawed at his petty heart. He had gained a subtle hypnotic influence over Hypatia, who helped him in his ceremonies, and he had now commissioned her to seek out his rival and pick up some magical link through which he might be destroyed.

The door opened, and the girl passed from the cold stone dusk of the stairs to a palace of rose and gold. The poet's rooms were austere in their elegance. A plain gold-black paper of Japan covered the walls; in the midst hung an ancient silver lamp within which glowed the deep ruby of an electric lamp. The floor was covered with black and gold of leopards' skins; on the walls hung a great crucifix in ivory and ebony. Before the blazing fire lay the poet (who had concealed his royal Celtic descent beneath the pseudonym of Swanoff) reading in a great volume bound with vellum.

He rose to greet her.

'Many days have I expected you,' he exclaimed, 'many days have I wept over you. I see your destiny – how thin a thread links you to that mighty Brotherhood of the Silver Star whose trembling neophyte I am – how twisted and thick are the tentacles of the Black Octopus whom you now serve. Ah! wrench yourself away while you are yet linked with us: I would not that you sank into the Ineffable Slime. Blind and bestial are the worms of the Slime: come to me, and by the Faith of the Star, I will save you.'

The girl put him by with a light laugh. 'I came,' she said, 'but to chatter about clairvoyance – why do you threat me with these strange and awful words?'

'Because I see that today may decide all for you. Will you come with me into the White Temple, while I administer the Vows? Or will you enter the Black Temple, and swear away your soul?'

'Oh, really,' she said, 'you are too silly – but I'll do what you like next time I come here.'

'Today your choice – tomorrow your fate,' answered the young poet.

And the conversation drifted to lighter subjects.

But as she left she managed to scratch his hand with a brooch, and this tiny blood-stain on the pin she bore back in triumph to her master; he would work a strange working therewith!

Swanoff closed his books and went to bed. The streets were deadly silent; he turned his thoughts to the Infinite Silence of the Divine Presence, and fell into a peaceful sleep. No dreams disturbed him; later than usual he awoke.

How strange! The healthy flush of his cheek had faded: the hands were white and thin and wrinkled: he was so weak that he could hardly stagger to the bath. Breakfast refreshed him somewhat; but more than this the expectation of a visit from his master.

The master came. 'Little brother!' he cried aloud as he entered, 'you have disobeyed me. You have been meddling again with the Goetia!'

'I swear to you, master!' He did reverence to the adept.

The newcomer was a dark man with a powerful cleanshaven face almost masked in a mass of jet-black hair.

'Little brother,' he said, 'if that be so, then the Goetia has been meddling with you.'

He lifted up his head and sniffed. 'I smell evil,' he said, 'I smell the dark brothers of iniquity. Have you duly performed the Ritual of the Flaming Star?'

'Thrice daily, according to your word.'

'Then evil has entered in a body of flesh. Who has been here?'

The young poet told him. His eyes flashed. 'Aha!' he said, 'now let us Work!'

The neophyte brought writing materials to his master: the quill of a young gander, snow-white; virgin vellum of a young male lamb; ink of the gall of a certain rare fish; and a mysterious Book.

The master drew a number of incomprehensible signs and letters upon the vellum.

'Sleep with this beneath the pillow,' he said: 'you will awake if you are attacked; and whatever it is that attacks you, kill it! Kill it! Kill it! Then instantly go into your temple and assume the shape and dignity of the god Horus; send back the Thing to its sender by the might of the god that is in you! Come! I will discover unto you the words and the signs and the spells for this working of magic art.'

They disappeared into the little white room lined with mirrors which Swanoff used for a temple.

Hypatia Gay, that same afternoon, took some drawings to a publisher in Bond Street. This man was bloated with disease and drink; his loose lips hung in an eternal leer; his fat eyes shed venom; his cheeks seemed ever on the point of bursting into nameless sores and ulcers.

He bought the young girl's drawings. 'Not so much for their value,' he explained, 'as that I like to help promising young artists – like you, my dear!'

Her steely virginal eyes met his fearlessly and unsuspiciously. The beast cowered, and covered his foulness with a hideous smile of shame.

The night came, and young Swanoff went to his rest without alarm. Yet with that strange wonder that denotes those who expect the unknown and terrible, but have faith to win through.

132

This night he dreamt — deliciously.

A thousand years he strayed in gardens of spice, by darling streams, beneath delightful trees, in the blue rapture of the wonderful weather. At the end of a long glade of ilex that reached up to a marble palace stood a woman, fairer than all the women of the earth. Imperceptibly they drew together — she was in his arms. He awoke with a start. A woman indeed lay in his arms and showered a rain of burning kisses on his face. She clothed him about with ecstasy; her touch waked the serpent of essential madness in him.

Then, like a flash of lightning, came his master's word to his memory — Kill it! In the dim twilight he could see the lovely face that kissed him with lips of infinite splendour, hear the cooing words of love.

'Kill it! My God! Adonai! Adonai!' He cried aloud, and took her by the throat. Ah God! Her flesh was not the flesh of woman. It was hard as india-rubber to the touch, and his strong young fingers slipped. Also he loved her — loved, as he had never dreamt that love could be.

But he knew now, he knew! And a great loathing mingled with his lust. Long did they struggle; at last he got the upper, and with all his weight above her drove down his fingers in her neck. She gave one gasping cry — a cry of many devils in hell — and died. He was alone.

He had slain the succubus, and absorbed it. Ah! With what force and fire his veins roared! Ah! How he leapt from the bed, and donned the holy robes. How he invoked the God of Vengeance, Horus the mighty, and turned loose the Avengers upon the black soul that had sought his life!

At the end he was calm and happy as a babe; he returned to bed, slept easy, and woke strong and splendid.

Night after night for ten nights this scene was acted and re-acted: always identical. On the eleventh day he received a postcard from Hypatia Gay that she was coming to see him that afternoon.

'It means that the material basis of their working is exhausted,' explained his master. 'She wants another drop of blood. But we must put an end to this.'

They went out into the city, and purchased a certain drug of which the master knew. At the very time that she was calling at the flat, they were at the boarding-house where she lodged, and secretly distributing the drug about the house. Its function was a strange one: hardly had they left the house when from a thousand quarters came a lamentable company of cats, and made the winter hideous with their cries.

'That' (chuckled the master) 'will give her mind something to occupy itself with. She will do no black magic for our friend awhile!'

Indeed the link was broken; Swanoff had peace. 'If she comes again,' ordered the master, 'I leave it to you to punish her.'

A month passed by; then, unannounced, once more Hypatia Gay knocked at the flat. Her virginal eyes still smiled; her purpose was yet deadlier than before.

Swanoff fenced with her awhile. Then she began to tempt him.

'Stay!' he said, 'first you must keep your promise and enter the temple!'

Strong in the trust of her black master, she agreed. The poet opened the little door, and closed it quickly after her, turning the key.

As she passed into the utter darkness that hid behind curtains of black velvet, she caught one glimpse of the presiding god.

It was a skeleton that sat there, and blood stained all its bones. Below it was the evil altar, a round table supported by an ebony figure of a Negro standing upon his hands. Upon the altar smouldered a sickening perfume, and the stench of the slain victims of the god defiled the air. It was a tiny room, and the girl, staggering, came against the skeleton. The bones were not clean; they were hidden by a greasy slime mingling with the blood, as though the hideous worship were about to endow it with a new body of flesh. She wrenched herself back in disgust. Then suddenly she felt it was alive! It was coming towards her! She shrieked once the blasphemy which her vile master had chosen as his mystic name; only a hollow laugh echoed back.

Then she knew all. She knew that to seek the left-hand path may lead one to the power of the blind worms of the Slime – and she resisted. Even then she might have called to the White Brothers; but she did not. A hideous fascination seized her.

And then she felt the horror.

Something – something against which nor clothes nor struggles were any protection – was taking possession of her, eating its way into her . . .

And its embrace was deadly cold . . . Yet the hell-clutch at her heart filled her with a fearful joy. She ran forward; she put her arms round the skeleton; she put her young lips to its bony teeth, and kissed it. Instantly, as at a signal, a drench of the waters of death washed all the human life out of her being, while a rod as of steel smote her even from the base of the spine to the brain. She had passed the gates of the abyss. Shriek after shriek of ineffable agony burst from her tortured mouth; she writhed and howled in that ghastly celebration of the nuptials of the Pit.

Exhaustion took her; she fell with a heavy sob.

When she came to herself she was at home. Still that lamentable crew of cats miauled about the house. She awoke and shuddered. On the table lay two notes.

The first: 'You fool! They are after me; my life is not safe. You have ruined me – Curse you!' This from the loved master, for whom she had sacrificed her soul.

The second a polite note from the publisher, asking for more drawings. Dazed and desperate, she picked up her portfolio, and went round to his office in Bond Street.

He saw the leprous light of utter degradation in her eyes; a dull flush came to his face; he licked his lips.

The Moors Murders

MIRIAM ALLEN DEFORD

The multiple murders committed by Ian Brady and Myra Hindley for which both are still serving life sentences are probably the most familiar and horrifying of this century. The couple's cold-blooded killing of a teenage homosexual and two young children was revealed when they were tried in May 1966 – a trial which also brought to light their obsession with sadism, Nazism and pornography. The story shocked the nation and has since come to be regarded as a phenomenon of our times. The Moors Murders exerted a special fascination for the American crime and mystery writer, Miriam Allen deFord, who has won several of the country's most prestigious prizes, including the Mystery Writers of America, 'Edgar' award for The Overbury Affair *(1960), the story of the imprisonment and poisoning in the Tower of London of the courtier who was the favourite of James I. She was also highly praised for two books about famous modern American criminals,* The Real Bonny and Clyde *(1968) and* The Real Ma Baker *(1970). Miss deFord has published a number of short stories which feature characters from history – including Cicero and Edgar Allan Poe – but here turns her attention to the extraordinary facts of the case of Ian Brady and Myra Hindley and their implications for us today.*

MULTIPLE MURDERS ARE far from uncommon – there have been at least four striking instances of them in this country within the past year. Murder for the thrill of killing is as old as human nature. What differentiates the Moors Murders in England from the common run of other wanton and motiveless cases of the destruction of human life is the character and personality of the two perpetrators set against the particular period in which these young people were born and have grown up. Sick eras produce sick people.

Strictly speaking, the main crime for which Ian Brady and Myra Hindley are now serving life sentences was not a Moors Murder at all, though Brady had planned to bury the corpse of Edward Evans in the

Pennine Moors, near the graves of his other victims, if he had not been forestalled by the panic-stricken appeal to the police by his *soi-disant* brother-in-law, David Smith – himself perhaps an accomplice and fundamentally a victim also of Brady's corrupting influence. Evans was killed in the house in Hattersley, near Manchester, in which Brady lived with his mistress, Myra Hindley, and her grandmother, Mrs. Maybury. The two other known victims, 12-year-old John Kilbride and 10-year-old Lesley Ann Downey, probably also were killed elsewhere and then buried a few hundred feet apart in the wild and desolate moors which were the guilty couple's 'home away from home' where they spent much of their leisure time from their office jobs, sometimes all night long.

Brady himself is almost a case history in alienated youth. The illegitimate son of a waitress in Glasgow, his father unknown, he was reared by a foster mother in the Gorbal slums. She was kind and motherly and treated him well. He was a bright child who did well at school, but already the aberrant streak in him was manifest; he tortured animals, bullied his schoolmates, and as a child of 11 he was already obsessed with Nazism, with the Storm Troopers as his ideals. Also, he had started his career as a thief and housebreaker, his first arrest and probation coming at 13, in 1951. He left school at 14 and went to work as a butcher's assistant, and after two more arrests and probation periods the Glasgow authorities decided he was beyond his foster mother's control and sent him south to Manchester to his mother, who had married and moved there. He was not yet 15.

To his thieving propensities and his delight in Nazism he had by now added an obsessive preoccupation with torture and sexual perversion; he had discovered deSade. To his companions he was known as 'Dracula.' He could not change his nature, but at first he seems to have made some effort toward normality; he changed his name to his stepfather's and went to work. But soon he was back in his old habits, and in 1955 he was sent to Borstal (the boys' reform school) for three years. Eight months after his release he got a job as an invoice clerk at a small chemical works in Gorton, another Manchester suburb. (He was a very satisfactory employee.) Two years later, he met there a new stenographer named Myra Hindley.

Psychopaths frequently have superior mentality; Brady reminds one constantly of Richard Loeb. He was good at his job, his interests were intellectual, but he was utterly anti-social. He worshipped naked power and made no secret of his leanings. It was his misfortune that he was born in the wrong country – he would have gone far under Hitler. As it was, his only outlet was the corruption of and hatred and contempt for those inferiors, all other human beings. A generation earlier he would have been a disciple of a misunderstood version of the philosophy of Nietzsche. This was the man with whom a wilful, undisciplined girl fell so madly in love that she remade herself into his image, became his devoted slave, followed him into murder, and proudly proclaimed in the witness box that she still loved him – while he did not even glance at her. So far as a psychopath can care for anyone except himself she did become Brady's absorbing interest; she was his creature.

Myra Hindley is four years Brady's junior. When she was four years old her sister Maureen was born, and her working mother handed her over to her own mother, Mrs. Maybury, to rear: the two lived near each other. Myra grew up a tomboy, a poor student, but essentially very much like other girls in a poor industrial neighborhood. What she most admired was strength. Brady was far from strong physically, but emotionally he fulfilled her dreams. She threw over a fiancé and devoted herself to winning Brady's attention. It took her a long time. But after her grandmother moved to Hattersley, Brady moved in too (ostensibly he was still living with his mother and stepfather), and the two became inseparable.

No consideration of the two principals in this case would be complete without some reference to David Smith, who married Maureen Hindley when he was 16 and she was 17, and thus became Myra's brother-in-law. Whether Smith actually took part in the murder of Edward Evans is open to question; he turned Queen's evidence and was free from prosecution. He probably brought Lesley Ann Downey to the house where she met her death – it is unlikely that there was any truth in Brady's assertion that he took her away again, alive. He is weak and vicious, with an easy acceptance of criminality, but he has none of the driving force of Ian Brady. When they planned a robbery together, Smith wanted blank cartridges in the guns. Brady would never have panicked, as Smith did, after the murder of Evans. By the time of the trial he had recovered his aplomb; he was brash and impudent on the stand, acknowledging proudly that he was being paid £1000 by a newspaper for his story – 'Money is gorgeous stuff.' His pregnant young wife, Myra's sister, was a mere bystander. Once she and Myra were close friends; they are no longer on speaking terms.

The first known murder was that of 12-year-old John Kilbride, who disappeared from a movie on November 23, 1968, and whose body was dug up on the moor, close to the grave of Lesley Ann Downey, and identified by the clothing. (Brady is still being questioned about the disappearances of other young people in this part of the North of England during the past few years. He had boasted to Smith that he had committed 'three or four' murders and would be committing another soon. But the moors are vast, and if Brady had not photographed Myra, with her dog, staring at the spot they frequented where Lesley Ann lay buried, these two might never have been discovered either.)

The boy had been sexually abused before his death. It was impossible to tell just how he had been killed, but in all probability – and in the case of the little girl also – he was suffocated. Smith certainly had no connection with this murder, and neither did Myra Hindley, though she was convicted of 'harboring' Brady knowing that he had killed John Kilbride.

There was much more circumstantial evidence in the murder of Lesley Ann. Among Brady's chief hobbies was photography, including pornographic photography. There is no doubt that the child, who had gone to a local fair with sixpence to spend, was picked up by somebody – probably Smith – and persuaded to go with him to Myra's grandmother's house to have her picture taken. (They were complete strangers.) She would have been promised some small sum, perhaps was flattered to be told that she was pretty enough to be wanted as a subject, and went innocently to a scene of horror that makes this one of the unpleasantest murders on record.

Most of the English newspapers forebore to publish all of the heartbreaking tape recording which Brady and Myra callously set going to preserve Lesley Ann's dreadful experience. The jury and the auditors in court heard her screams and protests, her pitiful plea that she must get back home in time for tea, her vain appeals. She had been stripped naked and either raped or otherwise abused. Her captors took photographs in obscene poses, which were with the tape in a suitcase they had packed with this and other incriminating material and checked.

139

When she kept on screaming she got on Myra's nerves; she slapped the girl and then they stuffed her mouth with rags to gag her. To finish off the recording in style they tuned in to a radio broadcast of Christmas music – it was Boxing Day, the day after Christmas in 1964. She was buried as she died, naked. When a neighbor's girl they made a protegee of, read aloud the newspaper account of a reward offered for Lesley Ann's recovery by her distraught mother, Myra made a flippant remark and laughed.

The murder of Edward Evans was of a very different nature. Brady remarked to Smith that this one was 'out of turn' and didn't count. Evans, only 17 was an overt homosexual. Brady had seen him once before in a 'drag club' in Manchester; Ian used to visit such places 'for fun,' to laugh at the habitués. In the course of his indoctrination of David Smith – they were planning a hold-up at the time – he thought David should have some personal experience in crime; for a start, how about 'rolling a queer'? 'The point was that if anything did go wrong, this person was unlikely to complain to the police, so there was no risk.'

On the evening of October 6, 1965, Ian and Myra drove to Gorton for some wine and then on to the Central Station at Manchester; Brady couldn't drive and Myra always drove them in her own car. There Brady saw Evans and decided to take him home with them, ostensibly for a drink. Why he thought a young apprentice engineer would have any money worth stealing is a problem; another version of his story is that this was just practice for Smith, in preparation for the robbery next Saturday.

So Smith had to be brought into the picture. It was past midnight by now and presumably David was asleep at his nearby home with Maureen. Brady sent Myra to his house with a supposed message for Maureen from their mother; then she asked Smith to 'walk her home' and pick up some wine bottles they had for him. Smith, who had been undressing to go to bed, did as she asked, and she left him standing inside the front door while she went 'to get the bottles.' His story is that he heard thumping sounds and Myra called, 'Dave, come and help me.' He went into the room and found a young man unknown to him writhing and screaming on the floor while Brady kept hitting him with a hatchet.

Brady had not waited for Smith's arrival. There is evidence that while Myra was gone he and Evans had had intimate relations, though Brady denied it, but just what precipitated his attack on Evans is unknown. From that point on, with Myra in and out of the room, there is no doubt that Brady kept slashing at Evans with the hatchet until the youth collapsed — Brady said Smith helped him by hitting Evans with his stick, Smith says he simply stood and watched, horrified. Finally, to stop his 'gurgling,' Brady strangled Evans with a cord.

Blood was everywhere, and they all three set to with cloths and mops to clean up. Then they tied the corpse in a polythene sheet and blankets. Their first idea was to carry it out between them, drive to the moor, and bury the victim at once, but they were afraid of a trail of blood, so they carried him to an upstairs bedroom — where the police found him. (They also found a cryptic 'plan' for disposing of a murder victim among Brady's belongings.)

One may ask, where was Mrs Maybury, the 77-year-old grandmother, during all this? She had been visiting Myra's uncle over Christmas, and Myra had refused to drive her home that night on the grounds that the roads were too bad.

All this practical demonstration had been too much for David Smith. He got himself home somehow, washed, vomited, and tried to sleep but couldn't, so he woke Maureen and told her what had happened. By this time they were both terrified. They armed themselves for protection with a knife and a screwdriver and, since they had no telephone, went to a nearby booth, where they phoned the police. It was the beginning of the end for Ian Brady and Myra Hindley.

The preliminary hearing was held in December, the trial in April and May of 1966. The judge was Justice Fenton Atkinson; the case was prosecuted, with two assistants, by Sir Elwyn Jones, Q.C., Attorney General; Brady's chief counsel was Emlyn Hooson, Q.C., Liberal M.P. for Montgomery, and Hindley's was Geoffrey Heilpern, Recorder of Salford. (During the trial Heilpern's sister-in-law was murdered in her dress shop in London by someone unknown.) Four of the 12 first picked for the jury were women, but they were all challenged by the defense and the jury was all male. No photographs were allowed, and the names of children who testified in the Kilbride and Downey cases were not published.

The jury took two hours and 14 minutes to convict Brady of all three murders and Hindley of the Downey and Evans murders and of harboring Brady in the Kilbride case. (For this last she received seven years.) This was the first important murder trial after the abolition of capital punishment in Britain; both defendants received concurrent life sentences on the murder charges.

Brady is in Durham Gaol, in solitary confinement at his own request; Myra Hindley, whose appeal was rejected, is in Holloway. (Her appeal was based on the fact that she was not given a separate trial. Brady did not appeal.) She took the rejection unemotionally, as both took their sentences; it was noted that the synthetic blonde Myra has by now become a brunette. (An odd reflection is that Brady, slender and dark-haired, would never be noticed in a crowd; Hindley, with her wedgeshaped jaw and cavernous eyes, is much nearer the Lombrosan picture of a born criminal, though in actuality it is Brady who is the born criminal, if such a thing exists, and if they had never met there is no likelihood that Myra would ever have deviated from the conventional norm.)

So what is one to make of this sorry case? Has it any relevance to our troubled and chaotic time? Among the books which were Brady's Bibles, besides the works of deSade and Hitler's 'Mein Kampf', were volumes about Goering and Eichmann and descriptions of Nazi genocide; there were also books with such titles as 'Kiss of the Whip,' 'Pleasures of the Torture Chamber,' 'The History of Torture and Cruelty,' and 'Corporal Punishment through the Ages.' As David Ware remarked in *Punch*, 'the pages devoted to Sade are the best thumbed . . . in the Reading Room of the British Museum.' Doubtless some of the crowd who shrieked 'Kill them!' as Brady and Hindley were taken to prison have been among those readers – but they have committed no murders. The Moors Murders are no argument for censorship; despite the complacency with which one London newspaper stated that the books the two read and passed on to Smith were 'the drugs' that 'poisoned their minds,' Anthony Boucher has commented that this is the first sadistic murder on record in which there was any evidence that the murderer had ever actually read deSade!

People like Ian Brady have existed in all times and all places. What developed his evil potentialities and brought them to fruition was the world into which he was born. This is a sick world in a sick age. There is hope for humanity's recovery, but there is no use in pretending that all is well with us. Perhaps if it were made possible for no child to be born unwanted, there would be fewer like Brady. But any child born in an urban slum has a tremendous handicap to start with. Just because he had so good a mind and so frustrated a personality, Ian Brady seized on his one means of fulfilment – the relentless pursuit of individual power and domination. In a healthy civilization, his bent would have been recognized early and he would have had assistance toward and opportunity for socially desirable ways to prove his superiority. We threw him away, after we had let him corrupt and ruin at least two other human beings.

A statement by the managing director of Madame Tussaud's Waxworks throws inadvertently a flood of light on the thin veneer of our normality. Brady and Hindley will not appear in the Chamber of Horrors, he says; in fact, the Chamber is now complete. 'However nasty the murderers were, they were at least executed, which gave them a touch of glamor.' While murder, either private or by the State, is popularly considered glamorous, we cannot call ourselves civilized, or justify amazement and revulsion at the emergence of an Ian Brady.

As Pamela Hansford Johnson said, 'A wound in the flesh of society . . . (has) cracked open.'

Section Two

THE EVIL LIVES ON

Monsieur de Néron

WILLIAM WALDORF ASTOR

Few names have remained higher on the list of infamy than that of Nero, the Roman Emperor from A.D. 54 to 68, who has been called a monster of debauchery, extravagance and tyranny. He it was who watched, amused, as Rome burned in July 64; who murdered both his mother and his wife; and who poisoned and executed indiscriminately all those who displeased him. He showed the greatest cruelty and intolerance to anyone of integrity and virtue, and when finally the Roman legions rose up in revolt against him, Nero only escaped justice by committing suicide. His crimes were truly horrendous and have since made his name an aphorism for evil and cruelty. In 'Monsieur De Néron', Willian Waldorf Astor employs the memoirs of a French antiquary to show how a monstrous evil can live on. Astor was the great-grandson of John Jacob Astor, the American millionaire who established a dynasty and left a legacy to found the New York public library. William Astor was also a millionaire businessman who after being active in American politics and serving as US minister in Italy from 1882–85, settled in England and published the Pall Mall Gazette *and* The Observer. *In 1916 he was made First Viscount Astor. Among Astor's many interests were history and writing, and he combined these two in a series of stories about famous characters from the past which he published in a collection entitled* Pharaoh's Daughter, *in 1900. 'Monsieur De Néron' is undoubtedly the best of these and is here returned to print for the first time since the early years of the century.*

I WAS BORN at St. Germain in the year 1830, and therefore, even if you know no more of figures than a *Ministre des Finances*, you will see that I am sixty-four years old. I am not an infirm man, though I no longer eat champagne suppers nor frequent public balls. The trifle of interest upon my savings, added to my pension – a mere pittance, such as one might expect from these Radical times – enables me to live without care, and to allow myself a few gratifications. I drink coffee in bed

147

every morning, as becomes an officer of the Second Empire, rise at twelve, and dine upon *la soupe* of the French soldier, followed by a Chateaubriand, or a grilled chicken, *arrosé* with a bottle of Léoville – good enough stuff to lubricate the whistle, as the frank-spoken English sailors say.

It was one afternoon, a week ago, when I had just finished dinner, that the Commissaire de Police of this Arrondissement waited upon me. I was pouring out a thimbleful of brandy and deliberating whether to go to the *matinée*, when the Commissaire followed Babette into my sitting-room unannounced. His muddy boots left a mark upon my ruby carpet, and he looked at me inquiringly, as though I were some curious and perhaps dangerous animal. I regretfully remembered another saying that comes to us from across the Channel, that an Englishman's house is his castle, and wondered how John Bull will relish a hangtail republic like ours when he looks up across his roast beef and pint-o'-bitter-draw-it-mild to see an inspector walk into his private room, while a couple of bobbies stand staring at the door.

The Commissaire's first words informed me that a dangerous character – he used the words with startling intensity – had fallen into the hands of the police, and that a paper found in his possession made allusion to me; that I must come instantly to the Préfecture, not precisely under arrest, but for the purpose of identifying the prisoner.

'Who is this prisoner?' I ejaculated.

'He passes under so many aliases that it is hard to tell his real name.'

'But it is monstrous to connect me with the criminals you find in the byways!'

'*Après tout*,' rejoined the Commissaire, with an elastic shrug, 'if Monsieur is clear of complicity, as of course he must be,' he added, with a queer smile, 'it will only be to inform us who this man is.'

'You attach great importance to him, then?'

The Commissaire drew in his breath with a hissing sound without speaking.

'So bad as that! . . . An Anarchist, perhaps?'

'*Bédam!*' was all the answer I received.

At the Préfecture de Police I was shown into the Préfet's private room. There were so many people crowded about the table at which he sat, that for a moment I did not distinguish which among them was the prisoner. Then two or three men moved aside, and I saw him standing handcuffed, with a *sergeant de ville* on each side. I recognised him at once as Monsieur de Néron, a man I had met at several periods of my life. His appearance was greatly changed since I first knew him, at Rome in the early sixties. He still had the burly, athletic figure of his younger days, and the smiling look of insolent triumph; but he had grown fat and bald, his eye had lost much of its fire, and his face had acquired that indescribable yet unmistakable look that stamps the absinthe drinker. No salutation or word of recognition was exchanged. Perhaps he was thinking, as I was, of what happened between us in '71, whereof I shall presently have occasion to speak.

The Préfet asked me questions till I nearly fainted from exhaustion. After that a *Juge d'Instruction* cross-questioned me in a way which showed that the prisoner was believed to be the supreme chief of the Anarchists in France, Spain, and Italy — a sort of ultimate 'Number One,' who makes the plans and touches the button, and, pouf! — a revolution. The straightforwardness of my story soon exculpated me from any connection with him — a circumstance doubtless greatly strengthened by the failure to discover anything more suspicious among my papers than some photographs of handsome women and half a dozen love letters dating from no matter how many bright years ago. Through the long course of my interrogatory, the prisoner never proffered a word, nor made the slightest interruption, merely regarding me from time to time with his insouciant, devil-may-care look. Whatever reasons his captors had for thinking him guilty of great crimes, he appeared to feel quite unconcerned, perhaps knowing that the fetters of justice have no more power to bind a malefactor of extraordinary force — a real *premier* in crime — than the webs spun by spiders at dawn can stop a wolf on his way to his lair. *Qui sait!* All I know is that upon presenting myself the next morning I was excused from further attendance, and soon it leaked out that Monsieur de Néron had mysteriously vanished in the night, leaving nothing behind but half a package of cigarettes. Impossible, you will say; yet we all know that things deemed impossible are continually happening. There was an *enquête* into the circumstances of his escape, and the guards who connived at it were severely punished, but that did not bring back the culprit. In the meantime my interrogatory was read over to me — a jumbled, unintelligible mass of questions and answers — and I was required to sign it as an acknowledgment of its accuracy. Before leaving the room a heedless impulse prompted me to offer to write the story of my acquaintance with Monsieur de Néron in more concise and direct form; whereas the Préfet bowed, as polite as a dancing-master, and the *huissier* showed me out. The next day, after dinner, Babette wheeled a large table to the light, laid upon it half a dozen sheets of foolscap and two artistically sharpened pencils, and I wrote the following memorandum:

I first met Monsieur de Néron at Rome in 1861. It was when the Emperor Napoleon had purchased the ruined Palace of the Caesars of Pope Pius IX., and had commissioned the celebrated archaeologist Pietro Rosa to excavate it. Those were the glorious days of old Rome, before it had been smeared with modern brick and stucco. True, one might come now and then upon a heap of offal higher than a man's head, and occasionally a throat was cut at midnight, but as the charming Romans said, *Cosa vuole*! – will not God care for His own at the last?

An uncle of mine had caused me to receive a military education; but upon his death, in 1852, I relinquished my chance of a commission, and devoted myself to a more congenial and lucrative career than the profession of arms. After some years of travel and study, I obtained a clerical appointment in connection with the researches being made by the Imperial Government amid the ruins of the Palatine Hill. One morning I was superintending the labours of a force of men, with my maps unrolled at my feet. The scene was one of such transcendent loveliness, with the violet Alban hills and the vast stretch of the green Campagna in the distance, that occasionally I strolled this way or that, to look about me and to breathe the soft Roman air, and revel in the deliciousness of the Italian sunshine. During one of these momentary absences, I observed a stranger, a young man, clean shaven, of powerful physique and commanding air, walking about contemplating the fragments that raised themselves in places above the greensward. I took him to be some visitor of distinction to whom a permit had been extended, and thinking it a pity that he should waste his time in mere idle speculation, approached him, with the remark, 'If you desire a guide, Monsieur, I will detail some one to accompany you!'

Before my sentence was finished, the stranger, who had turned to confront me, burst into an immoderate fit of laughter. I felt so mortified at this rudeness that I was moving away, when, laying his hand upon my arm, and restraining his merriment, he said:

'You will perhaps excuse the mirth your question excites in me when I give you some slight proof of how little I, of all others, stand in need of a guide in the Palace of the Caesars. Listen. You and your men are at this moment, so one of them told me, in search of a portico or side entrance to the structure raised by Caligula. You are searching for it in the wrong place: it is farther back, and a hundred yards to the left!'

I was as much displeased by this suggestion as I had been at his want of civility when I addressed him. Was it not absurd, as well as impertinent, that a casual visitor should assume to know better than Signor Rosa, under whose orders I was working?

'Nevertheless,' I replied, 'I am not informed upon what authority you speak; and, as for the position of the portico, it must evidently have opened upon the Via Sacra.'

'You are again mistaken,' answered the stranger. 'The Via Sacra did not pass, as you imagine, in a straight line before the Palace. When you dig it out, you will find that it bends away to the eastward.'

I looked at the man in silence. Was he mad – this babbler who knew the course of the Via Sacra, that had lain buried for centuries, and whose position the best of us could only conjecture?

'There is another mistake upon your map which lies unrolled yonder,' he added, talking as though he owned the ground we stood upon. 'The temple of Jupiter was built, not where you place it, but near those great trees, at the head of a little street, called, in ancient times, the Clivus Palatinus.' With that he gave me a nod, and, turning away, continued his stroll.

You may be sure I did not let the matter end there. A moment later my clerk was following him from a distance, and that afternoon he reported the stranger to be *il cavaliere di Nerone*, lodging in the Via Quattro Fontane.

His words were strange enough, and left me dazed; but, stranger still, the statements he made proved true. I remained several years in Rome, working as one of Signor Rosa's assistants. The portico was found at the spot indicated; the Via Sacra turned eastward, as he said; the Temple of Jupiter Stator, and even the Clivus Palatinus, revealed themselves at the point he had noted. And here I must plead guilty to having taken to myself the credit of these discoveries as the result of my own superior acumen. As soon as it appeared that the stranger was right about the portico, I announced the other facts he had communicated to me, and upon my prognostications proving correct, I became famous among antiquarians.

151

It goes without saying that I made inquiries concerning the Cavaliere di Nerone, which resulted in information of a nature to his discredit. Whence he came, no one knew. He had received an excellent education, and spoke French with such correctness as indicated a long residence in Paris. He was said to be indolent and gluttonous. He talked with gusto of Spanish bull-fights in which he had participated, and was known to the police for monstrous and demoniacal cruelty to animals, and, when they fell into his power, to young children. He possessed ability of a high order, frequented the Papal Court, always had plenty of money, and was evidently 'protected,' as the Romans call it, by the highest influence. He was fond of strolling about the ruins, knowing many of them, as it were, by intuition, and speaking of a few as recalling personal memories. Some of his time must, however, have been less innocently employed, for, although but twenty-three years old, he had already incurred the scandal of having compromised and abandoned two young women.

My phenomenal success with the buried Via Sacra and the Temple of Jupiter Stator ultimately brought me to the notice of the Emperor Napoleon. I was appointed one of his staff of literary secretaries, being employed in 1866 upon technical and geographical data for his 'Vie de Jules César,' and in 1867 upon confidential matters. I do not mean to insinuate that I was more favoured or trusted than others who were engaged in similar capacities; but I was industrious, I acquired the knack of quickly deciphering the Emperor's chirography, and away from my desk, or from the presence of my Imperial master, I forgot everything of a private nature that came under my notice.

In the summer of 1867 I was ordered to Compiègne, to take my turn for a fortnight as one of his Majesty's scribes. That year, as every one knows, was the climax of the Second Empire. The Exhibition was open, and the Czar, the King of Prussia, the Sultan, and the Emperor of Austria visited Paris. All the luxury and magnificence in which the pride of life and the lust of the flesh can steep themselves were there. To this day, when I listen to the love music of Strauss, whose waltzes were familiar novelties, I seem to behold again a semblance of that voluptuous dream. But to the Emperor – ill, harassed, haunted by forebodings – that year's cup was bitter. I had first seen him in 1857, when he was *par excellence* the man of nerve. Through almost daily contact I came to know him as the nerveless man. Ten years before, he strode upon the lines of a fixed purpose; now every step pointed towards a collapse.

On the day of my arrival at Compiègne I was surprised to see the Cavaliere di Nerone sitting after dinner upon a terrace in the midst of a brilliant group of men and women. I say surprised only in the sense that I had not expected to meet him, for Compiègne was the place to which all sorts of adventurers obtained access. The next day I heard that his name was now gallicised into 'Monsieur de Néron,' that he was still under the highest protection of the Pontifical Government, that he was the inventor of a fulminating powder of extraordinary destructiveness, with which some officers of the Bureau de l'Artillerie were experimenting. In appearance he was unchanged. There were the same athletic and burly proportions, the same thick-set neck and clean-shaven face, the same sensuous yet commanding eyes. My informant whispered further that he had left Rome two years previously on account of a defalcation in the Pontifical treasury in which he appeared to be implicated, and also that his name was connected at Compiègne with that of Mademoiselle X——, one of the beautiful girls with whom, as maids of honour, the Empress surrounded herself. Socially he was a favourite – as is often the case when a man has a scandal jingling at his heels: it is like tying a tin pan to a dog's tail – all the other dogs run after him.

One afternoon, some days later, my work being finished, and the Emperor having left the chateau for a drive, so that there was no chance of my services being required, I resolved to refresh myself by a walk through the forest. I had gone some distance when, on approaching a clearing, I heard excited voices. One was the voice of a woman, pleading in words that did not reach me; the other was that of a man – harsh, strident, producing a sound that I had never before heard the equal of. A few steps brought me to the edge of the trees, and there I halted. Thirty paces distant stood Mademoiselle X——, confronted by Monsieur de Néron. She had ceased to speak; her face was bathed in tears, and her hands were extended in mute supplication. And he! What a figure he was – dressed to perfection, twisting his *gants de suède* convulsively between his fingers, with red passionate face and livid eyes, and nostrils distended like an animal's! During the instant I stood there he poured forth his words with frenzied volubility, and – think of it – this angry raving of his was in Latin! Then suddenly he advanced and struck the lady a heavy slap in the face.

I sprang to the rescue, but halted at the first step. De Néron had turned upon his heel, and was striding away. Mademoiselle X—— was walking slowly towards me, with her face bent down and half covered by a handkerchief she held to it. For the lady's sake I would have interposed a moment before; but now, for the sake of the lady's *amour propre*, I drew back unnoticed, watching to see that she was not followed or further molested. She walked away sobbing, passing within a few yards of me, and disappeared among the trees.

I paused for some minutes, rooted to the spot where I had innocently trespassed upon a drama of grave import to at least one life. What may have been the story between these two I know not, nor at that moment did I concern myself with it. The perplexity that beset me was the fact that De Néron spoke to Mademoiselle X—— in Latin. Now, a man in a paroxysm of rage may curse and rant in the language most familiar to him, even though it be unknown to the person to whom the words are addressed. It is Nature's instinctive reversion to the mother tongue. But how could Latin be De Néron's mother tongue? Of course I shall be told that what he used was Italian, but this was not the fact. I speak Italian fluently, and am too good a Latin scholar to be mistaken. Moreover, it was Latin spoken as neither I nor any other living man had ever heard it used, with a rhythm of enunciation and a redundance of invective wholly different from the stilted aping of a dead language. Could it be that Monsieur de Néron spoke Latin in that paroxysmal frenzy because to him it was a living language, expressing things no modern and acquired tongue could phrase with equal force and fluency?

In the midst of these cogitations I noticed something lying upon the grass where they had stood, and found it to be one of De Néron's gloves. After breakfast on the morrow I led him aside. He remembered me at once, though I do not know whether he had previously noticed me during the week I had been at Compiègne.

'We met once in Rome,' I began, 'some years ago, among the ruins of the Palatine, with whose former construction you showed a miraculous knowledge.'

He smiled absently, nodded, and waited for me to continue.

'Chance brought me yesterday in sight of a painful scene a mile from here. I was stupefied to see a man strike a lady.'

He turned upon me his large face, beneath whose olive skin the hot blood flushed. Even in that moment's excitement I could not but admire the classic contour of his features, and thought him, as perhaps Mademoiselle X—— had thought him before me, as handsome as the sun-god whom Clytie loved.

Without another word I extended his glove, but he brushed it impatiently aside.

'Monsieur,' said he, 'you can carry my glove back to the place where you found it. You were pained, you say, to see me yesterday at a moment upon which another would have forborne to intrude. I remember you only too well during the Roman days to which you refer. I rendered you then a trifling service, which you acknowledged by having me dogged to my lodgings, and by causing offensive and injurious inquiries to be circulated about me. Shall I tell you in a word what I think of your conduct?'

'Do me the favour,' I exclaimed, 'to say that word in Latin, since that is the tongue in which, to judge from your performance yesterday, you express yourself with the greatest readiness.'

He winced at this thrust, and I saw a dangerous look leap to his eyes.

'Monsieur,' he exclaimed hotly, 'since you presume to allude again to what happened yesterday, you will be good enough to meet me tomorrow at sunrise at that identical spot, with your seconds, when we shall finish this discussion with very few words in any language.'

On the following morning the sun had not yet reached the horizon when, at a little before seven o'clock, I and my seconds, who were officers of my acquaintance, arrived upon the now familiar ground. It was a fine, crisp, October day, the air quite still, and the motionless branches of red and gold contrasting vividly with the brilliant emerald of the grass. I was a capital swordsman in those days, having been a fencer all my life, and having previously had two affairs upon the terrain, of which modesty forbids me to speak further than to say that one turned upon the question whether macaroni should or should not be flavoured with cheese, and that the other concerned a lady's photograph which my opponent had abstracted (by mistake, of course) from her album. I therefore felt quite unconcerned, and walked briskly up and down, humming a refrain from *La Belle Hélène*, while my seconds chatted softly and puffed at their cigars. When twenty minutes had elapsed, one of them approached me ceremoniously, as one soldier approaches another who is about to risk his life.

'I have the deep regret, mon cher,' he began, 'to inform you, with the concurrence of my colleague, that in our opinion it is evident that the Sieur de Néron will not come to this rendezvous. This evasion of his is identical with what he did last year, when he failed to meet Madame Mathilde's husband.'

Almost before the speaker had finished a martial figure appeared and saluted us all with a comprehensive wave of the hand, in which he held an open letter. This gentleman was Colonel B——, one of Monsieur de Néron's seconds, and the letter was written by the Cavaliere himself at midnight, informing the Colonel that, upon reflection, it appeared beneath his dignity to cross swords with one whom he was pleased to term 'an employé,' and that he was on the point of leaving for Paris. 'A greater piece of poltroonery never came to my knowledge,' added the Colonel, 'and I trust, gentlemen, that you will do me and my colleague the justice to exonerate us from all responsibility.'

Two years and nine months later, at the beginning of August 1870, the First French Army Corps occupied the line of the Lauter; and here I, serving as one of General Douay's volunteer aides, was in camp. The army was short of officers, as of everything else, and a graduate of St. Cyr would at least do to stop a Prussian bullet. I was sitting on the grass trying to repair my garments, and thinking to myself that, from all the disheartening news that circulated, the bottom was equally out of our march to Berlin. Suddenly a figure passed before me: it was De Néron, in uniform, covered with decorations, and no more disconcerted at the sight of me than if we had never laid eyes upon one another. I rose at once, and walked straight upon him.

'Monsieur,' I exclaimed, 'when one is a coward, one does not presume to stand in the ranks of brave men who are about to give their blood for their country.'

He regarded me fixedly, with magnificent indifference, breathing short a little from corpulency, which had gained upon him since our rencounter at Compiègne. He wore an artillery uniform, from which I inferred that his fulminating powder might have secured him a commission. He looked the very type of a fighting man – cool, resolute, imperturbable – yet I alone in all that camp knew him to be an arrant poltroon.

'Monsieur,' he replied without hesitation, 'I did not come here to bandy words or cross weapons with my brother officers. Within a few days – perhaps a few hours – we are to encounter a host of enemies.

156

Will not that suffice your ardour? And when that moment comes,' he pursued, laying his hand theatrically upon his breast, 'I will vie with you, as becomes a *preux chevalier*, in deeds of prowess; and when the victory is ours, if ours it is to be, I will, if you still require it, meet you when and where you please.'

'That,' I exclaimed, slapping my leg contemptuously, 'is what you said a couple of years ago, just before business called you in such haste from Compiègne.'

'Well,' he answered quietly, as though my taunt had passed him by, 'if we must fight, so shall it be. Curb your impatience for a day or two, and on the first battlefield we will shoot one another, *à l'Américaine*, on sight.'

De Néron was not wrong in anticipating a surfeit of fighting. Two days later, August 6th, those of us who held the village of Froeschewiller were violently attacked. I pass by the courage, the carnage, the horror, the despair of that evil day. As I stood watching the wild gallop of the cuirassiers to their destruction, I was wounded and my horse killed by the bursting of a shell. On our side it had already become a *sauve qui peut*, and I made my way painfully to the rear, whither thousands were straggling. Presently an officer rode past me covered with dust, and grasping a broken sword: in leaping a hedge his horse fell and threw him heavily. A moment later, passing where he lay, I recognised De Néron. Much as I disliked the man, the chivalry of a French officer bade me pause beside my intended adversary, even in the midst of that awful *débacle*, and offer him such assistance as one disabled man can give another. He grasped eagerly the proffered canteen, and, having slaked his thirst, thanked me and rose with difficulty to his feet.

'It is nothing,' he said, as we walked away together. Then, as though speaking to himself, he added, 'The amphitheatre never beheld a finer slaughter than the mangling and crippling and killing of those cuirassiers. By all the gods, what a sight!'

The retreat to Châlons was an arduous five days' journey, which De Néron and I made in company with a convoy of wounded. We no longer talked of fighting: there was sure to be enough of that without duels. Moreover, the extraordinary mystery which hung about this singular man exercised a witchery over me that nothing could shake off. I am no more inquisitive than most people, yet I would have given half a year's income to know the Cavaliere's true story. Events proved that I had not long to wait.

157

On the 12th of August we sat down to dine together *tête-à-tête* in a restaurant at Châlons. It was to be our last meeting, and we had agreed to part friends. On the morrow I, with my arm in a sling, was to return to Paris for a fortnight in the hospital, while he, having recovered from his concussion, should resume his service with Ducrot's Army Corps. We were finishing a bottle of champagne at the end of dinner, by way of refreshing our lips after the two bottles of Chambertin which had flavoured our repast. For three weeks we had been living upon coarse camp fare, glad during the retreat to get a single meal a day. The wine, the rest, and our table-talk together had brought us to a stage of good-natured comradeship on the strength of which I ventured to inquire the fate of his fulminating powder.

'It is the greatest military invention of the age,' he replied, coolly wiping his lips; 'and, had the army been supplied with my long-barrelled magazine cannon, and my annihilating shells, the Prussians could not have lived within seven miles of our line of battle. *Que voulez-vous?* the models are somewhere in the Ordnance Department, and could we have hastened them by – say a few years, an equipment of artillery would have been furnished to the Armée du Rhin, compared to which the Prussian batteries and your rumbling mitrailleuses are but coffee-mills.'

'And yet you are not a professional artillerist?'

'No; I pursue it as a profession of love.'

'A singular taste for a dilettante!'

'You might not think it so if you knew who and what I am.'

'Can you not see,' I ejaculated impatiently, 'that I am dying to know who and what you are? You are the most weird enigma ever heard of. You know things that have been forgotten for centuries, and my flesh creeps when I clasp your hand in mine, as though it were a hand that had plucked flowers and filled wine-cups ages ago.'

Monsieur de Néron listened to these extravagant words without emotion. 'I cannot tell you my story,' he answered, after a moment's hesitation: 'it is incredible, and you would no more believe it than a dozen others to whom it has been told.'

'As surely,' I rejoined, 'as the facts you told me about the position of the buried ruins on the Palatine proved true, will I believe any confidence about yourself.'

At these words Monsieur de Néron rose, paid for our dinner, and motioned me to follow. 'I cannot talk,' he explained, 'when there is any risk of being overheard. It is a fine starlight night, the streets are tolerably quiet, – walk with me half an hour, and I will recount to you a stranger story than is to be found in most fiction.

'Do you ever,' he asked, passing his arm familiarly through mine, 'experience a sudden spasmodic consciousness that the thing you are doing, or the words you are speaking, or the thought you are thinking, have been done or spoken or thought by you in some dim, bygone epoch? Of course you do. It is a sensation experienced by almost every one, and from it was derived our first perception of the possible transmigration of souls. With me that consciousness was habitual from childhood. As soon as I began to think, I perceived that I possessed two memories, and that one of them was a recollection of things that happened to me at some remote date, amid other scenes, and in the companionship of people I no longer met. When I was fourteen, I talked about this dual memory to a priest who came once a week to Rocca di Papa, where my mother lived; and he first laughed at my queer fancy, and presently became afraid of me. The next year I was put to school at a Jesuit seminary, and ventured, after a time, to make the same confidence to my tutor. He did not laugh, for Jesuits know that the truth, however grotesque, is never ridiculous; and, so far from being disconcerted, he gave me excellent advice. "You evidently believe," he said, "that somewhere, at some time long since past, you lived upon earth, and that the memory of that life haunts and follows and perplexes you now. Through the life you are living to-day appears to you to be woven the tissue of a life you know only in memory, but that you remember with perfect distinctness. My advice to you is to read, to study, to fill your mind with pictures of bygone times, and the semblance of many lands, and the names of a thousand illustrious men. Probe the past in every direction. If your theory is right, you should some day come upon a clue to this extraordinary dreamland. If there be nothing in it, the course of study I recommend will have made you no mean scholar."

'I took him at his word, and a month later sought him again with an open book in my hand. "Lucius Annoeus Seneca," I explained, pointing to the titlepage, "was the name of my tutor." "And who then the devil are *you*?" shouted the Jesuit, growing red in the face. "I have found my own name also," I replied triumphantly, "and here it is:

'"'Nero Claudius Caesar Drusus Germanicus.'"'

'The Jesuits would have no more to do with me, but I was provided for at the Collegio Romano by an all-powerful influence that has continually made itself felt. I acquired Latin by intuition, and gave my tutors the music of half a dozen of the love songs Acte used to sing, which they developed into superb anthems. At the age of sixteen I wrote my dreamlife from memory, and submitted it in the form of a prize essay, embracing newly discovered and authentic facts concerning the emperor Nero and his times. It made a profound sensation. Some of the Cardinals thought to test me. "If," they said, "this be indeed a case of direct transmigration, you will be able to take us to the spot on the Campagna where stood the freedman's house to which Nero fled, and where he died." I led them forth to a place I recognised, transfigured though it is, and bade the labourers dig. Four feet below the sod they uncovered the foundations of a villa. "Now," I said, "the atrium of this house was paved with red and yellow tiles"; and in the debris, all broken and displaced, we found a score of the red and yellow tiles I remembered. The only thing that still puzzled me was that I do not look quite as I used to do. You shake your head? Well, I received my robust figure from my mother, who was a handsome contadina; and, as to my father, knowing Rome as you must, you should have little difficulty in making a shrewd guess as to his identity. Little by little, in the course of my reading, the complete past became distinct. I remembered my first love, the beautiful freedwoman Acte; I recalled the poet Lucan, the Consul Laternus, Faenius Rufus, the Prefect of the Pretorians, and Calpurnius Piso, with whom I used to sup. But I sought in vain for my golden house at the foot of the Esquiline, or for the Roman Forum, where as a youth I sat administering justice, or for the gardens of Sallust, where I loved to lie in the deep shade and dream. They existed no more than did the face of Nero in the glass; for, you understand, it was my soul only that had survived, and with it my memory. All my youth I was consumed by a passionate love of that past to which my reveries by day and my visions at night reverted. I longed for the associations of that proud life, for the frenzied shouts of the populace, for the triumphant march-past of my legions, for chariot races, and the gasp of the stricken gladiator, for the lascivious songs of the dancing girls, and for the flutes of the Athenian slaves at night.'

'There was once a fire in Rome,' I dryly suggested.

'Yes, and to this day it makes me laugh to read your modern melodramatic version of it, and to find that I am guilty of something I had no more to do with than yourself.'

I had let the man run on, for he was evidently mad. 'We have wandered a bit,' I said, 'from that delight in your long-barrelled cannon and annihilating explosives concerning which we began to speak. Are these also derived from souvenirs of the Imperial Nero?'

'There is,' he answered slowly, speaking as though in mental pain, 'a wild beast in many men's natures; and why should not that evil thing, with its cruelty, its base passions, its delight in wrong, haunt a soul from one life to another? If that wild beast had been let sleep and not awakened, the story of my first life would have been different. But when once a tiger has tasted blood, it is too late to tame him.' Then, suddenly observing that we neared the house in which I had been lodged, he disengaged his arm from mine, nodded an abrupt good-night, and was presently lost among the moving groups of people.

The siege had come to an end, and the Commune was in possession of Paris. I had served from October until January, had escaped wounds, but not the exposure and privation of the trenches. In April I lay dangerously ill of typhoid fever, from which by the middle of May I was convalescent. It was a time of such horrors as Paris had not known since la Barthélemy. I was lodged in the Rue de Rivoli, within sound of the firing that went on day and night while the National troops broke into the city, and the Communards stood at bay, – almost within sight of the Colonne Vendôme when it fell, with the military supremacy of which it was the emblem. One evening Madame S—— whose *locataire* I was, came to my room in great agitation.

'Monsieur,' she said, bursting into tears, 'I appeal to you as a man and an officer for protection.'

'*Parbleu*, Madame!' I cried, 'what mean these strange words?'

'Protection, not for me, who am of an age to care for myself, but for my daughter – a child of fifteen.'

'Protection against whom?'

'Against an officer who has lodged here these two weeks.'

'And his name?'

'Le Chevalier de Néron.'

'My good woman,' I cried, beside myself with rage, weak as I was, 'have the kindness to take my card to Monsieur de Néron, and say I beg a few words with him immediately.'

The Chevalier, whom I had by this time come to regard as my evil genius, was out at the moment, but returned an hour later to secure some papers. Upon the receipt of my message, he came bounding upstairs to my room. His greeting died unspoken upon his lips before the cold gesture with which I motioned him to a chair.

'It appears, Monsieur,' I began, in a voice which I essayed to render calm, 'that I am fated always to hear revolting things of you. One of the worst reached my ears an hour ago. We will not discuss it, any more than we will resume our consideration of that crazy tale you confided to me at Châlons. You understand very well what I mean, and I order you to leave this house on the instant, and not enter it again under pain of being shot like the hound that you are.'

He looked at me for a moment in insolent silence. 'Yes,' he said at length, 'I see what it is. You were a fool and a beggar when I first knew you, – now you are a fool and rich. You are living in good quarters here, which means money, and nothing dulls the wits so much. In that, mark you, wealth differs from power, which, when it becomes supreme, ends in madness. As to the matter to which your insinuations point, recall, if you can, that Ode of Horace beginning

Faune, Nympharum fugientum amator,

and you will understand. Poppeia used to recite it divinely eighteen hundred years ago. The fair nymph below, who understands and believes my story, is none other than a Greek girl whom in that bygone age I loved beneath her native skies. Think you I would not know again the voluptuous imagination of my divine Euphrosyne, or that, wheresoever we meet, she could fail to follow me, even as a love-bird flies to its mate? But as for yourself, by Hercules, I have trifled with you too long. Hark? do you hear those explosions? I must be gone. I find here in Paris a sphere worthy of great deeds. It is I who all day long have been preparing the petroleuses. I saw Rome burn – tonight I shall see Paris in flames. But before I go, you shall receive from me the most excruciating death known to the ancients. With this bottle of petroleum I shall make of you a *feu d'artifice* similar to those I made of the early Christians—'

'Stay! . . . What's that?'

I had struggled to my feet, and pointed speechless to the window. Before us was the black line of the Tuileries, through whose casements the eager flames were leaping. He rushed astonished to the hall, where a corner window gave a wider view; and, springing after him, I closed and bolted the door.

★

162

That, Monsieur le Préfet, or reader, whoever you may be, is all I know of Monsieur de Néron. I am not astonished to hear to-day, after twenty-three years, that he is the ultimate Number One of the Renaissance that is to purge the world with dynamite. Nor does it surprise me, *Messieurs les policiers*, that he has slipped through your clumsy clutches. Have I an opinion about him, you ask? None whatever. I do not know whether he is more fool than knave, or whether he is more mad than many other equally eccentric people I have met in the course of a long and adventurous life.

A point that interests me is the query what I, an old and relatively helpless man, may personally expect from De Néron. His enmity I can now depend upon; and you, Monsieur le Préfet, intimate that he is at the head of a fraternity of Socialists that drawn up in single rank would encircle Paris. This fact alone is so conclusive a demonstration of the futility of nineteenth-century methods against Radicalism, that I shall not hesitate upon emergency to take the law into my own hands, as people say when they mean to break it. I do not know what Monsieur de Néron and his pals may be planning. Any night he or some of them may appear at my bedside to settle accounts with me in some such drastic fashion as would have delighted him in the fine old days he remembers. But this I know – that I sleep with an American revolver under my pillow, and that the American revolver is a weapon of great straightforwardness and clearness of purpose, or, as its Trans-Atlantic manufacturers would say in their expressive vernacular – it means business every time!

Herodes Redivivus

H.N.L. MUNBY

Gilles de Retz, the Baron of France in the early fifteenth century, was a man of prodigious wealth and unbridled sexual excesses. Having first served his country in battles against the English and then becoming the richest nobleman in Europe as a result of marrying a fabulously wealthy heiress, Catherine de Thouars, de Retz thereafter retreated to his huge estate and devoted himself to sexual perversions (especially with children) and a number of unsuccessful attempts to raise demons and spirits through the use of alchemy and magic. Later, as a result of a mounting tide of accusations that he had sexually abused hundreds of small boys and girls, murdered them and then decapitated the bodies, the former Marshall was brought to trial by the church. He was tortured to confess his guilt and burned at the stake in October 1440. Alan Munby, the author of 'Herodes Redivivus', worked for years as a librarian and was also a specialist in rare and antiquarian books. These have a habit of featuring in his stories, such as the one here which continues the theme of evil reappearing throughout history. (As a matter of interest, Munby actually wrote this story while a prisoner-of-war in Germany between 1943–5.)

I DON'T SUPPOSE that many people have heard of Charles Auckland, the pathologist, as he isn't the type of man who catches the public eye. What slight reputation he has got is of rather a sinister nature; for he has always tended to avoid the broad, beaten tracks of scientific research, and has branched off to bring light into certain dark cul-de-sacs of the human mind, which many people feel should be left unilluminated. Not that one would suspect it from his appearance. Some men who spend their lives studying abnormalities begin to look distinctly queer themselves, but not Auckland. To look at him one would put him down as a country doctor, a big red-faced man of about sixty, obviously still pretty fit, with a shrewd but kindly face. We belonged to the same club and for years had been on nodding terms,

164

but I didn't discover until quite recently that he was a book-collector, and that only accidentally. I went to refer to Davenport's *Armorial Bookbindings* in the club library, and found him reading it. He deplored its inaccuracies, and I offered to lend him a list of corrections and additions that I had been preparing. This led to further discussion on bindings, and finally he invited me to go back with him to his flat and see his books. It was not yet ten o'clock and I agreed readily.

The night was fine, and we strolled together across the park to Artillery Mansions, where he was living at the time. On arriving we went up in the lift, and were soon seated in the dining-room of his flat, the walls of which were lined with books from floor to ceiling. I was glad to see that one alcove was entirely filled with calf and vellum bindings, the sight of which sent a little thrill of expectation down my spine. I crossed the room to examine them, and my host rose too. A glance showed me that they were all of the class that second-hand booksellers classify comprehensively under the word 'Occult.' This, however, did not surprise me, as I knew of Auckland's interests. He took down several volumes, and began to expatiate on them – some first editions of the astrological works of Robert Fludd, and a very fine copy of the 1575 *Theatrum Diabolorum*. I expressed my admiration, and we began to talk of trials for witchcraft. He had turned aside to fetch a copy of Scot's *Discoverie* to illustrate some point in his argument when suddenly my eye became riveted on the back of a small book on the top shelf, and my heart missed a beat. Of course it couldn't be, but it was fantastically like it! The same limp vellum cover without any lettering, with the same curious diagonal tear in the vellum at the top of the spine. My hand shook a little as I took it down and opened it. Yes, it was the book. I read once more the title villainously printed on indifferent paper: *Herodes Redivivus seu Liber Scelerosae Vitae et Mortis Sanguinolentae Retzii, Monstri Nannetensis,* Parisiis, MDXLV. As I read the words memories came flooding back of that macabre episode which had overshadowed my schooldays. Some of the terror that had come to me twenty years before returned, and I felt quite faint.

'I say, you must have a nose for a rarity,' said Auckland, pointing to the volume in my hand.

'I've seen this book before,' I replied.

'Really?' he said. 'I'd be very glad to know where. There's no copy in any public collection in England, and the only one I've traced on the Continent is in the Ambrosian Library at Milan. I haven't even *seen* that. It's in the catalogue, but it's one of those books that librarians are very reluctant to produce. Can you remember where you've met it before?'

'I mean that I've seen this copy before,' I answered.

He shook his head dubiously. 'I think you must be mistaken about that. I've owned this for nearly twenty years, and before that it was the property of a man that you're most unlikely to have met. In fact, he died in Broadmoor fifteen years ago. His name was—'

'Race,' I interposed.

He looked at me with interest. 'I shouldn't have expected you to remember that,' he said. 'You must have been at school during the trial – not that it got much publicity. Thank God, there's legislation to prevent the gutter press from splashing that sort of stuff across their headlines.' He half smiled. 'You must have been a very precocious child – surely you were only a schoolboy at the time?'

'Yes,' I replied. 'I was a schoolboy – *the* schoolboy, one might say; the one who gave evidence at the trial and whose name was suppressed.'

He put down the book he was holding and looked hard at me. 'That's most extraordinarily interesting. I suppose you wouldn't be willing to tell me about it? As you know, cases of that sort are rather my subject. Of course, it would be in the strictest confidence.'

I smiled. 'There's nothing in my story that I'm particularly ashamed of,' I replied, 'though I must confess that I occasionally feel that if I'd been a little more intelligent the tragedy might have been averted. However, I've no objection at all. It's only of academic interest now. I haven't thought about the matter for years.'

He sat me down in an armchair and poured me out a large whisky-and-soda, then settled himself opposite me.

'Take your time about it,' he said. 'I'm a very late bird, and it's only a quarter to eleven.'

I took a long drink and collected my thoughts.

'I was at a large school on the outskirts of Bristol,' I began, 'and was not quite sixteen at the time of these events. Even in those days I was extremely interested in old books, a hobby in which I was encouraged by my housemaster. I never cut a great figure on the games field, and when it was wet or I was not put down for a game, I used to go bookhunting in Bristol. Of course, my purse was very limited and my ignorance profound, but I got enormous pleasure out of pottering round the shops and stalls of the town, returning every now and then with a copy of Pope's *Homer* or Theobald's *Shakespeare* to grace my study.

'I don't know whether you're acquainted with Bristol, but it's a most fascinating town. As one descends the hills towards the Avon, one passes from the Georgian crescents and squares of Clifton into the older maritime town, with its magnificent churches and extensive docks. Down by the river are many narrow courts and alleys, which are unchanged since the days when Bristol was a thriving mediaeval port. Much of this poorer area was out of bounds to the boys at school, but having exhausted the bookshops of the University area, I found it convenient to ignore this rule and explored every corner of the old town. One Saturday afternoon – it was in a summer term – I was wandering round the area between St. Mary Redcliffe and the old 'Floating Harbour,' and I discovered a little court approached through a narrow passage. It was a miserable enough place, dark and damp, but a joy to the antiquarian – so long as he didn't have to live there! The first floors of the half-timbered houses jutted out and very nearly shut out the sky, and the court ended abruptly in a high blank wall. At the end on the right was a shop – at least the ground-floor window was filled with a collection of books. They were of little interest, and from the accumulation of dust upon them it was obvious that they hadn't been disturbed for years. The place had a deserted air, and it was in no great hope of finding it open that I tried the door. But it did open, and I found myself in its dark interior. Books were every-where – all the shelves were blocked by great stacks of books on the floor with narrow lanes through which one could barely squeeze sideways, and over everything lay the same thick coating of dust that I'd noticed in the window. I felt as though I were the first person to enter it for years. No bell rang as I opened the door, and I looked round for the proprietor. I saw him sitting in an alcove at my right, and I picked my way through the piles of books to his desk. Did you ever see him yourself?'

'Only later in Broadmoor,' replied Auckland. 'I'd like you to describe in your own words exactly how he struck you at the time.'

'Well,' I resumed, 'my first impression of him was the extreme whiteness of his face. One felt on looking at him that he never went out into the sun. He had the unhealthy look that a plant gets if you leave a flower-pot over it and keep the light and air from it. His hair was long and straight and a dirty grey. Another thing that impressed me was the smoothness of his skin. You know how sometimes a man looks as though he has never had any need to shave – attractive in a young man but quite repulsive in an old one – well, that's how he looked. He stood up as I approached, and I saw he was a fat man, not grotesquely so but sufficiently to suggest grossness. His lips particularly were full and fleshy.

'I was half afraid of my own temerity in having entered, but he seemed glad to see me and said in rather a high-pitched voice:

'"Come in, my dear boy; this is a most pleasant surprise. What can I do for you?"

'I mumbled something about being interested in old books and wanting to look round, and he readily assented. Shambling round from pile to pile, he set himself deliberately to interest me. And the man was a fascinating talker – in a very little while he had summed up my small stock of bibliographical knowledge and was enlightening me on dates, editions, issues, values and other points of interest. It was with real regret that I glanced at my watch and found that I had to hurry back to school. I had made no purchase, but he insisted on presenting me with a book, a nicely bound copy of Sterne's *Sentimental Journey,* and made me promise to visit him again as soon as I could.'

'Have you still got the Sterne?' asked Auckland.

'No,' I said, 'my father destroyed it at the time of the trial.

'As the shop was in a part of the town that was strictly out of bounds, I didn't mention my visit to my housemaster, but on the following Thursday it was too wet for cricket and I returned to my newly found friend.

'This time he took me up to a room on the first floor, where there were more books and several portfolios of prints. Race, for such I discovered was his name, was a mine of information on the political history of the eighteenth century, and kept me enthralled by his exposition of a great volume of Gillray cartoons. The man had a sort of magnetism, and at that impressionable age I fell completely under his spell. He drew me out about myself and my work at school, and it was impossible for a boy not to feel flattered by the attention of so learned a man. It was easy to forget his rather repellent physical qualities when he talked so brilliantly.

'Suddenly we heard the shop door below opening, and with an exclamation of annoyance he descended the stairs to attend to the customer. A minute or two passed, and he did not return. I listened and could hear the murmur of conversation below. I idly pulled a book or two from the shelves and glanced at them, but there was little in the room that he had not already shown me. I went to the door and peered down over the stairs, but couldn't see what was going on. My ears caught a scrap of dialogue about the county histories of Somerset. I became bored.

'Across the landing at the top of the stairs was another room, the door of which was very slightly ajar. I'm afraid that I'm of a very inquisitive disposition. I pushed it open and peeped in. It was obviously where Race lived. There was a bed in one corner, a wardrobe, and a circular table in the middle of the room, but what caught my eye at once and held me spellbound was a picture over the fireplace. No words of mine can describe it.'

Auckland nodded. 'I saw it — an unrecorded Goya — in his most bloodcurdling vein — made his "Witches' Sabbath" look like a school treat! It was burned by our unimaginative police force. They wouldn't even let me photograph it.' He sighed.

I resumed. 'I went nearer to have a look at it. On the mantelpiece below it was a book — the book you've got now on your top shelf. I opened it and read the title page. Of course it meant nothing to me. Gille de Retz doesn't feature in the average school curriculum. Suddenly I heard a noise behind me and swung round. There was Race standing in the doorway. He had come up the stairs without my hearing me. I shall never forget the blazing fury in his eyes. His face seemed whiter than ever as he stood there, a terrifying figure literally shaking with rage.

'I quickly tried to make my apologies, but he silenced me with a gesture; then he snatched the book from my hands and replaced it on the mantelpiece. Still without speaking, he pointed to the door and I went quickly down the stairs. He followed me down into the shop. I was about to leave without another word when suddenly his whole manner changed. It was as though he had recollected some powerful reason for conciliating me. He laid a hand on my arm.

'"My dear boy," he said, "you must forgive my momentary annoyance. I am a methodical man, and I can't bear people touching the things in my room. I'm afraid that living as something of a recluse has made me rather fussy. I quite realise that you meant no harm. There are some very valuable books and pictures in there — not for sale, but my own private collection, and naturally I can't allow customers to wander in and out of it in my absence."

'I expressed my contrition awkwardly enough, for the whole situation had embarrassed me horribly and I felt ill at ease. He perceived this and added:

'"Now you mustn't worry about this – and least of all must you let it stop coming here. I want you to promise that you'll visit me as soon as you can again – just to show that you bear no ill-will. I'll hunt out some interesting things for you to look at."

'I gave him my promise and hurried back to school. In a day or two I had persuaded myself that I'd been imagining things, that some trick of the light had made him appear so distorted with rage. After all, why should a man get so angry about so little? As for the picture, it made comparatively little impression on my schoolboy mind. Much that it depicted was unintelligible to me at that time. I was, in any case, unlikely to be invited into the private room again. And so I resolved to pay a further visit to the shop.

'An opportunity didn't occur for nearly a fortnight, and when I did manage to slip down to Bristol, there was no mistaking how glad he was to see me. He was almost gushing in his manner. He had been as good as his word in finding more books to show me, and I spent a most pleasant afternoon. Race was as voluble as ever, but I got the impression that he was slightly distrait, as though he were labouring under some sort of suppressed excitement. Several times as I looked up from a book I caught him looking at me in a queer reflective way, which made me feel a little uncomfortable. When I finally said that I must go, he made a suggestion that he had never made before.

'"You've got very dusty," he said. "You really must wash your hands before you go. There's a basin downstairs – I'll turn on the light for you."

'As he said this, he stepped across the shop, opened a door and turned a switch, illuminating a long flight of stairs. I descended them. They were of stone and led apparently into a cellar. As I reached the bottom step the light was extinguished. I turned sharply and saw him standing at the head of the stairs – a fantastic, foreshortened figure at the top of the shaft, silhouetted in the doorway. He had his hands stretched out, holding on to the jambs of the door, and with the half-light of the shop behind him he looked like a misshapen travesty of a cross. I called out to him and started to remount the stairs, but as I did so he quickly closed the door without saying a word.

170

'I was terribly afraid. Of course, it might have been a joke but I knew inside me that it wasn't and that I was in the most deadly peril. I reached the top of the stairs and groped at the door, but there seemed to be no handle inside. I couldn't find the switch either, it must have been in the shop. I shouted, there was no reply. An awful horror gripped me – the dank smell of the stone cellar, the lack of air and the darkness, all conspired to undermine what little courage I possessed. I shouted again; then listened holding my breath. All at once I heard the outer shop door open and an unfamiliar footstep inside the shop. With all my strength I pounded on the door, shouting and screaming like a madman. The noise reverberating round the confined space nearly deafened me. I listened again for a second; voices were raised in the shop, but I caught no words. I shouted again until I felt my lungs would burst and hammered on the door until my fists were bruised. Suddenly it was flung open and I stumbled out, hysterical with fear and half-blinded by the daylight. Before me stood an old clergyman, behind him Race, who bore on his face the same look of malevolent fury that I had seen before.

'"What is the matter?" asked the clergyman. "How did you get shut in there?"

'It was then that I made my fatal mistake. All I wanted was to get away and never come back again. If I lodged a complaint I foresaw endless trouble, with the school authorities, even with the police. My terror had evaporated with the daylight, and I was feeling more than a little ashamed of myself.

'"I went down to wash my hands," I said. "The lights went out and I got frightened. I'm quite all right now, though."

'The clergyman looked enquiringly at Race, but the latter had recovered his self-possession.

'"The lights must have fused," he said; "they often do – it's the damp. I was just going to let him out when you came in. No wonder he was frightened. It's a most eerie place in the dark."

'The clergyman looked from him to me, as if inviting some comment from me, but I merely said, 'I ought to be getting back to school now.'

'We left the shop together, and as we walked through the passage out of the court I looked back, and there was Race standing on the step of his shop following us with baleful eyes. My companion seemed to be debating whether he would ask me a question, but he refrained.

I hardly liked to ask him to say nothing about the episode; he obviously wished to satisfy his curiosity, but we were complete strangers and, though old enough to be my grandfather, he seemed to be a diffident man. It was a curious relationship.

'He put me on to a bus, and I thanked him gravely. As we shook hands he said abruptly, "I shouldn't go there again," and turned away.

'For a few days I was on tenterhooks lest he should make any report of the occurrence to the school, but as the days became weeks and I heard no more, my mind became at rest. I had firmly decided that nothing would induce me to visit Race's shop again, and soon the whole episode assumed an air of unreality in my mind.'

I looked at my watch.

'Good Lord!' I said to Auckland, 'it's getting pretty late. Do you want to go to bed? We could have another session tomorrow.'

'Certainly not,' he replied. 'I find your story of the most absorbing interest. It fills in all sorts of gaps in my knowledge of the affair. If you don't mind sitting up, I should greatly appreciate it if you'd carry on.'

He refilled my glass and I settled myself more comfortably into my chair.

'Well,' I continued, 'I'm a bit diffident about telling the rest of the story. Up to now it's been pretty strange, but it has been sober fact; now we get into realms where I find myself a bit out of my depth.'

Auckland nodded. 'Never mind,' he said, 'let's have it. Just as it comes back to you – don't try to explain it, just tell me what happened.'

'A year passed and I was still at school,' I continued; 'I'd got into the Sixth Form and was working pretty hard for a scholarship. I'd also got into the House Cricket XI by some miracle, and so I couldn't be so free-and-easy about games as I had been previously. Public opinion forced me to take them fairly seriously. A dropped catch at a critical point in a match can make a schoolboy's life pretty good hell.

'At that age I used to sleep extraordinarily well – I still do for that matter. It was very rare for me to dream and then only of trivial affairs. But on the night of June 26th – I noted the date in my diary – I had the first of a couple of particularly horrible dreams. I dreamed most vividly that I was back in Race's shop. Every detail of that untidy interior passed in an accurate picture through my brain. I was standing in the middle of the shop, and it was dusk. Very little light came through those dusty windows piled high with books. Race himself was

172

nowhere to be seen. The door to the cellar which had such sinister associations for me was closed. Suddenly from the other side of it came a series of appalling screams and shouts, intermingled with muffled bangs and thumps on the door. I ran across and tried to open it, but it was locked. Then I darted out to the shop steps to see if anyone were at hand to assist me, but the court was deserted. I stood irresolute in the shop, and then all at once the cries seemed to get weaker and the banging on the door ceased. I listened and could hear the sounds of a struggle on the stairs gradually getting fainter as it reached the cellar below.

'At this point I awoke shivering with fright, bathed in a cold sweat. Sleep was impossible for me during the rest of the night. I lay and thought about my dream. It seemed so queer that I should dream, not of my own experience on the stairs, but from the point of view of an observer.

'The next night exactly the same thing occurred, and the horror of the scene so impressed me that I must have cried out in my sleep, for I found that I'd awakened several of the other boys in my dormitory. I couldn't bear the anticipation of having such a dream a third time, and I went to the House Matron on the following day and told her that I couldn't sleep. She moved me from the dormitory into the sick-room and gave me a sedative. On that night and thereafter I slept quite normally again.

"Not quite a fortnight later a further link was forged in this extraordinary chain of events. I was passing the local police-station and I stopped to read a notice posted outside about the protection of wild birds – I've always been a bit of an ornithologist. Along the railings in front of the building were hung the usual medley of notices – Lost, Found and Missing. My eye caught one more recent than the others – and I idly read it.

'I cannot, of course, remember the exact wording at this date, but it asked for information about a boy named Roger Weyland, aged fifteen and a half. He was described in detail, and I remember being struck at once by his similarity to myself. He had left his home at Clevedon after lunch on June 26th to bicycle into Bristol, where he intended to visit the docks. He was last seen near St Mary Redcliffe at about half-past five the same afternoon, and the police were asking anyone to come forward who could throw light on his whereabouts.

'I read and reread the notice. Its implication dawned on me at once.

It's no good asking why, but I assure you that at the moment I *knew* what had happened. My dream of the night of June 26th was still fresh in my memory, and even in the broad sunlit street I shuddered and was oppressed by a feeling of nameless horror.

'I debated what I should do. The police, I felt sure, would laugh at me. I could never bring myself to walk into the station and blurt out such a fantastic tale to some grinning sergeant. But I must tell someone; and after dinner that day I sought an interview with my housemaster. He was a most understanding man, and listened in patient silence while I told him the whole story. I must have spoken with conviction, because at the end of it he rang up a friend of his, a local Inspector of Police. Half an hour later I repeated my tale to him. He was very polite, asked one or two searching questions, but I could see that he was sceptical. He did, however, agree with my housemaster that Race's activities might profitably be looked into.

'If you followed the trial, I suppose you know all the rest – how they found the boy's body and Godknows-what other devilish things beside. My name was suppressed in the evidence, and I left school at the end of that term and went abroad for six months.

'One very odd thing about it all was that they never traced the clergyman. The police were most anxious to get him to corroborate my story, and my father was equally keen to find him – after all, he saved my life – and my father wanted to show some tangible appreciation of the fact, subscribe generously to one of his favourite charities or something. It's very queer really that the police, with all their nation-wide organisation, never got on to him. After all, there aren't a limitless number of clergymen, and the number of those in the Bristol area that afternoon must have been comparatively small. Perhaps he didn't like to come forward and be connected with such a business, but I don't think that's very likely – he didn't strike me as the sort of man who would shirk his obligations.

'That's really all that I can tell you, and I expect you knew some of that already.'

'A certain amount,' replied Auckland, 'but by no means all. I occasionally get asked questions by the police in this kind of case, and I did assist them on this occasion, though I wasn't called in evidence. Race had a damned good counsel in Rutherford, and managed to convince the jury that he was insane. If a man is sufficiently wicked, a British jury will often believe that he must be mad. And so he went to Broadmoor. Of course, he was as sane as you and I are.'

'How did you come to get hold of one of his books?' I asked.

'Through the good offices of the police,' he said. 'Perhaps as a sort of consolation prize for my distress at the destruction of the Goya. The book is really the clue to Race.

'It is a contemporary account of the activities of Gille de Retz, Marshal of France, hanged at Nantes in 1440. I expect you know a certain amount about him; he figures in all the standard works on Diabolism. The contemporary authorities are a bit vague on the exact number of children he murdered – Monstrelet says a hundred and sixty, but Chastellain and some others put it at a hundred and forty. But all this is general knowledge.

'What isn't so widely known is that every now and then he seems to reappear in history – at least the devilish practices, with which his name is associated, crop up again and again. He was quite a cult in seventeenth-century Venice, and there was a case in Bohemia in the middle of the last century. A variant of de Retz's name is de Rais and Race himself claimed to be a descendant; but I've no proof of this. The police failed to trace his parentage or to find any details about him before he appeared in Bristol just before the first World War. His shop has gone now; the whole of that area was pulled down in a recent slum-clearance scheme.

'The trial at Nantes in 1440 has always been an interest of mine, and I had a great find the last time I was in Paris. Some early Nantes archives had recently been acquired by the Bibliothèque Nationale, and I spent a happy week examining all the original documents relating to the examination of the woman, La Meffrie, who procured most of the children for de Retz. I've got transcripts of the most important. Would you care to borrow them? They are quite enthralling.'

'Not on your life,' I replied as I rose to take my leave. 'I came far too near to playing the principal rôle to read about such things with any pleasure. *You* may be able to take a detached, scientific view of the case, but, believe me, I've had enough of de Retz and all his works to last me a lifetime.'

The Borgia Heirloom

JULIAN SYMONS

Lucrezia Borgia also enjoys a notoriety for infamy which is almost the equal of her brother, Cesare. Biographies of this fifteenth-century noble-women have detailed her life of wantoness, vices and crimes, although some of the authors have suggested that she was not altogether to blame, but was very much under the influence of Cesare. Married three times, she was certainly involved in the assassination of the second of her husbands with her father and brother, and from them she also learned her dexterity with poison. Lucrezia was famous, too, for her love of scholarship, art and beautiful jewellery – and she may well have been the first noblewoman to have made a habit of wearing several rings on each of her fingers. A number of historical novelists and crime writ-ers have utilised the Borgia legend in stories of plotting and murder, but few have done so as cleverly as the doyan of English mystery authors, Julian Symons, in this brief little shocker, 'The Borgia Heirloom'. Symons has written a great deal about murder in fact and fiction – including Beyond Reasonable Doubt *(1960) about thirteen con-troversial murder cases, and* The Players and the Game *(1972) based on the infamous Moors Murders – as well as a series of cases of the resourceful detective Francis Quarles. Julian has always been fasci-nated by the violence which he says can exist behind the most respectable faces and uses this idea to dramatic effect in the next few pages.*

'AND NOW,' LADY X said, 'you may ask your questions.'

The young man repeated, perhaps for the sixth time, that it was very good of her to receive him, and give him lunch, and talk to him. At that, she merely inclined her head, told the maid that they would take coffee in the drawing room, and led the way there. She was very old, her skin the color of parchment, her hands liver spotted, thickly veined, the nails yellow and horny. Several rings – a large diamond, a sapphire-and-ruby cluster, a huge emerald – looked incongruous on them.

176

'It's not exactly questions.' The young man was American, his fair hair cut close to the head, his eyes round and innocent, his manner earnest. 'I'm doing this book on great unsolved British cases, they're so much subtler than our crude shootouts, and I'm trying to get accounts from people who actually knew the background and the characters. Official accounts don't really bring them to life.'

'I can do that for you.' Her laugh was a raven's caw, but she shook her head when, with a tentative air, he produced a notebook. 'Oh, no – no. Notebooks are for reporters, my dear young man. I understand you to be a real writer.'

He put away the notebook. He had, after all, a good memory.

'The place, as you know, was Gratchen Manor, where we are now – the home of my husband's family for more than a century. It is a pleasant place, one with an ambience that impresses itself on the characters of those who live in it. Do you understand me?'

The young American nodded. In truth, he was overawed by the great house, the portraits of grim-faced ancestors along the walls, the intimidating size of the dining room in which the two of them had eaten at one end of the long table, and of this drawing room with its grand piano, alcoves containing what was no doubt immensely valuable porcelain, great windows looking onto a terrace from which steps led down to what seemed acres of lawn. It seemed to him wrong that families should live in such large houses – and now not even a family, but one old woman and her housekeeper, plus a servant or two.

'This house and this English countryside formed the character of my husband, Tom, and our son Charlie. You would have had to know them to understand them. Tom – Sir Thomas – went to London two or three days each week, he was a director of this company and vice-chairman of that, but his heart was here at Gratchen. He took part in every local event, thought of himself as the squire, as his father and grandfather had been before him, employed half the people in the village, felt responsible for their moral welfare. A strange thing that, in this modern world, but it was so.'

The young man nodded. He had heard different tales in the village, where Sir Thomas was resented as a man who poked his nose into matters that did not concern him.

'And Charlie, Charlie was perfect. Everybody loved him.' She indicated a portrait, head and shoulders, of a weakly handsome young man in officer's uniform. 'I prayed for him to come through the war unharmed, and my prayers were answered. Then all I wanted was for him to marry the right girl and make this house their home. That will sound old-fashioned, too, I'm sure.'

Charlie's fellow officers had said he was pleasant enough, but thick as two blocks. Feeling that he should speak, the young American said, 'That was in nineteen forty-eight.'

'I believe so.' Lady X's small eyes were sharp within their folds of skin. 'I hope you do not expect dates and hours. This is a mystery without a solution. I am telling you what happened, no more.

'In the autumn, Charlie became engaged to Susan Baybridge. They had known each other from childhood, her father was a barrister, it was a suitable match in every way.' Lady X rose arthritically, took a silver-framed photograph from the top of the grand piano, and showed it to the young man. 'That was Susan at the time.'

The photograph showed a rather plain, heavy-featured girl with a determined chin. 'Charlie was involved in some kind of commercial activity in London, which his father seemed to think necessary. He came back here, of course, at weekends. You may imagine my incredulity when he arrived one weekend in company with a young woman and told us he intended to break his engagement with Susan and marry this – this woman. Her name was Deirdre O'Connor and she was alleged to be a fashion model. It was obvious to me at once that she was out for what she could get and had no feeling for Charlie. It was found later that she had granted her favors to half a dozen young men.

'I thought her an entirely unsuitable wife for Charlie, and told him so, and I told him also that his treatment of Susan was disgraceful. I was not surprised that when at last he told her that he wished to break off their engagement, there was a violent quarrel. In front of the servants.'

In front of the servants, he thought. It was certainly a different world. As if reading his thoughts, she said, 'It was another world we lived in here at Gratchen. And a better one.

'In the New Year, we gave a dinner party. Of course we invited Susan. She did some job in a scientific laboratory and we invited the director of the place, a tiresome man named Cleggit. There were other friends, including our local medical man, Dr. MacFarlane – a dozen altogether. Then, quite unexpectedly, Charlie came down, the woman with him. Susan had to meet the woman – it was most unpleasant for her.'

'Your son said he told you he was coming down and you must have forgotten.'

'I forget nothing.' Her gaze was withering. 'May I continue? Thank you. – We ate simple English food, which, even in those days of rationing, was not denied to us at Gratchen. A clear soup made with stock, roast beef accompanied by the usual vegetables, an apple charlotte. It was not a happy meal. Tom was already sick with the kidney disease from which he died six months later, Susan hardly spoke, the dreadful Deirdre talked too much and too loudly, and Charlie was obviously besotted by her. After dinner we came in here, and it was then that Deirdre behaved as if drunk or drugged. She staggered about, almost fell over when sitting down in a chair, a disgusting exhibition. Then she collapsed and was taken to lie down, Dr. MacFarlane attending her. He agreed with me that she had taken an overdose of drugs, and when we questioned Charlie he admitted that she used both cocaine and heroin. She was taken ill at nine-thirty. Just after midnight, she died.'

'But drugs didn't cause her death.'

'Dr. MacFarlane thought so at the time.'

'But Cleggit knew better. His pharmaceutical knowledge led him to suspect an alkaloid poison. He made sure that the wine glasses and coffee cups were preserved not washed up.'

'Cleggit was a busybody, a troublemaker.'

'And you know what was found in one coffee cup. Coniine, the drug derived from *conium maculatum*, the spotted hemlock. The poison Socrates took, the drug Keats said induced a drowsy numbness, the drug of which even a few drops may be a fatal dose. But how was it administered? That was what the police could never establish. It must have been from some kind of phial, but none was found. Your son poured the coffee, you added sugar, but none of the guests noticed anything unusual, and in any case Deirdre O'Connor took no sugar.'

The maid came in with a tray containing a coffee pot, two cups, a milk jug, and a bowl of sugar cubes. The young man continued 'Of course, there were suspects. Susan had reason enough to hate Deirdre. Your son might have found out about her other men friends. It was even suggested that your husband, knowing himself under sentence of death, might have been responsible.'

'That was ridiculous. If Cleggit had not been such a busybody, Dr. MacFarlane would have signed a death certificate. As it was, the affair broke up the family. Charlie went out to Australia, married a girl there, died five years ago without an heir. I am quite alone now.'

The young man's eyes were bright. He lowered his voice, almost whispered, as he said, 'You arranged the dinner party, you knew your son was coming, you invited Dr. MacFarlane. I think you did it.'

She seemed not to have heard him, poured the coffee into the two cups. 'It was all so long ago. Do you take milk?'

'What? Oh, no, thank you.'

'Sugar?'

'No sugar.' He leaned forward. 'Won't you tell me, now that it can do no harm, just for my satisfaction as an amateur criminologist, how you did it?'

The little eyes in the wrinkled face were amused, contemptuous. You are an impertinent young man. I said I was telling you a story to which there is no solution.' She passed him the coffee cup, then held up her veined, spotted hand with the bright rings on it. 'Would you believe that my hands were once admired? Nowadays people only look at the rings. The emerald is an heirloom, said to have belonged to a Borgia.'

What followed was so quick that if she had not drawn attention to her hand he would not have seen it. From the center of the great emerald ring a tiny stream of liquid shot into her cup. She gave her raven caw at his shocked, startled face and said, 'Liquid saccharin.'

The Silver Mirror

SIR ARTHUR CONAN DOYLE

The murder of Mary Queen of Scots' favourite, the Italian David Rizzio in 1566, is one of the most famous murder stories associated with the British monarchy. Rizzio, who was a courtier and musician, entered Mary's service in 1561 and rapidly made himself so invaluable to the Queen that three years later he was appointed her private foreign secretary. In 1565 he negotiated Mary's marriage with her cousin, Henry Stewart, Lord Darnley — with whom he was at first very friendly. But when Darnley became aware of Rizzio's undoubted influence over his wife as well as his strong political power, the new husband formed a plot with several other noblemen to have the Italian killed. Rizzio was summarily dragged from the Queen's presence and brutally murdered at Holyroodhouse on March 9, 1566. Scotsman Sir Arthur Conan Doyle, the creator of Sherlock Holmes and something of an amateur detective himself, was very intrigued by the Rizzio killing and utilised the facts in the story of 'The Silver Mirror' — a dramatic tale which neatly bridges the past and present and which is, in my opinion, long overdue for adaptation to the screen.

JAN. 3 — THIS affair of White and Wotherspoon's accounts proves to be a gigantic task. There are twenty thick ledgers to be examined and checked. Who would be a junior partner? However, it is the first big bit of business which has been left entirely in my hands. I must justify it. But it has to be finished so that the lawyers may have the result in time for the trial. Johnson said this morning that I should have to get the last figure out before the twentieth of the month. Good Lord! Well, have at it, and if human brain and nerve can stand the strain, I'll win out at the other side. It means office-work from ten to five, and then a second sitting from about eight to one in the morning. There's drama in an accountant's life. When I find myself in the still early hours, while all the world sleeps, hunting through column after column for those missing figures which will turn a respected alderman

181

into a felon, I understand that it is not such a prosaic profession after all.

On Monday I came on the first trace of defalcation. No heavy game hunter ever got a finer thrill when first he caught sight of the trail of his quarry. But I look at the twenty ledgers and think of the jungle through which I have to follow him before I get my kill. Hard work – but rare sport, too, in a way! I saw the fat fellow once at a City dinner, his red face glowing above a white napkin. He looked at the little pale man at the end of the table. He would have been pale, too, if he could have seen the task that would be mine.

Jan. 6. – What perfect nonsense it is for doctors to prescribe rest when rest is out of the question! Asses! They might as well shout to a man who has a pack of wolves at his heels that what he wants is absolute quiet. My figures must be out by a certain date; unless they are so, I shall lose the chance of my lifetime, so how on earth am I to rest? I'll take a week or so after the trial.

Perhaps I was myself a fool to go to the doctor at all. But I get nervous and highly strung when I sit alone at my work at night. It's not a pain – only a sort of fullness of the head with an occasional mist over the eyes. I thought perhaps some bromide, or chloral, or something of the kind might do me good. But stop work? It's absurd to ask such a thing. It's like a long-distance race. You feel queer at first and your heart thumps and your lungs pant, but if you have only the pluck to keep on, you get your second wind. I'll stick to my work and wait for my second wind. If it never comes – all the same, I'll stick to my work. Two ledgers are done, and I am well on in the third. The rascal has covered his tracks well, but I pick them up for all that.

Jan. 9. – I had not meant to go to the doctor again. And yet I have had to. 'Straining my nerves, risking a complete breakdown, even endangering my sanity.' That's a nice sentence to have fired off at one. Well, I'll stand the strain and I'll take the risk, and so long as I can sit in my chair and move a pen I'll follow the old sinner's slot.

By the way, I may as well set down here the queer experience which drove me this second time to the doctor. I'll keep an exact record of my symptoms and sensations, because they are interesting in themselves – 'a curious psycho-physiological study,' says the doctor – and also because I am perfectly certain that when I am through with them they will all seem blurred and unreal, like some queer dream betwixt sleeping and waking. So now, while they are fresh, I will just make a note of them if only as a change of thought after the endless figures.

There's an old silver-framed mirror in my room. It was given me by a friend who had a taste for antiquities, and he, as I happen to know, picked it up at a sale and had no notion where it came from. It's a large thing – three feet across and two feet high – and it leans at the back of a side-table on my left as I write. The frame is flat, about three inches across, and very old; far too old for hall-marks or other methods of determining its age. The glass part projects, with a bevelled edge, and has the magnificent reflecting power which is only, as it seems to me, to be found in very old mirrors. There's a feeling of perspective when you look into it such as no modern glass can ever give.

The mirror is so situated that as I sit at the table I can usually see nothing in it but the reflection of the red window curtains. But a queer thing happened last night. I had been working for some hours, very much against the grain, with continual bouts of that mistiness of which I had complained. Again and again I had to stop and clear my eyes. Well, on one of these occasions I chanced to look at the mirror. It had the oddest appearance. The red curtains which should have been reflected in it were no longer there, but the glass seemed to be clouded and steamy, not on the surface, which glittered like steel, but deep down in the very grain of it. This opacity, when I stared hard at it, appeared to slowly rotate this way and that, until it was a thick, white cloud swirling in heavy wreaths. So real and solid was it, and so reasonable was I, that I remember turning, with the idea that the curtains were on fire. But everything was deadly still in the room – no sound save the ticking of the clock, no movement save the slow gyration of that strange woolly cloud deep in the heart of the old mirror.

Then, as I looked, the mist, or smoke, or cloud, or whatever one may call it, seemed to coalesce and solidify at two points quite close together, and I was aware, with a thrill of interest rather than of fear, that these were two eyes looking out into the room. A vague outline of a head I could see – a woman's by the hair, but this was very shadowy. Only the eyes were quite distinct; such eyes – dark, luminous, filled with some passionate emotion, fury or horror, I could not say which. Never have I seen eyes which were so full of intense, vivid life. They were not fixed upon me, but stared out into the room. Then as I sat erect, passed my hand over my brow, and made a strong conscious effort to pull myself together, the dim head faded into the general opacity, the mirror slowly cleared, and there were the red curtains once again.

A sceptic would say, no doubt, that I had dropped asleep over my figures, and that my experience was a dream. As a matter of fact, I was never more vividly awake in my life. I was able to argue about it even as I looked at it, and to tell myself that it was a subjective impression – a chimera of the nerves – begotten by worry and insomnia. But why this particular shape? And who is the woman, and what is the dreadful emotion which I read in those wonderful brown eyes? They come between me and my work. For the first time I have done less than the daily tally which I had marked out. Perhaps that is why I have had no abnormal sensations to-night. To-morrow I must wake up, come what may.

Jan. 11. – All well, and good progress with my work. I wind the net, coil after coil, round that bulky body. But the last smile may remain with him if my own nerves break over it. The mirror would seem to be a sort of barometer which marks my brain pressure. Each night I have observed that it had clouded before I reached the end of my task.

Dr. Sinclair (who is, it seems, a bit of a psychologist) was so interested in my account that he came round this evening to have a look at the mirror. I had observed that something was scribbled in crabbed old characters upon the metal work at the back. He examined this with a lens, but could make nothing of it. 'Sanc. X. Pal.' was his final reading of it, but that did not bring us any further. He advised me to put it away into another room; but, after all, whatever I may see in it is, by his own account, only a symptom. It is in the cause that the danger lies. The twenty ledgers – not the silver mirror – should be packed away if I could only do it. I'm at the eighth now, so I progress.

Jan. 13. – Perhaps it would have been wiser after all if I had packed away the mirror. I had an extraordinary experience with it last night. And yet I find it so interesting, so fascinating, that even now I will keep it in its place. What on earth is the meaning of it all?

I suppose it was about one in the morning, and I was closing my books preparatory to staggering off to bed, when I saw her there in front of me. The stage of mistiness and development must have passed unobserved, and there she was in all her beauty and passion and distress, as clear-cut as if she were really in the flesh before me. The figure was small, but very distinct – so much so that every feature, and every detail of dress, are stamped in my memory. She is seated on the extreme left of the mirror. A sort of shadowy figure crouches down beside her – I can dimly discern that it is a man – and then behind them is cloud, in which I see figures – figures which move. It is not a mere picture upon which I look. It is a scene in life, an actual episode. She crouches and quivers. The man beside her cowers down. The vague figures make abrupt movements and gestures. All my fears were swallowed up in my interest. It was maddening to see so much and not to see more.

But I can at least describe the woman to the smallest point. She is very beautiful and quite young – not more than five-and-twenty, I should judge. Her hair is of a very rich brown, with a warm chestnut shade fining into gold at the edges. A little flat-pointed cap comes to an angle in front and is made of lace edged with pearls. The forehead is high, too high perhaps for perfect beauty; but one would not have it otherwise, as it gives a touch of power and strength to what would otherwise be a softly feminine face. The brows are most delicately curved over heavy eyelids, and then come those wonderful eyes – so large, so dark, so full of overmastering emotion, of rage and horror, contending with a pride of self-control which holds her from sheer frenzy! The cheeks are pale, the lips white with agony, the chin and throat most exquisitely rounded. The figure sits and leans forward in the chair, straining and rigid, cataleptic with horror. The dress is black velvet, a jewel gleams like a flame in the breast, and a golden crucifix smoulders in the shadow of a fold. This is the lady whose image still lives in the old silver mirror. What dire deed could it be which has left its impress there, so that now, in another age, if the spirit of a man be but worn down to it, he may be conscious of its presence?

One other detail: On the left side of the skirt of the black dress was, as I thought at first, a shapeless bunch of white ribbon. Then, as I looked more intently or as the vision defined itself more clearly, I perceived what it was. It was the hand of a man, clenched and knotted in agony, which held on with a convulsive grasp to the fold of the dress. The rest of the crouching figure was a mere vague outline, but that strenuous hand shone clear on the dark background, with a sinister suggestion of tragedy in its frantic clutch. The man is frightened – horribly frightened. That I can clearly discern. What has terrified him so? Why does he grip the woman's dress? The answer lies amongst those moving figures in the background. They have brought danger both to him and to her. The interest of the thing fascinated me. I thought no more of its relation to my own nerves. I stared and stared as if in a theatre. But I could get no further. The mist thinned. There were

185

tumultuous movements in which all the figures were vaguely concerned. Then the mirror was clear once more.

The doctor says I must drop work for a day, and I can afford to do so, for I have made good progress lately. It is quite evident that the visions depend entirely upon my own nervous state, for I sat in front of the mirror for an hour to-night, with no result whatever. My soothing day has chased them away. I wonder whether I shall ever penetrate what they all mean? I examined the mirror this evening under a good light, and besides the mysterious inscription 'Sanc. X. Pal.,' I was able to discern some signs of heraldic marks, very faintly visible upon the silver. They must be very ancient, as they are almost obliterated. So far as I could make out, they were three spear-heads, two above and one below. I will show them to the doctor when he calls to-morrow.

Jan. 14. – Feel perfectly well again, and I intend that nothing else shall stop me until my task is finished. The doctor was shown the marks on the mirror and agreed that they were armorial bearings. He is deeply interested in all that I have told him, and cross-questioned me closely on the details. It amuses me to notice how he is torn in two by conflicting desires – the one that his patient should lose his symptoms, the other that the medium – for so he regards me – should solve this mystery of the past. He advised continued rest, but did not oppose me too violently when I declared that such a thing was out of the question until the ten remaining ledgers have been checked.

Jan. 17. – For three nights I have had no experiences – my day of rest has borne fruit. Only a quarter of my task is left, but I must make a forced march, for the lawyers are clamouring for their material. I will give them enough and to spare. I have him fast on a hundred counts. When they realise what a slippery, cunning rascal he is, I should gain some credit from the case. False trading accounts, false balance-sheets, dividends drawn from capital, losses written down as profits, suppression of working expenses, manipulation of petty cash – it is a fine record!

Jan. 18. – Headaches, nervous twitches, mistiness, fullness of the temples – all the premonitions of trouble, and the trouble came sure enough. And yet my real sorrow is not so much that the vision should come as that it should cease before all is revealed.

But I saw more to-night. The crouching man was as visible as the lady whose gown he clutched. He is a little swarthy fellow, with a black, pointed beard. He has a loose gown of damask trimmed with

186

fur. The prevailing tints of his dress are red. What a fright the fellow is in, to be sure! He cowers and shivers and glares back over his shoulder. There is a small knife in his other hand, but he is far too tremulous and cowed to use it. Dimly now I begin to see the figures in the background. Fierce faces, bearded and dark, shape themselves out of the mist. There is one terrible creature, a skeleton of a man, with hollow cheeks and eyes sunk in his head. He also has a knife in his hand. On the right of the woman stands a tall man, very young, with flaxen hair, his face sullen and dour. The beautiful woman looks up at him in appeal. So does the man on the ground. This youth seems to be the arbiter of their fate. The crouching man draws closer and hides himself in the woman's skirts. The tall youth bends and tries to drag her away from him. So much I saw last night before the mirror cleared. Shall I never know what it leads to and whence it comes? It is not a mere imagination, of that I am very sure. Somewhere, some time, this scene has been acted, and this old mirror has reflected it. But when – where?

Jan. 20. – My work draws to a close, and it is time. I feel a tenseness within my brain, a sense of intolerable strain, which warns me that something must give. I have worked myself to the limit. But to-night should be the last night. With a supreme effort I should finish the final ledger and complete the case before I rise from my chair. I will do it. I will.

Feb. 7. – I did. My God, what an experience! I hardly know if I am strong enough yet to set it down.

Let me explain in the first instance that I am writing this in Dr. Sinclair's private hospital some three weeks after the last entry in my diary. On the night of January 20 my nervous system finally gave way, and I remembered nothing afterwards until I found myself, three days ago, in the home of rest. And I can rest with a good conscience. My work was done before I went under. My figures are in the solicitors' hands. The hunt is over.

And now I must describe that last night. I had sworn to finish my work, and so intently did I stick to it, though my head was bursting, that I would never look up until the last column had been added. And yet it was fine self-restraint, for all the time I knew that wonderful things were happening in the mirror. Every nerve in my body told me so. If I looked up there was an end of my work. So I did not look up till all was finished. Then, when at last with throbbing temples I threw down my pen and raised my eyes, what a sight was there!

The mirror in its silver frame was like a stage, brilliantly lit, in which a drama was in progress. There was no mist now. The oppression of my nerves had wrought this amazing clarity. Every feature, every movement, was as clear-cut as in life. To think that I, a tired accountant, the most prosaic of mankind, with the account-books of a swindling bankrupt before me, should be chosen of all the human race to look upon such a scene!

It was the same scene and the same figures, but the drama had advanced a stage. The tall young man was holding the woman in his arms. She strained away from him and looked up at him with loathing in her face. They had torn the crouching man away from his hold upon the skirt of her dress. A dozen of them were round him – savage men, bearded men. They hacked at him with knives. All seemed to strike him together. Their arms rose and fell. The blood did not flow from him – it squirted. His red dress was dabbled in it. He threw himself this way and that, purple upon crimson, like an over-ripe plum. Still they hacked, and still the jets shot from him. It was horrible – horrible! They dragged him kicking to the door. The woman looked over her shoulder at him and her mouth gaped. I heard nothing, but I knew that she was screaming. And then whether it was this nerve-racking vision before me, or whether, my task finished, all the overwork of the past weeks came in one crushing weight upon me, the room danced round me, the floor seemed to sink away beneath my feet, and I remembered no more. In the early morning my landlady found me stretched senseless before the silver mirror, but I knew nothing myself until three days ago I awoke in the deep peace of the doctor's nursing home.

Feb. 9. – Only to-day have I told Dr. Sinclair my full experience. He had not allowed me to speak of such matters before. He listened with an absorbed interest. 'You don't identify this with any well-known scene in history?' he asked, with suspicion in his eyes. I assured him that I knew nothing of history. 'Have you no idea whence that mirror came and to whom it once belonged?' he continued. 'Have you?' I asked, for he spoke with meaning. 'It's incredible,' said he, 'and yet how else can one explain it? The scenes which you described before suggested it, but now it has gone beyond all range of coincidence. I will bring you some notes in the evening.'

Later. – He has just left me. Let me set down his words as closely as I can recall them. He began by laying several musty volumes upon my bed.

'These you can consult at your leisure,' said he. 'I have some notes here which you can confirm. There is not a doubt that what you have seen is the murder of Rizzio by the Scottish nobles in the presence of Mary, which occurred in March 1566. Your description of the woman is accurate. The high forehead and heavy eyelids combined with great beauty could hardly apply to two women. The tall young man was her husband, Darnley. Rizzio, says the chronicle, 'was dressed in a loose dressing-gown of furred damask, with hose of russet velvet.' With one hand he clutched Mary's gown, with the other he held a dagger. Your fierce, hollow-eyed man was Ruthven, who was new-risen from a bed of sickness. Every detail is exact.'

'But why to me?' I asked, in bewilderment. 'Why of all the human race to me?'

'Because you were in the fit mental state to receive the impression. Because you chanced to own the mirror which gave the impression.'

'The mirror! You think, then, that it was Mary's mirror — that it stood in the room where the deed was done?'

'I am convinced that it was Mary's mirror. She had been Queen of France. Her personal property would be stamped with the Royal arms. What you took to be three spear-heads were really the lilies of France.'

'And the inscription?'

'"Sanc. X. Pal." You can expand it into Sanctae Crucis Palatium. Someone has made a note upon the mirror as to whence it came. It was the Palace of the Holy Cross.'

'Holyrood!' I cried.

'Exactly. Your mirror came from Holyrood. You have had one very singular experience, and have escaped. I trust that you will never put yourself into the way of having such another.'

The Late Eugene Aram

HENRY HERRING

Eugene Aram has gone down in history as one of the cleverest murder-ers of the eighteenth century. Not just because he led a double life as a rigid, disciplinarian schoolmaster and a petty criminal who specialised in receiving stolen goods and later turned to murder, but also as a result of being eulogised in a poem by Thomas Hood, 'The Dream of Eugene Aram'. Although the poem was not written until seventy years after his execution in 1759, the irony would undoubtedly have appealed to Aram for he had also tried to be a poet. The profligate scholar was responsible for the killing of a shoemaker whose body was not discovered for fourteen years while he led his double life. Arrested as a result of being given away by a confederate, Aram tried to avoid the death penalty by pleading that the bones of his victim could well have been those of a saint thought to have been interred in the same area that the body was found. However, after being found guilty, he attempted suicide the night before his execution and had to be dragged half-dead to the gallows. A number of writers have followed Thomas Hood in utilising Aram's intriguing story, including Henry Herring, a popular turn-of-the-century mystery novelist, best known for The Burglars' Club *published in 1906. In 'The Late Eugene Aram', the notorious man who led two lives reappears once again to utilise his well-honed powers of deception.*

AT THAT TIME I was engaged on my well-known work on Druidical Vestiges. I wanted absolute seclusion in which to arrange my notes and write my book, and I cast about for a suitable place. I was fortunate enough to hear of an ideal spot in the heart of the broad-acred county, on the fringe of the moors and the dales, and within easy access of York withal. The house was picturesque in itself and in its position. It was situated on the edge of the great reservoir that had just been made for some distant town. It was the old manor house of the district, and had been saved from destruction by the pleading of local antiquarians.

190

It now stood on a little peninsula jutting into the lake, and it took my fancy at first sight. On three sides was water, on the fourth a delightful old English garden of sunflowers, hollyhocks, yew hedges and box. It was, I say, an ideal place for my work.

The engineer had lived there for the past five years, superintending the building of the works, and when I looked over the house he was busy packing up his belongings. I naturally asked him how he liked the place, and if there were any special disadvantages connected with it.

To the first question he replied that he liked it uncommonly; to the latter he did not reply at all. I pressed for an answer, and he reluctantly admitted there was a special disadvantage; and then he added inconsequently that possibly I might call it an attraction.

'My dear sir,' I replied, 'if I take this house I shall be here twelve months at least, and if I find anything objectionable about the premises it will totally upset my plans. I think you ought to give me full particulars, you really ought to be candid with me.'

'Well,' said the engineer, 'the fact is the house is haunted by the ghost of a local celebrity. I didn't mind it when I got used to it, but at first I objected to it considerably; and possibly you might never get to like it.'

'I do object to ghosts,' I answered; 'and I don't think I should ever get used to one, far less ever grow to like it. What form does this one take?'

'It is the ghost of Eugene Aram,' he replied. 'He was born near here and lived for some time in the house. I have never heard of anyone else seeing the appearance, and haven't spoken about it to anyone but you. The thing only came when I was alone. I didn't relish its presence at all at first, but I grew to like it. You see, I was very lonely here. Most of my spare time I've had nobody but my dog with me, and the evenings are long. It's wonderful how you take to a ghost under such conditions. A man, a dog, and a ghost get on uncommonly well together in the country when they understand each other. Besides, Aram is wonderfully well-informed. He isn't a chain-clanking ghost. He's a man of talent.'

'A murderer, I believe.'

'I'm afraid so. Aram swears he isn't; but the best of us might do that under the circumstances. However, he's quite harmless now, and, frankly speaking, I'm sorry to leave him.'

I carefully thought over the matter, and finally decided to take the place, despite the incubus attached. The engineer was a man of education and taste, and if he could stand the ghost for five years I ought to be able to bear the infliction for one. Besides, it would be an experience.

So I fixed up the tenancy, moved books and furniture there, and commenced my work.

For the next two months I was so busy arranging my voluminous notes that I had little time for anything else, but when at last I got them into order, and had fairly started my book, I thought a little relaxation advisable. I found this in returning the friendly visits of my neighbours. Only one of the latter interested me, and that on account of his valuable library. Mr. Leigh had no literary tastes himself, and he smiled at my enthusiasm about his possessions.

These were at once a delight and a sorrow to me, for they had been horribly neglected. This was particularly the case with the manuscripts, which were mottled and foxed with mildew, and thickly coated with the dust of ages. It was pitiable to see them in this condition. Illuminated missals had long since lost their colouring, and the Greek, Latin, Saxon, and other manuscripts were fast becoming undecipherable. Many of them were so already.

They were evidently spoils of the demolition of the neighbouring monastery, and the best preserved, and to me the most interesting, was the diary of a priestly Pepys of the fourteenth century, old abbey accounts that would scarcely have borne an auditor's scrutiny, and a bundle of monkish love-letters – no doubt mere theoretical exercises to an imaginary divinity, but evincing undoubted genius in the Ars Amatoria.

Mr. Leigh let me ferret at will among these treasures, and from them I hoped to get enough material for several magazine articles. This research afforded a pleasing intermission to my Druidical work, which progressed apace.

I well remember the evening of the day in which I completed the first chapter of my book. I was walking about my room, declaiming from the MS. in my hands. As I ended, expressions of applause came from the fireside. I looked up in astonishment. There, sitting in the chair, was the ghost of Eugene Aram.

Owing to its non-appearance I had long since put this down to be an hallucination of the engineer, and I don't mind admitting I was startled when actually confronted by the apparition. However, I tried not to show this, and had sufficient presence of mind to reply to its applause with a casual 'I'm glad you like it.'

'I do. It's interesting – remarkably interesting, Mr. Smilax,' said Aram. 'You've a pretty talent for original research.'

'Thank you,' I modestly replied. 'Did you ever do anything in that direction?'

'A little – just a little. I discovered a European affinity in Celtic roots, as possibly you remember.'

'I can't say that I do,' I replied.

'Such is fame! 'sighed Aram. 'Nevertheless, I assure you that my discovery gained me some little distinction among the savants of my day, just as your own theories will no doubt do for you. I hope you will meet with greater recognition from posterity,' he added politely. Then in a harsh voice, 'Will you kindly tell that dog of yours to stop its hideous noise?'

Gyp, with bristling hair, was growling ferociously.

'Down, Gyp, down! Be quiet! 'I commanded. But Gyp wouldn't. For the first time in her life she disobeyed me, and I was obliged to turn her out of the room.

Aram was evidently annoyed at his reception, for on my return to the room he said stiffly—

'Your dog, sir, seems less well behaved than that of your predecessor. In my own day a cur that snarled at a gentleman was—

What happened under those particular circumstances was not forthcoming, for my housekeeper entered at that moment with sugar and hot water, and the ghost faded into nothingness before she was in view. Gyp followed at her heels, sniffing uneasily, and evidently upset by recent events.

From that short and inauspicious interview began my acquaintance with Eugene Aram's ghost, an acquaintance that ripened into something approaching a friendship, and which threatened at one time to have a most disastrous influence on my career.

From that night forward Aram regularly put in an appearance whenever I was alone, and it grew to be a matter of course for me to find the intangible shade of the departed murderer seated opposite. Like the engineer, I soon got used to it, and would have regretted its absence, but Gyp never overcame her first feelings of repugnance, and nightly I had to eject her from the room.

Aram was indeed a wonderfully well-informed man. His knowledge

193

of the classics was remarkable. In a weak moment I agreed to rub up my Homer with him, and he led me at a gallop through the Iliad. But he was altogether too deep and enthusiastic a linguist for me, and our first coolness arose through my objecting to learn Hebrew.

'You'll be sure to find it useful sometimes, Smilax,' said Aram.

'I simply haven't room for it in my head, and I've no wish to learn it either,' I replied firmly.

'If you'd prefer Celtic or Arabic, I should be just as pleased to teach you,' he urged. 'Or we could take up Chaldee.'

'I don't wish to appear ungrateful, Aram,' I answered, 'but I can't do anything of the sort. I'm not good at languages. I only agreed to Homer to please you, and I don't understand half we read.'

Aram sighed regretfully. 'There's little love of pure learning in these days,' he said. 'I wanted to read Cesar's Commentaries with the engineer, but he used unnecessarily expressive language, and flatly refused. I hoped better things of you – a man of literary tastes.'

I felt I had behaved somewhat unhandsomely, and the next night I strove to make amends by my sympathetic attention to his version of his domestic troubles, pecuniary difficulties, and all the events that culminated in his trial and sentence. He was so singularly able in his manipulation of facts, and so plausible in their interpretation, that he left me firmly convinced that if ever an innocent man was hanged, that man was Eugene Aram.

It was about a month after his first appearance that conversation turned upon Mr. Leigh's manuscripts, and the disgraceful state in which they were.

'What a pity it is they don't belong to you!' said Aram after a pause. 'Leigh couldn't appreciate them if he tried, and he doesn't even do that.'

'Yes, things are a bit unequally distributed,' I admitted.

'Don't you think intelligent men should try to remedy the inequality?' continued Aram. 'If I were flesh and blood I should certainly try to do so in this particular instance.'

'What do you mean?' I asked.

'What I said,' replied Aram, as he faded away.

I went to bed that night thinking over his words. Yes, it was a pity, a great pity, those priceless manuscripts should belong to a country squire who didn't even look after them. What loving care would I not give to them, did they belong to me! But now they were absolutely rotting away. If they were mine, I— And so musing, I fell asleep.

The next day I had arranged to run over to the Grange to continue my excerpts from the manuscripts. Never had they seemed so forlorn. I was gingerly handling one time-stained piece – Saxon it seemed to me, from the faint indications of writing that were discernible, and mentally I anathematised its owner.

'A confounded shame, isn't it?' said a familiar voice. I looked round, and in the daylight saw the dim outline of Aram.

'Now, if I were you I should take that home, where you can clean it up and restore it, and investigate it at your leisure. It looks like a valuable original. You could bring it back any time.'

He spoke so naturally and plausibly that I only saw the reasonableness of his suggestion. I could, as he said, easily take it away and clean it, and investigate it at home. Aram's help would be invaluable. Mr. Leigh was away, so I couldn't ask his permission, but I would tell him what I had done next time I saw him, and he was too good-natured to consider I had taken a liberty.

'Well, perhaps you are right,' I said to Aram, as I put the manuscript carefully in my pocket.

I fancied I heard a sort of chuckle from the ghost, but on facing Aram it appeared he was suffering from a severe cold.

That evening was spent by me in removing as best I could the deposit of centuries from the manuscript, and by restoring the writing from a recipe of Aram's.

'Smilax,' said the latter, after an hour's careful and eager examination of what was thus disclosed, 'you've got a find here, and no mistake. It's eleventh century, or early twelfth, and it seems to be a continuation of the Saxon Chronicle – A Northern continuation, as one can see from the verbal inflections. It's a find that will perpetuate your name – or should I say Leigh's?' he added unkindly. 'But this is only a fragment. You must bring the other sheets, and we'll work together at them. You'll have to throw over the Druids till we've done it.'

'Nonsense,' I replied. 'What if it is as you say? This is only a philological curiosity. You can't expect me to throw over my work for it. I'm hanged if I do.'

Aram winced. 'I don't think it very kind of you to make that remark, Smilax,' he said. 'If you knew what hanging meant you would not talk about it so lightly.'

'I'm sorry if I hurt your feelings, Aram,' I rejoined; 'but I don't think you had any right to ask me to give up my work for something more congenial to your tastes.'

'Well, perhaps there will be no need for you to do so,' he went on; 'but I hope you'll help me with this Chronicle in the evenings. It will be the first bit of real work I've done for a hundred and forty years, and it will be a contribution to history.'

Aram spoke so feelingly, and his object seemed so laudable, that with very little persuasion I agreed to his suggestion, and each time I went to the Grange I brought away with me a further portion of the manuscripts. Much of them was hopelessly illegible, but there still remained enough that could be deciphered to occupy Aram with the evenings of three months, and I took down his translation.

I remember very well meeting Mr. Leigh on his return. I had part of the precious Chronicle in my pocket, just abstracted from his collection. Somehow there didn't seem an opening for telling him about it. At any rate, I said nothing. I told Aram that I hadn't mentioned the matter to Mr. Leigh, and he agreed that it was quite unnecessary to do so.

'Mankind is never corrupted at once; villainy is progressive, and declines from right, step by step, till every regard of probity is lost and every sense of moral obligation perishes.'

So said Aram at his trial, and I can from my own experience vouch for the accuracy of his statement so far as it affects the purloining of Old English manuscripts.

Piece by piece I transferred the Chronicle from Mr. Leigh's possession to my own. There only remained two more to bring, when one night I said jokingly to Aram:

'Now, suppose Leigh came upon me just as I was pocketing one of these things. What would you advise me to do?'

'Kill him,' said Aram.

I stared at him in horror. 'You'd have me commit murder?' I said at last.

'That's it,' he replied. 'And you'd do it well. You're a man after my own heart.'

He was just a little premature. I hadn't progressed quite so far in villainy as that. Perhaps in another week I might have been ready, but I wasn't just then.

Aram's speech thoroughly aroused me to the seriousness of the situation. For the first time I realized that he was slowly dragging me to perdition by his insidious suggestions. I was now a thief – possibly a confirmed thief – but there was still time to save myself from worse. I thought it all out, and before I went to sleep I had taken two resolves – to make restitution and to get rid of Aram.

It's simply amazing how easy it is to be good if you only try.

I just walked over to Leigh's the next morning with a parcel under my arm.

'I've been cleaning these manuscripts of yours,' I said, opening the parcel and showing them. 'I took them to my place to do, and I hope you don't mind.'

'Not at all, Mr. Smilax,' said Leigh cheerfully. 'You can have them if they're any good to you.'

'You don't mean it?' I gasped. 'Why, man, it's a continuation of the Saxon Chronicle.'

'If it had been the *Sporting Chronicle* I could have appreciated it, Smilax,' said Leigh. 'As it isn't, I'll pass it on to you, for you seem to get more amusement out of those rags than I should have thought possible.'

I was simply overwhelmed by the gift. And to think that Aram had actually suggested murder for its possession!

'Aram,' said I that night, 'there'll be no need for me to kill Mr. Leigh; he has given me the manuscripts.'

'Then all I can say is that he's just about as big a fool as you, if such a thing were possible,' said Aram; and then he relapsed into moody silence.

From that night one thought surged uppermost in my mind. Aram must go, before he led me into fresh mischief. But how to get rid of him? I dared not suggest he should leave the place, for I knew he would stick more closely to it than ever if he saw I wanted him to go.

I don't mind admitting that previous to my meeting with Aram I had given very little attention to ghosts. I had even doubted the existence of such things; but I could do so no longer when I was in nightly communion with one. Naturally my interest in the whole question of *post-mortem* appearances was aroused, and I had resolved to go fully into the matter as soon as the Druids were off my hands. In the meantime I had sent for a few psychical books, magazines, and pamphlets, and had discussed them with Aram.

I now turned to this literature to see if it afforded me any escape from the ghost. There was an article on Exorcism that interested me, but I hesitated at the services of a professional exorcist except as a last resort, as I did not wish to make the matter public property. Then there was a column or two on Incantations. I tried a few of the simpler formulae prescribed, but they did not act. They only served to irritate Aram, who got the impression it was some Druidical rite I was practising upon him.

In the general matter of these numbers there seemed to be nothing that would be of immediate us to me in my difficulty, but among the advertisements one in particular attracted my attention.

'PSYCHE AND CO., GHOST AND SPECTRE PURVEYORS,' it ran. 'Mansions haunted at moderate cost. Large stock of ghosts kept. An assorted batch of Crusaders just to hand. Send for catalogue. N.B. – Good prices given for ghosts of repute. Exchanges effected.'

My heart lightened as I read this singular advertisement. Here, it seemed to me, was a possibility of relief. I had a ghost of repute, and if only Psyche and Co. would take charge of him I might rid myself of the incubus – might even be a monetary gainer by the transaction, judging from the terms of the advertisement,

I wrote at once to the firm in question, and in due course came this reply:

'Archipelago Street, Soho.

'Dear Sir, – In reply to your favour of yesterday's date, we are willing to purchase the ghost of the late E. Aram, Esq., from you if you can satisfy us as to its authenticity. As we are rather overstocked with eighteenth century *revenants* at the moment, we cannot offer you more than twenty-five guineas for its possession. Should you accept our terms, a representative will at once wait upon you to effect the removal desired.

'We are, dear sir,
'Faithfully yours,
'PSYCHE & CO.'

Agree to the terms? Of course I would. I wrote off accepting them by that day's post, and then anxiously awaited the arrival of the firm's representative.

He was a little man with large eyes, sharp nose, thin lips, and pallid cheeks. He seemed to be a smart business man, and thoroughly up in his calling.

'I expect to have no difficulty at all in removing Mr. Aram,' he said in reply to my first question. 'I have taken the trouble of making myself acquainted with his interesting career, and I think I can offer him an inducement to transfer.'

'I suppose you will have to arrange the details personally with him?' I queried.

'Certainly; and as soon as possible. You say he appears nightly. If you will tell him this evening that I specially desire to make his acquaintance – of course saying nothing about my object – you will probably be able to arrange an interview. I have no doubt whatever of the result of one. I will stay in my bedroom till you call me down.'

'Aram,' said I, at a later hour, 'a friend of mine has come to-day from London who is particularly desirous of meeting you. Have you any objection to his joining us now? I thought I would ask your permission.'

'Deuced considerate of you, Smilax,' sneered Aram. 'Who is he?' Then he added suspiciously: 'I don't absolutely object to you, but I might to your friends.'

'Well, if you don't like him, you can – er – fade away,' I replied. 'But I think you'll take to him. Try him on my recommendation, anyway.'

'Well,' said Aram, after a moment's reflection, 'you can show him in. But no tricks, mind, or you'll suffer for it.'

It was certainly high time I got rid of Aram. He had never threatened me before.

I called for Mr. Vigo, who entered and was introduced. The conversation began with the weather and the state of the crops. Finally Vigo said:

'Mr. Aram. Perhaps your friend hasn't told you why I am here. The fact is, I want you to better your position. A ghost of your European celebrity is simply wasted here. I know a place where you would be heartily welcomed, and appreciated in a manner befitting your eminence.'

'Ah!' said Aram suspiciously.

'I may as well be frank with you,' continued Vigo. 'I'm the representative of Psyche and Co., of London, who deal in articles – er – gentlemen – like yourself.'

'I know you,' said Aram. 'I've heard of you from friends, and it's little I know to your advantage. You make a good thing out of your *employees*, and yet you keep them short of pocket-money, and make 'em be in at dusk every night they're off duty.'

'You are misinformed, Mr. Aram,' said Vigo earnestly. 'I assure you that any such obnoxious rules have long since been cancelled by our firm. If it were a question of hours or pocket-money, I'm sure we should be able to satisfy you. However, I'm not wanting you to join our stock. I think I've got a permanent billet for you, and one that will suit you down to the ground. One of her Majesty's judges – Mr. Justice Dormer – a hanging judge, as they call him – has just bought a fine old mansion in Devonshire, and his wife wants a ghost for it. She has applied to us herself for one, as his lordship does not approve of the idea. Now, if you would take up your residence there, you would oblige a lady and have splendid opportunities for annoying one of her Majesty's judges – a hanging judge, I think I said. I believe you have no special reason to like them, Mr. Aram?'

Aram's eyes brightened. 'You're right, sir; I haven't,' he said. 'I'll admit you have taken my fancy by what you propose. One of that kidney caused me a lot of temporary inconvenience and cut short a very promising career. I'd like to take it out of another. King's Bench?'

'Yes,' Mr. Vigo said.

Aram glided up and down in visible excitement.

'I should be sorry to leave you, Smilax,' he said, stopping suddenly.

'Oh, don't mind me,' I put in hastily.

'We were getting to know each other uncommonly well, Mr. Vigo,' said Aram; 'and I was anticipating a merry time this coming Christmas; but dash me, sir, your offer suits me better! Smilax is only a poor soul, after all. I think I could do better with a hanging judge. I'll go.'

My joy at this announcement almost overcame my politeness, and it was with difficulty I could fittingly express my regret at losing him. 'You'll write soon,' I said mechanically.

'Vigo will, no doubt,' said Aram grimly. 'And if I don't take to the job I shall come back. Hurry up the Druids, Smilax; and don't forget the Chronicle. Why, there are those last sheets I must stay to finish.'

'No, no,' I cried. 'I can do them quite well myself. If I get stuck I'll let you know through Mr. Vigo, and you can run over for an odd evening.'

'Well,' said Aram doubtfully, 'perhaps that will do; but if you make a mess of that translation, I'll either haunt you myself or put a friend up to the job. Stapleton Manor, Devon, did you say, Vigo? I'll be there to-morrow night if the wind settles. Good-bye, Smilax. Don't fret,' and the ghost of Eugene Aram slowly faded out of sight.

A fortnight later I heard from Psyche and Co. that Aram had taken up his quarters in Stapleton Manor, much to the judge's indignation. A cheque for twenty- five guineas was enclosed in the letter.

I now had leisure to resume my work on the Druids. I finished the book during the last week of my tenancy, and then I took a well-earned holiday, chiefly on the strength of Psyche's cheque, for from a monetary point of view the Druids were not satisfactory. I was in Algiers when I read the following in the *Atlas*:

'It is with extreme regret we have to announce the retirement from the bench of Mr. Justice Dormer, who has recently evinced undoubted signs of klepto- and even homicidal mania. The matter was brought before the notice of the Lord Chancellor, who at once recognized that only one course was open. It is deeply to be regretted that the once brilliant intellect of Mr. Justice Dormer should have given way under the strain of official work, and we can only hope that the pure air and quiet seclusion of his Devonshire estate will ultimately restore him to his formal mental vigour.'

I was sorry for Mr. Justice Dormer, very sorry; but he really ought to have had enough moral strength to resist Aram's insidious prompt-ings. His case was indeed hopeless if his friends were relying on the Devonshire seclusion to effect a cure.

I published the translation of the English Chronicle in due course. It created quite a little sensation, and my friends considered it unac-countable modesty on my part that on the title-page was 'Translated from the original manuscripts by E. A.'

Now, for the first time, will they understand that in this I only did justice to a brilliant though unscrupulous scholar.

The Mirror of Cagliostro

ROBERT ARTHUR

Count Alessandro di Cagliostro was an Italian who claimed to have discovered the 'elixir of immortal youth'. In fact the title was self-styled, and his real name was Giuseppe Balsamo and he had been born the son of humble parents in the thieves' kitchen quarter of Palermo. Cagliostro was actually a self-styled magician who, with a little knowledge of chemistry and medicine gained from some monks in Caltagirone, in time became known, alternatively, as one of the greatest alchemists and charlatans of the eighteenth century. To his practise of necromancy he also added crime, forgery and blackmail, and was involved in the notorious 'Affair of the Diamond Necklace' in 1785 in which the villainous Comtessa de la Motte tried to implicate Cardinal de Rohan in the theft of an heirloom. Cagliostro paid for his involvement in the affair with a year in the Bastille. In 1789 the Inquisition seized him for starting what they said was a fraudulent occult society and he was sentenced to death. However, the sentence was commuted to life imprisonment in the fortress of San Leone, near Urbino, and here Cagliostro remained until his death in 1795. The Count's roguish life on both sides of the law – as well as the debate about the extent of his magical powers – has been featured in works by Dumas, Goethe and Walpole as well as, more recently, a film by Orson Welles. Here Robert Arthur, the American writer and radio and television personality who was associated for many years with Alfred Hitchcock, offers a new addition to the legend of the man who claimed to have found the secret of eternal youth . . .

London, 1910
THE GIRL'S EYES were open. Her face, which had been so softly young, flushed with champagne and excitement, was a thing of horror now. Twisted with shock, contorted with the final spasm of life ejected from the body it had tenanted, her face was a mask of terror, frozen so until the rigor of sudden death should release its hold. Only then

202

would her muscles relax and death be allowed to wipe away the transformation he had wrought.

Charles, Duke of Burchester, wiped his fingers delicately on a silk handkerchief. For a moment, looking down at the girl, Molly Blanchard, his eyes lighted with interest. Was it truly possible that in death the eyes photographed, as he had been told, the last object that sight registered?

He bent over the girl huddled on the crimson carpet of the small private dining room of Chubb's Restaurant, and stared into the blue eyes that seemed to start from the contorted face. Then he sighed and straightened. It was, after all, a fairy tale. If the story had been true, her dead eyes should have mirrored two tiny, grinning skulls, one in each — for a skull had been the last thing she had seen in life. *His* skull.

But the blue eyes were cold and blank. He had seen in them reflection from one of the tapers that burned upon the table, still set with snowy linen and silver dishes from which they had dined.

He amended the thought. From which Molly had dined. Dined as she, poor lovely creature from some obscure group of actors, had never dined before. He had dined afterwards. She had dined upon food, but he had dined upon life.

He felt replete now. It was a pity he had not been able to restrain his impulse to kill. London was a city of infinite interest in this, the twentieth century. He should have planned on a prolonged stay, to explore it fully, but temptation had been too great, after so long an abstinence.

He moved swiftly now. The cheap necklace of glass beads, which the girl's mind had seen as rare diamonds, he allowed to remain about the throat where they glistened against the blue marks of strangling fingers. But he took his cloak from a hook and threw it over his shoulders. He retrieved his hat and let himself out the door without a backward glance for the empty husk that lay upon the rug.

A waiter in red livery was coming down the hall, past the series of closed doors that led to the famous — and infamous — private dining rooms of Chubb's. Charles stopped him.

'I leave,' he said. 'My friend —' he nodded toward the closed door — 'wishes to be undisturbed so that she may compose herself. Please see to it.'

A coin slipped from one hand to the other, and the servitor nodded.

'Very good, Sir,' he said. No titles and no names were used at Chubb's. They were, however, well known to both proprietor and all the help. A pity.

Charles walked down the long corridor, down the steps which led to the street without imposing upon one the necessity of exposing himself to the view of the crowd in the dining rooms below. As he let himself out, the eight-foot tall doorman, cloaked in crimson with a black shakko upon his head – a sight more goggled at in these days by tourists from puritanical America than even Windsor Castle – raised a hand. A hansom cab arrived in place precisely on the moment that his steps carried him to the curb.

Without looking back, Charles tossed a coin over his shoulder. The giant doorman casually retrieved it from the air as a dozen beggars and street loungers leaped futilely for it.

'Burchester House,' Charles said to the coachman.

He settled back to stare with hungry eyes upon this, the new London of which he had seen so little – and could have seen so much if he had not let himself be carried away by the soft sweet temptation of Molly Blanchard's life so that . . .

But it was futile to dwell upon it. There would be other occasions. As they rolled through the dark streets he let himself relive the moment when he had placed the necklace about Molly's throat, telling her to look deep into his eyes. The heady delight of the instant when her trusting eyes had seen behind the mask of flesh which he now wore. The almost intolerable joy of her struggles.

He realized that the hansom had stopped. For how long had he been living again those delights, unaware? There was not, after all, infinity ahead of him yet. Pursuit would be hot after him soon, and he was as vulnerable now as a new-hatched chick.

He stepped from the cab and flung the driver money. Charles, still with the down of youth upon his pink and white cheeks, strolled with the gait of a man much older and more experienced into the great, three-storied stone mansion which was the London residence of the Burchesters.

Inside, someone came scurrying out of the shadows of the almost dark parlor.

'Charles, my son,' his mother began, in a voice that trembled.

'Later, mother,' he said sharply, and brushed past her. 'I am going to my studio. I will be occupied for some time.' He started up the stairs toward the tower room where he kept his paints and canvases. Behind him he heard his mother whimpering. He paid no heed. As he reached the second floor he increased his pace. It would not do to be late in getting back to his sanctuary.

An hour later, with his mother weeping outside his door and the men from Scotland Yard hammering on it, Charles, Duke of Burchester, flung himself from the casement window and jellied himself on the cobblestones below.

Paris, 1963

The Musée des Antiquités Historique was a small brick building, twisted out of shape by the pressure of time and its neighbors. It stood at the end of one of Paris' many obscure streets, so narrow and twisting that no driver of even the smallest car, entering one, could be sure of finding room enough to turn around to get out again.

Beyond the Musée flowed the Seine, and if the waters of the Seine gave off any glint of light this overcast day, the glint was wholly lost in passing through the grime that darkly frosted the windows of the office of the curator, Professor Henri Thibaut.

Thibaut himself was ancient enough to seem one of the museum's exhibits, rather than its curator. But his eyes still snapped, and he spoke with a swift crispness that strained Harry Langham's otherwise excellent understanding of French.

'Cagliostro?' Thibaut said, and the word seemed to uncoil from his lips like a tiny serpent of sound. 'Count Alexander Cagliostro, self-styled. Born in 1743, died in 1795. A man of great controversy. By some denounced as a fraud. By others acclaimed as a miracle worker – a veritable magician. Ah yes, my young colleague from America, I have studied his life. Your information is entirely correct.'

'Good,' Harry Langham said. He smiled. At thirty-five he still seemed younger than his age, although a carefully acquired professorial manner helped counterbalance his youthful aspect.

'Frankly, sir,' he added, 'I had just about given up hope of getting any decent information about Cagliostro to make my summer in Europe worthwhile. I'm an associate professor of history at Boston College – my period is the 18th Century – and I am working for my doctorate, you see. I have chosen Count Cagliostro as the subject for my thesis. This is my last day in France. Only last night I heard of you – heard that you yourself had once written a thesis on the life of Cagliostro. I'm here, hoping you will assist me.'

'Ah.' Thibaut took a cigarette from an ivory box and lit it. 'And from what viewpoint do you approach your subject? Do you propose to expose him as one of history's great frauds? Or will you credit him with powers bordering on the magical?'

'That's my problem,' Harry Langham said frankly. 'To play it safe I ought to call him a mountebank, a faker, a great charlatan. But I can't. I started thinking that, and now – now I believe that he may really have had mystic powers. His life is wrapped in such mystery—'

'And you wish to clarify the mystery?' Thibaut said, his tone sardonic. 'You will write your thesis about Cagliostro. You will win an advanced degree. You will get a promotion. You will make more salary. You will marry some attractive woman. All from the dusty remains of Cagliostro. N'est-ce pas?'

'Well – yes.' Harry Langham laughed, a bit uneasily. 'Cagliostro – thesis – promotion – money – marriage. Almost like an equation, isn't it?'

'It is indeed.' With a sudden motion, Thibaut ground out his cigarette. 'Except that the answer is wrong.'

'How do you mean?'

'Cagliostro can bring you only grief. Go back to America and erase the name of Cagliostro from your memory!'

'But Professor!' Harry reflected that the French became excited easily, and the thought made his tone amused. 'You yourself wrote a thesis about the man.'

'And destroyed it.' Thibaut sank back into his chair. 'Some things our world will not accept. The truth about Count Cagliostro is one of them.'

'But he's been dead for nearly two hundred years!'

'M'sieu Langham,' Thibaut said, reaching again for the cigarettes in the ivory box, 'Evil never dies. No, no. Do not answer. There is little I can do to help you. I destroyed my thesis and all my notes. 'However, if you should go to London—'

'I go there tomorrow,' Harry told him. 'I sail from Southampton in a week. I hope to find some material on Cagliostro in the British Museum.'

'You will find little of value,' the Frenchman said. 'To the British,

Cagliostro was a charlatan. But attend. Seek in the old furniture shops for a plain desk with a hinged lid, the letter "C" carved into it in ornate scrolls. Once it belonged to Cagliostro. Later it was acquired by one of the Dukes of Burchester. I have reason to believe that certain of Cagliostro's papers were hidden in a secret drawer in this desk and may possibly still be there.'

'A plain desk with a hinged lid, the letter "C" carved into it.' Harry Langham's expression was eager. 'That would be a find indeed. I certainly thank you, Professor Thibaut.'

The older man eyed him sadly.

'I still repeat my advice – tear up your thesis, forget the name. But you are young, you will not do it. Very well, I shall make one more suggestion. Go – now, today – to the Church of St. Martin.'

'St. Martin?'

'I will give you the address. Find the caretaker, give him ten new francs. Tell him you wish to see the tomb of Yvette Dulaine.'

'Yvette Dulaine?'

'She was buried there in 1780.'

'But I don't understand – I mean, what point is there in seeing the tomb of a girl who died in 1780?'

'I said she was buried then.' Thibaut's gaze was inscrutable. 'Insist that the caretaker open the tomb for you. Then do whatever you must do. Au revoir, my young friend.'

In the age-wracked Museum of Historic Antiquities, it had been easy to smile at the melodramatic earnestness of the French. Here, with the streets of Paris Lord alone knew how many feet above his head, moving down a narrow stone passageway slippery with seepage of water, holding aloft his own candle and following the flickering flame borne by the rheumatic old man in front of him, Harry found it less easy to smile.

They had gone down endless steps, along corridors that turned a dozen times. How old was this church anyway, and how far into the bowels of the earth did its subterranean crypts go? The whole thing was too much like an old movie for Harry Langham's taste. Except that the smell of damp corruption in the air, the shuffle of the old man's shoes on the rock flooring, and the scamper of rats in the darkness carried their own conviction.

They passed another room opening off the corridor, a room into which the bobbing candle flames sent just enough light to show old, elaborately carved stone tombs in close-joined ranks.

'Is this it?' Harry asked impatiently, as his guide paused. 'We must be there by now. We have had time enough to travel halfway across Paris.'

'Patience, my son.' The caretaker's tone was unhurried. 'Those who lie here can not come to us. We must go to them.'

'Then let's hurry it up. This is my last day in Paris. I have a thousand things to tend to.'

They went on, around another turning, down some stairs and came into a low-ceilinged room dug from solid rock. The tombs here were simpler. Many had only a name and a date. In the light from the two candles, they lay like sleeping monsters of stone, jealously hiding within them the bones of the humans they had swallowed.

'Are we there at last?' Harry Langham's tone was ironic. 'Thank heaven for that! Now which of these dandy little one-room apartments belongs to Miss Yvette Dulaine? I've come this far. I'll see it, but then I'm heading back for fresh air.'

'None of these,' the caretaker said quietly. 'She lies over here, la pauvre petite. Come.'

He skirted the outer row of tombs and paused, lifting his candle high. In a crude niche in the stone a tomb apart from the others had been placed. It could have been no plainer – stone sides, a stone slab on top, the date *1780* cut into the top, no other inscription.

'She is here. It is only the second time in this century that she has been disturbed.'

Harry stared skeptically at the simple tomb. His shoes were damp and he felt chilled as well as somehow disappointed.

'Well?' he asked. 'What am I supposed to do? Say ooh and aah? Why isn't her name on it – just the date? How do I know this is even Yvette Dulaine's tomb?'

The caretaker straightened painfully. He held his candle up and stared into Harry's face.

'You are American,' he said. 'When this tomb was closed, your nation had but begun its destiny. You have much to learn.'

'Look,' Harry said, controlling his impatience with an effort. 'I agree we have a lot to learn. But I can't see I'm learning much here, looking at some chunks of stone that hide a lady who died one hundred and eighty-odd years ago.'

'Ah.' The other spoke gently. 'If she had but died.'

'If she had but—' Harry stared at him 'What are you talking about? They don't bury you unless you're dead. Believe me, I know.'

'M'sieu's knowledge is no doubt formidable.' The other's tone was gentle, the sarcasm in his words. 'Let us now disturb the peace of Mlle Dulaine for but one moment more. We shall open her tomb.'

'Now really, that's hardly necessary—' Harry began, but stopped when the caretaker handed him his candle and grasped the bottom end of the slap top. He tugged; inch by inch the heavy stone moved, screeching its protest. Harry had no special desire to see some mouldering bones. He had avoided such a tourist attraction as the catacombs of Paris, just because he didn't care for morbid reminders of man's mortality. He liked his life – and death – in the pages of books. Both life and death were neat and tidy there and could be studied without emotion. He did not look into the open tomb until the caretaker straightened and motioned with his hand.

'Perceive,' he said. 'Look well upon the contents of this tomb, which the good fathers left nameless so that the poor one inside would not disturb the thoughts of the living.'

Still holding the candles, Harry bent over. As he did so, the flames flickered wildly, as if buffeted by drafts from all sides, though no breath of air stirred there. And the shadows they created made the girl in the tomb seem to smile, as if she would open her eyes and speak.

Her face was madonna-like in its perfection of ivory beauty. Heavy black tresses, unbound, flowed down upon her breast. Her hands, small and exquisite, were crossed upon her bosom. She wore something white and simple which exposed her wrists and arms. As he bent over her Harry's hand shook and one of the candles dropped a blob of molten wax upon her wrist. He so completely expected her to move, to cry out at the pain, that when she did not he felt a sudden wild rage. At her, for seeming so alive, so beautiful and so desirable. At Thibaut for sending him here on a fool's errand. At the shriveled gnome of a caretaker for wasting his time on so childish a deception.

'Damn you!' he cried. 'She's a wax figure! What kind of tomfoolery is this?'

With surprising strength, the caretaker thrust the stone lid back into place. Harry had one last glimpse of the young and lovely face with the lips that seemed about to speak, and then it was gone. And he could not explain why he felt doubly cheated, doubly angered.

'So!' he shouted. 'You didn't want me to get another look! You knew I was going to touch her and see that she really was wax. Admit it and tell me why you bothered with this nonsense. Or is this a standard tourist attraction that you've rigged up to bring in a little income from gullible Americans?'

The Frenchman faced him with dignity, reaching for and taking back his candle. 'M'sieu,' he said. 'As I remarked, you are young, you have much to learn. Once, Mlle Dulaine attracted the attention of a certain Count Cagliostro. She refused him. He persisted. She rejected him utterly. One night she vanished from her home. The next day, servants of Count Cagliostro found her lying in his rooms, at the base of a great mirror as if she had been admiring herself. The Count was held blameless; he was far from Paris at the time.

'Mlle Dulaine seemed asleep, but did not waken. There was no mark on her. Yet she did not breathe and her heart did not beat. A week passed. A month. She remained unchanged. She did not begin that return to dust which is the fate of us all. So her sorrowing parents consigned her to the good fathers of the church, and they placed her here. She has remained as you see her, since the year 1780.'

'That's idiotic,' Harry said, shakily. 'Such things aren't possible. She's a wax figure. She's certainly not dead.'

'No, M'sieu. She is not dead. Yet she is not alive. She exists in some dark dimension it is not well to think of. The Count Cagliostro took his revenge upon her. She will sleep thus, until the very stones of Paris become dust around her. Now let us go. As you reminded me, you have many things to do.'

'Wait a minute. I want to see that girl — that figure — again.'

Harry's breathing was harsh in the silence; he felt his pulse pounding — with fury? with bafflement? — he couldn't tell what emotion he felt. But the caretaker was already moving toward the stairs.

In a moment he would be gone. Harry wanted to tear the stone slab off that tomb and satisfy himself. But to linger even a moment would mean to be lost in those stygian depths without a guide.

Furious, he followed the flickering candle that was already becoming small in the darkness.

It was easy, in the daylight above, to regain his composure and laugh at himself for being tricked. It was easy, next day in London, when he met Bart Phillips, his closest friend at the university, who had spent the summer in London working toward his doctorate in chemistry, to entertain him with an elaborate account of the mummery he had gone through. It was easy to erase the lingering doubt that the girl had indeed been a wax figure.

Easy – until he found the mirror.

He found it in a dingy secondhand shop in Soho, called Bob's Odds and Ends. The desk he was seeking he had traced to an auction house which had suffered a fire. Presumably the desk had burned with many other rare pieces. But Bob's Odds and Ends had been mentioned in connection with the sale of the furnishings of Burchester House, residence of ducal line now extinct.

Bob himself, five feet tall and four feet around the waist, did not bother to remove the toothpick from between his unusually bad teeth when Harry, with Bart in protesting tow, asked about the desk. 'No, guvnor,' the untidy fat man said. 'No such article 'ere. Probably Murchison's got it, them wot 'ad the fire.'

'Come on, Harry,' Bart said. 'One last day in London and still you're dragging me to junk shops. Let's go get something to drink and see if we can't make a date with those girls from Charlestown we met.'

'Don't 'urry off, gents,' Bob said plaintively, unhooking fat thumbs from a greasy vest. 'Got somethin' pretty near as good. 'Ow would you like to buy th' mirror wot killed th' Duke of Burchester 'imself?'

'Mirror?' Harry asked, the word tugging at his memory.

'Come on, Harry!' Bart exploded, but Harry was already following the fat man toward the dark recesses of the shop.

The mirror was a tall, oval pier glass, hinged so that it could be adjusted. It stood in a corner. As the fat man swung it out, it rolled on a sloping stretch of floor, toppled sideways, and would have crashed down upon him if he had not sidestepped numbly. The mirror fell to the floor with a violence that should have sent flying glass for a dozen feet.

The proprietor looked at it calmly, then heaved it upright.

'That's 'ow it killed th' duke,' he observed. 'Fell on 'im. And 'im with an 'atchet in his 'and, like he was trying to smash it. But this glass can't smash. Unbreakable, it is.'

'What's unbreakable?' Bart asked, following them.

'This mirror, according to the man,' Harry said.

211

'Nonsense. Glass can't be made unbreakable,' Bart said. 'Good Lord, it's all painted over with black paint. It's no earthly use to anyone. Come on, I'm dying of thirst.'

'But, gents, it's a rare mirror, it is,' the fat man said sadly. 'Without that paint, it'd be worth a pretty sum. Besides, it's an 'aunted mirror. It killed th' duke 'isself, and it stood in a closet for almost fifty years before that. Ever since th' duke's brother, wot was the duke then, murdered a girl in Chubb's Restaurant back in 1910, then jumped out th' window into th' courtyard an' broke his neck when the Bobbies came for 'im.'

'Come on, Harry,' Bart groaned. But Harry, on the verge of turning away, saw the faint glint of glass near the bottom where something sharp had scratched a few square inches of the black paint which covered the mirror's surface. It seemed to him the bit of glass reflected light, and he stooped to look into it.

He stared for a long minute, until Bart became alarmed and grabbed him by the shoulder.

'Harry!' he said. 'My God, man, you're the color of putty. Are you sick?'

Harry Langham looked at him without seeing him.

'Bart,' he said, 'Bart – I saw a face in that mirror.'

'Of course you did. Your own.'

'No. I saw the face of that girl, Yvette Dulaine, who lies beneath St. Martin's Church in Paris. She was holding a candle, and looking out at me, and she tried to speak to me. I could read her lips. She said, "Sauvez-moi!" Save me!'

'What in God name has happened to Harry Langham?' Bart Phillips demanded, and ran his fingers through bristling red hair. 'He's missed his classes two days in a row. Mrs. Graham, is he sick?'

The middle-aged woman, who might have stepped from one of the stiff portraits on the walls of the rundown Beacon Street house, compressed her lips.

'I don't know what has happened to him, Professor Phillips,' she said. 'He hasn't been himself for a week, not since he received word that mirror was due to be landed. Then since they delivered it two days ago he has not left his room. He makes me leave his meals outside the door. I have always considered Professor Langham a very fine lodger, but if this goes on – Well!'

She uttered the final exclamation to Bart Phillips' back as he took the broad, curving stairs of the once elegant house two at a time.

At the top, Bart hesitated outside Harry's door. Some dirty dishes sat on the floor just beside it. He tested the knob, found the door unlocked, and quietly pushed it open.

In the center of the big, old-fashioned room, Harry was on his knees before the oval pier glass, laboriously scraping away at the black paint which covered its surface. From time to time he paused to wet a rag in turpentine, rub down the surface he had scraped, and then begin again.

The younger man walked quietly up behind him. The glass, he saw, was now nearly free of obscuring paint. It shone with an unusual clarity, giving the effect of a great depth. Then Harry saw his reflection and leaped up.

'Bart!' he shouted. 'What are you doing here? Why have you broken into my room?'

'Easy, boy, easy,' Bart said, putting a hand on his shoulder. 'What's the matter, are you in training for a nervous breakdown? I've been coming in your room without knocking for years.'

'Yes — yes, of course.' Harry Langham rubbed his forehead wearily. 'Sorry, Bart. I'm edgy. Not enough sleep, I guess.'

Bart looked at the flecks of paint on the floor, and rapped the mirror with his knuckle. Harry started to protest, and subsided.

'At a guess,' Bart said, 'you have been working on this old looking glass since it got here. Now honestly, Harry, aren't you being — well, illogical? I mean, you think you saw a girl's face mysteriously looking out at you from this mirror, back in London. You've been on pins and needles ever since waiting for it to arrive — you've hardly been over to see us, and I must say that Sis is hurt, since she kind of got the idea you planned to propose. Tell me the truth — are you expecting that girl is going to appear in this mirror again? Is that what you've had all along in the back of your mind?'

'I don't know.' Harry dropped into a chair and stared at himself in the mirror. 'I tell you, Bart — I just don't know. I feel I have to get this mirror clean again. Then — well, I don't know what. But I have to get it clean.'

'In other words, a neurotic compulsion,' Bart told him. 'Under an old church in Paris you saw a wax figure. Later your imagination played a trick on you—'

'It wasn't imagination!' Harry Langham leaped to his feet with a fury that astonished them both. 'I saw her. I tell you I saw her!'

He stopped, breathing harshly. His friend had fallen back a step in surprise.

'I – I'm sorry, Bart. Look, maybe I am being – unreasonable. Just let me get this mirror cleaned, and some sleep, and I'll be myself. And I'll come to dinner tomorrow night with you and Laura. How's that?'

'Well – all right.' Bart said. 'And you'll cover your classes Monday? I officially announced you had a virus, but I can't cover for you any more.'

'I'll be at my classes. And thanks, Bart.'

When Bart had left, Harry dropped into the chair again and stared at the gleaming mirror. It seemed to shine with a light which was not reflection, yet he could discover no source for it.

'Yvette!' he said. 'Yvette? Are you there? If you are – show yourself.'

He knew he was acting ridiculously. Yet he did not care. He wanted to see her face again – the face he had seen in a tomb in Paris, the face he had seen in a bit of mirror in London, the face he saw in his dreams now.

Nothing happened. After a long moment, he got to work again with scraper, turpentine and steel wool.

The paint stuck doggedly. Twilight had dimmed the room to semi-darkness by the time the glass finally showed no trace of black remaining.

Exhausted, Harry sank back into his chair and stared at it. It was curious how brilliant a reflection it gave. Even in the twilight it showed every detail of his room. His studio couch, his bookshelves, his pictures, his hi-fi set – they seemed three dimensional.

He sighed with fatigue and his vision blurred. The reflection in the mirror clouded like wind-rippled water. He rubbed his eyes and once again the image was clear. The handsome black-and-white striped wallpaper, the crystal chandelier for candles, the old rosewood harpsichord, the enormous Oriental rug on the floor, the hunting-scene tapestry on one wall—

Harry Langham sat up abruptly. The room in the mirror was a place he had never seen in his life. It bore no more resemblance to his own room than – than—

And then she entered.

She wore something simple – he had never had an eye for clothes, he only knew it was elegant and expensive and of a style two centuries old. Her black hair was bound up in coiled tiers. She carried a candle, and as she came toward him from one of the doorways that showed in the shadowy sides of the room, she paused to light the candelabra atop the harpsichord. Then she turned toward the man who was watching, his breathing quick and shallow, his pulse hammering. It was she. Yvette Dulaine, whose body lay buried beneath St. Martin's Church.

He thought she was going to step into the room with him. But she stopped as if at an invisible barrier, and gave him a glance of infinite beseechment. Her lips moved. He could hear no sound, but he could read the words.

'Sauvez moi! M'sieu, je vous implorer. Sauvez-moi!'

'How?' he cried. 'Tell me how?'

She made a gesture of helpless distress. A ripple swept across the mirror and she was gone. Harry Langham sprang to his feet.

'Come back!' he shouted. 'Yvette, come back!'

Behind him the door opened. He turned in a fury, to see Mrs. Graham bearing a tray of food.

'What are you doing?' he shouted at her. 'Why did you break in? You sent her away! You frightened her!'

The woman drew herself up in starchy dignity.

'I am not accustomed to being spoken to that way, Professor Langham,' she said. 'I knocked, and heard you say "Come". I have brought your dinner. I would prefer that you arrange to lodge elsewhere as soon as this month is up.'

She set down the tray and marched like a grenadier out of the room.

Harry passed a hand hopelessly over his forehead. The sight of the food on the tray revolted him. He thrust it away and turned back to the mirror, which now was dull and lifeless in the almost darkened room.

'Yvette,' he whispered. 'Please! Please come back. Tell me how I can help you.'

The mirror did not change. He flung himself into the chair and stared at it as if the very intensity of his willing would make it light again, would reveal the strange and elegant room it had shown before.

215

The room darkened, until he could no longer see the mirror. Then his fingers, gripping the arms of the chair, relaxed. Exhaustion overcame his willpower, and he slept.

It was the booming of a clock that woke him. Or was it a voice, speaking insistently in his ear? Or a sound as of a thousand tinkling chimes intermingled? Or all three? He opened his eyes, and saw before him the mirror, light emanating from it. Once again it showed the strange room. The candles in the crystal chandelier glittered. And an elegantly dressed gentleman, who leaned against the harpsichord and watched, smiled.

'You are awake, m'sieu,' he said, and now Harry heard the words clearly. 'That is good. I have been waiting to speak to you.'

Harry Langham rubbed his eyes, and sat up.

'Who are you?' he asked. 'Where is she? Yvette, I mean.'

'I am Count Lafontaine, at your service.' The man bowed, 'And Mademoiselle Dulaine will be here. She is waiting for you to join us. To save us.'

'Save you?'

'We are both victims of an evil done long ago, before even your great-grandfather was born. The evil of the most evil of living men, Count Alexander Cagliostro. But with your help, that evil can be undone.'

'How?' Harry demanded.

'In a moment I shall tell you. But here comes Mlle Dulaine. Will you not join us?'

Harry rose to his feet, feeling strangely light, disembodied.

'Join you?' he asked. And even as he spoke he was aware that his senses were dulled, his mind sleepy. 'Is it possible?'

'Just step forward.' The Count held out his hand, 'I will assist you.'

Beyond the man, Harry saw the girl come slowly into the room. She came toward him, slowly, on her face a look of infinite appeal.

'Yvette!' he cried. 'Yvette!' He took two steps forward, and felt his hand grasped by the cold, inhuman fingers of the man within the mirror. The pull but assisted his unthinking impulse. For a moment he felt like a swimmer breasting icy water, shoulder deep. Then the sensation was gone and he was within the room in the mirror.

He looked with exultation into the eyes of the girl.

'Yvette!' he said. 'I'm here. I'm here to save you.'

'Alas, m'sieu,' she said. 'Now you too have been trapped. Look.'

He turned. The Count Lafontaine bowed to him, formally.

'A thousand thanks, my young friend,' he said. 'It is half a century since last I left the world of the mirror. I am hungry for the taste of life again – very hungry.'

He kissed the tips of his fingers and flung the kiss to them.

'Adieu, mes enfants,' he said. 'Console each other in my absence.'

He strode confidently forward, and beyond him Harry saw, as through a window, his own room, dimly lit. The Frenchman stepped into the room and approached the chair where Harry had been seated, and now the shadowed figure in the chair, which he had not noticed before, was suddenly clear and vivid. 'That's me!' he gasped. 'Yvette – that's me – asleep in the chair.'

She stood beside him, her coiled dark hair coming to his shoulders, and infinite regret tinged her voice.

'Your body, M'sieu Langham. *You* are here, in the world of the mirror, this dark dimension which is not life and is not death and yet partakes of both. In your sleep he spoke the words of his spell and evoked your spirit forth from your body without your awareness. Now he will inhabit your body – for an hour, a day, a decade, I do not know.'

'He?' Harry shook his head, fighting the sense of languor and oppression. 'But who is he? He said—'

'He is the Count Alexander Cagliostro, M'sieu. And see – he lives again, in your body.'

As they spoke, the figure that had emerged from the mirror world turned to smile at them with sardonic triumph. Then it settled down upon Harry's sleeping body, blended with it, vanished – and Harry saw himself rise, stretch and yawn and smile.

'Ah, it's good to be alive again, with a young body, a strong body.' It was his voice speaking and in English – his voice, subtly accented.

'Now, au revoir. The night is still young.'

'No!' Harry flung himself forward – and was stopped by an impalpable barrier. The glass of the mirror – yet it did not feel like glass. It felt like an icy net which for an instant yielded, then gathered resistance and threw him back. 'You can't!' he cried. 'Come back!'

'But I can,' said Count Cagliostro reasonably, in Harry's own voice. 'And I shall come back when it pleases me. Meanwhile, it is best that none save myself should be able to see you.'

217

He raised his hand in the air and drew it downward, speaking a dozen words in rolling Latin. And Harry faced only darkness — an empty darkness that stretched beyond him, for an infinitude of time and space.

He lunged into it, and found himself spinning dizzily in a black void where there was neither substance nor direction. There was only a cube of light, from the mirror room, swiftly dwindling into a tiny gleam.

'Come back! You will be lost forever, M'sieu. I pray you, return!'

The words, faint and faraway, steadied his whirling senses. He saw the light, focused his thoughts on the room it represented, on the girl, and once more he stood beside her, with the candles flickering warmly above them and the hungry blackness behind him.

'Mon Dieu, I feared you were gone!' Her voice was unsteady. 'M'sieu, we are alone here together. Even the consolation of death and the sweet sleep of eternity is denied us. At least, let us keep each other company and take what comfort we may from that.'

'Yes, you're right.' Harry passed a trembling hand over his face. 'And maybe we'd better start with you telling me what in God's name has happened to us.'

It did not require many words, Harry thought dully, half stretched out upon a tapestried couch as he listened to the soft tone of Yvette's voice. She had rejected Cagliostro — and with a smile he had promised her that she would have all eternity in which to regret her decision. Then one night in her sleep a strange compulsion had taken her will, and she had gone to his home, admitted herself, and gone up to his empty room — to find him smiling at her from within the mirror. He had spoken — She had left her body behind crumpled on the floor — and she had joined him in the world of the mirror. Then he — his own body many miles away — had left her alone there until the time came for him to take final refuge himself in the world between life and death of which the mirror was a door that he had opened.

'But he died in 1795 in prison,' Harry protested.

'No, m'sieu. They but said he had died. His body is buried somewhere, as is mine, and like mine, it does not change. His spirit sought refuge here, in this sanctuary he planned long in advance. And from time to time he found means to escape, as he has now, in your body. Over the years, the crimes committed by various hands, yet all

218

animated by the spirit of Cagliostro, would fill a library of horrors. One has heard of the Marquis de Sade. Yet the Marquis was but a man interested in things magical – until he encountered the mirror and met the gaze of Cagliostro. Then, m'sieu, the name of de Sade became synonymous with evil.

'Later, given but little choice, he assumed the flesh of a drunken servant who had entree only to the lowest of London's dives. It was then he acquired a nickname which you will know. Jacques.'

'Jacques?'

'Jacques, the Ripper. Never was he caught, this Jacques. He froze to death in a gutter one winter night – but only after the spirit of Cagliostro had safely quitted his mortal flesh.

'And then young Charles, Duke of Burchester, acquired a desk and the mirror for his studio. And so fell into Cagliostro's power. But the evil Count was too greedy. The first night he killed a girl almost in public and must flee back to this, his place of safety. Charles, himself again, tried to break the mirror. When he could not, when the men of the police came for him, he covered the mirror with black paint, and then he threw himself from his window and was dashed to death on the stones below.

'Now, m'sieu –' her gaze was compassionate – 'he is free again in your body. And the hunger is strong within him. I would speak words of consolation, but unfortunately I cannot.'

'But what is he doing?' Harry started to his feet. 'My God, Yvette, isn't there any way to know what he is up to and to stop him?'

'It is possible to know what he is doing,' she said at last, 'for the spirit still is connected with the body, though but faintly. But he can not be stopped. He is the master, we are his prisoners. And it is not wise to know what your body does at his orders.'

'I must know, I have to know!' Harry declared feverishly.

'Then lie back, stare at the burning candles, and let your mind empty itself . . .'

He was in a bar somewhere. A crowded, noisy, smoky dive. Impression of laughter, of voices. Of a face looking up into his. A hungry face, over-painted, yet still with some youthful sweetness in it not quite destroyed. They were moving. They were outdoors. They were strolling down a narrow street toward the waterfront, and light and sound here left behind.

The girl was petulant. She did not want to go. But he laughed, and with a hand on her elbow, urged her onward. They came to a railing, with the dark water swirling below, and a mist curling around them.

'No, I'll show you what I promised you,' he was saying. 'But first we must remove these.'

He deftly removed from her ears the cheap, dangling crystal earrings, dropped them into his pocket.

'Why did you do that?' Her voice was shrill, angry. 'You can't treat me like that.'

'Your beauty should be unadorned. Look into my eyes.'

She looked and her gaze grew fixed. In his eyes she saw the black void of eternity, and rising from it the grinning skull-face of Death. She did not struggle, did not scream as his hungry fingers closed around her throat. Only when it was too late did she fight, so deliciously, so rewardingly. When he dropped her over into the rolling waters below and saw them suck her down with hungry swiftness, he felt again deliciously warm and full . . .

'M'sieu! M'sieu!'

He opened his eyes. Yvette was shaking him, her face concerned.

'M'sieu, you looked so distressed! I told you it was not wise—'

'I'm a murderer,' Harry groaned. 'I killed her – killed that girl for the sheer lust of killing . . .'

'Comfort yourself, m'sieu. You did not. It was he, Cagliostro, slaking his hunger for life. It is thus his spirit feeds, grows strong – on the life of those he sacrifices.'

'But it was my hands that choked her – Oh, my God, what are we going to do?'

He stood up, his hands clenched. 'Can't we do *anything*?'

'Nothing, alas. He lives – in your body. We are shadows of the spirit trapped between life and death. Someday he will return and you will once more regain your body—'

'To be accused of all the infamous crimes he committed!' Harry cried. 'To pay for them. But first, I'll break this mirror. That's one thing I won't fail to do.'

Her gaze was wistful.

'If only that could be. Then I could at last die and be at rest. But you will not do what you think. Others have tried and failed. This mirror can not be broken by human hand – only he himself, Cagliostro, can break it. No – do not ask. I can not answer how or why these things are. He has the knowledge. I have not. Now, you must distract yourself. Come – let me show you this world.'

He let her take his hand, and numbly followed as she led.

There were doorways to the great room, several of them. She led him through one and he found himself in a small, book-lined library, where alchemical apparatus crowded tables, and a small, white-globed lamp burned with a bright fierceness. A book lay open, revealing mystic symbols. A giant spider squatted upon it and stared at them with glistening pinpoint eyes.

'His library,' Yvette said. 'Once the mirror stood in this room in the world of reality. Everything the mirror reflected since it was made exists in this dark and fathomless dimension, if only it was reflected long enough; and his arts can call it into being.'

'Like a time exposure being developed,' Harry muttered to himself.

'Pardon?'

'I was just thinking. What lies beyond?'

'There are many rooms and a garden and even a pond. I will show you.'

There were indeed other rooms, but Harry viewed them without interest. There was a garden where fruit trees bloomed, and a pool that reflected the sunlight of a sun not seen for two centuries. But when he would have gone on, through other doors, Yvette held him back.

'No, m'sieu. Beyond there is nothing. Darkness. Emptiness. Where one can become lost and wander until the end of time. And in the darkness there are – creatures.'

She shivered as she spoke the word. But Harry persisted in his exploration. He opened a closed door – and there beyond it did indeed lie abysmal darkness. There were sounds in the darkness . . . flutings and wailings like no sounds he had ever heard before. And something darker than darkness itself drifted past as they watched, accompanied by the sound of a myriad of tiny bells. Swiftly Yvette slammed the door.

'Please, m'sieu,' she panted. 'Promise me. Never go into the darkness. Even Cagliostro knows not what it is or what creatures inhabit it.'

'All right, Yvette.' Harry agreed. 'I promise. Let's go back. Maybe Cagliostro has returned. Maybe he'll be ready to give up my body now.'

They returned through rooms of a dozen different sorts, one of them

221

plainly the cabin of a ship. In the room of the mirror, the candles still burned as they had before, unconsumed and eternal. The wall of blackness which was the mirror remained in place. But even as they entered, it dissolved, became a window beyond which was Harry's study where Cagliostro sat at a table, eating breakfast and reading a newspaper.

He smiled smugly at them.

'I hope you have become well acquainted, mes enfants. I have waited for your return. M'sieu Langham, this body you have loaned me is a splendid one, so strong, so handsome, so indefatigable. I shall enjoy its use for a long time, I think. This time I make no foolish mistakes. I have begged the most humble pardon of Mrs. Graham, your good landlady, and she has forgiven me. This evening I dine with your friend, Bart, and his sister Laura, with whom I gather you have — what is the word? — an understanding. I must make amends to them for your behaviour.

'Ah, my good friend, this Boston of yours is a most interesting city. Cold and reserved in appearance, yet it has its under-current of wickedness quite as naughty as London or Paris. I enjoyed myself last night. I was rash, perhaps, but fortunately I escaped detection. And now my motto is to be — discretion.'

He rose and tossed down his napkin.

'Now, I shall rest,' he said, and yawned. 'Last night was — fatiguing. Tonight may be the same. Au 'voir.'

He swept his hand downward with a roll of unknown words, and blackness sprang into place.

Wretchedly, Harry turned to the girl.

'How long were we?' he asked. 'A dozen hours have passed since last night, but it seemed like only a few minutes — half an hour, perhaps.'

'There is no time here,' Yvette told him. 'An hour may seem a day, a day an hour. You will become used to it, M'sieu Harry. Compose yourself — think not of Cagliostro.'

She seated herself at the harpsichord and began to play a light, tinkling tune to which she sang in a sweet soprano. Harry flung himself down on the tapestried couch and listened. Gradually he relaxed. His mind ceased to throb and burn with turbulent thoughts. But as it did, other images, other sounds and sensations entered it.

Voices. Bart and Laura. Laughter. Wine.

★

'It's good to see you acting normal again, Harry. You had us worried.'

'I don't wonder, old man. That mirror delusion – you brought me to my senses. Guess I worked too hard in Paris.'

'Then there wasn't any girl in the mirror?' Laura's voice. Laura's smile. Laura's hand lightly on his arm as her eyes begged for assurance.

'If there was, she looked like me and needed a shave.' Laughter. 'Besides, what good would a girl in a mirror be?' More laughter. 'You'll see for yourself. When we set up house-keeping.'

'Goodness. Is that a proposal? Or a proposition?' Wide, hopeful eyes, lips that hide a trembling eagerness.

'Look, you two – while you debate the question, I have to see a graduate student of mine who's working on an interesting line of experiment.' Bart, rising, leaving. 'I won't be back until late.'

'Tactful Bart.'

'A nice brother. I like him. Harry—'

'Yes?'

'Whether it was a proposal or a proposition, it's a little sudden. Since you got back from Europe, I've hardly seen you. Why, I think you've kissed me once.'

'An oversight I plead guilty to. I can only say I'm prepared to make amends. Like this.'

Warm lips. Tremulous response becoming breathless excitement.

'Harry! What *kind* of overwork did you do in Paris? What research were you engaged in, anyway?'

'Can not we go elsewhere? . . . This is better. My dear . . .'

Breathless excitement becoming recklessness.

'Harry! You mustn't!'

'Oh, yes, my dear I must.'

'And I thought you were so prim and proper – even though I liked you.'

'And I thought you the same. How wrong we can be about people! Now . . .'

'Stop!' Harry leaped to his feet, pressing his fists to his forehead, shutting out the damnable sensations from his distant body.

'M'sieu Harry.' Yvette rose and came to him. Gently she touched his forehead. 'It is Cagliostro again. You must not try to know what it is he does.'

'I can't help it.' Harry groaned. 'My God, I never thought that Laura—'

'Do not speak of it. Shall I read to you? Shall we walk in the garden?'

'No, no . . . Yvette.'

'Yes?'

'Cagliostro controls whether or not we can see the world outside the mirror – and whether it can see us.'

'That is true. He has charms that control it. If he speaks but the words, we can see and be seen but not heard. Or hear, but not be seen. And the greatest charm, that of drawing the spirit from the body and transporting it within the mirror. Alas, m'sieu, I crave your pardon.'

'For what?'

'It was I – I who enticed you here. I could not help myself. Cagliostro worked magic that brought you to that shop in London where the mirror lay – he had waited long for the right moment. It was he who enabled you to see me. It was his doing that you determined you must own the mirror, must see me.'

'I did feel – possessed,' Harry admitted. 'But don't blame yourself, Yvette. Even without Cagliostro you would have attracted me.'

'You are gallant, I thank you.'

'But what I started to say, if Cagliostro has charms, we can learn. We are not entirely helpless.'

'Learn them? It is true, his books, his philters, his mystic objects are within his study—'

But in the study, where the white-globed lamp burned with an undying brilliance, Harry groaned and pushed away the strange books, the ancient parchments, after he had leafed through them.

'I can't read them. They're not Latin. Maybe Sanskrit. Maybe Sumerian. Maybe some language that died before history began.'

'It is true,' the girl told him, 'Cagliostro has said that his magic is older than history, that it comes from a race so ancient no trace is left.'

'And I don't believe in magic. That's one trouble. I belong to the twentieth century. Even here – even a victim of it – I still can't believe in magic!'

'Oui,' Yvette agreed, 'belief is necessary. Without belief, the magic does not work. But then one must have faith in God, as well as in evil, m'sieu.'

'Yes, of course?' His eyes lighted. 'And what is magic to one age is mere science to another. So why shouldn't science to one age be magic to another? Yvette, help me work this out.'

'Anything I can do, anything,' she said. 'Sometimes Cagliostro had me help him. He said that in things mystic the female principal helps. Wait.'

She took pins from her hair, let her tresses tumble down over her shoulder. From a drawer beneath the bookshelves she withdrew an odious object – the dried and shrunken head of a man who once had had flaming red hair and a red beard. She sat facing him, the head upon her lap.

'Now, m'sieu,' she said. 'This head – Cagliostro swore it was the head of one of the thieves crucified with the true Christ. Perhaps. But now I look like a sorceress, I will sit in silence, and you shall study.'

'Good girl!' He plunged anew into an effort to make sense of the books, the cabalistic symbols. In his mind he thought of them as simply equations which produced certain results. So categorized, he was able to believe in them. After all, this mirror world – was it so much more than a photograph caught on celluloid, or a motion picture electronically impressed upon magnetic tape? Perhaps the people in pictures felt and thought!

And wasn't it Asimov, right here in Boston, who had said that some day the entire personality of a man could be put on tape, to remain forever, to be reproduced again whenever and as often as desired? What would existence inside a magnetized tape be? What thoughts would the man there think?

Perhaps his analogies were faulty, but they helped give him confidence. Yvette sat in silence as he worked, with feverish intensity. He deciphered a word, a sentence, for Cagliostro had translated into a doggerel of Italian, French and Latin the older, unknown language – which might, after all, be the scientific language of a long dead race.

As Yvette had said, there was no time in this place. At intervals he paused and put his fingers to throbbing temples. Then he was aware of sensations from the world of life. His classrooms. Students listening with rapt intensity they had never paid before. Himself speaking with brilliant detail of life in London, in Paris, in the 18th Century. A girl in the back row, blond, with a face as soft as a camelia. A girl who paused after class at his request. 'Miss Lee, you are very silent. Yet I

225

think you are hiding a genuine intelligence. Are you afraid of me?'

'Afraid of you? Oh professor, I couldn't ever be that.'

'You need confidence. You need – awareness. I would like to talk to you about yourself. Tonight?'

. . . Night. His car. Driving. Lights. Stopping.

'Professor. What – what are you doing?'

'Look into my eyes, child. You are not afraid of me?'

'I – I – no, I trust you. I trust you forever and always.'

'That is good. Now come.'

He forced his thoughts back to the books before him. He translated, worked out probable sequences, guessed where he had to. Still the awareness crept into his mind whenever he relaxed.

'Harry – I haven't seen you for so long.'

'Working on my new thesis, Laura. That fraud Cagliostro – I've torn him up. The new one is to be a comparison of social life in London and Paris in the 18th Century.

'It sounds quite exciting.'

'It will be masterly. But I must make up for my neglect. My darling—'

'Harry! But —'

'No buts. Did you know that among the Romans—'

Doggedly he resumed work. But the outside impressions pressed in more strongly.

An alley. Blare of music. A girl, provocative in a red dress. She smiled into his eyes . . . And lay cold, moments later, in a shadowed corner . . . Another girl. Walking home from a bus. A scream. A struggle, sweet in its intensity . . .

'No,' he groaned. 'No, Yvette! The things he is doing! The things *I* am doing! Even if I conquer him – I can't live. Not with what I have done.'

'Poor M'sieu Harry,' she said. 'But can you conquer him? Suppose you force him to return here and give back your body, what then? This mirror – it too is under a spell. It can be broken only by Cagliostro.'

'Maybe,' Harry said grimly. 'But it hasn't been tested in an atomic explosion. In any case I'm pretty sure that, bathed in hydrofluoric acid, it would dissolve. Or dropped into molten glass it too would melt.'

'But then—' Horror touched her features. 'But then I would be lost forever in the darkness that lies outside, lost among the beings whose nature I know not. Only if the glass is broken is the spell broken. Only then can spirit and body reunite and blessedly find eternal sleep together.'

'I see. But Cagliostro must be removed from the world. If the mirror were dropped into the ocean where it is a mile deep . . .'

She shuddered. But nodded.

'He must be removed, oui,' she said. 'What happens to me – it is not important. Continue, m'sieu.'

'I think I'm on the track.' He pronounced some words, crudely. 'Does that sound familiar?'

'Yes!' her face lighted. 'It is what he speaks when he wishes to hear but not be seen. But it sounds like this—' She corrected his pronunciation. He repeated after her, the strange, rolling syllables. 'And this?' He spoke again, making a motion with his hand.

'When he wishes to see and be seen. Like this.' She corrected once more. 'And his hands – I'm not sure – there is a certain movement . . .'

He tried, but did no better. Then he stiffened. They heard voices. Real voices. For the first time.

'Yvette!' he whispered. 'We've won the first round. We can hear. Come, the other room. He is there, speaking to someone.'

They moved swiftly back to the great room where one wall of seething darkness represented the mirror. And words came through it.

'Professor Langham?'

'Associate Professor only, I'm afraid.'

'I'm Sergeant Burke, Homicide.'

'So Mrs. Graham said. Homicide. Intriguing. What can I do for you, Sergeant?'

'Where were you at three this morning?'

'Here in my room. Working on my thesis. May I ask why you are interested?'

'A girl was strangled outside the Fishnet Bar last night.'

'I don't believe I've heard of the place.'

'One of your students was there. He believes he saw you with the girl who was killed.'

'I am a very ordinary type, Sergeant. And one of my students – in a bar at three in the morning? No wonder they learn so little – academically speaking, of course.'

227

'He described you pretty closely.'

'Perhaps because he has seen me in class for weeks. Let me assure you, Sergeant, based on their classwork, the powers of recognition and description of my students are limited.'

'Maybe so. Do you know a girl named Elsie Lou Lee?'

'Of course. One of my students. A shy thing.'

'She committed suicide last night. Cut her throat with a razor blade. Her last words were, "He said he wished I was dead and out of the way, so I'm going to die!"'

'A suggestible type, may I remark?'

'Her landlady describes you as the man who sometimes called for her.'

'Believe me, Sergeant, my description would fit twenty thousand men in Boston. I assure you I am too discreet to – fraternize – with a female student.'

'Yeah, I suppose so. But frankly – well, we've had eight women killed in this city in four months. Eight! All young, all without motive. I have to check out everybody.'

'Quite understandable.'

'So – I haven't any warrant – but if you'd be willing to come down and make a statement at Headquarters . . .'

'With the greatest of pleasure. Let us go.'

Footsteps. A door closing. Silence.

'If only we'd had the rest of the charm,' Harry groaned. 'So that the Sergeant could have seen us! Then we'd have had him for sure.'

'He would have returned to the mirror,' Yvette said sadly. 'It is you who would have paid.'

'Even so – Let's keep trying. Tell me again what he said and how he moved his hands.'

Repetition. Endless. Timeless. Then abruptly the curtain of black vanished and they saw, through the window of the mirror, into his room. In time to see the door open and Laura enter.

She looked distraught and haggard. She advanced swiftly, calling in case Harry might be in the bedroom.

'Harry! Harry, are you here? I must talk to you!'

'Laura!' Harry cried. 'Here. Here!'

She did not turn. She crossed the room, looked into the bedroom, then came and sat back on the studio couch, nervously pulling off her gloves.

'She does not hear,' Yvette said. 'There yet remains some part of the charm incorrect.'

'Laura!' Harry groaned. 'Please, for God's sake, look this way!'

She did not immediately look toward the mirror. But as she sat, nervously playing with her gloves, her gaze swept the room – and finally stopped upon the mirror. And then she saw them.

Slowly, unbelievingly, she rose to her feet and approached them.

'Harry?' she whispered. 'Harry?'

'Yes,' he said, then realized she could not hear. He nodded instead. 'Call the police!' He mouthed the words carefully but she stared at him with numb incomprehension. He turned to Yvette. 'Quickly!' he said. 'Paper and pen!'

Yvette ran. But before she returned, Harry saw himself enter the room. Cagliostro, as himself. And Laura, turning, stared from the man in the doorway to the image in the mirror with mounting disbelief and horror.

'Ah,' said Cagliostro, approaching her. 'Our friends have learned some tricks. I underestimated M'sieu Langham. Now you know.'

'Know what?' Laura asked huskily. 'Harry, I don't understand.'

'You will, my dear. Alas. My plans were so well made. Marriage, a long and honorable career on the faculty. Unlimited opportunities to indulge my little hobby unsuspected – all professors seem so harmless. Now it must end. But perhaps there is still a chance—'

'Laura, look out!' Harry shouted, futilely, Cagliostro approached her – and then his hands were around her throat, throwing her back across the bed, controlling her struggles until she lay still. Breathing hard, he rose. He looked into the mirror.

'Blame yourself, M'sieu Langham,' he said. 'But then, I was growing tired of her. A possessive type. If I can but get her to the river, it is possible I may yet bluff your stupid police into believing in my innocence.'

He turned, and was drawing a blanket over Laura when the door burst open and Bart exploded into the room.

'Harry!' he shouted. 'Where's Laura! Mrs. Graham said she came up here. My God, man, don't you know you were seen with that Lee girl only last night before she—'

Abruptly he was silent, staring at the still figure only half concealed.

'Laura fainted, Bart,' Cagliostro said soothingly. 'If you will go for a doctor—'

229

'Murderer!' The words were a strangled sob as Bart flung himself at the other man. Cagliostro stepped aside and Bart sprawled on the bed atop his sister's body. Before he recovered, Cagliostro held a needle-sharp paperknife he had snatched from the desk.

'My young friend,' he said suavely, 'usually I kill only women. But in your case I will make an exception.'

With the litheness of a fencer he came forward, the point extended. But he was unacquainted with the game called football. The younger man lunged low, caught him around the knees, and flung him backwards. His body stopped only because it came into contact with the face of the mirror. And a myriad of cracks streaked the glass to its every corner.

'The glass!' Yvette said in fervent joy, as she and Harry saw Cagliostro crumple forward, with the paperknife still in his hand. 'Cagliostro himself has broken it!'

Bart Phillips saw the cracked glass, and for just an instant he was aware of the two figures within the glass, figures already twisting and distorting as the glass came loose. A shower of a thousand sharp fragments fell across the prone man on the floor. In one fragment, Bart saw a single eye staring out at him. In another, a pair of lips murmured, 'Merci.'

Then the reflections were gone and the man on the floor groaned and with difficulty rolled over. The paperknife emerged from his ribcase beside the heart, and dark blood stained his shirt and coat.

'Harry!' Bart dropped to his knee. 'Harry, *why*, *why*?'

'I am not your doltish friend Harry, M'sieu,' the dying man said. 'He is lost in some strange dimension where there is neither light, nor time, nor space.' His English now was accented. His features flowed, firmed. They became hook-nosed, sharp-jawed, the features of a man of middle age who has seen far too much of life.

'I am Count Alexander Cagliostro.' The words came with difficulty and were punctuated with blood issuing from the mouth. 'And I go now, his body mine, to meet the death which has awaited me patiently for almost two hundred years.'

He fell back, limp, and in a space of seconds his skin became a loathsome corruption, his hair powdered, and the white bone showed through. The corruption became horror. The horror dried, became dust, and the very bones beneath it melted like wax, falling in upon themselves. A moment later and there were but fragments mixed with dust.

The Skull of the
Marquis De Sade

ROBERT BLOCH

*The Marquis Donatien Alphonse François de Sade is the man whose
life and crimes gave rise to the word 'Sadism' to describe a form of sexual perversion that delights in the infliction of cruelty. Born in Paris in
1740, he fought as a soldier for several years in the Seven Years War.
In 1772, however, he was arrested and condemned to death at Aix for
his 'cruel sexual vices', but twice escaped from prison. Finally he was
committed to an asylum where he wrote his scandalous novels,* Justine
(1791), La Philosophie dans le Boudoir *(1793) and* Les Crimes
de l'Amour *(1800). He died mad at Charenton in 1814 having
given a new word to the language. De Sade's fame has continued to
grow in numerous works of fact and fiction as well as in the study of
sexual perversions. Robert Bloch, author of one of the most famous novels of sexual obsession,* Psycho, *which was filmed by Alfred Hitchcock
in 1960, has also been fascinated by the legend of the Marquis de Sade
and the continuing interest in him. Like* Psycho, *'The Skull of the
Marquis de Sade' has also been filmed, as* The Skull *(1965) starring
Peter Cushing, Christopher Lee, Patrick Wymark and Jill Bennett.*

CHRISTOPHER MAITLAND SAT back in his chair before the fireplace and
fondled the binding of an old book. His thin face, modeled by the
flickering firelight, bore a characteristic expression of scholarly preoccupation.

Maitland's intellectual curiosity was focused on the volume in his
hands. Briefly, he was wondering if the human skin binding this book
came from a man, a woman or a child.

He had been assured by the bookseller that this tome was bound in
a portion of the skin of a woman, but Maitland, much as he desired to
believe this, was by nature skeptical. Booksellers who deal in such
curiosa are not overly reputable, as a rule, and Christopher Maitland's

years of dealing with such people had done much to destroy his faith in their veracity.

Still, he hoped the story was true. It was nice to have a book bound in a woman's skin. It was nice to have a *crux ansata* fashioned from a thighbone; a collection of Dyack heads; a shriveled Hand of Glory stolen from a graveyard in Mainz. Maitland owned all of these items, and many more. For he was a collector of the unusual.

Maitland held the book up to the light and sought to distinguish pore-formation beneath the tanned surface of the binding. Women had finer pores than men, didn't they?

'Beg pardon, sir.'

Maitland turned as Hume entered. 'What is it?' he asked.

'That person is here again.'

'Person?'

'Mr. Marco.'

'Oh?' Maitland rose, ignoring the butler's almost grotesque expression of distaste. He suppressed a chuckle. Poor Hume didn't like Marco, or any of the raffish gentry who supplied Maitland with items for his collection. Hume didn't care for the collection itself, either – Maitland vividly remembered the old servant's squeamish trembling as he dusted off the case containing the mummy of the priest of Horus decapitated for sorcery.

'Marco, eh? Wonder what's up?' Maitland mused. 'Well – better show him in.'

Hume turned and left with a noticeable lack of enthusiasm. As for Maitland, his eagerness mounted. He ran his hand along the reticulated back of a jadeite *tao-tieh* and licked his lips with very much the same expression as adorned the face of the Chinese image of gluttony.

Old Marco was here. That meant something pretty special in the way of acquisitions. Perhaps Marco wasn't exactly the kind of chap one invited to the Club – but he had his uses. Where he laid hands on some of the things he offered for sale Maitland didn't know; he didn't much care. That was Marco's affair. The rarity of his offerings was what interested Christopher Maitland. If one wanted a book bound in human skin, old Marco was just the chap to get hold of it – if he had to do a bit of flaying and binding himself. Great character, old Marco!

'Mr. Marco, sir.'

Hume withdrew, a sedate shadow, and Maitland waved his visitor forward.

Mr. Marco oozed into the room. The little man was fat, greasily so; his flesh lumped like the tallow coagulating about the guttering stump of a candle. His waxen pallor accentuated the simile. All that seemed needed was a wick to sprout from the bald ball of fat that served as Mr. Marco's head.

The fat man stared up at Maitland's lean face with what was meant to be an ingratiating smile. The smile oozed, too, and contributed to the aura of uncleanliness which seemed to surround Marco.

But Maitland was not conscious of these matters. His attention was focused on the curious bundle Marco carried under one arm – the large package, wrapped in prosaic butcher's paper which somehow contributed to its fascination for him.

Marco shifted the package gingerly as he removed his shoddy gray ulster. He did not ask permission to divest himself of the coat, nor did he wait for an invitation to be seated.

The fat little man merely made himself comfortable in one of the chairs before the fire, reached for Maitland's open cigar case, helped himself to a stogie, and lit it. The large round package bobbed up and down on his lap as his rotund stomach heaved convulsively.

Maitland stared at the package. Marco stared at Maitland. Maitland broke first.

'Well?' he asked.

The greasy smile expanded. Marco inhaled rapidly, then opened his mouth to emit a puff of smoke and a reply.

'I am sorry to come unannounced, Mr. Maitland. I hope I'm not intruding?'

'Never mind that,' Maitland snapped. 'What's in the package, Marco?'

Marco's smile expanded. 'Something choice,' he whispered. 'Something tasty.'

Maitland bent over the chair, his head outthrust to throw a vulpine shadow on the wall.

'What's in the package?' he repeated.

'You're my favorite client, Mr. Maitland. You know I never come to you unless I have something really rare. Well, I have that, sir. I have that. You'd be surprised what this butcher's paper hides, although it's rather appropriate. Yes, appropriate it is!'

'Stop that infernal gabbling, man! What is in the package?'

Marco lifted the bundle from his lap. He turned it over gingerly, yet deliberately.

'Doesn't seem to be much,' he purred. 'Round. Heavy enough. Might be a medicine ball, eh?' Or a beehive. I say, it could even be a head of cabbage. Yes, one might mistake it for a head of common cabbage. But it isn't. Oh no, it isn't. Intriguing problem, eh?'

If it was the little man's intention to goad Maitland into a fit of apoplexy, he almost succeeded.

'Open it up, damn you!' he shouted.

Marco shrugged, smiled, and scrabbled at the taped edges of the paper. Christopher Maitland was no longer the perfect gentleman, the perfect host. He was a collector, stripped of all pretenses – quivering eagerness incarnate. He hovered over Marco's shoulder as the butcher's paper came away in the fat man's pudgy fingers.

'Now!' Maitland breathed.

The paper fell to the floor. Resting in Marco's lap was a large, glittering silver ball of – tinfoil.

Marco began to strip the tinfoil away, unraveling it in silvery strands. Maitland gasped as he saw what emerged from the wrappings.

It was a human skull.

Maitland saw the horrid hemisphere gleaming ivory-white in the firelight – then, as Marco shifted it, he saw the empty eye sockets and the gaping nasal aperture that would never know human breath. Maitland noted the even structure of the teeth, adherent to a well-formed jaw. Despite his instinctive repulsion, he was surprisingly observant.

It appeared to him that the skull was unusually small and delicate, remarkably well preserved despite a yellow tinge hinting of age. But Christopher Maitland was most impressed by one undeniable peculiarity. The skull was *different*, indeed.

This skull did not grin!

Through some peculiar formation or malformation of cheekbone in juxtaposition of jaws, the death's-head did not simulate a smile. The classic mockery of mirth attributed to all skulls was absent here.

The skull had a sober, serious look about it.

Maitland blinked and uttered a self-conscious cough. What was he doing, entertaining these idiotic fancies about a skull? It was ordinary enough. What was old Marco's game in bringing him such a silly object with so much solemn preamble?

Yes, what *was* Marco's game?

The little fat man held the skull up before the firelight, turning it from time to time with an impressive display of pride.

234

His smirk of self-satisfaction contrasted oddly with the sobriety set indelibly upon the skull's bony visage.

Maitland's puzzlement found expression at last. 'What are you so smug about?' he demanded. 'You bring me the skull of a woman or an adolescent youth—'

Marco's chuckle cut across his remark. 'Exactly what the phrenologists said!' he wheezed.

'Damn the phrenologists, man! Tell me about this skull, if there's anything to tell.'

Marco ignored him. He turned the skull over in his fat hands, with a gloating expression which repelled Maitland.

'It may be small, but it's a beauty, isn't it?' the little man mused. 'So delicately formed, and look – there's almost the illusion of a patina upon the surface.'

'I'm not a paleontologist,' Maitland snapped. 'Nor a grave robber, either. You'd think we were Burke and Hare! Be reasonable, Marco – why should I want an ordinary skull?'

'Please, Mr. Maitland! What do you take me for? Do you think I would presume to insult your intelligence by bringing you an ordinary skull? Do you imagine I would ask a thousand pounds for the skull of a nobody?'

Maitland stepped back.

'A thousand pounds?' he shouted. 'A thousand pounds for *that*?'

'And cheap at the price,' Marco assured him. 'You'll pay it gladly when you know the story.'

'I wouldn't pay such a price for the skull of Napoleon,' Maitland assured him. 'Or Shakespeare, for that matter.'

'You'll find that the owner of this skull tickles your fancy a bit more,' Marco assured him.

'Enough of this. Let's have it, man!'

Marco faced him, one pudgy forefinger tapping the osseous brow of the death's-head.

'You see before you,' he murmured, 'the skull of Donatien Alphonse François, the Marquis de Sade.'

2

Giles de Retz was a monster. Torquemada's inquisitors exercised the diabolic ingenuity of the fiends they professed to exorcise. But it remained for the Marquis de Sade to epitomize the living lust for pain.

235

His name symbolizes cruelty incarnate – the savagery men call 'sadism'.

Maitland knew de Sade's weird history, and mentally reviewed it.

The Count, or Marquis, de Sade was born in 1740, of distinguished Provencal lineage. He was a handsome youth when he joined his cavalry regiment in the Seven Years' War – a pale, delicate, blue-eyed man, whose foppish diffidence cloaked an evil perversity.

At the age of twenty-three he was imprisoned for a year as the result of a barbaric crime. Indeed, twenty-seven years of his subsequent life he spent in incarceration for his deeds – deeds which even today are only hinted at. His flagellations, his administration of outer drugs and his tortures of women have served to make his name infamous.

But de Sade was no common libertine with a primitive urge toward the infliction of suffering. He was, rather, the 'philosopher of pain' – a keen scholar, a man of exquisite taste and breeding. He was wonderfully well-read, a disciplined thinker, a remarkable psychologist – and a sadist.

How the mighty Marquis would have squirmed had he envisioned the petty perversions which today bear his name! The tormenting of animals by ignorant peasants, the beating of children by hysteric attendants in institutions, the infliction of senseless cruelties by maniacs upon others or by others upon maniacs – all these matters are classified as 'sadistic' today. And yet none of them are manifestations of de Sade's unnatural philosophy.

De Sade's concept of cruelty had in it nothing of concealment or deceit. He practiced his beliefs openly and wrote explicitly of such matters during his years in prison. For he was the Apostle of Pain, and his gospel was made known to all men in *Justine*, *Juliette*, *Aline et Valcour*, the curious *La Philosophie dans le Boudoir* and the utterly abominable *Les 120 Journées*.

And de Sade practiced what he preached. He was a lover of many women – a jealous lover, willing to share the embraces of his mistresses with but one rival. That rival was Death, and it is said that all women who knew de Sade's caresses came to prefer those of his rival, in the end.

Perhaps the tortures of the French Revolution were indirectly inspired by the philosophy of the Marquis – a philosophy that gained circulation throughout France following the publication of his notorious tomes.

When the guillotine arose in the public squares of the cities, de Sade emerged from his long series of imprisonments and walked abroad among men maddened at the sight of blood and suffering.

He was a gray, gentle little ghost — short, bald, mild-mannered and soft-spoken. He raised his voice only to save his aristocratic relatives from the knife. His public life was exemplary during these latter years.

But men still whispered of his private life. His interest in sorcery was rumored. It is said that to de Sade the shedding of blood was a sacrifice. And sacrifices made to certain things bring black boons. The screams of pain-maddened women are as prayer to the creatures of the Pit. . . .

The Marquis was cunning. Years of confinement for his 'offenses against society' had made him wary. He moved quite cautiously and took full advantage of the troubled times to conduct quiet and unostentatious burial services whenever he terminated an amour.

Caution did not suffice, in the end. An ill-chosen diatribe directed against Napoleon served as an excuse for the authorities. There were no civil charges; no farcical trial was perpetrated.

De Sade was simply shut up in Charenton as a common lunatic. The men who knew his crimes were too shocked to publicize them — and yet there was a satanic grandeur about the Marquis which somehow precluded destroying him outright. One does not think of assassinating Satan. But Satan chained—

Satan, chained, languished. A sick half-blind old man who tore the petals from roses in a last gesture of demoniac destructiveness, the Marquis spent his declining days forgotten by all men. They preferred to forget, preferred to think him mad.

In 1814, he died. His books were banned, his memory desecrated, his deeds denied. But his name lived on — lives on as an eternal symbol of innate evil. . . .

Such was de Sade, as Christopher Maitland knew him. And as a collector of *curiosa*, the thought of possessing the veritable skull of the fabulous Marquis intrigued him.

He glanced up from revery, glanced at the unsmiling skull and the grinning Marco.

'A thousand pounds, you said?'

'Exactly,' Marco nodded. 'A most reasonable price, under the circumstances.'

'Under what circumstances?' Maitland objected. 'You bring me a skull. But what proof can you furnish me as to its authenticity? How did you come by this rather unusual *memento mori*?'

'Come, come, Mr. Maitland – please! You know me better than to question my source of supply. That is what I choose to call a trade secret, eh?'

'Very well. But I can't just take your word, Marco. To the best of my recollection, de Sade was buried when he died at Charenton, in 1814.'

Marco's oozing grin expanded.

'Well, I can set you right about *that* point,' he conceded. 'Do you happen to have a copy of Ellis's *Studies* about? In the section entitled *Love and Pain* there is an item which may interest you.'

Maitland secured the volume, and Marco riffled through the pages.

'Here!' he exclaimed triumphantly. 'According to Ellis, the skull of the Marquis de Sade was exhumed and examined by a phrenologist. Phrenology was a popular pseudo-science in those days, eh? Chap wanted to see if the cranial formation indicated the Marquis was truly insane.

'It says he found the skull to be small and well formed, like a woman's. Exactly your remark as you may recall!

'But the real point is this. The skull wasn't reinterred.

'It fell into the hands of a Dr. Londe, but around 1850 it was stolen by another physician, who took it to England. That is all Ellis knows of the matter. The rest I could tell – but it's better not to speak. Here is the skull of the Marquis de Sade, Mr. Maitland,

'Will you meet my offer?

'A thousand pounds,' Maitland sighed. 'It's too much for a shoddy skull and a flimsy story.'

'Well – let us say eight hundred, perhaps. A quick deal and no hard feelings?'

Maitland stared at Marco. Marco stared at Maitland. The skull stared at them both.

'Five hundred, then,' Marco ventured. 'Right now.'

'You must be faking, Maitland said. 'Otherwise you wouldn't be so anxious for a sale.'

Marco's smile oozed off again. 'On the contrary, sir. If I were trying to do you, I certainly wouldn't budge on my price. But I want to dispose of this skull quickly.'

'Why?'

For the first time during the interview, fat little Marco hesitated. He twisted the skull between his hands and set it down on the table. It seemed to Maitland as if he avoided looking at it as he answered.

'I don't exactly know. It's just that I don't fancy owning such an item, really. Works on my imagination. Rot, isn't it?'

'Works on your imagination?'

'I get ideas that I'm being followed. Of course it's all nonsense, but—'

'You get ideas that you're followed by the police, no doubt, Maitland accused. 'Because you stole the skull. Didn't you, Marco?'

Marco averted his gaze. 'No,' he mumbled. 'It isn't that. But I don't like skulls – not my idea of ornaments, I assure you. Squeamish I am, a bit.

'Besides, you live in this big house here. You're safe. I live in Wapping now. Down on my luck at the moment and all that. I sell you the skull. You tuck it away here in your collection, look at it when you please – and the rest of the time it's out of sight, not bothering you. I'll be free of it knocking around in my humble diggings. Matter of fact, when I sell it, I'll vacate the premises and move to decent lodgings. That's why I want to be rid of it, really. For five hundred, cash in hand.'

Maitland hesitated. 'I must think it over,' he declared. 'Give me your address. Should I decide to purchase it, I'll be down tomorrow with the money. Fair enough?'

'Very well.' Marco sighed. He produced a greasy stub of pencil and tore a bit of paper from the discarded wrappings on the floor.

'Here's the address,' he said.

Maitland pocketed the slip as Marco commenced to enclose the skull in tinfoil once more. He worked quickly, as though eager to obscure the shining teeth and the yawning emptiness of the eye-sockets. He twisted the butcher's paper over the tinfoil, grasped his overcoat in one hand, and balanced the round bundle in the other.

'I'll be expecting you tomorrow,' he said. 'And by the way – be careful when you open the door. I've a police dog now, a savage brute. He'll tear you to pieces – or anyone else who tries to take the skull of the Marquis de Sade.'

3

It seemed to Maitland that they had bound him too tightly. He knew that the masked men were about to whip him, but he could not understand why they had fastened his wrists with chains of steel.

Only when they held the metal scourges over the fire did he comprehend the reason — only when they raised the white-hot rods high above their heads did he realize why he was held so securely.

For at the fiery kiss of the lash Maitland did not flinch — he convulsed. His body, seared by the hideous blow, described an arc. Bound by thongs, his hands would tear themselves free under the stimulus of the unbearable torment. But the steel chains held, and Maitland gritted his teeth as the two black-robed men flogged him with living fire.

The outlines of the dungeon blurred, and Maitland's pain blurred too. He sank down into a darkness broken only by the consciousness of rhythm — the rhythm of the savage, sizzling steel flails that descended upon his naked back.

When awareness returned, Maitland knew that the flogging was over. The silent, black-robed men in masks were bending over him, unfastening the shackles. They lifted him tenderly and led him gently across the dungeon floor to the great steel casket.

Casket? This was no casket. Caskets do not stand open and upended. Caskets do not bear upon their lids the raised, molded features of a woman's face.

Caskets are not spiked, inside.

Recognition was simultaneous with horror.

This was the Iron Maiden!

The masked men were strong. They dragged him forward, thrust him into the depths of the great metal matrix of torment. They fastened wrists and ankles with clamps. Maitland knew what was coming.

They would close the lid upon him. Then, by turning a crank, they would move the lid down — move it down as spikes drove in at his body. For the interior of the Iron Maiden was studded with cruel barbs, sharpened and lengthened with the cunning of the damned.

The longest spikes would pierce him first as the lid descended. These spikes were set so as to enter his wrists and ankles. He would hang there, crucified, as the lid continued its inexorable descent. Shorter spikes would next enter his thighs, shoulders and arms. Then, as he struggled, impaled in agony, the lid would press closer until the smallest spikes came close enough to penetrate his eyes, his throat, and — mercifully — his heart and brain.

Maitland screamed, but the sound served only to shatter his

eardrums as they closed the lid. The rusty metal grated, and then came the harsher grating of the machinery. They were turning the crank, bringing the banks of spikes closer to his cringing body. . . .

Maitland waited, tensed in the darkness, for the first sharp kiss of the Iron Maiden.

Then, and then only, he realized that he was not *alone* here in the blackness.

There were no spikes set in the lid! Instead, a figure was pressed against the opposite iron surface. As the lid descended, it merely brought the figure closer to Maitland's body.

The figure did not move, or even breathe. It rested against the lid, and as the lid came forward Maitland felt the pressure of cold and alien flesh against his own. The arms and legs met his in unresponsive embrace, but still the lid pressed down, squeezing the lifeless form closer and closer. It was dark, but now Maitland could see the face that loomed scarcely an inch from his eyes. The face was white, phosphorescent. The face was – *not a face!*

And then, as the body gripped his body in blackness, as the head touched his head, as Maitland's lips pressed against the place where lips *should* be, he knew the ultimate horror.

The face that was *not* a face was the skull of the Marquis de Sade!

And the weight of charnel corruption stifled Maitland and he went down into darkness again with the obscene memory pursuing him to oblivion.

Even oblivion has an end, and once more Maitland woke. The masked men had released and were reviving him. He lay on a pallet and glanced toward the open doors of the Iron Maiden. He was oddly grateful to see that the interior was empty. No figure rested against the inside of the lid. Perhaps there had been no figure.

The torture played strange tricks on a man's mind. But it was needed now. He could tell that the solicitude of the masked ones was not assumed. They had subjected him to this ordeal for strange reasons, and he had come through unscathed.

They anointed his back, lifted him to his feet, led him from the dungeon. In the great corridor beyond, Maitland saw a mirror. They guided him up to it.

Had the torture changed him? For a moment Maitland feared to gaze into the glass.

But they held him before the mirror, and Maitland stared at his reflection – stared at his quivering body, on which was set the grim, unsmiling death's-head of the Marquis de Sade!

4

Maitland told no one of his dream, but he lost no time in discussing Marco's visit and offer.

His confidant was an old friend and fellow-collector, Sir Fitzhugh Kissroy. Seated in Sir Fitzhugh's comfortable study the following afternoon, he quickly unburdened himself of all pertinent details.

Genial, red-bearded Kissroy heard him out in silence.

'Naturally, I want that skull,' Maitland concluded. But I can't understand why Marco is so anxious to dispose of it at once. And I'm considerably worried about its authenticity. So I was wondering – you're quite an expert, Fitzhugh. Would you be willing to visit Marco with me and examine the skull?'

Sir Fitzhugh chuckled and shook his head.

'There's no need to examine it,' he declared. 'I'm quite sure the skull, as you describe it, is that of the Marquis de Sade. It's genuine enough.'

Maitland gaped at him.

'How can you be so positive?' he asked.

Sir Fitzhugh beamed. 'Because, my dear fellow – that skull was stolen from me!'

'What?'

'Quite so. About ten days ago, a prowler got into the library through the French windows facing the garden. None of the servants were aroused, and he made off with the skull in the night.'

Maitland rose. 'Incredible, he murmured. 'But of course you'll come with me, now. We'll identify your property, confront old Marco with the facts, and recover the skull at once.'

'Nothing of the sort,' Sir Fitzhugh replied. 'I'm just as glad the skull was stolen. And I advise you to leave it alone.

'I didn't report the theft to the police, and I have no intention of doing so. Because that skull is – unlucky.'

'Unlucky?' Maitland peered at his host. 'You, with your collection of cursed Egyptian mummies, tell me that? You've never taken any stock in such superstitious rubbish.'

'Exactly. Therefore, when I tell you that I sincerely believe that skull is dangerous, you must have faith in my words.

Maitland pondered. He wondered if Sir Fitzhugh had experienced the same dreams that tormented his own sleep upon seeing the skull. Was there an associative aura about the relic? If so, it only added to the peculiar fascination exerted by the unsmiling skull of the Marquis de Sade.

'I don't understand you at all,' he declared. 'I should think you couldn't wait to lay hands on that skull.'

'Perhaps I'm not the only one who can't wait,' Sir Fitzhugh muttered.

'What are you getting at?'

'You know de Sade's history. You know the power of morbid fascination such evil geniuses exert upon the imagination of men. You feel that fascination yourself; that's why you want the skull.

'But you're a normal man, Maitland. You want to *buy* the skull and keep it in your collection of *curiosa*. An abnormal man might not think of buying. He might think of stealing it – or even killing the owner to possess it. Particularly if he wanted to do more than merely own it; if, for example, he wanted to *worship* it.'

Sir Fitzhugh's voice sank to a whisper as he continued, 'I'm not trying to frighten you, my friend. But I know the history of that skull. During the last hundred years it has passed through the hands of many men. Some of them were collectors, and sane. Others were perverted members of secret cults – worshippers of pain, devotees of Black Magic. Men have died to gain that grisly relic, and other men have been – sacrificed to it.

'It came to me quite by chance, six months ago. A man like your friend Marco offered it to me. Not for a thousand pounds, or five hundred. He gave it to me as a gift because he was afraid of it.

'Of course I laughed at his notions, just as you are probably laughing at mine now. But during the six months that the skull has remained in my hands, I've suffered.

'I've had queer dreams. Just staring at the unnatural, unsmiling grimace is enough to provoke nightmares. Didn't you sense an emanation from the thing? They said de Sade wasn't mad – and I believe them. He was far worse – he was *possessed*. There's some thing *unhuman* about that skull. Something that attracts others, living men whose skulls hide a bestial quality that is also unhuman or inhuman.

'And I've had more than my dreams to deal with. Phone calls came, and mysterious letters. Some of the servants have reported lurkers on the grounds at dusk.'

'Probably ordinary thieves, like Marco, after a valuable object,' Maitland commented.

'No,' Sir Fitzhugh sighed. 'Those unknown seekers did more than attempt to steal the skull. *They came into my house at night and adored it!*

'Oh, I'm quite positive about the matter, I assure you! I kept the skull in a glass case in the library. Often, when I came to see it in the morning, I found that it had been moved during the night.

'Yes, moved. Sometimes the case was smashed and the skull placed on the table. Once it was on the floor.

'Of course I checked up on the servants. Their alibis were perfect. It was the work of outsiders – outsiders who probably feared to possess the skull completely, yet needed access to it from time to time in order to practice some abominable and perverted rite.

'They came into my house, I tell you, and worshipped that filthy skull! And when it was stolen, I was glad – very glad.

'All I can say to you is, keep away from the whole business! Don't see this man Marco, and don't have anything to do with that accursed graveyard relic!'

Maitland nodded. 'Very well,' he said. I am grateful to you for your warning.'

He left Sir Fitzhugh shortly thereafter.

Half an hour later, he was climbing the stairs to Marco's dingy attic room.

5

He climbed the stairs to Marco's room; climbed the creaking steps in the shabby Soho tenement and listened to the curiously muffled thumping of his own heartbeat.

But not for long. A sudden howl resounded from the landing above, and Maitland scrambled up the last few stairs in frantic haste.

The door of Marco's room was locked, but the sounds that issued from within stirred Maitland to desperate measures.

Sir Fitzhugh's warnings had prompted him to carry his service revolver on this errand; now he drew it and shattered the lock with a shot.

Maitland flung the door back against the wall as the howling reached the ultimate frenzied crescendo. He started into the room, then checked himself.

Something hurtled toward him from the floor beyond; something launched itself at his throat.

Maitland raised his revolver blindly and fired.

For a moment sound and vision blurred. When he recovered, he was half-kneeling on the floor before the threshold. A great shaggy form rested at his feet. Maitland recognized the carcass of a gigantic police dog.

Suddenly he remembered Marco's reference to the beast. So that explained it! The dog had howled and attacked. But – why?

Maitland rose and entered the sordid bedroom. Smoke still curled upward from the shots. He gazed again at the prone animal, noting the gleaming yellow fangs grimacing even in death. Then he stared around at the shoddy furniture, the disordered bureau, the rumpled bed—

The rumpled bed on which Mr. Marco lay, his throat torn in a red rosary of death.

Maitland stared at the body of the little fat man and shuddered.

Then he saw the skull. It rested on the pillow near Marco's head, a grisly bedfellow that seemed to peer curiously at the corpse in ghastly *camaraderie*. Blood had spattered the hollow cheekbones, but even beneath this sanguinary stain Maitland could see the peculiar solemnity of the death's-head.

For the first time he fully sensed the aura of evil which clung to the skull of de Sade. It was palpable in this ravaged room, palpable as the presence of death itself. The skull seemed to glow with actual charnel phosphorescence.

Maitland knew now that his friend had spoken the truth. There *was* a dreadful magnetism inherent in this bony horror, a veritable Elixir of Death that worked and preyed upon the minds of men – and beasts.

It must have been that way. The dog, maddened by the urge to kill, had finally attacked Marco as he slept and destroyed him. Then it had sought to attack Maitland when he entered. And through it all the skull watched, watched and gloated just as de Sade would gloat had his pale blue eyes flickered in the shadowed sockets.

Somewhere within the cranium, perhaps, the shriveled remnants of his cruel brain were still attuned to terror. The magnetic force it focused had a compelling enchantment even in the face of what Maitland knew.

That is why Maitland, driven by a compulsion he could not wholly explain or seek to justify, stooped down and lifted the skull. He held it for a long moment in the classic pose of Hamlet.

Then he left the room, forever, carrying the death's-head in his arms.

Fear rode Maitland's shoulders as he hurried through the twilit streets. Fear whispered strangely in his ear, warning him to hurry, lest the body of Marco be discovered and the police pursue him. Fear prompted him to enter his own house by a side door and go directly to his rooms so that none would see the skull he concealed beneath his coat.

Fear was Maitland's companion all that evening. He sat there, staring at the skull on the table, and shivered with repulsion.

Sir Fitzhugh was right, he knew it. There *was* a damnable influence issuing from the skull and the black brain within. It had caused Maitland to disregard the sensible warnings of his friend; it had caused Maitland to steal the skull itself from a dead man; it had caused him now to conceal himself in this lonely room.

He should call the authorities; he knew that. Better still, he should dispose of the skull. Give it away, throw it away, rid the earth of it forever. There was something puzzling about the cursed thing – something he didn't quite understand.

For, knowing these truths, he still desired to possess the skull of the Marquis de Sade. There was an evil enchantment here; the dormant baseness in every man's soul was aroused and responded to the loathsome lust which poured from the death's-head in waves.

He stared at the skull, shivered – yet he knew he would not give it up; could not. Nor had he the strength to destroy it. Perhaps possession would lead him to madness in the end. The skull would incite others to unspeakable excesses.

Maitland pondered and brooded, seeking a solution in the impassive object that confronted him with the stolidity of death.

It grew late. Maitland drank wine and paced the floor. He was weary. Perhaps in the morning he could think matters through and reach a logical, sane, conclusion.

Yes, he was upset. Sir Fitzhugh's outlandish hints had disturbed him; the gruesome events of the late afternoon preyed on his nerves.

No sense in giving way to foolish fancies about the skull of the mad Marquis . . . better to rest.

Maitland flung himself on the bed. He reached out for the switch and extinguished the light. The moon's rays slithered through the window and sought out the skull on the table, bathing it in eerie luminescence. Maitland stared once more at the jaws that should grin and did not.

Then he closed his eyes and willed himself to sleep. In the morning he'd call Sir Fitzhugh, make a clean breast of things, and give the skull over to the authorities.

Its evil career – real or imaginary – would come to an end. So be it.

Maitland sank into slumber. Before he dozed off he tried to focus his attention on something . . . something puzzling . . . an impression he'd received upon gazing at the body of the police dog in Marco's room. The way its fangs gleamed.

Yes. That was it. There had been no blood on the muzzle of the police dog. Strange. For the police dog had bitten Marco's throat. No blood – how could that be?

Well, that problem was best left for morning too. . . .

It seemed to Maitland that as he slept, he dreamed. In his dream he opened his eyes and blinked in the bright moonlight. He stared at the table top and saw that the skull was no longer resting on its surface.

That was curious, too. No one had come into the room, or he would have been aroused.

If he had not been sure that he was dreaming, Maitland would have started up in terror when he saw the stream of moonlight on the floor – the stream of moonlight through which the skull was rolling.

It turned over and over again, its bony visage impassive as ever, and each revolution brought it closer to the bed.

Maitland's sleeping ears could almost hear the thump as the skull landed on the bare floor at the foot of the bed. Then began the grotesque process so typical of night fantasies. The skull climbed the side of the bed!

Its teeth gripped the dangling corner of a bed sheet, and the death's-head literally whirled the sheet out and up, swinging it in an arc which landed the skull on the bed at Maitland's feet.

The illusion was so vivid he could feel the thud of its impact against the mattress. Tactile sensation continued, and Maitland felt the skull rolling along up the covers. It came up to his waist, then approached his chest.

Maitland saw the bony features in the moonlight, scarcely six inches away from his neck. He felt a cold weight resting on his throat. The skull was moving now.

247

Then he realized the grip of utter nightmare and struggled to awake before the dream continued.

A scream rose in his throat – but never issued from it. For Maitland's throat was seized by champing teeth – teeth that bit into his neck with all the power of a moving human jawbone. The skull tore at Maitland's jugular in cruel haste. There was a gasp, a gurgle and then no sound at all.

After a time, the skull righted itself on Maitland's chest. Maitland's chest no longer heaved with breathing, and the skull rested there with a curious simulation of satisfied repose.

The moonlight shone on the death's-head to reveal one very curious circumstance. It was a trivial thing, yet somehow fitting under the circumstances.

Reposing on the chest of the man it had killed, the skull of the Marquis de Sade was no longer impassive. Instead, its bony features bore a definite, unmistakably *sadistic* grin.

The Sword of Jean Lafitte

KIRK MASHBURN

Jean Lafitte was one of the great maritime swashbucklers of American history during the opening two decades of the nineteenth century. Born in 1780, he became the leader of a ferocious band of privateersmen and smugglers who preyed on Spanish commercial ships off the coasts of Louisianna and Texas as they were sailing through the Bay of Mexico. Lafitte was widely known as the 'Robin Hood of Barataria' after the bay not far from New Orleans on the Mississippi Delta where he and his men hid out after their daring and usually successful raids. In January 1815, Lafitte added to his legend by helping Andrew Jackson defeat the British in the Battle of New Orleans. His death about 1825 is, though, shrouded in mystery: some sources claim he died during a bombardment of the port of Galveston; others that he was sunk by an English ship that had been dogging his heels for years to bring him to justice. In any event, Lafitte was a hero to the people of the South regardless of the number of seamen he had ruthlessly put to death on the blade of his fearsome sword. Legends of Lafitte's swordsmanship are, in fact, told all around the Bay of Mexico, and Kirk Mashburn, a prolific writer of historical dramas for the popular American magazines of the thirties, forties and fifties, has drawn on one of these for the following story. It is an evocative tale with a chilling finale.

MY ACQUAINTANCE WITH Jean Lafitte, in the beginning, was of the most casual nature. In short, my household was one of a considerable number that maintained the prosperity of his really excellent grocery.

When, shortly after the removal of my residence to New Orleans, I discovered the name of the grocer with whom my wife had established trade, it impressed me as being singularly unsuited to his occupation. As a matter of fact, I thought it ridiculous that any commonplace career should appeal to one who bore the name, and who, my wife informed me, claimed descent of that olden Robin Hood of Barataria.

I am possessed of a romantic streak which even the exigencies of

249

modern business have not been entirely able to overcome, and for some time this led me into the habit of personally settling my monthly account at Lafitte's.

I was not disappointed with Lafitte's personal appearance, for he proved to be a small, courtly-mannered individual, with excellently modeled head and features. A slightly swarthy complexion but served to set off his fine eyes to better advantage, although I observed a touch of pathos in their depths, and an expression of faintly bitter resignation, which I then could not account for. I had the explanation, some time afterward, when I accidentally discovered that the parish records vouchsafed descent to my grocer, not from the gallant Jean, but from his less appealing brother, Pierre Lafitte, and a mulatto mistress. Such lack of fastidiousness on the pirate's part promptly dispelled my fanciful interest in his progeny, and thereafter I substituted the use of the mails for the payment of my grocery bills, instead of presenting my checks in person.

More than a year passed, following the cessation of my periodic visits to his establishment, before I again (as I thought) came into contact with the grocer, under peculiar circumstances. I happened to be hunting ducks at the time, near the eastern reaches of Barataria Bay, and it struck me as a singular coincidence that I should find him in the same country where his picturesque ancestor once held sway.

I had become separated from the other members of my party, and the realization that I had hopelessly lost my bearings was gradually forced upon me. In attempting to retrace my steps toward the distant quarter in which I believed my companions to be, I was further confused to come upon a small bayou, which failed to impress me with any sense of familiarity.

While engaged in seeking a place where the heavy, sluggish water was shallow enough for me to wade across in my hip-boots without the necessity of a thorough wetting. I was relieved to observe the figure of what I took to be another hunter, upon the opposite side of the bayou.

I succeeded in crossing the stream without much difficulty, and hastened to accost the stranger — about whom there was something vaguely familiar. As I approached him, it suddenly dawned upon me that he was none other than that Jean Lafitte who sold me groceries. Simultaneously, I observed that his nondescript and yet picturesque attire would more appropriately have served that other Lafitte, who possibly stood upon the same ground when Barataria was a pirate stronghold.

A long, sleeveless cloak, curiously faded and weathered, and conveying an impression of impossible age, draped from his shoulders to below the tops of equally aged leather knee-boots. A broad-brimmed, lowcrowned hat, of apparently the same vintage as cloak and boots, drooped over the sallow face, where care appeared to have graven deeper lines than I remembered. I thought, for a moment, that the fellow seemed vexed as I hailed him. He hesitated for a perceptible instant, and then, slightly shrugging his shoulders, answered my greeting civilly enough, although without cordiality.

'I am certainly glad to see you, Lafitte,' I said, and observed that he gave a slight start as I pronounced the name, and regarded me with uncalled-for surprise.

'Indeed, *Monsieur*?' he questioned.

Lafitte spoke English with the curious inflection so often encountered in the southern parishes of Louisiana, even upon the tongues of some who are of a third or fourth generation of born Americans. He had never before addressed me as '*Monsieur*', however, and the use of the French title struck me as an affectation, possibly impelled by some conceit associated with his present surroundings. 'I surely am,' I affirmed. 'I've been floundering around in this confounded swamp all morning, and just about decided that I don't know where I am. I haven't even heard a gunshot for the last hour or more.'

'In which direction does *Monsieur* desire to proceed?' asked Lafitte.

'Back to that so-called railroad, at Le Boeuf station,' I informed him, conscious of a rising distaste for his continued use of the French mode of address.

'That is fortunate,' nodded Lafitte, 'for I am bound in the same general direction, and I shall be more than pleased to guide *Monsieur* to Le Boeuf.'

There it was again, and my rather childish irritation gave vent to expression as I reminded him, a trifle shortly.

'You've sold me enough groceries as *Mister* Stuart to be able to get along without all that '*Monsieur*' foolishness, haven't you, Lafitte?'

I was immediately ashamed of the outburst, for which there was little enough real reason, but consoled myself with the reflection that the damned nigger – even if he was almost white – was a bit too fond of histrionics.

251

None the less, my rebuke produced a dangerous gleam in Lafitte's deep eyes, and he stiffened ominously. The appearance of swiftly mounting wrath gave way, however, to an almost immediate expression of quizzical surprise, and what appeared to be sudden and amused comprehension. I confess to a distinct relief at seeing the blaze die out of those brilliant eyes, for the momentary flash, brief as it was, had given me a glimpse of something potentially dangerous in their depths. I repeat, therefore, that I experienced a relief even disproportionate to the incident when Lafitte lifted his shoulders in their habitual gesture and smiled, amusedly – a little contemptuously, I have since believed.

'So,' he queried, 'you buy groceries from one Jean Lafitte, in New Orleans, and because you consider him a very commonplace person, object that I – he – finds it natural, so close to Barataria Bay, to speak in the fashion of that – that *other* – Jean Lafitte?'

I answered him with his own trick, by shrugging my shoulders, whereat he faintly smiled again, and nodded.

'Please pardon my unwitting offense, Mr Stuart. One will surely be safe in asserting that Jean Lafitte – the grocer – highly values your good will.'

I was strongly suspicious that the rascal found something in his last statement to furnish him secret amusement; but I could not be sure, so offered no comment beyond a noncommittal grunt.

The fact was that Lafitte impressed me in a curious and vaguely disquieting manner. I was at a loss to account for the indefinable antipathy his presence inspired in me; for even in Barataria, and despite what I then considered his theatrical manner, I refused to regard him as other than a moderately prosperous grocer – and a not-quite-white grocer, at that.

We trudged on in silence for a while, Lafitte setting a course almost at right angles to the direction I had been following. Finally, partly as a relief to the monotonous lack of conversation, which my guide seemed indifferently disposed to remedy, and partly to shake off the unreasonable disquiet which I experienced in his proximity, I hazarded a remark.

'I did not know you were in the habit of taking holidays in the Barataria country, Lafitte,' I said.

'Nor am I,' was his grave reply. 'I have not had a holiday, in Barataria or elsewhere, in more years than you would be likely to credit, should I tell you just how many.'

'Does one flounder through these swamps on business, then?' I asked, with a short laugh. At the same time, I noticed a fact that had previously escaped my definite attention: in addition to his queer attire, neither was Lafitte armed for hunting, as well as I was able to determine.

'More men have sought these swamps with serious intent than have come for pleasure,' moodily answered Lafitte, breaking the thread of my thoughts. There was another flash of that latent ferocity I had previously noted as he added, 'Some few have come to bide here the hour of vengeance!'

I made no comment; nor did Lafitte seem to expect any. I could make neither heads nor tails of his erratic talk, and, what with the wild and positively uncanny expression that frequently replaced the air of calm melancholy I had grown to associate with him, I began to entertain an uneasy suspicion that the fellow might be more or less unbalanced mentally – although the idea was certainly discounted by what I knew of him.

At about this time, however, I was further perplexed to observe that, although we were almost constantly on boggy ground, and frequently wading in mud or shallow water, Lafitte's boots and long cloak were utterly free of any stain in witness of the fact. The full shock of this phenomenon did not strike me until I afterward recalled it, in the light of later events. My attention was diverted, at the moment, by the appearance of the Mississippi River levee, which confronted us as we broke through a concealing patch of tall sugar-cane.

The wretched little railroad track ran almost in the shadow of the levee, and Lafitte informed me that Le Boeuf station was only about two miles above us, around the bend of the river. He suggested that I might see for myself from the embankment, and as its summit furnished an easy and natural highway to my destination, we made the ascent.

Sure enough, I discerned the settlement at no great distance up the river.

At this juncture, Lafitte called my attention to a vessel that was rounding a lower bend of the great river which rolled majestically below us, and forging slowly upstream in our direction. His face retained a mask of impassivity, but his eyes were like glowing coals, alive with suppressed but exultant excitement.

Examining the craft, which was smaller than the usual ships of commerce, and yet had one funnel more than is customary, I remarked to Lafitte that she seemed to be some sort of small warship. This fact, in itself, afforded me no clue to the reason of his interest, but he nodded an eager affirmative.

'Ah!' he exclaimed; 'a warship, indeed! And does *Monsieur* observe the flag she flaunts?'

'Why yes,' I acknowledged, after a moment's further gazing, 'it is the Mexican flag; and, as we are expecting her arrival for general overhauling in the dry dock of my company at Algiers, I assume her to be the gunboat *Tampico.*'

'It *is* the *Tampico*,' agreed Lafitte. It did not occur to me to ask how he came to be so assured of this fact, since I happened to know that the gunboat carried no nameplate – and even if it had, he could not possibly have made it out at that distance. Instead, I remarked as an afterthought:

'It is quite possible that I shall go with her when she returns to Mexico, if the authorities will permit it. Her commander is an old friend of mine, and he has several times asked me to make a voyage with him. As I have to go to Vera Cruz, anyway, to inspect another gunboat before placing a bid to repair it also, I may take advantage of his offer at this time.'

To my great surprise, Lafitte vehemently shook his head, and urged, 'Do not follow your plan, *Monsieur* – you *must* not!'

Displeased at the receipt of such peremptory advice, I was upon the point of making a curt reply, but the fellow was so evidently in earnest that curiosity concerning his motive in objecting to a plan that did not in the least concern him, let me to question him.

'Pray, why not?' I demanded.

'Because,' slowly answered Lafitte, 'Captain Manuel de Ruiz, your friend and the gunboat's commander, *is marked for the vengeance of Jean Lafitte!*'

I do not know what reply I made to this amazing statement, or whether I said anything at all, but I do know that my last doubt as to Lafitte's mental condition left me, then and there. Probably he understood my thought, which would make clear his reason for explaining to me as much as he did – although why *he* should care for my opinion is beyond me.

'*Monsieur*,' he began, 'they will tell you that Jean Lafitte – *the* Jean

Lafitte – perished in Galveston; or at sea, under the guns of this or that man-of-war – some say an American, and some say an English vessel. But they are wrong! When an American warship bombarded Galveston, of which Lafitte was then governor, it is true that he was forced to flee the island. But he fled, *Monsieur*, not to sea, where every man's hand was against him, but to the mainland.

'The fugitive governor sought sanctuary in old Mexico, where he had many friends. But, alas! he had also many enemies, and treachery brought him full into the eager clutches of the chief of them all: one Don Manuel de Ruiz, the governor of Matamoras.'

Lafitte's face contracted with a spasm of fierce and somehow terrifying hate at the mention of the name, and he broke off his narrative to glare malevolently at the approaching gunboat.

'De Ruiz was not one to pass by the opportunity to settle an old grudge,' he continued, 'which was only the more bitter because unjust. His end was attained by the simple and expedient use of a firing squad, unattended by such superfluous trifles as formality or pretense of justice.'

'But where,' I interposed, 'is your authority for such statements? With proof, your story becomes an important contribution to history; but without such proof – and that of a very definite nature – it remains nothing more than another of many interesting tales about the same subject.'

'*Monsieur*,' replied Lafitte, with an enigmatic expression in his eyes, and contempt in his voice, 'I, *who know*, tell you what is the truth. Proof I have none; but I do not seek to write history, and I am little concerned with what fate history may assign to Jean Lafitte. What does concern me is the fact that, as the Mexican governor's ragged *soldados* riddled his body with an uneven volley, Lafitte cursed de Ruiz with his final breath, *and swore vengeance on him, and all who bore his name after him*! And, *Monsieur*, the last de Ruiz, the great-grandson and namesake of the murderer of Jean Lafitte, commands that teakettle, yonder.'

'At any rate,' I remarked a trifle maliciously, 'he does command it, so that Lafitte's curse can not have been entirely efficacious.'

'Ah!' snarled my fanciful grocer (I still thought of him in that light, and found the fact amusing), with an air of baffled rage. 'Yet, *Monsieur*, the original de Ruiz sickened and died of a malady that baffled his physicians, shortly after the 'execution' of his enemy. The Mexican had laughed at Lafitte's curse, but there were those who remembered and

255

shuddered, and peons who crossed themselves with dread, when the governor shrieked the Baratarian's name in the last agony of death!'

There was a pause, while the speaker seemed to be reviewing a personal knowledge of the event he had just described, so detached and earnest was his expression. There was about him, also, an air of gloating over that knowledge; but, even so, I could not forbear another sly gibe at his story.

'Yet, his great-grandson prospers,' I remarked. 'He is still a young man, and he will be a power in Mexico, some day, if he lives.'

'If he lives,' significantly agreed Lafitte. He regarded me for a moment with a stony stare. 'Would you know why he lives – why, indeed, his family was not wiped out long before he was born? Then, *Monsieur*, I will tell you: it is because they buried the sword of Jean Lafitte with his great-grandfather!'

I think that I snorted outright at this statement, but Lafitte continued his remarkable narrative without seeming to notice.

'The superstition of the governor's wife, who had a carefully ignored strain of Indian blood in her veins, caused her to seek counsel of her old Indian nurse, and the old *ama* advised her mistress to do a strange thing. There is, or was, *Monsieur*, a belief among some of the native tribes of old Mexico, that if a warrior's weapons be buried with his slayer, the malignant spirit of the former would be bereft of much of its power to harm either the spirit of his foe, when death should claim him also, or those living ones beloved of that foe. . . .

'*Monsieur*, there is often wisdom in what is termed the superstition of ignorant savages! Since the death of that old de Ruiz, his descendents have struggled against something more than mere ill fortune, and they have never greatly prospered in the end – but, at least, they have survived, thanks to the 'superstition' of an old Indian woman.'

I was strongly tempted to laugh, but something checked the impulse. By now, I was firmly convinced that there was a very decided quirk in my grocer's mental make-up. His appearance and manner, as well as his extraordinary conversation, caused me to wonder if his present visit to the old haunts of his pirate ancestor had not, through an association of ideas, finally developed a previously obscure obsession, and caused him to confuse the identity, as well as the real or fancied wrongs, of that other Jean Lafitte with his own. I remember, also, that I found time to be amused that his vanity had caused him to ignore the fact that he had less to do with Jean Lafitte than with his brother, Pierre.

I decided to be on my way to Le Boeuf, and thanked my guide for his services. He courteously assured me of his pleasure at having been of some slight assistance, and then added a final admonition against my proposed trip aboard the *Tampico*.

'A revolution brews in Mexico, *Monsieur*,' he gravely informed me, 'and strange things often happen when the passions of men are set loose, like wolves, to harrass their fellows. The gates of hell have waited overlong for Jean Lafitte, and I have a premonition that his buried sword shall again see the light. Keep off de Ruiz's tinpot, *Monsieur!*'

I should certainly have answered him in short and impatient fashion, except that, with a final courtly bow, Lafitte turned and climbed swiftly down the levee, and vanished into the cane patch through which we had recently come.

I watched him go with a feeling strangely like relief, and vaguely noticed that the tall, close-growing cane stalks did not even waver to mark his passage. I thought nothing of that fact at the time, and, dismissing my late guide with a shrug, I turned toward Le Boeuf.

It was then mid-afternoon, and I found on arrival at the settlement that my companions had not yet returned from the hunt. As I had eaten nothing since a very early breakfast, my first interest was to satisfy my hunger. Afterward, my mind was chiefly occupied with the attempt to invent some sort of excuse plausible enough to forestall, or at least diminish, the inevitable chaffing to which I should soon be subjected for losing myself – to say nothing of my failure to bag a single duck.

For this reason, I completely forgot my encounter with Lafitte, for the time being, and so made no mention of it to the rest of the party. When it later recurred to me, back home in New Orleans, I casually remarked to my wife that she need not be surprised to hear, at any time, that her grocer had been committed to a lunatic asylum. Naturally, this statement called for explanation, and when I had given it in complete detail, my better half regarded me with a quizzical air.

'You don't mean that all this happened three days ago?' she asked.

I nodded agreement, unsuspecting of the surprise in store for me.

'Then *you* had better be careful,' dryly commented my wife,

257

'because I happen to know that Lafitte was run down and rather severely injured by an automobile, *ten* days ago, and has been confined to his bed ever since!'

'Bunk!' I scoffed. 'He may have been hurt, but he was surely up and out last Saturday.'

'It's not bunk, and he wasn't up,' insisted my wife, 'because I went to the store Saturday afternoon to select some things personally, and Dr. Marvin was there at the same time. I heard one of the clerks ask him how long it would be before Lafitte would be able to get about, and the doctor told him that it would be ten days or two weeks. I shouldn't be at all surprised,' was her added and somewhat severe comment, 'if your duck-hunting party was like some of the fishing parties you and your precious friends go on.'

'Not a drop,' I hastily assured her, 'not a single drop!'

I was answered with an eloquent sniff, and I was aware that the subject was better dropped. While my wife is probably the finest woman in the world, and ordinarily reasonable, those of my readers who have been married for any length of time will at once understand my aversion to debate with her, along certain lines.

In the meantime, the *Tampico* had been put in our dry dock that very day, and I was so busily engaged in superintending the preparations for her speedy repairing that I again forgot my adventure in the Barataria swamps. Otherwise, I should have mentioned it to Captain de Ruiz sooner than I did. When we were about two-thirds finished with the job, however, we were quietly asked to work night and day, to get the ship finally conditioned, and de Ruiz confided to me that, although his government had succeeded in suppressing the news up to the moment, a revolution was actually under way in Mexico.

This at once recalled to my mind the warning Lafitte had given me, and I told de Ruiz the story. Although I dealt as humorously as possible with the matter of the supposed curse on the captain's family – and, for that matter, on the captain himself – he, to my great surprise, seemed to regard it as not altogether a joke.

'Why,' I remonstrated, seeing him suddenly so grave, 'surely you don't take serious stock in such rubbish?'

'There is a guarded story in my family similar to the one told you on the levee,' he quietly informed me. 'How do you account for your grocer's knowing of it? Then, too, what of the fact, attested by your own wife and your family physician, that your Lafitte was in bed with a

258

broken leg, to say nothing of a few ribs, at the same time you were talking to someone you thought was he?'

'You have me there,' I confessed. 'I can't figure it out any more than you can, but you may be sure of one thing: there is some perfectly logical explanation. One other thing, also – that explanation is not that I was drunk, as my wife more than half suspected!'

'*Quien sabe?*' murmured de Ruiz, with a shrug.

'"Who knows" what?' I demanded. 'Whether or not I was drunk?'

'No, no!' denied the captain, with a hearty chuckle in which I joined, although not quite so heartily.

'At any rate,' I nodded, 'I am going to Vera Cruz with you, if you will take me, and your consul general will grant the necessary permission.'

It happened that permission was readily granted me, and the upshot of it was that when the *Tampico* slipped down the river from New Orleans, I sailed aboard her.

Once we had passed the bar at the mouth of the Mississippi, we steamed away at full speed; for de Ruiz had urgent instructions to reach Vera Cruz with all possible dispatch. The first night out passed without incident, and I was beginning to enjoy the trip immensely. I do not hesitate to assert that, regardless of what may be said of their colleagues in the army, the commissioned personnel of Mexico's half-dozen gunboats is made up of men who, on the whole, are remarkably likable and intelligent. Had those on board the *Tampico* all been insufferable boors and hopeless morons, the captain's private stores contained the wherewithal, in unlimited quantity and variety, to make us all feel comfortably fraternal.

I confess (with the hope that this may never be read by my wife) to having taken some pains, on our second night out, to avoid belittling hospitality – in bottled form – by refusing it. We expected to raise Vera Cruz sometime the following day, with war and disaster in the immediate offing; so de Ruiz, his *teniente* and I sat in the captain's tiny *salón* until late, smoking and talking, with drinks at respectable intervals.

It may be that I drank too much – although I think not – or it may have been the sultry weather and the closeness of my stuffy little stateroom that caused me to dream as I did, when I finally turned in. At any rate, I dreamed: and rather remarkably.

It seemed that I saw a disorderly group of swarthy men, battering in the door of what I took to be a tomb, or burial crypt. I had the impression that they were Mexicans of the viler sort, and more or less intoxicated, judging from the manner in which they staggered about, and the inefficient way they handled the iron bars with which they finally forced the door.

I saw them drag out a moldy casket and batter it open. What they hoped to find, I could not guess; but when they shattered the coffin and exposed its contents, there appeared to be nothing but a heap of musty bones. But there was something else – one of the villains stooped and held up an object that I could not at first distinguish, but which I presently saw to be a rust-encrusted sword of antique pattern, such as one sees in the shops of dealers in such objects on the Rue Royal, in New Orleans. With evident disgust, the fellow flung the rusty weapon back upon the ground. Then my dream faded into nothingness.

It was hardly daylight when I was awakened by insistent rapping upon the door of my stateroom. When I finally dispelled the cobwebs from my sleepy brain, sufficiently to rise and open the door, my early caller proved to be Captain de Ruiz. I stared at him for a moment, still stupid with sleep, and then it dawned upon me that my friend appeared shaken and distressed, and I hastily bade him enter.

He slumped into a sitting position upon the side of my bunk, while I waited for the explanation of his unseasonal visit. He seemed greatly to have regained his composure since I first opened the door, and hesitant to speak – ashamed, almost.

Then he told me, in exact detail, of a dream from which he had just awakened. And his dream, in every respect, was identical with my own! To be sure, this occasioned me some surprise, but the cause of the renewed agitation when I told him that we had dreamed in duplicate still did not occur to me.

'What's so exciting about it?' I wanted to know. 'It's curious, certainly, but I don't see any reason to be upset.'

'*La espada!*' cried de Ruiz.

'The sword?' I stupidly repeated. Then the light dawned. 'You mean—?'

'The sword of Jean Lafitte,' de Ruiz answered my unspoken question. 'It was my great-grandfather's tomb we saw. *He* has his sword – Lafitte, I mean.'

'Nonsense!' I sharply informed him – partly to cover up my own puzzlement. I was not so very sure, myself.

'I have not the matter-of-factness of you Americans, my friend. Besides, I have heard this tale of the sword of Jean Lafitte too many times from my old Indian nurse – that, and other things. I am absolutely convinced that drunken *revolucionistas* – or drunken *federalistas: quien sabe?* – unearthed the sword last night. Perhaps they thought to find treasure in the tomb. Perhaps—'

He permitted the sentence to remain unfinished; and, after a moody moment, smiled as if in self-ridicule, and lighted a cigarette. His composure seemed quite restored, and he still smiled as I good-naturedly chaffed him about his superstitions. It was still faintly in evidence as he left me, but I noticed that his face was dead-white.

Moodily, I proceeded to dress myself, after first ringing for an orderly to bring me a small cup of black coffee, in the hope of dispelling the weight which seemed to have settled upon my spirits. The coffee heartened me somewhat, and having no desire for further breakfast, I sought the deck to try if the early morning air would not additionally stimulate my mind to cheerful thoughts.

To my dismay, it had precisely the opposite effect. The sulking sun, hardly clear of the horizon, was a murky ball anything but provocative of cheerfulness. The air was still and sultry, and seemed even more depressing on the deck than in the close confines of my meager stateroom.

'I am glad we shall make Vera Cruz this afternoon,' confided Lieutenant Morales, the *Tampico's* second in command. 'I am afraid there is going to be some foul weather. I don't like the looks of things.'

'I don't like it, either,' I muttered; but whether I had reference to the weather, as Morales naturally understood, or to the uneasy and apparently unfounded forebodings that oppressed my mind, I hardly knew myself.

My own unrest, I gradually observed, seemed to be shared quite generally, although nobody else appeared conscious of the pervading air of gloom. I am afraid that most of the officers had imbibed a little too freely the night before – as, indeed, I may have also done – in a last merry fling before facing the serious duties awaiting them. Swollen heads and fuzzy palates would have accounted for their sourness, but nothing of the sort explained the sullen uneasiness with which the members of the crew went about their varied routine. The very atmosphere seemed surcharged with dismal prophecy.

Then, late in the forenoon, with our port but a few scant hours away, it happened.

Lieutenant Morales had just imparted the information that the captain had remained locked in his stateroom all morning, denying entrance to all save his orderly, who reported him to be drinking prodigiously – already hopelessly drunk, in fact. Hardly had the words been uttered, when de Ruiz gave them the lie, by himself appearing on deck. If he was drunk, I thought, he certainly carried his liquor well. There was a noticeable firmness to his step as he strode past where we stood, without appearing to notice us, and climbed the ladder to the bridge.

I noticed that his eyes were unnaturally bright, and Morales directed attention, wonderingly, to a detail even more remarkable, under the circumstances.

'*Porque la espada?*' he asked, of no one in particular.

I also wondered 'why the sword,' now that I observed it hanging at the captain's side. He was in fatique uniform, and just barely disheveled, and the glittering, ornamented weapon looked out of harmony with the rest of his ensemble, had it not been incongruous in the first place.

The nameless, half-formed dread which had oppressed me all morning now seemed stronger than ever, and I had a sudden conviction that my intuition was about to be justified.

'*Mira!*' ejaculated Morales, clutching my arm.

I looked as he bade, and beheld de Ruiz upon the bridge with his gleaming sword drawn, thrusting before him at the empty air. Followed the most remarkable exhibition of swordplay it has ever been my lot to witness. The captain's blade leaped in and out like a thing alive, glittering dully ominous in the grudging rays of the murky sun. Cut and thrust, thrust and parry. While the gaping crew looked on, de Ruiz handled his sword exactly as if it crossed another, held in the hand of a deadly opponent. Yet, the bridge was empty, save for him alone!

From where I watched, spellbound, the captain's pallor was easily discernible, and I could see, also, his clenched teeth, and the desperate set of his jaw. Drunk or sober, it was a deadly serious business to him, at any rate. He seemed to be getting a shade the worst of his imaginary encounter, for he slowly retreated to the bridge ladder, and having gained it, leaped swiftly down upon the deck, after a whirlwind of thrusting that might have been to give him the instant's respite necessary to accomplish the feat in safety.

Swiftly de Ruiz turned, and I distinctly heard his growl of cornered rage, as his sword again leaped up to ward and fend. He was strictly on the defensive, now, and gradually backed to the companion stairs. Inch by inch, step by step, he seemed forced relentlessly backward. Finally, with the same preliminary fury of thrusting that had marked his descent of the bridge ladder, the captain disappeared below.

Officers and crew surged forward to follow, but Morales awoke from the stupefaction into which he had been thrown with the rest of us, at seeing his commander fight an apparently desperate duel with thin air, and hastily posted a couple of marines at the head of the stairway to hold back the crew. Then he fairly leaped down the precarious flight of steps, I immediately behind him, and several officers close upon my heels. We rushed pellmell for the captain's *salón*, where we could hear de Ruiz moving about, swearing with low vehemence that ended, even as we ran, in a sudden, choked groan.

As the lieutenant gained the doorway of the *salón*, he stopped short; so that I almost bowled him over, so close was I behind him. I was taller than he, and could easily see over his shoulder – and what I saw caused me to gape quite as much as he probably was doing.

I have spoken of de Ruiz fighting an *imaginary* duel (and how else was I to describe it?), but I saw him now with head thrown back in agony, his pale face working horribly. With one hand, he strove to support himself against a table at his side; the other hand was clutched above his left breast. It was upon this other hand that my gaze was riveted with horror: for, as his knees buckled under his weight, and he crashed sideways upon the table, I saw that his fingers were red with the unmistakable stain of the blood that welled between them.

Upon the polished mahogany table against which de Ruiz fell was a small bottle, half filled with fiery, colorless tequila, which rocked precariously upon its bottom at the crash. Such is the complexity of the human mind that it takes remarkable cognizance of trifles associated with habit, even when focused upon other and far graver matters. Therefore, as Morales leaped to catch the captain as he slid from the table to the floor, I, quite involuntarily, rescued the half-bottle of tequila, to prevent it spilling and marring the beautiful surface of the table.

The ship's medical officer, who had been in the group at my heels, stepped in and helped Morales turn the captain on his back. His examination was very brief. He spoke to the lieutenant, and Morales sprang from his knees with his face sternly set.

'Someone,' he snapped at the wide-eyed officers grouped about the doorway, 'has taken advantage of circumstances to assassinate Captain de Ruiz in the interval before we followed him below. Señor Montalvo, have the kindness to immediately inform the guards at the companionway that none are to pass them until my further order, and bring me men to conduct a thorough search. In the meantime, the rest of you will patrol the corridor, and permit none to leave or enter. Go!'

Having literally spat out his orders, the lieutenant and the doctor took up the captain's body, and, between them, carried it in and laid it upon the bunk in the adjoining stateroom. With a vague feeling that I also should do something, and there being nothing better at hand, I walked over and picked up de Ruiz's sword from the floor.

As I stooped to recover it, I noticed a second sword, which had escaped attention because it had been thrown well under the table (or had rolled there). Curious, I retrieved the strange weapon, and then felt the hair prickle on the back of my neck. This sensation was not due to the significant stain upon the point, but wholly to something inherent in the sword itself. It was an ancient rapier, and very rusty; of a sort in use a hundred years and more ago.

Shakily I turned toward the door, impelled by I know not what, and saw (or, at least, I *thought* I saw) a shadowy figure in the passage, that made a mocking, significant gesture in my direction, ere it moved on in the direction of the stairway.

With the ancient sword in my hand, I leaped into the passage, bringing a sharp challenge from a guard at the far end. The corridor was absolutely empty, except for that one guard, and he, sauntering up, assured me when questioned that no one else had passed.

None the less, I felt that I had surely seen a face that I had seen before (I never could forget those eyes!), and I had had a fleeting impression of a wide, drooping hat above it, and of a shadowy form draped in a long, weathered, sleeveless cloak. These I remembered, also!

I *knew*, then, that the rotten sword in my hand was the same one I had seen in my dream – the same that poor de Ruiz had seen in *his* dream. The sword of Jean Lafitte!

I cast it through an open porthole, and put out my other hand to steady myself, for my knees felt suddenly and strangely weak. It was then I discovered that I had all along held tight to the tequila bottle. It was a small bottle, and only half full; but tequila is a terribly potent liquid. I didn't care: I was glad of it.

I drained the bottle, almost at a gulp.

Jack's Little Friend

RAMSEY CAMPBELL

As I mentioned in the first part of this collection, no one could be in any doubt about the continuing influence of the legend of Jack the Ripper. Indeed, as I write these notes in the winter of 1993, controversy is raging over the latest book claiming to 'solve' the mystery of Jack's identity. In The Diary of Jack the Ripper, *the Liverpool cotton merchant, James Maybrick, who was poisoned by his wife in 1889, is said to have been the writer of the* Diary *in which he confesses to the Ripper's crimes. Like so many books before – and so many of the suspects – the* Diary *has its supporters and its detractors, all of whom help to add a little more frisson to the whole mystery surrounding the mass killer. Among the recent short stories to deal with the legend, 'Jack's Little Friend' by Ramsey Campbell is by far the most ingenious, and in its tale of demonic possession supports my theme of the continuance of evil. Liverpool-born Ramsey is among the very best writers of horror fiction in Britain today, having skillfully developed his craft during the past quarter of a century since his first Lovecraftian pastiches were published while he was still a teenager. The following tale is another example of why his work has been so widely praised – 'He is the nearest thing we have to an heir to M.R. James,' The* Times *declared recently – and also won so many awards. The reasons are there to see in the following pages . . .*

IT'S AFTERNOON WHEN you find the box. You're in the marshes on the verge of the Thames below London. Perhaps you live in the area, perhaps you're visiting, on business or on holiday. You've been walking. You've passed a power station and its expressionless metallic chord, you've skirted a flat placid field of cows above which black smoke pumps from factory chimneys. Now reeds smear your legs with mud, and you might be proposing to turn back when you see a corner of metal protruding from the bearded mud.

You make your way toward it, squelching. It looks chewed by time, and you wonder how long it's been there. Perhaps it was dumped here recently; perhaps it was thrown out by the river; possibly the Thames, belaboring and dragging the mud, uncovered the box. As the water has built the box a niche of mud so it has washed the lid, and you can make out dates scratched on the metal. They are almost a century old. It's the dates that provoke your curiosity, and perhaps also a gesture against the dull landscape. You stoop and pick up the box, which frees itself with a gasp of mud.

Although the box is only a foot square it's heavier than you anticipated. You skid and regain your balance. You wouldn't be surprised if the box were made of lead. If anyone had thrown it in the river they would certainly have expected it to stay sunk. You wonder why they would have bothered to carry it to the river or to the marshes for disposal. It isn't distinguished, except for the dates carved on the lid by an illiterate or clumsy hand – just a plain box of heavy grey metal. You read the dates:

31/8/1888
8/9/1888
30/9/1888
9/11/1888

There seems to be no pattern. It's as if someone had been trying to work one out. But what kind of calculation would be resolved by throwing away a metal box? Bewildered though you are, that's how you read the clues. What was happening in 1888? You think you read somewhere that expeditions were returning from Egypt around that date. Have you discovered a lost archaeological find? There's one way to know. But your fingers slip off the box, which in any case is no doubt locked beneath its coat of mud, and the marsh is seeping into your shoes; so you leave off your attempts to open the lid and stumble away, carrying the box.

By the time your reach the road your excitement has drained somewhat. After all, someone could have scratched the dates on the lid last week; it could even be an understated practical joke. You don't want to take a heavy box all the way home only to prise from its depths a piece of paper saying APRIL FOOL. So you leave the box in the grass at the side of the road and search until you find a metal bar. Sorry if I'm aborting the future of archaeology, you think, and begin to lever at the box.

But even now it's not as easy as you thought. You've wedged the box and can devote all your energy to shifting the lid, but it's fighting you. Once it yields an inch or two and then snaps shut again. It's as if it were being held shut, like the shell of a clam. A car passes on the other side of the road and you begin to give in to a sense of absurdity, to the sight of yourself struggling to jemmy open an old box. You begin to feel like a tourist's glimpse. Another car, on your side this time, and dust sweeps into your face. You blink and weep and cough violently, for the dust seems to have been scooped into your mouth. Then the sensation of dry crawling in your mouth recedes, and only the skin beneath your tongue feels rough. You wipe your eyes and return to the box. And then you drop the bar, for the box is wide open.

And it's empty. The interior is as dull as the exterior. There's nothing, except on the bottom a thin glistening coat of what looks like saliva but must be marsh water. You slam the lid. You memorize the dates and walk away, rolling your tongue around the floor of your mouth, which still feels thick, and grinning wryly. Perhaps the hitch-hiker or whoever finds the box will conceive a use for it.

That night you're walking along a long dim street toward a woman. She seems to be backing away, and you can't see her face. Suddenly, as you rush toward her, her body opens like an anemone. You plunge deep into the wet red fronds.

The dream hoods your brain for days. Perhaps it's the pressure of work or of worry, but you find yourself becoming obsessive. In crowds you halt, thinking of the dates on the box. You've consulted such books as you have immediate access to, but they didn't help. You stare at the asymmetrical faces of the crowd. Smoke rises from their mouths or their jaws work as they drive forward, pulled along by their set eyes. Imagine asking them to help. They wouldn't have touched the box, they would have shuffled on by, scattering their waste paper and condoms. You shake your head to dislodge the crawling thoughts. You aren't usually so misanthropic. You'll have to find out what those dates mean. Obviously your brain won't give you much peace until you do.

So you ask your friend, the one who knows something about history. And your friend says 'That's easy. They're the dates of Jack the Ripper,' and tells you that the five murders everyone accepts as the Ripper's work were committed on those dates. You can't help smiling, because you've just had a flash of clarity: of course you must have recognized the dates subconsciously from having read them somewhere, and the recognition was the source of your dream. Then your friend says 'Why are you interested?'

You're about to answer, but your tongue sticks to the floor of your mouth for a moment, like the lid of the box. In that moment you think: why should your friend want to know anyway? They've no right to know, they aren't entitled to a fee for the consultation. You found the box, you'll conduct the enquiry. 'I must have read the dates somewhere,' you say. 'They've been going round in my head and I couldn't remember why.'

On the way home you play a game with yourself. No, that bus shelter's no good, too open. Yes, he could hide in that alley, there would be hardly any light where it bends in the middle. You stop, because the skin beneath your tongue is rough and sore, and hinders your thoughts. You explore the softness beneath your tongue with one finger, and as you do so the inflammation seems to draw into itself and spare you.

Later you ponder Jack the Ripper. You've read about him, but when you leaf through your knowledge you realize you're not so well informed. How did he become the Ripper? Why did he stop? But you know that these questions are only your speculations about the box, disguised.

It's inconvenient to go back to find the box, but you manage to clear yourself the time. When you do think at first you've missed the place where you left the box. Eventually you find the bar, but the box has gone. Perhaps someone kicked it into the hedges. You search among the cramped roots and trapped crisp-bags until your mouth feels scraped dry. You could tell the local police, but then you would have to explain your interest, and they would take the credit for themselves. You don't need the box. Tomorrow you'll begin to research.

And so you do, though it's not as easy as you expected. Everyone's fascinated by the Ripper these days, and the library books are popular. You even have to buy a paperback of one of them, glancing sideways as you do so at the people browsing through the book. The sunlight glares in the cracks and pores and fleshy bags of their faces, giving them a sheen like wet wax: wax animated by simple morbid fascination. You shudder and hurry away. At least you have a reason for reading the book, but these others haven't risen above the level of the mob that gloated squirming over reports of the Ripper's latest killing. You know how the police of the time must have felt.

You read the books. You spread them across the table, comparing

269

accounts. You're not to be trapped into taking the first one you read as definitive. Your friends, and perhaps your spouse or lover as well, joke and gently rebuke you about your singlemindedness. No doubt they talk about it when you're not there. Let them. Most people seem content to relive, or elaborate, the second-hand. Not you.

You read. 31/8/1988: throat cut twice, head nearly severed, disembowelled twice. 8/9/1888: handkerchief wrapped around almost severed neck, womb missing, intestines cast over shoulder, relatively little blood in the yard where the corpse was found. 30/9/1988: two women, one with windpipe severed; the other, less than an hour later, with right eye damaged, earlobe cut off, intestines over shoulder, kidney and entrails missing. 9/11/1888: throat cut, ears and nose missing, also liver, and a mass of flesh and organs on the bedside table. There's a photograph of her in one book. You stare at it for a moment, then you slam the book and stare at your hands.

But your hands are less real than your thoughts. You think of the Ripper, cutting and feeling his way through the corpses, taking more time and going into more detail with each murder. The last one took two hours, the books tell you. A question is beginning to insist on an answer. What was he looking for?

You aren't sleeping well. You stare at the lights that prick your eyeballs behind your lids and theorize until you topple wakefully into sleep. Sometimes you seem almost to have found a pattern, and you gasp in crowds or with friends. They glance at you and you meet their gaze coldly. They wouldn't be capable of your thoughts, and you certainly don't intend to let them hinder you. But even as their dull gaze falls away you realize that you've lost the inspiration, if indeed it were one.

So you confine yourself to your home. You're glad to have an excuse to do so, for recently you've been growing hypersensitive. When you're outside and the sunlight intensifies it's as though someone were pumping up an already white-hot furnace, and the night settles around you like water about a gasping fish. So you draw the curtains and read the books again.

The more you read the stranger it seems. You feel you could understand the man if a missing crucial detail were supplied. What can you make of his macabre tenderness in wrapping a handkerchief around the sliced throat of Annie Chapman, his second victim? A numbed denial of his authorship of the crime, perhaps? If there were relatively little blood in the yard then surely the blood must have soaked into the Ripper's clothes, but in that case how could he have walked home in broad daylight? Did he cut the windpipe of Elizabeth Stride because he was interrupted before he was able to do more, or because she had seen too much for him simply to leave her and seek a victim elsewhere? An hour later, was it his frustration that led him to mutilate Catherine Eddowes more extensively and inventively than her predecessors? And why did he wait almost twice as long as hitherto before committing his final murder, that of Mary Kelly, and the most detailed? Was this the exercise of a powerful will, and did the frustration build up to an unprecedented climax? But what frustration? What was he looking for?

You turn to the photograph of Mary Kelly again, and this time you're able to examine it dispassionately. Not that the Victorian camera was able to be particularly explicit. In fact, the picture looks like a piece of early adolescent pornography on a wall, an amateur blob for a face and a gaping darkness between the legs. You suck your tongue, whose underside feels rough and dry.

You read the Ripper's letters. The adolescent wit of the rhymes often gives way to the childish illiteracy of some of the letters. You can understand his feelings of superiority to the victims and to the police; they were undoubtedly at least as contemptible as the people you know. But that doesn't explain the regression of the letters, as if his mind were flinching back as far as possible from his actions. That's probably a common trait of psychopaths, you think: an attempt to reject the part of them that commits the crimes.

Your mind is still frowning. You read through the murders again. First murder, nothing removed. Second, the womb stolen. Third, kidney and entrails stolen. A portion of kidney which had been preserved in spirits was sent to the police, with a note saying that the writer had eaten the rest. Fourth, the liver removed and the ears and nose, but the womb and a three-month-old fetus untouched. Why? To sate the hunger which motivated the killings, presumably, but what hunger was that? If cannibalism, surely he would never have controlled himself sufficiently to preserve a portion of his food with which to taunt the police? If not, what worse reality was he disguising from the police, and perhaps from himself, as cannibalism?

You swallow the saliva that's pooling under your tongue and try to grasp your theories. It's as if the hunger spat out the kidney. Not literally, of course. But it certainly seems as if the Ripper had been trying

271

to sate his hunger by varying the delicacies, as if it were a temperamental pet. Surely the death of Mary Kelly couldn't have satisfied it for good, though.

Then you remember the box. If he had externalized the hunger as something other than himself, could his mind have persuaded him that the hunger was alive independent of him and might be trapped? Could he have used one of the portions of Mary Kelly as a lure? Would that have seemed a solution in the grotesque algebra of his mind? Might he have convinced himself that he had locked his hunger away in time, and having scratched the dates on the box to confirm his calculations have thrown it in the river? Perhaps the kidney had been the first attempted lure, insufficiently tempting. And then – well, he could hardly have returned to a normal life, if indeed he had left one, but he might have turned to the socially acceptable destruction of alcoholism and died unknown.

The more you consider your theory the more persuasive it becomes. Perhaps you can write it up as an article and sell it somewhere. Of course you'll need to pursue your research first. You feel happy in a detached unreal way, and you even go to your companion willingly for the first time in, now you think about it, a long while. But you feel apart from the moist dilation of flesh and the hard dagger thrust, and are glad when it's over. There's something at the back of your mind you need to coax forward. When you've dealt with that you'll be able to concentrate on other things.

You walk toward her. The light is flickering and the walls wobble like a fairground corridor. As you approach her, her dress peels apart and her body splits open. From within the gap trails a web toward which you're drawn. At the center of the web hangs a piece of raw meat.

Your cry wakes you but not your companion. Their body feels like burning rubber against you, and you flinch away. After a minute you get out of bed. You can't stand the sensation, and you want to shake off the dream. You stare from the window; the darkness is paling, and a bird sings tentatively. Suddenly you gasp. You'll write that article now, because you've realized what you need. You can't hope to describe the Ripper or even to meet a psychopath for background. But there's one piece of first-hand research you can do that will help you to understand the Ripper. You don't know why you didn't read your dream that way at once.

Next day you begin searching. You read all the cards you can find in shop windows. They aren't as numerous or as obvious as you expected. You don't want to find yourself actually applying for a course of French lessons. You suppose there are magazines that would help you, but you're not sure where to find them. At last, as the streets become grimmer, you notice a group of young men reading cards in a shop window. They nudge each other and point to several of the cards, then they confer and hurry toward a phone box. You're sure this time.

You choose one called Marie, because that was what Mary Kelly used to call herself. No particular reason, but the parallel seems promising. When you telephone her she sounds dubious. She asks what you want and you say 'Nothing special. Just the usual.' Your voice may be disturbing her, because your tongue is sticking somehow to the floor of your mouth, which feels swollen and obstructive. She's silent for a moment, then she says 'All right. Come up in twenty minutes,' and tells you where she is.

You hadn't realized it would be as swift as that. Probably it's a good thing, because if you had to wait much longer your unease might find you excuses for staying away. You emerge from the phone box and the sunlight thuds against your head. Your mouth is dry, and the flesh beneath your tongue is twitching as if an insect has lodged there. It must be the heat and the tension. You walk slowly toward your rendezvous, which is only a few streets away. You walk through a maze of alleys to keep in the shade. On either side of you empty clothes flap, children shout and barks run along a chain of dogs.

You reach your destination on time. It's in a street of drab shops: a boarded betting shop, a window full of cardigans and wool, a Chinese take-away. The room you want is above the latter. You skid on trodden chips and shielding your face from the eyes of the queue next door, ring the bell.

As you stare at the new orange paint on the door you wonder what you're going to say. You have some idea and surely enough money, but will she respond to that? You understand some prostitutes refuse to talk rather than act. You can hardly explain your interest in the Ripper. You're still wondering when she opens the door.

She must be in her thirties, but her face has aged like an orange and she's tried to fill in the wrinkles, probably while waiting for you. Her eyelashes are like unwashed black paint-brushes. But she smiles slightly,

273

as if unsure whether you want her to, and then sticks out her tongue at a head craning from next door. 'You rang before,' she says, and you nod.

The door slams behind you. Your hand reaches blindly for the latch; you can still leave, she'll never be able to pursue you. Beneath your tongue a pulse is going wild. If you don't go through with this now it will be more difficult next time, and you'll never be rid of the Ripper or of your dreams. You follow her upstairs.

Seeing her from below you find it easy to forget her smile. Her red dress pulls up and her knickers, covered with whorls of color like the eye of a peacock's tail, alternately bulge and crease. The hint of guilt you were beginning to feel retreats: her job is to be on show, an object, you need have no compunction. Then you're at the top of the stairs and in her room.

There are thick red curtains, mauve walls, a crimson bed and telephone, a color TV, a card from Ibiza and one from Rhyl. Behind a partition you can see pans and knives hanging on hooks in the kitchen area. Then your gaze is wrenched back to her as she says 'Go on then, tell me your name, you know mine.'

Of course you don't. You're not so stupid as to suppose she would display her real name in the window. You shake your head and try to smile. But the garish thick colors of the room are beginning to weigh on you, and the trapped heat makes your mouth feel dry, so that the smile comes out soured.

'Never mind, you don't have to,' she says. 'What do you want? Want me to wear anything?'

Now you have to speak or the encounter will turn into a grotesque misunderstanding. But your tongue feels as if it's glued down, while beneath it the flesh is throbbing painfully. You can feel your face prickling and reddening, and rooted in the discomfort behind your teeth a frustrated disgust with the whole situation is growing.

'Are you shy? There's no need to be,' she says. 'If you were really shy you wouldn't have come at all, would you?' She stares into the mute struggle within your eyes and smiling tentatively again, says 'Can't you talk?'

Yes, you can talk, it's only a temporary obstruction. And when you shift it you'll tell her that you've come to use her, because that's what she's for. An object, that's what she's made herself. Inside that crust of makeup there's nothing. No wonder the Ripper sought them out.

274

You don't need compassion in a slaughterhouse. You try to control your raw tongue, but only the throbbing beneath it moves.

'I'm sorry, I'm only upsetting you. Never mind, love,' she says. 'Nerves are terrible, I know. You sit down and I'll get you a drink.'

And that's when you have to act, because your mouth is filling with saliva as if a dam has burst, and your tongue's still straining to raise itself, and the turgid colors have insinuated themselves into your head like migraine, and tendrils of uneasiness are streaming up from your clogged mouth and matting your brain, and at the core of all this there's a writhing disgust and fury that this woman should presume to patronize you. You don't care if you never understand the Ripper, so long as you can smash your way out of this trap. You move toward the door, but at the same time your hand is beckoning her, it seems quite independent of you. You haven't reached the door when she's in front of you, her mouth open and saying 'What?' And you do the only thing that seems, in your blind violent frustration, available to you.

You spit into her open mouth.

For a moment you feel free. Your mouth is clean and your tongue can move as you want it to. The colors have retreated, and she's just a well-meaning rather sad woman using her talents as best she can. Then you realize what you've done. Now your tongue's free you don't know what to say. You think perhaps you could explain that you sneezed. Perhaps she'll accept that, if you apologize. But by this time she's already begun to scream.

You were so nearly right most of the time. You realized that the stolen portions of Mary Kelly might have been placed in the box as a lure. If only you'd appreciated the implications of this: that the other mutilations were by no means the act of a maniac, but the attempts of a gradually less sane man to conceal the atrocities of what possessed him. Who knows, perhaps it had come from Egypt. He couldn't have been sure of its existence even when he lured it into the box. Perhaps you'll be luckier, if that's luck, although now you can only stand paralyzed as the woman screams and screams and falls inertly to the floor, and blood begins to seep from her abdomen. Perhaps you'll be able to catch it as it emerges, or at least to see your little friend.

Was Crippen a Murderer?

ANTHONY BERKELEY

Apart from being arguably the most famous killer of the twentieth century, Dr Hawley Harvey Crippen is also the only murderer whose name has passed into the language as an expletive. And if we accept the premise of the next few pages he may not even have been guilty at all. The story of the American-born doctor who was hanged at Pentonville Gaol on 23 November, 1910 for the murder of his wife has been told in numerous books, stories and films. His love for his mistress, Ethel le Neve, and the arrest of the runaway lovers on board the SS Montrose bound for Canada where le Neve was so ill-fittingly disguised as a boy as to excite the attention of the ship's captain, is the unique element of the case which has kept the public's interest alive. That and the puzzling facts about Crippin and the circumstances of his wife's death which Anthony Berkeley examines here. Berkeley, one of England's most distinguished mystery writers and a man who so shunned personal publicity that his own life is shrouded in secrecy, is also well-known for having created the outrageous detective Roger Sheringham and founded London's famous Detective Club. The case of Dr Crippen clearly fascinated Berkeley and its influence is to be found in his novels, Malice Aforethought *(1931) about a doctor who murders his wife; and* Before the Fact *(1932) in which a husband seems bent on poisoning his wife. (This story was filmed by Alfred Hitchcock in 1941 starring Cary Grant). Berkeley wrote 'Was Crippen a Murderer?' in 1937 as part of a series,* Great Unsolved Crimes.

IT IS IRONICAL that the name of the man who, of all the classical murderers, was the least certainly guilty, should have become almost a synonym for the word 'murderer.' It is no less ironical that a man whose chief characteristics were his kindness and gentle charm should be remembered only as an inhuman monster.

Few murder cases have remained as famous as that of unfortunate little Hawley Harvey Crippen. Many people to-day have never heard of Seddon, whose case, within a year or two of Crippen's, aroused almost as much interest at the time; yet who is there even now who does not think he knows all about Crippen?

In point of fact he knows very little about Crippen: not even the most important thing of all, namely the very great possibility, amounting almost to probability, that Crippen never committed murder at all.

At the time of his tragedy Hawley Crippen was nearly fifty years old. Here is an interesting point for a beginning. I have never seen any statistics regarding the age of murderers, but one would be inclined to say off-hand that few are as old as this.

If murder is in the blood, it will come out before half a century. Moreover Crippen's alleged crime was one of passion. Is not fifty a little late in life to begin committing murder for love? We may bear the point in mind later.

Crippen is usually referred to as 'Dr.' Actually, he was not a qualified medical man. He underwent a sketchy kind of training in his own country (he was a native of Michigan, U.S.A.) and in 1883 when he was twenty-one years old, paid a visit to London where he attended several London hospitals in a haphazard way.

The only degree he ever achieved was a diploma in 1883 as an ear and eye specialist at the Ophthalmic Hospital in New York, which may or may not have given him the right to call himself a 'doctor,' but certainly did not make him one. In view of the profession he was practising in London at the time of his wife's death, this point will also become important.

After obtaining his diploma, Crippen practised during the next fifteen years at a variety of places, including Detroit, Santiago, Salt Lake City, New York, Philadelphia, and Toronto, never staying more than two years in any of them; though whether this was due to restlessness of disposition or inability to make a living, we do not know,

In 1887 he married for the first time; his wife died three or four years later leaving a son who, at the time of his father's trial, was living in California. In 1893 he fell in love with a young girl who was not too young to have acquired a bad reputation even at the age of seventeen. This girl passed under the name of Cora Turner. Her mother was a German and her father a Russian Pole, and her real name was Kunigunde Mackamotzki; so that Cora Turner was certainly a change towards simplicity.

Crippen married her and, in 1900, brought her to London, when he obtained the post of manager of the English branch of a patent medicine firm.

If Crippen really did murder his wife, it cannot be denied that Mrs. Crippen almost brought the deed upon herself. She was not a pleasant woman. Possessed of an almost pathologically swollen vanity, she fancied herself for honours on the music-hall stage; at one time, indeed, she expected to bring the world to her feet in grand opera, though her voice was no better than that of any of the young women who, at that time, used to sing ballads in the drawing-room after supper.

In any case, arrived in London, Cora Crippen made all preparations to take it by storm. She chose the stage name of 'Belle Elmore,' she laid in a huge stock of expensive gowns, she joined the Music-hall Ladies' Guild, she did in fact everything except make a success on the stage; for she only appeared on it once, and was then promptly hissed off it by the audience.

Soured by this reception, and the impossibility of obtaining another engagement, Mrs. Crippen proceeded to take it out of the indulgent little husband who had paid for all the gowns, the singing-lessons, the agents' fees, and everything else: for at this time Crippen adored his shrewish wife, believing in her talents when no one else did.

She hen-pecked him unmercifully, quarrelled with him, insulted him before his friends, and did not draw the line at assuaging her wounded vanity with the attentions, and more than the attentions, of other men.

In short, Cora Crippen did what so many stupid, shrewish wives have done before her and literally drove her amiable little husband out of love with her.

And to drive out of love with his wife a man who has been accustomed to love is tantamount to driving him into the arms of another woman. Mrs. Crippen drove her husband into the arms of a typist at his office, Ethel Le Neve.

All this, of course, took time. It was 1900 when the Crippens came to London; it was 1910 when Cora Crippen died; and during those ten years there is no doubt that Crippen's home life was becoming more and more intolerable. Between him and Miss Le Neve there sprang up a love which, on Crippen's side at any rate, was to prove stronger than the fear of death.

And then Mrs. Crippen died.

There is no need to give the events which followed in any close detail, for they are still well known. Crippen made blunder after blunder – so incredibly foolish that there is surely some inference to be drawn from that very foolishness. He pawned his wife's jewellery quite openly; some of it he gave to Miss Le Neve, and let her wear it openly; he had even bought the hyoscin from which his wife was to die quite openly from a chemist who knew him well and had signed the book in his own name.

If these were indeed the acts of a deliberate murderer, then surely a more stupid murderer never existed. I suggest that they were not the acts of a deliberate murderer.

Then, by this small detail and that, an inaccuracy here and there, suspicion was aroused among Mrs. Crippen's friends; information was lodged at Scotland Yard, and a Detective-Inspector went to Hilldrop Crescent to interview Crippen.

The Inspector viewed the visit as a formality; Crippen's demeanour confirmed his expectation that it was all nothing but a mare's nest. But three days later a small point took the Inspector up to Hilldrop Crescent again – and Crippen had fled. If Crippen had stood his ground then, neither you nor I would ever have heard of him.

The events that followed roused the excitement of two continents. It was not merely a case of an insignificant little man being wanted for wife murder; every romantic ingredient was present to turn the affair into the greatest of all classical murder hunts.

There was the identification of the pair on the liner *Montrose* by means of the new-fangled wireless telegraphy; there was the fact that Ethel Le Neve was disguised as a boy; there was the fact that the dead wife's body had been not merely buried under the cellar floor, but dismembered first – and dismemberment invariably rouses the public's horror; there was the dramatic chase of the *Montrose* across the Atlantic by Inspector Dew in a faster boat, with the eyes of the whole world on the race except only those of the *Montrose*'s own passengers; there was the love affair which had caused the whole tragedy; and there was finally, the character of Crippen himself as it began to leak out – a gentle, affectionate, mild, precise little man in late middle age, the last little man in the whole world, one would have said, to commit a callous and inhuman murder.

Inspector Dew did reach America first. Crippen was arrested on the *Montrose* when she docked, brought back to England, tried, condemned and hanged. On the evidence before them the jury could have returned no other verdict. Miss Le Neve, tried separately as an accessory after the fact, was acquitted. The letters Crippen wrote to her from prison as he awaited execution are among the most touching documents ever penned.

What, then, is the truth? How can it be asserted, in face of these facts, that Crippen never did commit murder? What considerations, pointing to this conclusion, never came before the jury at all?

It is always easy to argue, on one side or the other. Facts alone can determine truth; and there is one fact in Crippen's case which appears to me insurmountable, in the absence of any greater facts to confute it.

Unfortunately, however, it is a fact of psychology; and psychology, even psychological fact, carries little or no weight in a court of law. Evidence may be given as to character, but it influences little but the sentence. And yet it is character that determines action.

The insurmountable fact is this: there is overwhelming evidence that Crippen was mild, gentle and kindly – and mild, gentle, kindly men simply do not commit murder. That is surely incontrovertible. One does not remain gentle and throwing off the mask, reveal oneself kindly for forty-eight years and then, suddenly as a fiend.

That elementary fact of psychology has been recognised for at least two thousand years. It is, after all, a long time since the rule was laid down that *nemo fuit repente turpissimus* (no one ever became vile all of a sudden). And there is no evidence that Crippen ever slid at all down the path of vileness; it is just assumed that he took in one single bound.

Admit that one psychological fact, if to prove no more than that there is something queer behind the scenes here, and instantly the whole case becomes full of difficulties.

Take, for instance, the choice of poison. Very little was known in 1910 about hyoscin, or henbane. It had never been used in a case of murder. It was, I fancy, not even in the British Pharmacopoeia. Why did Crippen choose it?

Consider Crippen's profession. He was not a bona fide doctor, nor did he practice as such. He filled a succession of posts in firms concerned with patent medicines. Almost up to his last moments he was engaged in compiling a formula for a patent medicine of his own, to be called *Sans Peine*.

He was, in fact, used to dealing with drugs, but not in the way of the recognised prescriptions: he was used to experimenting with them.

Now put these two considerations together, and look at them in the light of a very curious piece of evidence which was certainly never put forward at the trial, for it was not known then. This evidence takes us from an insignificant villa in London to no less a place than the Royal Palace in St. Petersburg, Russia.

It has been reliably established that, at just about the sane time as Crippen was dabbling with hyoscin here, the Court Magician, or Conjurer, at St. Petersburg, a man named Papus, was dosing the Tsar and Tsarina with a mixture of hyoscin and hashish, which was said to produce singularly pleasing effects, the admixture of hashish having been found to neutralise much of the toxic properties of hyoscin. What does this give us? It shows us that at this time, the quacks of Europe were experimenting with hyoscin, of which all they knew for certain was that it had properties as a narcotic. And Crippen was a quack.

This seems not only to offer a possible explanation of Crippen's very puzzling choice of a drug; but it goes some way, too, to suggest that his intention was not murderous. That suggestion is more than strengthened by the absence of any concealment of the purchase – the last thing, surely, that one would expect with a guilty intention.

Now, it is a theory of my own that dismemberment seldom enters into any plan of calculated murder. That is to say, when dismemberment occurs it almost amounts to proof that murder had not been planned ahead, and shows that the killing was, if not accidental, at any rate decided only on the spur of the moment.

But a poisoning is never decided on the spur of the moment. Therefore a poisoning, followed by dismemberment, which in turn is followed only by ordinary burial, and not by some such method as a piecemeal burning of the body, carries all the appearances of unexpected instead of expected death.

If, further, we admit dismemberment as indicative of an absence of plan, we see more and more evidence to the same effect. When obvious blunder after obvious blunder is made the conclusion is difficult to resist that nothing was thought out in advance.

Yet the use of poison for purposes of murder is equally strong evidence of premeditated planning. The only way of reconciling these opposing factors in the case of Crippen is that he did not intend to kill with his poison.

What, then, did he intend to do?

The late Sir Edward Marshall Hall, who believed strongly in Crippen's innocence, propounded a theory to answer this question which seems to me from every point of view convincing. It was his belief that Crippen, knowing of hyoscin only as a narcotic, used it upon his wife, not with any intention of killing her, but in order to put her into a drugged sleep so that he could spend the evening with Miss Le Neve.

This, I think, is what must have happened. But Crippen, in his ignorance, either administered an overdose or perhaps mixed his hyoscin with some agent which did not neutralise it sufficiently. In any case he discovered that he had killed instead of drugged, and lost his head. For plainly he did lose his head. Crippen was not of the stuff of which murderers are made.

There is, actually, a piece of evidence supporting this theory which came out at the trial, though its significance was missed then. On the night before her death Mrs. Crippen had some friends in, who left at about midnight. At Miss Le Neve's trial her landlady gave evidence that one night at the end of January Miss Le Neve came home very late in a state of considerable distress, quite horror-stricken, in fact, as if she had suffered a great shock, and the time mentioned was *two o'clock in the morning*. Mrs. Crippen died on January 31. If Crippen had intended to murder his wife he would not have had Miss Le Neve in the house at the time. If Miss Le Neve was in the house, it may be almost certainly said that murder was not intended.

All these considerations convince me that Crippen was innocent of premeditated murder. That he was responsible for his wife's death is, of course, indubitable, and the defence he adopted, of a blank denial of every thing, was the worst possible one. At worst he was guilty only of manslaughter.

Why, then, did he not make a clean breast of the facts and plead manslaughter, or even accident?

The answer to that question is one of the most striking features of the whole case. He was in fact pressed to do this, but he refused. His reason was that to substantiate his plea he would have to admit that Miss Le Neve was in the house that night; and, if anything went wrong with the case and the jury did bring in a verdict of murder, this might have been prejudicial to Miss Le Neve.

He was almost assured of an acquittal from the murder charge if he permitted this defence, but on the quite slender danger of entangling Miss Le Neve he decided upon almost certain death for himself.

I always feel very sorry for Crippen. He has been dreadfully maligned. I cannot believe that he was a monster. Certainly he was, as the late Lord Birkenhead said of him, 'a brave man and a true lover.'

Darling Adolf

RAY BRADBURY

The evil influence of Adolf Hitler and Nazism are still a major factor in the world today almost half a century after the horrors they perpetrated on mankind were ostensibly brought to an end. Admirers of the Führer and his infamous Third Reich are said to be growing in numbers throughout Europe in the wake of increasing political unrest and the growth of racism, and many commentators are worried that the lessons of the Second World War are already being forgotten or ignored by the latest generations. Certainly the interest in Hitler has never been greater: there is a constant flow of books examining his life and the activities of the Reich under his leadership. But there are plenty of writers who are also very concerned about this influence, as American's foremost living writer of fantasy and science fiction, Ray Bradbury, extemporizes in this next story, 'Darling Adolf'. Utilising the background of the making of yet another film about Hitler, Ray makes all too evident the terrible power that is still inherent in the man's name and what he stood for. 'Darling Adolf' may well be the most salutory tale in this whole collection . . .

THEY WERE WAITING for him to come out. He was sitting inside the little Bavarian café with a view of the mountains, drinking beer, and he had been in there since noon and it was now two-thirty, a long lunch, and much beer, and they could see by the way he held his head and laughed and lifted one more stein with the suds fluffing in the spring breeze that he was in a grand humor now, and at the table with him the two other men were doing their best to keep up, but had fallen long behind.

On occasion their voices drifted on the wind, and then the small crowd waiting out in the parking lot leaned to hear. What was he saying? and now what?

'He just said the shooting was going well.'

'What, where?!'

284

'Fool. The film, the film is shooting well.'

'Is that the director sitting with him?'

'Yes. And the other unhappy one is the producer.'

'He doesn't look like a producer.'

'No wonder! He's had his nose changed.'

'And him, doesn't he look *real*?'

'To the hair and the teeth.'

And again everyone leaned to look in at the three men, at the man who didn't look like a producer, at the sheepish director who kept glancing out at the crowd and slouching down with his head between his shoulders, shutting his eyes, and the man between them, the man in the uniform with the swastika on his arm, and the fine military cap put on the table beside the almost-untouched food, for he was talking, no, making a speech.

'That's the Führer, all right!'

'God in heaven, it's as if no time had passed. I don't believe this is 1973. Suddenly it's 1934 again, when first I saw him.'

'Where?'

'The Nuremberg Rally, the stadium, that was the autumn, yes, and I was thirteen and part of the Youth and one hundred thousand soldiers and young men in that big place that late afternoon before the torches were lit. So many bands, so many flags, so much heartbeat, yes, I tell you, I could hear one hundred thousand hearts banging away, we were all so in love, he had come down out of the clouds. The gods had sent him, we knew, and the time of waiting was over, from here on we could *act*, there was nothing he couldn't *help* us to do.'

'I wonder how that actor in there feels, playing him?'

'Sh, he hears you. Look, he waves. Wave back.'

'Shut up,' said someone else. 'They're talking again. I want to hear—'

The crowd shut up. The men and women leaned into the soft spring wind. The voices drifted from the café table.

Beer was being poured by a maiden waitress with flushed cheeks and eyes as bright as fire.

'More beer!' said the man with the toothbrush mustache and the hair combed forward on the left side of his brow.

'No, thanks,' said the director.

'No, no,' said the producer.

'More beer! It's a splendid day,' said Adolf. 'A toast to the film, to us, to me. Drink!'

The other two men put their hands on their glasses of beer.

'To the film,' said the producer.

'To darling Adolf.' The director's voice was flat.

The man in the uniform stiffened.

'I do not look upon myself—' he hesitated, 'upon *him* as darling.'

'He was darling, all right, and you're a doll.' The director gulped his drink. 'Does anyone mind if I get drunk?'

'To be drunk is not permitted,' said Der Führer.

'Where does it say that in the script?'

The producer kicked the director under the table.

'How many more weeks' work do you figure we have?' asked the producer, with great politeness.

'I figure we should finish the film,' said the director, taking huge swigs, 'around about the death of Hindenburg, or the *Hindenburg* gasbag going down in flames at Lakehurst, New Jersey, whichever comes first.'

Adolf Hitler bent to his plate and began to eat rapidly, snapping at his meat and potatoes in silence.

The producer sighed heavily. The director, nudged by this, calmed the waters. 'Another three weeks should see the masterwork in the can, and us sailing home on the *Titanic*, there to collide with the Jewish critics and go down bravely singing "*Deutschland Uber Alles*."'

Suddenly all three were voracious and snapping and biting and chewing their food, and the spring breeze blew softly, and the crowd waited outside.

At last, Der Führer stopped, had another sip of beer, and lay back in his chair, touching his mustache with his little finger.

'Nothing can provoke me on a day like this. The rushes last night were so beautiful. The casting for this film, ah! I find Göring to be incredible. Goebbels? Perfection!' Sunlight dazzled out of Der Führer's face. 'So. So, I was thinking just last night, here I am in Bavaria, me, a pure Aryan—'

Both men flinched slightly, and waited.

'—making a film,' Hitler went on, laughing softly, 'with a Jew from New York and a Jew from Hollywood. So amusing.'

'I am not amused,' said the director, lightly.

The producer shot him a glance which said: the film is not finished yet. Careful.

'And I was thinking, wouldn't it be fun . . .' Here Der Fuhrer

286

stopped to take a big drink,' . . . to have another . . . ah . . . Nuremberg Rally?'

'You mean for the *film*, of course?'

The director stared at Hitler. Hitler examined the texture of the suds in his beer.

'My God,' said the producer, 'do you know how much it would cost to reproduce the Nuremberg Rally? How much did it cost Hitler for the original, Marc?'

He blinked at his director, who said, 'A bundle. But he had a lot of free extras, of course.'

'Of course! The Army, the Hitler Youth.'

'Yes, yes,' said Hitler. 'But think of the publicity, all over the world? Let us go to Nuremberg, eh, and film my plane, eh, and me coming down out of the clouds? I heard those people out there, just now: Nuremberg and plane and torches. *They* remember. *I* remember. I held a torch in that stadium. My God, it was beautiful. And now, now I am exactly the age Hitler was when he was at his prime.'

'He was never at his prime,' said the director. 'Unless you mean hung-meat.'

Hitler put down his glass. His cheeks grew very red. Then he forced a smile to widen his lips and change the color of his face. 'That is a joke, of course.'

'A joke,' said the producer, playing ventriloquist to his friend. 'I was thinking,' Hitler went on, his eyes on the clouds again, seeing it all, back in another year. 'If we shot it next month, with the weather good. Think of all the tourists who would come to watch the filming!'

'Yeah. Bormann might even come back from Argentina.'

The producer shot his director another glare.

Hitler cleared his throat and forced the words out: 'As for expense, if you took one small ad, *one* mind you! in the Nuremberg papers one week before, why, you would have an army of people there as extras at fifty cents a day, no, a quarter, no, *free!*'

Der Führer emptied his stein, ordered another. The waitress dashed off to refill. Hitler studied his two friends.

'You know,' said the director, sitting up, his own eyes taking a kind of vicious fire, his teeth showing as he leaned forward, 'there is a kind of idiot grace to you, a kind of murderous wit, a sort of half-ass style. Every once in a while you come dripping up with some sensational slime that gleams and stinks in the sun, buster. Archie, *listen* to him.

287

Der Führer just had a great bowel movement. Drag in the astrologers! Slit the pigeons and filch their guts. Read me the casting sheets.'

The director leaped to his feet and began to pace.

'That *one* ad in the paper, and all the trunks in Nuremberg get flung wide! Old uniforms come out to cover fat bellies! Old armbands come out to fit flabby arms! Old military caps with skull-eagles on them fly out to fit on fat-heads!'

'I will not sit here—' cried Hitler.

He started to get up but the producer was tugging his arm and the director had a knife at his heart: his forefinger, stabbing hard.

'Sit.'

The director's face hovered two inches from Hitler's nose. Hitler slowly sank back, his cheeks perspiring.

'God, you *are* a genius,' said the director. 'Jesus, your people *would* show up. Not the young, no, but the old. All the Hitler youth, your age now, those senile bags of tripe yelling "*Sieg Heil*," saluting, lighting torches at sunset, marching around the stadium crying themselves blind.'

The director swerved to his producer.

'I tell you, Arch, this Hitler here has bilge for brains but this time he's on target! If we don't shove the Nuremberg Rally *up* this film, I quit. I mean it. I will simply walk out and let Adolf here take over and direct the damned thing himself! Speech over.'

He sat down.

Both the producer and Der Führer appeared to be in a state of shock.

'Order me another goddamn beer,' snapped the director.

Hitler gasped in a huge breath, tossed down his knife and fork, and shoved back his chair.

'I do not break bread with such as you!'

'Why, you bootlicking lapdog son of a bitch,' said the director. 'I'll hold the mug and you'll do the licking. Here.' The director grabbed the beer and shoved it under Der Führer's nose. The crowd, out beyond, gasped and almost surged. Hitler's eyes rolled, for the director had seized him by the front of his tunic and was yanking him forward.

'Lick! Drink the German filth! Drink, you scum!'

'Boys, boys,' said the producer.

'Boys, crud! You know what this swill-hole, this chamberpot Nazi, has been thinking, sitting here, Archibald, and drinking your beer? Today Europe, tomorrow the world!'

'No, no, Marc!'

'No, no,' said Hitler, staring down at the fist which clenched the material of his uniform. 'The buttons, the buttons—'

'Are loose on your tunic and inside your head, worm. Arch, look at him pour! Look at the grease roll off his forehead, look at his stinking armpits. He's a sea of sweat because I've read his mind! Tomorrow the world! Get this film set up, him cast in the lead. Bring him down out of the clouds, a month from now. Brass bands. Torchlight. Bring back Leni Reifenstahl to show us how she shot the Rally in '34. Hitler's lady-director friend. Fifty cameras she used, fifty she used, by God, to get all the German crumbs lined up and vomiting lies, and Hitler in his creaking leather and Göring awash in his blubber, and Goebbels doing his wounded-monkey walk, the three superfags of history aswank in the stadium at dusk, make it all happen again, with this bastard up front, and do you know what's going through his little graveyard mind behind his bloater eyes at this very moment?'

'Marc, Marc,' whispered the producer, eyes shut, grinding his teeth. 'Sit down. Everyone sees.'

'Let them see! Wake up, you! Don't you shut your eyes on me, too! I've shut my eyes on you for days, filth. Now I want some attention. Here.'

He sloshed beer on Hitler's face, which caused his eyes to snap wide and his eyes to roll yet again, as apoplexy burned his cheeks.

The crowd, out beyond, hissed in their breath.

The director, hearing, leered at them.

'Boy, is this funny. They don't know whether to come in or not, don't know if you're real or not, and neither do I. Tomorrow, you bilgy bastard, you really dream of becoming Der Führer.'

He bathed the man's face with more beer.

The producer had turned away in his chair now and was frantically dabbing at some imaginary breadcrumbs on his tie. 'Marc, for God's sake—'

'No, no, seriously, Archibald. This guy thinks because he puts on a ten-cent uniform and plays Hitler for four weeks at good pay that if we actually put together the Rally, why Christ, History would turn back, oh turn back, Time, Time in thy flight, make me a stupid Jew-baking Nazi again for tonight. Can you see it, Arch, this lice walking up to the microphones and shouting, and the crowd shouting back, and him *really* trying to take over, as if Roosevelt still lived and Churchill wasn't six feet deep, and it was all to be lost or won again, but mainly won, because *this* time they wouldn't stop at the Channel but just cross on over, give or take a million German boys dead, and stomp England and stomp America, isn't *that* what's going on inside your little Aryan skull, Adolf? *Isn't* it!'

Hitler gagged and hissed. His tongue stuck out. At last he jerked free and exploded:

'Yes! Yes, goddamn you! Damn and bake and burn you! You dare to lay hands on Der Führer! The Rally! Yes! It must be in the film! We must make it again! The plane! The landing! The long drive through streets. The blonde girls. The lovely blond boys. The stadium. Leni Reifenstahl! And from all the trunks, in all the attics, a black plague of armbands winging on the dusk, flying to assault, battering to take the victory. Yes, yes, I, Der Führer, I will stand at that Rally and dictate terms!

He was on his feet now.

The crowd, out beyond in the parking lot, shouted.

Hitler turned and gave them a salute.

The director took careful aim and shot a blow of his fist to the German's nose.

After that the crowd arrived, shrieking, yelling, pushing, shoving, falling.

They drove to the hospital at four the next afternoon

Slumped, the old producer sighed, his hands over his eyes. 'Why, why, why are we going to the hospital? To visit that— monster?'

The director nodded.

The old man groaned. 'Crazy world. Mad people. I never saw such biting, kicking, biting. That mob almost killed you.'

The director licked his swollen lips and touched his half-shut left eye with a probing finger. 'I'm okay. The important thing is I hit Adolf, oh, how I hit him. And now—' He stared calmly ahead. 'I think I am going to the hospital to finish the job.'

'Finish, *finish*?' The old man stared at him.

'Finish.' The director wheeled the car slowly around a corner. 'Remember the twenties, Arch, when Hitler got shot at in the street and not hit, or beaten in the streets, and nobody socked him away for-ever, or he left a beer hall ten minutes before a bomb went off, or was in that officers' hut in 1944 and the briefcase bomb exploded and *that* didn't get him. Always the charmed life. Always he got out from under

290

the rock. Well, Archie, no more charms, no more escapes. I'm walking in that hospital to make sure that when that half-ass extra comes out and there's a mob of krauts to greet him, he's walking wounded, a permanent soprano. Don't try to stop me, Arch.'

'Who's stopping? Belt him one for me.'

They stopped in front of the hospital just in time to see one of the studio production assistants run down the steps, his hair wild, his eyes wilder, shouting.

'Christ,' said the director. 'Bet you forty to one, our luck's run out again. Bet you that guy running toward us says—'

'Kidnapped! Gone!' the man cried. 'Adolf's been taken away!'

'Son of a bitch.'

They circled the empty hospital bed; they *touched* it.

A nurse stood in one corner wringing her hands. The production assistant babbled.

'Three men it was, three men, three men.'

'Shut up.' The director was snowblind from simply looking at the white sheets. 'Did they force him or did he go along quietly?'

'I don't know, I can't say, yes, he was making speeches, making speeches as they took him out.'

'Making speeches?' cried the old producer, slapping his bald pate. 'Christ, with the restaurant suing us for broken tables, and Hitler maybe suing us for—'

'Hold on.' The director stepped over and fixed the production assistant with a steady gaze. '*Three* men, you say?'

'Three, yes, three, three, three, oh, three men.'

A small forty-watt lightbulb flashed on in the director's head.

'Did, ah, did one man have a square face, a good jaw, bushy eyebrows?'

'Why . . . yes!'

'Was one man short and skinny like a chimpanzee?'

'Yes!'

'Was one man big, I mean, slobby fat?'

'How did you *know*?'

The producer blinked at both of them. 'What goes on? What—'

'Stupid attracts stupid. Animal cunning calls to laughing jackass cunning. Come on, Arch!'

'Where?' The old man stared at the empty bed as if Adolf might materialize there any moment now.

'The back of my car, quick!'

From the back of the car, on the street, the director pulled a German cinema directory. He leafed through the character actors. 'Here.'

The old man looked. A forty-watt bulb went on in his head.

The director riffled more pages. 'And here. And, finally, here.'

They stood now in the cold wind outside the hospital and let the breeze turn the pages as they read the captions under the photographs.

'Goebbels,' whispered the old man.

'An actor named Rudy Steihl.'

'Göring.'

'A hambone named Grofe.'

'Hess.'

'Fritz Dingle.'

The old man shut the book and cried to the echoes.

'Son of a bitch!'

'Louder and funnier, Arch. Funnier and louder.'

'You mean right now out there somewhere in the city three dumbkopf out-of-work actors have Adolf in hiding, held maybe for ransom? And do we *pay* it?'

'Do we want to finish the film, Arch?'

'God, I don't know, so much money already, time, and—' The old man shivered and rolled his eyes. 'What if – I mean – what if they don't *want* ransom?'

The director nodded and grinned. 'You mean, what if this is the true start of the Fourth Reich?'

'All the peanut brittle in Germany might put itself in sacks and show up if they knew that—'

'Steihl, Grofe, and Dingle, which is to say, Goebbels, Göring, and Hess, were back in the saddle with dumbass Adolf?'

'Crazy, awful, mad! It couldn't happen!'

'Nobody was ever going to clog the Suez Canal. Nobody was ever going to land on the Moon. Nobody.'

'What do we do? This waiting is horrible. Think of something, Marc, think, think!'

'I'm thinking.'

'And—'

This time a hundred-watt bulb flashed on in the director's face. He sucked air and let out a great braying laugh.

'I'm going to help them organize and speak up, Arch! I'm a genius. Shake my hand!'

He seized the old man's hand and pumped it, crying with hilarity, tears running down his cheeks.

'You, Marc, on their side? helping form the Fourth Reich!?'

The old man backed away.

'Don't hit me, help me. Think, Arch, think. What was it Darling Adolf said at lunch, and damn the expense! What, what?'

The old man took a breath, held it, exploded it out, with a final light blazing in his face.

'Nuremberg?' he asked.

'Nuremberg! What month is this, Arch?'

'October!'

'October! October, forty years ago, October, the big, big Nuremberg Rally. And this coming Friday, Arch, an Anniversary Rally. We shove an ad in the international edition of *Variety*: RALLY AT NUREMBERG. TORCHES. BANDS. FLAGS. Christ, he won't be able to stay away. He'd shoot his kidnappers to be there and play the greatest role in his life!'

'Marc, we can't afford—'

'Five hundred and forty-eight bucks? For the ad plus the torches plus a full military band on a phonograph record? Hell, Arch, hand me that phone.'

The old man pulled a telephone out of the front seat of his limousine.

'Son of a bitch,' he whispered.

'Yeah.' The director grinned, and ticked the phone. 'Son of a bitch.'

The sun was going down beyond the rim of Nuremberg Stadium. The sky was bloodied all across the western horizon. In another half-hour it would be completely dark and you wouldn't be able to see the small platform down in the center of the arena, or the few dark flags with the swastikas put up on temporary poles here or there making a path from one side of the stadium to the other. There was a sound of a crowd gathering, but the place was empty. There was a faint drum of band music but there was no band.

Sitting in the front row on the eastern side of the stadium, the director waited, his hands on the controls of a sound unit. He had been waiting for two hours and was getting tired and feeling foolish. He could hear the old man saying:

293

'Let's go home. Idiotic. He won't come.'

And himself saying, 'He will. He must,' but not believing it.

He had the records waiting on his lap. Now and again he tested one, quietly, on the turntable, and then the crowd noises came from lily-horns stuck up at both ends of the arena, murmuring, or the band played, not loudly, no, that would be later, but very softly. Then he waited again.

The sun sank lower. Blood ran crimson in the clouds. The director tried not to notice. He hated nature's blatant ironies.

The old man stirred feebly at last and looked around.

'So this was the place. It was really *it*, back in 1934.'

'This was it. Yeah.'

'I remember the films. Yes, yes. Hitler stood – what? Over there?'

'That was it.'

'And all the kids and men down there and the girls there, and fifty cameras.'

'Fifty, count 'em, fifty. Jesus, I would have liked to have been here with the torches and flags and people and cameras.'

'Marc, Marc, you don't *mean* it?'

'Yes, Arch, sure! So I could have run up to Darling Adolf and done what I did to that pig-swine half-ass actor. Hit him in the nose, then hit him in the teeth, then hit him in the *blinis*! You *got* it, Leni? Action! *Swot*! Camera! *Bam*! Here's one for Izzie. Here's one for Ike. Cameras running, Leni? Okay. *Zot*! Print!'

They stood looking down into the empty stadium where the wind prowled a few newspapers like ghosts on the vast concrete floor.

Then, suddenly, they gasped.

Far up at the very top of the stadium a small figure had appeared.

The director quickened, half rose, then forced himself to sit back down.

The small figure, against the last light of the day, seemed to be having difficulty walking. It leaned to one side, and held one arm up against its side, like a wounded bird.

The figure hesitated, waited.

'Come on,' whispered the director.

The figure turned and was about to flee.

'Adolf, no!' hissed the director.

Instinctively, he snapped one of his hands to the sound-effects tape deck, his other hand to the music.

The military band began to play softly.

The 'crowd' began to murmur and stir.

Adolf, far above, froze.

The music played higher. The director touched a control knob. The crowd mumbled louder.

Adolf turned back to squint down into the half-seen stadium. Now he must be seeing the flags. And now the few torches. And now the waiting platform with the microphones, two *dozen* of them! *one* of them real.

The band came up in full brass.

Adolf took one step forward.

The crowd roared.

Christ, thought the director, looking at his hands, which were now suddenly hard fists and now again just fingers leaping on the controls, all to themselves. Christ, what do I do with him when I get him down here? What, *what*?

And then, just as insanely, the thought came. Crud. You're a director. And that's *him*. And this *is* Nuremberg.

So . . .?

Adolf took a second step down. Slowly his hand came up in a stiff salute.

The crowd went wild.

Adolf never stopped after that. He limped, he tried to march with pomp, but the fact was he limped down the hundreds of steps until he reached the floor of the stadium. There he straightened his cap, brushed his tunic, resaluted the roaring emptiness, and came gimping across two hundred yards of empty ground toward the waiting platform.

The crowd kept up its tumult. The band responded with a vast heartbeat of brass and drum.

Darling Adolf passed within twenty feet of the lower stands where the director sat fiddling with the tape-deck dials. The director crouched down. But there was no need. Summoned by the '*Sieg Heils*' and the fanfare of trumpets and brass, Der Führer was drawn inevitably toward that dais where destiny awaited him. He was walking taller now and though his uniform was rumpled and the swastika emblem torn, and his mustache moth-eaten and his hair wild, it was the old Leader all right, it was him.

The old producer sat up straight and watched. He whispered. He pointed.

Far above, at the top of the stadium, three more men had stepped into view.

My God, thought the director, that's the team. The men who grabbed Adolf.

A man with bushy eyebrows, a fat man, and a man like a wounded chimpanzee.

Jesus. The director blinked. Goebbels. Goring. Hess. Three actors at liberty. Three half-ass kidnappers staring down at . . .

Adolf Hitler climbing up on the small podium by the fake microphones and the real one under the blowing torches which bloomed and blossomed and guttered and smoked on the cold October wind under the sprig of lilyhorns which lifted in four directions.

Adolf lifted his chin. That did it. The crowd went absolutely mad. Which is to say, the director's hand, sensing the hunger, went mad, twitched the volume high so the air was riven and torn and shattered again and again and again with '*Sieg Heil, Sieg Heil, Sieg Heil!*'

Above, high on the stadium rim, the three watching figures lifted their arms in salute to their Führer.

Adolf lowered his chin. The sounds of the crowd faded. Only the torch flames whispered.

Adolf made his speech.

He must have yelled and chanted and brayed and sputtered and whispered hoarsely and wrung his hands and beat the podium with his fist and plunged his fist at the sky and shut his eyes and shrieked like a disemboweled trumpet for ten minutes, twenty minutes, half an hour as the sun vanished beyond the earth and the three other men up on the stadium rim watched and listened and the producer and the director waited and watched. He shouted things about the whole world and he yelled things about Germany and he shrieked things about himself and he damned this and blamed that and praised yet a third, until at last he began to repeat, and repeat the same words over and over as if he had reached the end of a record inside himself and the needle was fastened to a circle track which hissed and hiccuped, hiccuped and hissed, and then faded away at last into a silence where you could only hear his heavy breathing, which broke at last into a sob and he stood with his head bent while the others now could not look at him but looked only at their shoes or the sky or the way the wind blew dust across the field. The flags fluttered. The single torch bent and lifted and twisted itself again and talked under its breath.

At last, Adolf raised his head to finish his speech.

'Now I must speak of them.'

He nodded up to the top of the stadium where the three men stood against the sky.

'They are nuts. I am nuts, too. But at least I know I am nuts. I told them: crazy, you are crazy. Mad, you are mad. And now, my own craziness, my own madness, well, it has run itself down. I am tired.

'So now, what? I give the world back to you. I had it for a small while here today. But now you must keep it and keep it better than I would. To each of you I give the world, but you must promise, each of you to keep your own part and work with it. So there. Take it.'

He made a motion with his free hand to the empty seats, as if all the world were in his fingers and at last he were letting it go.

The crowd murmured, stirred, but said nothing loud.

The flags softly tongued the air. The flames squatted on themselves and smoked.

Adolf pressed his fingers onto his eyeballs as if suddenly seized with a blinding headache. Without looking over at the director or the producer, he said, quietly:

'Time to go?'

The director nodded.

Adolf limped off the podium and came to stand below where the old man and the younger director sat.

'Go ahead, if you want, again, hit me.'

The director sat and looked at him. At last he shook his head.

'Do we finish the film?' asked Adolf.

The director looked at the producer. The old man shrugged and could find nothing to say.

'Ah well,' said the actor. 'Anyway, the madness is over, the fever has dropped. I have *made* my speech at Nuremberg. God, look at those idiots up there. Idiots!' he called suddenly at the stands. Then back to the director, 'Can you think? They wanted to hold me for ransom. I told them what fools they were. Now I'll go tell them again. I had to get away from them. I couldn't stand their stupid talk. I had to come here and be my own fool in my own way for the last time. Well . . .'

He limped off across the empty field, calling back quietly:

'I'll be in your car outside, waiting. If you want, I am yours for the final scenes. If not, no, and that ends it.'

The director and the producer waited until Adolf had climbed to the top of the stadium. They could hear his voice drift down, cursing those other three, the man with the bushy eyebrows, the fat man, and the ugly chimpanzee, calling them many things, waving his hands. The three backed off and went away, gone.

Adolf stood alone high in the cold October air.

The director gave him a final lift of the sound volume. The crowd, obedient, banged out a last '*Seig Heil.*'

Adolf lifted his free hand, not into a salute, but some sort of old, easy, half-collapsed mid–Atlantic wave. Then he was gone, too.

The sunlight went with him. The sky was no longer bloodcolored. The wind blew dust and want-ads from a German paper across the stadium floor.

'Son of a bitch,' muttered the old man. 'Let's get out of here.'

They left the torches to burn and the flags to blow, but shut off the sound equipment.

'Wish I'd brought a record of Yankee Doodle to march us out of here,' said the director.

'Who needs records. We'll whistle. Why not?'

'Why not'

He held the old man's elbow going up the stairs in the dusk, but it was only halfway up, they had the guts to try to whistle.

And then it was suddenly so funny they couldn't finish the tune.

A Bride in the Bath

PETER LOVESEY

George Joseph Smith was the bigamist who preyed on defenceless women during the early years of this century and was subsequently tried in 1915 in a case that has become famous as the 'Brides in the Bath' murders. He was also one of the first killers to leave a courtroom with the expletive 'Crippin!' ringing in his ears from the packed public galleries. Smith was an unmitigated rogue who married, successively, three young women, each of whom died mysteriously in their baths. It was the perception of the father of the last of these brides who saw similarities between his daughter's death and his son-in-law's two earlier tragedies that alerted the police and finally led Smith to trial. The hearing at the Old Bailey also revealed that Smith had married each of the women bigamously, for he was actually still married to a certain Beatrice Thornhill whom he had wed in 1898. The horrific details of how Smith had drowned each of his brides as they lay soaking in their baths made headlines around the world and earned him the death sentence on the fateful day of Friday the Thirteenth in August 1915. Peter Lovesey has made a speciality of crime and mystery novels set in the Victorian era – in particular the cases of Sergeant Cribb which recently formed the basis of a popular television series, Cribb, *starring Alan Dobie – as well as a number of outstanding short stories featuring famous killers such as William Corder, the Red Barn murderer, and George Joseph Smith whose evil* modus operandi *is at work again in the following pages . . .*

'SORRY, DARLING. I mean to have my bath and that's the end of it!' With a giggle and a swift movement of her right hand, Melanie Lloyd closed the sliding door of her bathroom. The catch fastened automatically with a reassuring click. Her husband William, frustrated on the other side, had installed the gadget himself. 'None of your old-fashioned bolts or keys for us,' he had announced, demonstrating it a week before the wedding. 'The door secures itself when you slide it across from the inside. You can move it with one finger, you see, but once closed, it's as safe as your money in the bank.'

She felt between her shoulders for the tab of her zipper. William could wait for her. Sit in bed and wait while she had a leisurely bath. What was the purpose of a luxurious modern bathroom if not to enjoy a bath at one's leisure. William, after all, had spent *weeks* before the wedding modernizing it. 'Everything but the kitchen sink,' he had joked. 'Mixer taps, spray attachment, separate shower, bidet, heated towel rails, and built-in cupboards. You shall bathe like a queen, my love. Like a queen.'

Queenly she had felt when she first stepped through the sliding door and saw what he had prepared for her. It was all there exactly as he had promised, and more. Ceramic mosaic tiles. Concealed lighting. Steam-proof mirrors. And the floor – wantonly impractical! – carpeted in white, with a white fur rug beside the bath. There was also a chair, an elegant antique chair, over which he had draped a full-length lace negligee. 'Shameless Victoriana,' he had whispered. 'Quite out of keeping with contemporary design, but I'm incurably sentimental.' Then he had kissed her.

In that meeting of lips she had shed her last doubts about William, those small nagging uncertainties that would probably never have troubled her if Daddy had not kept on so. 'I'm old-fashioned, I know, Melanie, but it seems to me an extraordinarily short engagement. *You* feel that you know him, I've no doubt, but he's met your mother and me only once – and that was by accident. The fellow seemed downright evasive when I questioned him about his background. It's an awkward thing to do, asking a man things like that when he's damned near as old as you are, but, hang it, it's a father's right to know the circumstances of the man who proposes marrying his daughter, even if he is past fifty. Oh, I've nothing against his age; there's plenty of successful marriages on record between young women and older men. Nothing we could do to stop you, or would. You're over twenty-one and old enough to decide such things for yourself. The point is that he knew why I was making my inquiries. I wasn't probing his affairs from idle curiosity. I had your interests at heart, damn it. If the fellow hasn't much behind him, I'd be obliged if he'd say so, so that I can make a decent contribution. Set you both up properly. I would, you know. I've never kept you short, have I? Wouldn't see you come on hard times for anything in the world. If only the fellow would make an honest statement . . .'

One didn't argue with Daddy. It was no use trying to talk to him about self-respect. Every argument was always swept aside by that familiar outpouring of middle-class propriety. God, if anything drove her into William Lloyd's arms, Daddy did!

She stepped out of the dress and hung it on one of the hooks provided on the wall of the shower compartment. Before removing her slip she closed the Venetian blind; not that she was excessively modest, nor, for that matter, that she imagined her new neighbors in Bismarck Road were the sort who looked up at bathroom windows. The plain fact was that she was used to frosted glass. When she and William had first looked over the house – it seemed years ago, but it could only have been last April – the windows, more than anything else, had given her that feeling of unease. There were several in the house – they had been common enough in Victorian times when the place was built – small oblong frames of glass with frostwork designs and narrow stained-glass borders in deep red and blue.

They would have to come out, she decided at once, if William insisted on living there. They seemed so out of keeping, vaguely ecclesiastical, splendid in a chapel or an undertaker's office, but not in *her* new home. William agreed at once to take them out – he seemed so determined to buy that one house. 'You won't recognize the place when I've done it up. I'll put a picture window in the bathroom. The old frames need to come out anyway. The wood's half-rotten outside.' So the old windows went and the picture window, a large single sheet of glass, replaced them. 'Don't worry about ventilation,' William assured her. 'There's an exhaust fan built in above the cabinet there.' He had thought of everything.

Except frosted glass. She *would* have felt more comfortable behind frosted glass. But it wasn't *contemporary*, she supposed. William hadn't consulted her, anyway. He seemed to know about these things. And there *were* the Venetian blinds, pretty plastic things, so much more attractive than the old brown pelmet they replaced.

She fitted the plug and ran the water. Hot and cold came together from a lion's-head tap; you blended the water by operating a lever. Once you were in the bath you could control the intake of water with your foot, using a push-button mechanism. What would the first occupants of 9 Bismarck Road, eighty years ago, have thought of that?

Melanie reviewed the array of ornamental bottles on the shelf above the taps. Salts, oils, crystals, and foam-baths were prodigally provided.

She selected an expensive bath oil and upended the bottle, watching the green liquid dispersed by the cascading water. Its musky fragrance was borne up on spirals of steam. How odd that William should provide all this and seem unwilling for her to use it! Each evening since Monday, when they had returned from the honeymoon, she had suggested she might take a bath and he had found some pretext for discouraging her. It didn't matter *that* much to her, of course. At the hotel in Herne Bay she had taken a daily bath, so she didn't feel desperately in need of one immediately they got back. It was altogether too trivial to make an issue of, she was quite sure. If William and she *had* to have words some time, it wasn't going to be about bath nights, at any rate. So she had played the part of the complaisant wife and fallen in with whatever distractions he provided.

Tonight, though, she had deliberately taken him by surprise. Nightie and book she had hidden in the towel chest earlier in the day, so when she hesitated at the head of the stairs as they came to bed he was quite unprepared. You don't go for a late-night bath empty-handed, even when your bathroom has every convenience known to the modern home designer. She was sliding the bathroom door across before he realized what had happened. 'Sorry, darling. I mean to have my bath and that's the end of it!'

The door slid gently across on its runners and clicked, the whole movement perfectly timed, without a suspicion of haste, as neatly executed as a pass in the bull-ring. That was the way to handle an obstructive husband. Never mind persuasion and pleading; intelligent action was much more dignified, and infinitely more satisfying. Besides, she *had* waited till Friday.

She tested the water with her hand, removed her slip, took her book and plastic shower cap from the towel chest, shook her mass of flaxen hair, and then imprisoned it in the cap. She turned, saw herself unexpectedly in a mirror, and pulled a comical face. If she had remembered, she would have brought a face-pack – the one thing William had overlooked when he stocked the cosmetic shelf. She wasn't going into the bedroom to collect one now, anyway. She took off the last of her underclothes and stepped into the bath.

It was longer than the bath at home or the one in the hotel. Silly, really: neither William nor she was tall, but they had installed a 6 foot 6 inch bath – 'Two metres, you see,' the salesman had pointed out, as though that had some bearing on their requirements. Over the years it would probably use gallons more hot water, but it was a beautiful shape — made for luxuriating — with the back at the angle of a deck chair on the lowest notch, quite unlike the utility five-footer at home, with its chipped sides and overhanging geyser that allowed you enough hot water to cover your knees and no more. William had even insisted on a sunken bath. 'It will sink to four inches below floor level, but that's the limit, I'm afraid, or we'll see the bottom of it through the kitchen ceiling.'

Accustomed to the temperature now, she pressed the button with her toe for more hot water. There was no hurry to rise from this bath. It wouldn't do Mr. William Lloyd any harm to wait. Not simply from pique, of course; she felt no malice toward him at all. No, there was just a certain deliciousness — a man wouldn't understand it even if you tried to explain — in taking one's time. Besides, it was a change, a relief if she was honest, to enjoy an hour of solitude, a break from the new experience of being someone's partner, accountable for every action in the day from cooking a dinner to clipping one's toenails.

She reached for a book — one she had found on William's bookshelf with an intriguing title, *Murder is Methodical*. Where better to read a thriller than in a warm bath behind a locked door? There hadn't been much opportunity for reading in the last three weeks. Or before, for that matter, with curtains to make and bridesmaids to dress.

She turned to the first page. Disappointing. It was not detective fiction at all. Just a dreary old manual on criminology. 'William Palmer: the Rugeley Poisoner' was the first chapter. She thumbed the pages absently. 'Dr. Crippen: a Crime in Camden Town.' How was it that these monsters continued to exert such a fascination on people, years after their trials and executions? The pages fell open at a more whimsical title — from her present position, anyway — 'George Joseph Smith: the Brides in the Baths.'

Melanie smiled. That chapter ought to have a certain piquancy, particularly as one of the first place names to catch her eye was Herne Bay. Strange how very often one comes across a reference to a place soon after visiting there. With some slight stirring of interest she propped the book in the chromium soap holder that bridged the sides of the bath, dipped her arms under the water, leaned back and began to read.

George Joseph Smith had stayed in Herne Bay, but not at the New Excelsior. Wise man! If the food in 1912 was anything like the apologies for cuisine they dished up these days, he and his wife were far better off at the house they took in the High Street. But it wasn't really a honeymoon the Smiths – or the Williamses, as they called themselves – spent at Herne Bay, because they had been married two years before and he had deserted her soon after, only to meet her again in 1912 on the prom. at Weston-super-Mare. In May they had come to Herne Bay and on July 8th they made mutual wills. On July 9th, Smith purchased a new five-foot bath. Bessie, it seemed, decided to take a bath on the 12th, a Friday. At 8:00 a.m. next morning a local doctor received a note: 'Can you come at once? I am afraid my wife is dead.' On July 16th she was buried in a common grave, and Smith returned the bath to the supplier, saying he did not require it after all. Smith inherited £2,500.

£2,500. That must have been worth a lot in 1912. More, almost certainly, than the £5,000 policy William had taken out on her life. Really, when she considered it, the value of money declined so steadily that she doubted whether £5,000 would seem very much when they got it in 1995, or whenever it was. They might do better to spend the premiums now on decorating some of the rooms downstairs. Super to have a luxury bathroom, but they would have to spend a lot to bring the other rooms up to standard. 'Insurance policies are security,' William had said. 'You never know when we might need it.'

Well, security seemed important to him, and she could understand why. When you'd spent your childhood in an orphanage, with not a member of your family in the least interested in you, security was not such a remarkable thing to strive for. So he should have his insurance – it was rather flattering, anyway, to be worth £5,000 – and the rest of the house would get decorated in due course.

There was another reason for insurance which she did not much like to think about. For all his energy and good looks William was fifty-six. When the policy matured he would be over eighty, she fifty-two. No good trying to insure him; the premiums would be exorbitant.

For distraction she returned to the book and read of the death of Alice Burnham in Blackpool in 1913. Miss Burnham's personal fortune had amounted to £140, but the resourceful George Joseph Smith had insured her life for a further £500. She had drowned in her bath a month after her wedding, on a Friday night in December. Strange, that Friday night again! Really, it was exquisitely spine-chilling to be sitting in one's bath on a Friday night reading such things, even if they had happened half a century ago.

The Friday bath night, in fact, she learned as she read on, was an important part of Smith's infamous system. Inquest and funeral were arranged before there was time to make contact with the relatives, even when he wrote to them on the Saturday. Alice Burnham, like Bessie Mundy, was buried in a common grave early the following week. 'When they're dead, they're dead,' Smith had explained to his landlord.

Melanie shuddered slightly and looked up from the book. The appalling callousness of the murderer was conveyed with extraordinary vividness in that remark of his. For nearly twenty years he had exploited impressionable girls for profit, using a variety of names, marrying them, if necessary, as unconcernedly as he seduced them, and disappearing with their savings. In the early encounters, those who escaped being burdened with a child could consider themselves fortunate; his later brides were lucky if they escaped with their lives.

It was reassuring for a moment to set her eyes on her modern bathroom, its white carpet and ceramic tiles. Modern, luxurious, and *civilized*. Smith and his pathetic brides inhabited a different world. What kind of bathroom had those poor creatures met their fates in? She had a vision of a cheap tin bath set on cold linoleum and filled from water jugs, illuminated by windows with colored-glass panels. Not so different, she mused, from the shabby room William had converted – transformed, rather – for her into this dream of a modern bathroom. Lying back in the water, she caught sight of the cornice William had repainted, highlighting the molding with gold paint. So like him to preserve what he admired from the past and reconcile it with the strictly contemporary.

Friday night! She cupped some water in her hands and wetted her face. George Joseph Smith and his crimes had already receded enough for her to amuse herself with the thought that his system would probably work just as well today as it did in 1914. The postal service hadn't improved much in all those years. If, like Daddy, you insisted on living without a telephone, you couldn't get a letter in Bristol before Monday to say that your daughter had drowned in London on Friday evening.

How dreadfully morbid! More hot water with the right toe and back to the murders, quite remote now. When had Smith been tried and executed. – 1915 – well, her own William had been alive then, if only a baby. Perhaps it wasn't so long. Poor William, patiently waiting for her to come to bed. It wouldn't be fair to delay much longer. How many pages to go?

She turned to the end to see, and her eyes were drawn at once to a paragraph describing the medical evidence at Smith's trial. 'The great pathologist, Sir Bernard Spilsbury, stated unequivocally that a person who fainted while taking a bath sitting in the ordinary position would fall against the sloping back of the bath. If water were then taken in through the mouth or nose it would have a marked stimulating effect and probably make the person recover. There was no position, he contended, in which a person could easily become submerged in fainting. A person standing or kneeling might fall forward on the face and then might easily be drowned. Then, however, the body would be lying face downward in the water. The jury already knew that all three women had been found lying on their backs, for Smith's claim that Miss Lofty was lying on her side was nonsense in view of the size of the bath at Bismarck Road.'

Bismarck Road! Melanie jerked up in the water and read the words again. Extraordinary. God, how horrible! It couldn't possibly be. She snatched up the book and turned back the pages, careless of her wet hands. There it was again! 'Margaret made her will and bequeathed everything, nineteen pounds (but he had insured her life for £700) to her husband. Back at Bismarck Road, Highgate, a bath was installed that Friday night. Soon after 7:30 the landlady, who was ironing in her kitchen, heard splashes from upstairs and a sound which might have been wet hands being drawn down the side of the bath. Then there was a sigh. Shortly after, she was jolted by the sound of her own harmonium in the sitting room. 'Mr. John Lloyd,' alias George Joseph Smith, was playing *Nearer, My God, to Thee*.

Mr. John Lloyd! Mr. John *Lloyd*. That name. Was it possible? William said he knew nothing of his parents. He had grown up in the orphanage. A foundling, he said, with nothing but a scrap of paper bearing his name; abandoned, apparently, by his mother in the summer of 1915. The summer, she now realized, of the trial of George Joseph Smith, alias John Lloyd, the deceiver and murderer of women. It was too fantastic to contemplate. Too awful . . . An unhappy coincidence. She refused to believe it.

But William – what if he believed it? Rightly or wrongly believed himself the son of a murderer? Might that belief have affected his mind, become a fixation, a dreadful, morbid urge to re-live George Joseph Smith's crimes?

It would explain all those coincidences: the honeymoon in Herne

Bay; the insurance policy; the house in Bismarck Road; the new bath. Yet he had tried to keep her from having a bath, barred the way, as if unable to face the last stage of the ritual. And tonight she had tricked him and she was there, a bride in the bath. And it was Friday.

Melanie's book fell in the water and she sank against the back of the bath and fainted. An hour later her husband, having repeatedly called her name from outside the bathroom, broke through the sliding door and found her. That, at any rate, was the account William Lloyd gave of it at the inquest. She had fainted. Accidental death. A pity Sir Bernard Spilsbury could not have been in court to demonstrate that it was impossible. Even in a two-meter bath.

Forget–Me–Not

BERNARD TAYLOR

*The name Christie and the address 10, Rillington Place, are enough
to bring a shiver to all those who were alive when this middle-aged mass
murderer and sexual psychopath butchered at least six women to death
in the early fifties. The extraordinary events in the case of John
Reginald Halliday Christie began when he allowed Timothy Evans,
another tenant of the building in which they both lived in Notting Hill
Gate, to be hanged for a murder he himself had committed. Christie's
own guilt was not in fact exposed until he had left Rillington Place and
a new tenant in his former flat discovered the bodies of three women
behind a papered-over cupboard. A police search revealed another female
corpse under the floorboards and two more in the garden. When he was
arrested, the outwardly respectable and mild-mannered Christie admitted to the killings, claiming that his motives had been sexual – he said
he had strangled one of the women while they were actually having
intercourse. The horrors that Christie perpetrated on the women he had
lured to his flat left the judge and jury at the Old Bailey aghast and
earned him the death sentence. As he went to the gallows in Pentonville
on 15 July, 1953, there were few people who doubted that Timothy
Evans had suffered a terrible miscarriage of justice. Christie is the evil
influence in Bernard Taylor's deceptively chilling story, 'Forget-Me-
Not'. Taylor, who is a painter, actor, scriptwriter and novelist, is the
author of two bestselling horror novels,* The Godsend *(which was
filmed with Malcolm Stoddard and Cyd Hayman) and* Sweetheart,
Sweetheart, *as well as* Cruelly Murdered, *a radical re-examination
of the Victorian murder mystery of the killing of Constance Kent. The
author's knowledge of the Christie murders is also very evident in the
following pages.*

'THAT'S THE HOUSE where Christie lived . . .'

Sandra followed the direction of the young man's pointing finger
and saw, through the window, below them, a shabby cul-de-sac.

'The one at the end,' he said. 'Right next to that factory wall.'

Quickly, Sandra shifted her gaze, but there was only time to catch the briefest glimpse of the drab-looking terrace house before the tube train – travelling overground for this stretch – took them past. The house vanished from sight.

'Who is Christie?' she asked in her New York accent; she was a stranger to England, and curious about everything.

'Who *was* Christie,' he corrected her. 'Reginald Halliday Christie . . . Oh, – just a harmless-looking little man who killed – *murdered* – a number of women. He was hanged for it.'

'Really?' Sandra thought of the very ordinary house she had just seen. 'And he lived there?'

'Yes. And committed all the murders there.'

She shivered slightly, in spite of the warm September air. The young man went on:

'His victims were all female. Most of them were —' he broke off suddenly, grinning. 'Listen to me,' he said, '— a fine introduction to London for you!'

She laughed. 'No, no, it's fascinating! Anyway, I want to know everything – the good and the bad.' She paused, then added: 'It's funny, but somehow I never thought of associating London with any kind of violence . . .'

'Oh, we have our share,' he said, then, changing the subject, asked: 'Have you got a place to stay?'

'Yes, I've booked into a hotel for a while.' Just till I can find a room or an apartment . . .'

'That might not be so easy.'

She smiled, undeterred. 'I'll find something. I'll start looking tomorrow. I've got a whole week before I start school.'

Sandra, pretty, blond, twenty-six years old, had come to London from the U.S.A. to teach in the London Education system – just for a year, on an exchange basis. For months she had looked forward to it, and now the actual day of her arrival was here; it was one of the most exciting days of her life.

'The next stop is yours,' the young man said. He had been scribbling on a piece of paper and now, as she stood up, he handed it to her. 'My name and 'phone number,' he explained. 'Perhaps when you're settled you might give me a ring . . .' He looked hopeful, smiling. Sandra smiled back.

'Thanks. I'll do that.' She stuffed the note into her pocket and picked up her two suit-cases. 'You've been a great help. Honestly, I don't know how I'd have managed.'

He was eager to be even more helpful. 'Can you find your way to the hotel?' he asked.

She nodded. 'I got me a street map. An *A to Z*.' (She pronounced it Zee) 'I'll get there okay.' The tube was slowing. She moved towards the doors. 'Bye. And thanks again.'

He turned to wave a hand. 'Goodbye. Nice to meet you. Don't forget – 'phone me . . .'

Outside the station she looked at the slip of paper he had given her. *David Hampshire*, she read. Below the name was his telephone number. 'Yeh, maybe I *will* give him a call,' she said to herself.

With the help of her *A to Z* it was relatively easy to locate the hotel, and the room to which she was then shown looked cosy and inviting. Left alone, she kicked off her shoes, lit a cigarette and lay back on the bed. She was relaxed. There was no one to drag her into conversation; no one to tell her that she shouldn't smoke: she was wonderfully comfortable and alone. 'But don't get too comfortable, girl,' she told herself. 'Don't get too settled. You've got to go out and find something a little more permanent. And if David was right, that is not going to be *easy*.' She was not worried, though, the hunting might be fun. And anyway, one thing was certain: she was going to adore her stay in London – absolutely adore it.

David proved to be right. Finding something a little more permanent proved to be very difficult. My God! she thought, it's as bad as New York! It seemed that no matter how swift she was to answer the ads in the papers, or those in the shop windows, she was always just that bit too late; the room or the flat was always gone. But she'd get *something*, she told herself; she wasn't easily daunted. In the meantime the hotel made a comfortable haven.

It was during her flat-searching that she found, in a small corner-bookshop, the volume on Christie. As soon as she saw the title: *Reginald Christie, Mass Murderer*, she remembered her conversation on the tube with David. The book was secondhand and at a ridiculously low price. Sorting out the still-strange coins from her purse she handed them, along with the book, to the assistant. 'I'll take it,' she said.

She began to read the book that same afternoon, continuing with it into the evening. And even when she went down to the little café she took it with her to study over her steak pie and chips.

The story was absolutely fascinating. Reginald Halliday Christie was known to have killed at least seven women – by strangulation – and then to have secreted their bodies either in the house or the adjoining garden. His wife had been one of the victims, and a young tenant of the house another. Equally horrifying to Sandra, with her sheltered upbringing, was the fact that after killing each of the women he had undressed them and – and . . . She closed her eyes tight. The image in her mind was to terrible to bear. Later, when she took up the book again, she came upon a photograph of the house. The sight of it caused her to catch at her breath. *Ten, Rillington Place*, she read . . . But was that the name she had seen on the street sign . . .? No, surely not. Quickly she flicked through the pages to the appendix. Yes, there it was: *Ruston Close*. That was the name she had seen. After Christie's trial and execution the local authorities had – for obvious reasons – renamed the ugly little dead-end street. She remembered suddenly that David had pointed out the house just before she had got off the tube. With a strange little thrill she realised that *Ruston Close* was very, very near . . .

That night she found herself thinking more about the house where Christie had lived. And the things that had happened there. Stop it! she admonished herself; she was getting morbid! What she needed was to start work – to meet people, make a few nice friends . . . She thought of David. He had said he'd be glad to hear from her – maybe she'd give him a ring. Yes, that was a good idea. For some minutes she made a concerted effort to find the scrap of paper on which he had written his telephone number but, meeting with no success, she gave up the attempt. She'd find it later; there was plenty of time. She went back to her reading.

All at once, there was Christie, staring at her from the page. He had a thin, rather gaunt aspect. The hair on his domed head was thinning, and the cold, pale eyes that peered out through the steel-rimmed spectacles were merciless. He had been photographed standing in the tiny, untidy garden of his home, standing with his plump, smiling wife . . . Sandra found herself addressing the unfortunate, unattractive victim:

'You poor, poor thing,' she whispered, 'you wouldn't be smiling if you *knew* . . .'

Her first day at school the following Monday was very tiring. But that was to be expected, – teaching was never an easy job, no matter *what* the age of your pupils. Sandra was given a class of eleven-year-olds, – a vital, noisy group that left her, at four o'clock, feeling drained and exhausted. She departed through the school gates with aching feet, a throat sore from constant shouting, and a mouth that was dry and dusty from the chalk-laden air. Reaching Edgware Road tube station, she got on the train and settled back with a sigh of relief; her first day was *over*. The feeling was only temporary, though, – she'd have to face another day tomorrow, *and* the day after, *and* the day after that. The days stretched before her into infinity. 'Don't worry,' she told herself, 'it's just because you're not used to it. It'll be alright in time . . .' And there was another problem, also: the need for a flat of her own. The worry nagged like a toothache. She'd try again this weekend, she decided – really make an all-out effort. There had to be something somewhere. She lit a cigarette and, gazing from the window, idly noted the stations as they passed by; after Edgware Road came Paddington, then Royal Oak, then Westbourne Park, then Ladbroke Grove, then – And suddenly *the house* was there, – Christie's house – standing forlorn and dirty at the end of the cul-de-sac, shadowed by the tall, grey, ugly chimney. She turned as the train sped past, craning her neck to catch that last little glimpse. Every day that week she saw the house. Sitting on the tube, she found herself counting the stations, – almost impatient – just waiting for the street to come in sight. And always, at the end of the street was the house. But it looked so – innocuous, she thought. It was hard to believe that *that* was the scene of so many hideous crimes.

And yet . . . there was something about the place, that last tired-looking three-storey dwelling. Something about the whole street. And then she realised what it was that gave it all that air of – difference: the street was uninhabited. No people walked there, no children played. The windows were dark and empty – some of them boarded up.

In the mornings, on the way to school, she couldn't see the house, – the train, running on the left tracks, was too far over, affording her no possible view. But on the way back – well – that was a different matter. Her days at school could be bearable when there was something to look forward to. And Sandra *did* look forward to the house. Each teaching day, with thumping heart and damp palms, she watched, waited for the house to come in view. Soon – she could *see* – the house was waiting for *her*.

She needed something to look forward to at this time. Somehow, her life was becoming increasingly lonesome. It just wasn't that easy to make friends. For some people it was, but not for Sandra. The warm, satisfying relationships she had envisaged seemed somehow never to materialize. Why was it? she wondered. She had tried, too. Though there was, at school, no one with whom she thought she'd really like to be friends, she had, even so, made two or three half-hearted attempts to strike up more than the passing acquaintanceship. But her attempts were not very successful, and she was forced to continue with the amusements of her own designing.

Having no television set and no radio, she spent a great deal of her time reading, getting the books from the local library. Many of the books she read were about Christie. Reginald . . . Halliday . . . Christie . . . What a name! she thought. The syllables just rolled off the tongue . . . *Reginald . . . Halliday . . . Christie . . . Beautiful*. She felt she was beginning to know him so well – she almost thought of him as – Reginald . . . But that was silly.

One afternoon, returning from school, she looked down at the street and saw workmen moving about. And there was a bulldozer and other machines of demolition! 'My *God*!' she whispered; then louder: '*They're knocking it down*!' A woman on the opposite seat looked up from her knitting and gave her an odd, uncomprehending glance.

And they *were* knocking it down. The next day on her return Christie's house was just a pile of rubble, and the workmen were start- ing on the house next door.

At school, in the staff-room, one of the young teachers came to her holding out a newspaper. 'Here,' he said, 'you're the one who's always reading about Christie . . .' He pointed to a short column on the back page. Concealing her eagerness, she took the paper from him, read the words. It only told her what she already knew. But *why* tear it down? she asked herself. The reason given here: *space needed for redevelopment* – was just not good enough. It was *Christie's* house. They shouldn't have done it. It just wasn't fair.

Smiling, shrugging, as if not really interested, she handed the paper back to its owner.

It was that same evening that she found the flat. She had stopped at a small shop to buy cigarettes (– she was smoking far too much these days –) when she saw the card in the window. *Flat to Let*, it said. *Suit young working person. £6 per week*. Yes, she could afford that much, she reckoned. Quickly she made a note of the address, then set off at once to find it.

And now it was hers. She had paid Malaczynski, the Polish landlord, a month's rent in advance, and told him that she'd be moving in the very next day. She'd take the day off school, she decided. (She didn't feel like going anyway; there was nothing to look forward to anymore.)

There were three flats available, the landlord had told her, so she could have her choice. She chose the one on the first floor. At the moment the ground-floor flat was occupied by the landlord himself; 'But only for a short time,' he had explained. 'I'll be moving to another house this coming weekend.' Then, continuing in his accented English: 'Will you mind being here on your own for a while? It won't be long before the other flats are let.'

'Oh, no,' she had assured him. 'It won't bother me in the least.' Nor would it. She had her *own place* – *at last*. Nothing would bother her now.

The next day she paid her hotel bill and moved into the flat. Now at last, she had finally arrived. She stood in her bed-sitting room and looked around her. She had just the two rooms, – this one which was fairly large, – and a smaller kitchen next door. The bathroom was on the floor above, and she'd have to share it with the coming tenant, – whoever that might turn out to be. But it didn't matter. The flat was hers. It was small, but it was hers.

All the walls were a sort of greyish white. Not attractive. But she'd repaint them in time, she thought. For the present they'd look alright with a bit of colour added: – a few pictures, ornaments. It was going to be fun shopping for things. She could make the place – she was sure – really attractive. Though it was by no means perfect, – particularly to a sophisticated New Yorker – it had endless possibilities.

After she had unpacked, she spent a long time arranging her few things, trying – futiley – to add a touch of her own personality. It couldn't be done, she discovered; – not in a day. It could only come with living there.

In the course of her sorting-out she came across David Hampshire's name and 'phone number. She put the scrap of paper carefully between the leaves of her address book. She would invite him round for supper, she decided, – but not just yet; – not till she was well and truly settled.

She stayed up late that night, cleaning and scrubbing. There was so much to be done when moving into a new place. Eventually, totally exhausted, she got into bed and lay there, smoking a cigarette. She gazed about her. The room didn't look quite so bare, anyway. On the wall nearest the foot of the bed she had pinned a postcard-size reproduction of Murillo's *Peasant Boy Leaning on a Sill*. She had bought the small print at the National Gallery during her first days in London. She loved the soft, muted tones of the picture and the boy's wide, happy smile. Next to it, making something of a contrast, she had displayed the photograph of Christie and his wife. She had torn the picture from her book.

Lying there, very comfortable, she made vague plans of what she would do with the flat. She'd have to make a list of all the things that were needed, – and there were so many things – still, it would all come, gradually. Sighing, she put out her cigarette. She felt tired, but happy. Switching off the small lamp, she turned over to go to sleep.

Four hours later she was still wide-awake. In spite of her great exhaustion from the hectic day, sleep just would not come. Shifting restlessly, she was aware of the dawn lightening the pale curtains at the window. She gave a groan of exasperation – she *had* to get some rest. At last, some time after, she drifted off.

She awoke hours later, having slept right through the strident ringing of her alarm clock. She saw with a shock that the time was after eleven! – it was no good going in to school now. She'd 'phone in and explain. Anyway, she remembered, next week was half-term holiday; it hardly seemed worth going in – not just for those few remaining hours.

She made good use of the rest of the day. After her 'phone call to the headmistress, Sandra went out shopping. She bought china, saucepans, cutlery, – those items necessary for the furnishing of a home. And that evening she cooked supper for herself – no more eating out at cafés. The meal was a pleasant – though somewhat lonely – affair, and she experienced a real sense of achievement. After that, she washed the dishes, then read for a few hours.

She wasn't sure when the idea came to her, – or whether it had been there all the time, just waiting to be acknowledged. But it was the picture of Christie that actually *set* it. It had to be. For one thing, his eyes followed her all the time. And every time she looked up from her book, he was looking at her. She had to go there. She had to go to the place where Reginald Christie had lived and breathed – and killed.

It was very late when she left the house. The last tubes had gone, and only the occasional car disturbed the silence of the dingy street. Her footsteps echoing on the pavements, she walked in the general direction of Ruston Close. She had consulted her *A to Z*, and knew exactly which way to go.

And suddenly it was there.

She came upon it all at once, and the shock of the expected discovery almost took her breath away. Her heart beating wildly, she stood at the entrance to the close, gazing before her at the familiar shape of the chimney, only slightly darker than the dark night sky.

Everything was so quiet. On her right a cinema poster flapped against a wall – it was the only sound in the stillness. Nothing else moved. Completely deserted, the cul-de-sac stretched dark and forbidding before her, the windows of the remaining houses like dead, blind eyes.

Sandra found that she was holding her breath. She exhaled, slowly. The atmosphere – there *was* an atmosphere – poured over her. The place had its own feeling; and it reached out to her as she stood there on the street corner, clutching at her with soft, grasping fingers, drawing her in.

She tried to walk softly, but the cold wind that swirled around the corner followed her, buffeting, so that her raincoat flapped noisily against her legs. No moon or stars were visible; the old street was all a dark greyness, almost at one with the sky.

And then she had reached the end. Standing beneath the chimney, she peered into the gloom of the place where Christie's house had stood.

As she gazed, shivering, the moon appeared from behind a cloud. All at once the scene was lit up before her, and she saw in the sudden light that the house-wall on the right – the one adjoining the factory wall – had not, like all the others, been torn down. It stood there still. And there, yawning in the wall – like grotesque mouths – were the fireplaces, – *Christie's* fireplaces. Scraps of torn, discoloured wallpaper still adhered to some of the surfaces around.

Crossing over the rubble, she touched the wall with the tips of her fingers, then, gaining courage, she laid her whole hand, flat, against it. Underneath her palm the wallpaper was brittle and flaking. After a moment, she took hold of a piece of the paper . . . and pulled . . . There was a loud tearing noise, and a strip – about nine inches long and four inches wide – came away in her grasp. She had taken the piece from an area just above her own head. It might well, she thought, be an area that Reginald (*Christie!* she corrected herself) had actually touched; have actually leaned his own domed, balding head against. Carefully she eased the strip – it was made from several thicknesses – into a roll, then tucked it away inside her coat.

Arriving back at the downstairs entrance to her own flat, she let herself in and climbed the stairs. The silence was as complete as that which she had just left. It would be even more silent when the landlord left tomorrow . . .

In her room, she unrolled the paper and laid it flat on the table. She was pleased. It made a nice souvenir. Then, later, she pasted it on the greying wall – just to the right of the gas fire, slightly above the level of her head. She studied the result judiciously for some moments, then, with a smile of satisfaction, she climbed into bed. But once again, rest did not come easily. It was only after tossing and turning for a very long time that she eventually dropped off into a fitful, uneasy sleep, – a sleep disturbed by dreams that kept her peace at bay.

Next day she awoke very late. Still, it being Saturday, this time it didn't matter. She lay in bed looking at Reginald's wallpaper. It really stood out against the dull background of the painted wall. The paper had been so affected by dirt and age that it was difficult to determine what its original colour had been. Probably blue, she decided at last; blue with some kind of small design on it. Flowers? Yes, perhaps, but she couldn't possibly identify what species. She gazed at the paper for a long, long time. Yes, definitely flowers, she decided, and the background most certainly blue. It had probably been quite pretty when newly bought. She felt rather smug; for one thing, she hadn't remembered tearing off such a large piece. With a last look, she turned over and went back to sleep.

She stayed up very late again on Saturday night, then slept well into the afternoon of the following day. She awoke about two o'clock, feeling sluggish and heavy-headed, – not feeling like getting up at all. Anyway, there was nothing she had planned to do, no shopping could be done, and there was no one she had planned to see, so the day – or what was left of it – was her own. She could do exactly as she pleased. Later on, she thought, she'd get up and make herself a snack – something light – maybe a boiled egg. But she wasn't really hungry. Propping up the pillows behind her head, she sat up, lit a cigarette, and reached for her book. It was a new one from the library, all about

317

famous trials. There was a particularly interesting chapter on Reginald.

She forgot about eating until it was quite late. Hardly worth it now, she thought. She'd just have a cup of coffee and a biscuit.

As she waited for the water to boil, her thoughts went back to her own home in New York City, – the home she had shared with her parents and her four sisters. My God! Sandra thought, if my mother could see me now she'd have a fit! There had always been so much emphasis placed on regular habits – regular meals and regular sleeping times. But Sandra had wanted this independence, this solitude. They were all part of her reasons for coming to this strange city.

All around her, the house was as silent as a tomb. There was no longer even the soft, considerate movements of the landlord to disturb the stillness. He had left the day before, and, until the new tenants moved in she would be completely alone.

Having no intention of going out, there seemed little purpose in getting dressed, so when the coffee was made she carried it back to bed. Over the rim of the cup she gave a casual glance at the strip of wallpaper. Then she looked harder, studying intently the size, the shape and the colour of the piece. It seemed different somehow. But *how*? And *how could* it? No. It was silly, such a thing just wasn't possible. She stared at it, unblinking. But it was true. It *was* different. The piece of paper had grown bigger.

She hardly stirred from the house all that week, except to go to the shop for cigarettes and the odd items of food; not so much for the latter, as she had found that her appetite had decreased considerably.

And there was the silence in the house. It was complete. She began to wish that she owned a television set, a radio or a record-player. It was as if the silence, unchecked, seemed to gain in potency and, with Reginald's wallpaper, grew with each passing day.

Friday came, then Saturday, then Sunday, and then Monday loomed up over her head, threatening, and suddenly she knew that she just could not face the prospect of school that day. She couldn't face those children in the classroom, the idle talk with the other teachers during the breaks between sessions. She'd just have to telephone in again, tell them she was sick. They'd understand. She got to the telephone on the ground floor and started to dial the school's number. Half-way through she stopped, replaced the receiver, then turned and went back up the stairs to her room. There was no need to call them, anyway, she rationalized later; *they* would call *her* as soon as they discovered her absence. But then, in a moment the thought came to her: How could they? No one at the school was aware of her new address or telephone number. She had not even told her parents, she realised, – in fact she had not even *written* to her parents since before leaving the hotel. Only Mr. Malaczynski, the landlord, knew of her whereabouts, and he didn't really count.

Monday went by in silence. Tuesday morning came. She forced herself to get up, and began to get ready for school. There was a pounding in her head, and a constricted feeling at her temples as if a metal band had been placed there and was being slowly tightened. The pain was throbbing. She sat down on the chair and pulled on her boots. The wallpaper had spread inches during the night.

She was fully dressed. It was time to go. But the thought of facing those people – the teachers, the children – All those questions that would have been asked: 'Has anyone seen or heard from Miss Timms?' 'Does anyone know Miss Timms' address . . .?' And the questions and the comments when she *did* get there: 'Where were you . . .? What happened . . .? You should have let us know . . . Are you ill . . .? Why didn't you telephone . . .?' All those looks, all those words . . .

It was the thought of the looks, the faces, the words that settled the matter. She took off all her clothes, threw them over the back of the chair and got back into bed.

She was awakened some hours later by someone tapping at her door. She got out of bed and slipped on her dressing-gown. 'Who is it?' she called.

The landlord's voice came to her, the Polish accent strong: 'It's Mr. Malaczynski . . .'

Sandra opened the door a few inches. 'Yes, what is it?'

He smiled broadly at her. 'It's just that—' He broke off, gazing at her with concern. 'Are you alright?'

'Yeh. I'm fine. Why?'

'You . . . You don't look well . . . Are you ill?'

She felt a growing impatience under the well-meaning questions. 'Of course I'm not ill. What did you want?' Her tone was slightly sharp.

'I'm very sorry,' he said, wilting a little under the edge on her voice, 'I just wanted to tell you that if you hear footsteps above, there is no need to be frightened. Mr. Robertson, the new tenant, is moving in

319

today. He is an old man. He will not cause you worry with rock-and-roll music.' He smiled again, trying to break through the impatient, cold exterior she presented. He added lamely: 'He will be here soon.'

There seemed to be nothing more to say. They looked at each other for a few seconds, and Sandra, trying to ease the warmth into her voice, said: 'Thank you, very much . . . ' He smiled back at her, grateful. 'Thank *you*,' he answered, and moved towards the stairs.

When he had gone from sight, she closed the door and walked over to the mirror. She stood there, gazing at her reflection.

She certainly didn't look one hundred per cent, she had to admit. Her face was drawn and pale, and the lines around her eyes made her look older than her twenty-six years. And her hair needed washing, she observed. It hung limp, lifeless and uncombed to her shoulders. She'd do it tomorrow, she decided. About seven o'clock she heard the arrival of the new tenant; she could hear the soft movements of his feet as he moved around the floor above. What was his name? Robertson? Yes, that's what Malaczynski had said. Perhaps they could be friends. It might be nice to talk to someone. Just a little talk. Just something to relieve the silence . . .

The days went by. And each day was like the one before. The only way of actually seeing that time had progressed was by watching the wallpaper. It looked different each time she awoke. Always it grew during the night – some nights more than others. The silence grew with it.

The arrival of Mr. Robertson upstairs had made no difference to the house at all. It was just as quiet. Other people were plagued with neighbours who played their radios and their records too loudly – not so Sandra. Mr. Robertson had none of these and lived as silently as herself. The only evidence of his presence was the soft sound of his feet as he occasionally moved about the room. These faint noises did nothing to alleviate the stillness. They just seemed to emphasise it. The stillness grew louder all the time, and the paper seemed to feed upon the stillness. Yes! *That* was what was *happening*. She suddenly realised. Although normally silent – the house – throughout the day, – it was at night when the silence became absolute, so strong, so complete that it was almost tangible. And it was during the night that the wallpaper seemed to grow at such an alarming rate . . .

All the plans for transforming the ugly little flat into something that was truly her own were now forgotten. They had ceased to be important. Sandra sat on the bed, a cup of cold, untouched coffee in her hand, looking about her. What was happening to her? She didn't understand it. How long had she been here in this room — three weeks? four? She shivered violently. The room was cold, and she had run out of shillings for the meter. She'd have to go down to the shop to get some more. Sighing, she put down her cup and began to get dressed.

As she moved quietly about, the idea came into her mind that she should buy herself a radio. She had seen more inexpensive transistors not too far away. And she could just about afford it from the little she had left of her savings. The idea added impetus to her movements and she finished dressing quickly, anxious to be out. As she turned towards the door she caught sight of her reflection. Hurriedly she crossed to the sink and splashed cold water on her face. (The soap she had bought on her first day lay unused, still in its wrapper). Then she raked a hand through her tangled hair.

First of all she got the supply of shillings. She got them from the bank — two pound's worth. Now, she thought, she'd get that radio.

It was while she stood outside the entrance to the bank, wondering which way to go, that the weakness came over her. Suddenly she felt that her legs were about to give way. Her knees wobbled she thought she was about to fall and she clutched at the wall for support.

'Are you feeling alright, love . . .?'

She turned at the soft voice and tried to focus on the man who stood there, leaning towards her. For a moment she stared at herself, mirrored in the lenses of his steel-rimmed glasses, and then she turned, swinging away on her unsteady feet.

Back in her room, she collapsed, gasping, on the bed. It was a long time before she gathered the strength to undress and get in between the sheets. On the other wall, Reginald's paper was enormous.

Later, feeling calm again, she lay back and studied the paper. It had spread now in all directions, reaching out to the right as far as the mirror, and on the left almost as far as the shabby wardrobe. But she was no longer shocked by it. It had long since ceased to amaze her in any way. She looked at it now with acceptance, interest. After all, there was nothing she could *do* about it.

With the change in its size, the wallpaper had also changed in quality, — or, rather than that, — it appeared to be *newer*. In fact it looked brand-new, now. She wondered how she could ever have had to *decide* on its colour; it was quite obviously blue, a rather pretty blue. Likewise, the flowers that dotted its surface were now easily identifiable. They were the prettiest forget-me-nots, always among her favourite flowers. She thought: so goddamn English, too, and found herself smiling. The wallpaper was like a fungus – a creeping, thriving, rapacious, beautiful, beautiful fungus.

After a while, she got out of bed, lit the gas fire and put on some water for coffee. Nervously she stretched out a hand and touched the paper. It felt slightly damp, yet the other walls – the grey ones – were quite dry under her fingers. Gently she tried to insert a fingernail under the edge of the paper, but she couldn't do it – the paper was too firmly fixed. With the second try – in a different spot – she only succeeded in breaking her nail. Without any sense of disappointment, she picked up her coffee and moved back to the bed.

School, her job as a teacher her home in New York, – all seemed to be disconnected somehow. None of it was real. Not any more. These were the only things that were real: this room, this silence, and Reginald's forget-me-not wallpaper.

The paper had spread *so far* now. It had reached the far end of the wall and was beginning to turn the corner. There seemed to be no pattern to its actual movement – it just seemed to move, creeping, spreading, rather like liquid spilt on a polished surface. Some areas of the wall would be left bare, she noticed, then, later, she would see that they had been filled in. The paper was relentless and very, very thorough.

Even the little postcard of the peasant boy was not safe. She had pinned it up on the wall far away from the paper, and even though the mass of paper had not yet reached it, she could see that the lovely little picture had become infected. It started with just a tiny dot of blue down in one corner. She had noticed it one morning – her eyes seemed to be drawn to it – a little spot that had surely not been in the original. She knew what was happening. The little peasant boy did not, though, and – like Mrs. Christie in the photograph – he smiled his smile, unaware of the nearness of the evil. Unconcerned, he continued to lean on the sill, his tanned, peasant-boy's face beaming, while the forget-me-nots grew up around him. Sandra thought the picture was prettier. It's a pity, she thought, that Murillo can't be here to see it. Looking towards the photograph of Reginald and his wife, she was not surprised to see that it remained exactly as before. No forget-me-nots grew on that one. Looking closer, she saw that the paper was spreading *underneath* it.

Nothing was staying the same. Nothing. Even the quality of the silence was changing. Looking towards the window she saw the reason why. Snow was falling, thick and fast, the great soft shapes tumbling against the pane, settling. They fell without sound, insulating her more completely against the outside world.

And suddenly, she began to grow afraid. It had to stop. Everything had to stop. She had to do something. She didn't know what she was afraid of, but the fear grew, unexplainable, threatening, at any moment it would engulf her. She knew at once that she had to see someone, talk to someone. But who? There was no one she knew. Not Mr. Robertson; she had only glimpsed him on the stairs on two or three occasions. He had nodded to her, smiling, a slow-moving, sad old man of seventy-odd. He couldn't help. *Who* then?

David. David Hampshire. She saw his face before she thought of his name; that nice young man who had been so helpful on the tube that day of her arrival.

She took the piece of paper bearing his 'phone number and snatched a handful of coins from the shelf. Then, throwing on a coat and slippers, she went downstairs. Carefully, her hands trembling, she dialled his number.

'Hello . . .?' And there was his voice.

'Hello . . .? David?'

'Yes. Who's that?'

She paused, then said quickly: 'Sandra Timms.'

'Who?'

Oh, God, oh Jesus, he'd forgotten. 'I'm the girl you met on the tube. The American girl . . .' She could hear herself almost whimpering. 'Don't you remember . . .? You helped me . . .'

And then she heard the smile in his voice as recollection returned.

'Oh, yes!' he said. 'Yes, of course, I remember. How are you? Have you been okay?'

She began to blurt out her need for help. She had not meant to do this; she had meant to ask him to come round to see her, to tell him then – to do it more – casually. But somehow the desperation inside her had taken over, and she was pleading with him.

'Help me. You've got to help me.'

'But what's wrong?' he asked, his voice loaded with concern.

323

'I don't know – I don't know – I don't know . . .!'

'Right, listen,' he said, forcing the calmness into the situation, 'tell me where you are. I'll drive round straight-away.' He took up a pencil 'Give me your address.'

She was almost incoherent, but he managed to write down the address she gabbled out.

'I'll be there in fifteen minutes.'

'Yes, yes! Please hurry . . . *Please hurry*!' And she was gone.

David heard the click of the receiver and put the phone down. As he reached for his coat he looked at the address he had scribbled on the note pad. He stopped, gazing at it. Perhaps she was having some kind of joke with him – *some joke* on a night like *this*! He screwed the paper into a ball and tossed it into the wastebasket. It doesn't make sense, he thought, there was no longer any such address as *10, Rillington Place*.

Reaching her own room, Sandra ran in and closed the door behind her. In her absence the wallpaper had spread even further. Almost three walls were covered now, and the peasant boy had been completely wiped out. Reginald continued to smile.

Fifteen minutes, he had said. Fifteen minutes. She could hold out that long. It wasn't very long. Not too long. She could try counting them off, – that might help. Count the seconds: One, two, three, four, five, six, seven . . . She closed her eyes, shutting out the forget-me-nots that grew all around her. Eight . . . nine . . . ten . . . Now the silence was getting in the way. Where was she? Eight . . . nine . . . ten . . . eleven . . . She tried to shut her ears to the silence but it was no good. It got through. Whatever you did it got through. Make some coffee, smoke a cigarette, do *something*. Act naturally. The paper had crept onto the fourth wall now. It was moving faster than ever. She hurried to the kitchen, lit the gas under the kettle. That's it – be steady – be calm. Get the jar of coffee – don't spill any. One spoonful . . . sugar . . . milk ready . . . the wallpaper had got into the kitchen too. There were forget-me-nots everywhere. Take no notice. David will be here soon. Everything will be alright then. You can wait till then. Not long now. The water's boiling. The sound of the steam and the gas are the only sounds. Turn off the gas, pour on the water. Silence. The coffee's made. Add the milk. Sip it slowly,. Concentrate . . . concentrate . . . She looked at the clock. Half an hour had gone by since she had called David! What had happened to him? Why wasn't he here? Fifteen minutes, he had told her. It was over half an hour . . . She sipped at the

324

coffee. It was stone-cold, and she put it down in disgust. She moved from the kitchen, back into the larger room, walking slowly, forcing her way through the silence. The silence was like the sea, and it was rising, moment by moment. Reginald liked the silence. He smiled into it from his forget-me-not heaven. Would David *never* come?

Yes! He was *here*! At *last*! The gentle tap at her door had taken her completely by surprise. She pressed herself against the silence, pushing a way through. She got to the door, opened it. She saw the thin face, the smile, and the blue eyes behind the glasses. She spun, and the sweet, sweet forget-me-not fungus lurched, reaching out. The whole room was blue, quivering in silence. Then the man spoke. After a second, the silence itself was shattered.

'I wonder if I could borrow a little milk?' the man on the landing had said, holding out an empty cup. 'I've just moved in downstairs . . .' The girl – dirty, emaciated, her tangled hair hanging about her face – just stood there in the open doorway staring at him dumbly from wide, frightened eyes. He smiled at her, adding: 'My name is Reg,' and suddenly she screamed. Her voice echoed in the quiet house – the sound of something in pain. The screams continued, the loudness cutting into the snowbound silence. When the screaming stopped her mouth went on moving, opening and closing like the mouth of a ventriloquist's dummy.

A Case of Coincidence

RUTH RENDELL

The serial killer has become the most infamous figure in crime in recent years. Cases like that of the American Jeffrey Dahmer who killed at least seventeen young men and kept the heads of his victims in his fridge, have horrified the public as much as that of the Russian Andrei Chikatilo who is said to have slaughtered over fifty women and children. In fiction, Thomas Harris's best-selling novel, The Silence of the Lambs, *which has also been turned into a hugely successful movie starring Anthony Hopkins, has given a new meaning to the word cannibal. Creating any story about a serial killer presents the serious author with a number of problems – not the least of them being the risk of nauseating the reader with protracted descriptions of the murders – and there are probably few contemporary writers better able to succeed at this difficult task than Ruth Rendell, one of the acknowledged 'Queens of Crime Fiction'. Ruth is a great admirer of George Simenon's* Maigret *thrillers, and like* la patron, *her best-known character, Detective Chief Inspector Wexford, tends to build up a psychological portrait of the criminal he is pursuing by observing all of his or her little foibles. The psychology of 'The Wrexlade Strangler' is the focus of this final story in the collection which brings it to a brilliant finale on a note that is both tense . . . and surprising.*

OF THE SEVERAL obituaries which appeared on the death of Michael Lestrange not one mentioned his connection with the Wrexlade murders. Memories are short, even journalists' memories, and it may be that the newspapermen who wrote so glowingly and so mournfully about him were mere babes in arms, or not even born, at the time. For the murders, of course, took place in the early fifties, before the abolition of capital punishment.

Murder is the last thing one would associate with the late Sir Michael, eminent cardiac specialist, physician to Her Royal Highness the Duchess of Albany, and author of that classic work, the last word on its subject, so succinctly entitled *The Heart*. Sir Michael did not destroy life, he saved it. He was as far removed from Kenneth Edward Brannel, the Wrexlade Strangler, as he was from the carnivorous spider which crept across his consulting room window. Those who knew him well would say that he had an almost neurotic horror of the idea of taking life. Euthanasia he had refused to discuss, and he had opposed with all his vigour the legalizing of abortion.

Until last March when an air crash over the North Atlantic claimed him among its two hundred fatalities, he had been a man one automatically thought of as life-enhancing, as having on countless occasions defied death on behalf of others. Yet he seemed to have had no private life, no family, no circle to move in, no especially beautiful home. He lived for his work. He was not married and few knew he ever had been, still fewer that his wife had been the last of the Wrexlade victims.

There were four others and all five of them died as a result of being strangled by the outsized, bony hands of Kenneth Edward Brannel. Michael Lestrange, by the way, had exceptionally narrow, well-shaped hands, dextrous and precise. Brannel's have been described as resembling bunches of bananas. In her study of the Wrexlade case, the criminologist Miss Georgina Hallam Saul, relates how Brannel, in the condemned cell, talked about committing these crimes to a prison officer. He had never understood why he killed those women, he didn't dislike women or fear them.

'It's like when I was a kid and in a shop and there was no one about,' he is alleged to have said. 'I had to take something, I couldn't help myself. I didn't even do it sort of of my own will. One minute it'd be on the shelf and the next in my pocket. It was the same with those girls. I had to get my hands on their throats. Everything'd go dark and when it cleared my hands'd be round their throats and the life all squeezed out . . .'

He was twenty-eight, an agricultural labourer, illiterate, classified as educationally subnormal. He lived with his widowed father, also a farm worker, in a cottage on the outskirts of Wrexlade in Essex. During 1953 he strangled Wendy Cutforth, Maureen Hunter, Ann Daly and Mary Trenthyde without the police having the least suspicion of his guilt. Approximately a month elapsed between each of these murders, though there was no question of Brannel killing at the full moon or anything of that sort. Four weeks after Mary Trenthyde's death he was arrested and charged with murder, for the strangled body of Norah Lestrange had been discovered in a ditch less than a hundred yards from his cottage. They found him guilty of murder in November of that same year, twenty-five days later he was executed.

'A terrible example of injustice,' Michael Lestrange used to say. 'If the M'Naughten Rules apply to anybody they surely applied to poor Brannel. With him it wasn't only a matter of not knowing that what he was doing was wrong but of not knowing he was doing it at all till it was over. We have hanged a poor idiot who had no more idea of evil than a stampeding animal has when it tramples on a child.'

People thought it amazingly magnanimous of Michael that he could talk like this when it was his own wife who had been murdered. She was only twenty-five and they had been married less than three years.

It is probably best to draw on Miss Hallam Saul for the most accurate and comprehensive account of the Wrexlade stranglings. She attended the trial, every day of it, which Michael Lestrange did not. When prosecuting counsel, in his opening speech, came to describe Norah Lestrange's reasons for being in the neighbourhood of Wrexlade that night, and to talk of the Dutchman and the hotel at Chelmsford, Michael got up quietly and left the court. Miss Hallam Saul's eyes, and a good many other pairs of eyes, followed him with compassion. Nevertheless, she didn't spare his feelings in her book. Why should she? Like everyone else who wrote about Brannel and Wrexlade, she was appalled by the character of Norah Lestrange. This was the fifties, remember, and the public were not used to hearing of young wives who admitted shamelessly to their husbands that one man was not enough for them. Michael had been obliged to state the facts to the police and the facts were that he had known for months that his wife spent nights in this Chelmsford hotel with Jan Vandepeer, a businessman on his way from The Hook and Harwich to London. She had told him so quite openly.

'Darling . . .' Taking his arm and leading him to sit close beside her while she fondled his hand. 'Darling, I absolutely have to have Jan, I'm crazy about him. I do have to have other men, I'm made that way. It's nothing to do with the way I feel about you, though, you do see that, don't you?'

These words he didn't, of course, render verbatim. The gist was enough.

'It won't be all that often, Mike darling, once a month at most. Jan can't fix a trip more than once a month. Chelmsford's so convenient for both of us and you'll hardly notice I'm gone, will you, you're so busy at that old hospital.'

But all this came much later, in the trial and in the Hallam Saul book. The first days (and the first chapters) were occupied with the killing of those four other women.

Wendy Cutforth was young, married, a teacher at a school in Ladeley. She went to work by bus from her home in Wrexlade, four miles away. In February, at four o'clock dusk, she got off the bus at Wrexlade Cross to walk to her bungalow a quarter of a mile away. She was never seen alive again, except presumably by Brannel, and her strangled body was found at ten that night in a ditch near the bus stop.

Fear of being out alone which had seized Wrexlade women after Wendy's death died down within three or four weeks. Maureen Hunter, who was only sixteen, quarrelled with her boyfriend after a dance at Wrexlade village hall and set off to walk home to Ingleford on her own. She never reached it. Her body was found in the small hours only a few yards from where Wendy's had been. Mrs Ann Daly, a middle-aged widow, also of Ingleford, had a hairdressing business in Chelmsford and drove herself to work each day via Wrexlade. Her car was found abandoned, all four doors wide open, her body in a small wood between the villages. An unsuccessful attempt had been made to bury it in the leaf mould.

Every man between sixteen and seventy in the whole of that area of Essex was closely examined by the police. Brannel was questioned, as was his father, and was released after ten minutes, having aroused no interest. In May, twenty-seven days after the death of Ann Daly, Mary Trenthyde, thirty-year-old mother of two small daughters and herself the daughter of Brannel's employer, Mark Stokes of Cross Farm, disappeared from her home during the course of a morning. One of her children was with its grandmother, the other in its pram just inside the garden gate. Mary vanished without trace, without announcing to anyone that she was going out or where she was going. A massive hunt was mounted and her strangled body finally found at midnight in a disused well half a mile away.

All these deaths took place in the spring of 1953.

The Lestranges had a flat in London not far from the Royal Free Hospital. They were not well off but Norah had a rich father who was in the habit of giving her handsome presents. One of these, for her twenty-fifth birthday, was a Triumph Alpine sports car. Michael had a car too, the kind of thing that is called an 'old banger'.

As frontispiece to Miss Hallam Saul's book is a portrait photograph of Norah Lestrange as she appeared a few months before her death. The face is oval, the features almost too perfectly symmetrical, the skin flawless and opaque. Her thick dark hair is dressed in the high fashion of the time, in short smooth curls. Her make-up is heavy and the dark, greasy lipstick coats the parted lips in a way that is somehow lascivious. The eyes stare with a humourless complacency.

Michael was furiously, painfully jealous of her. When, after they had been married six months, she began a flirtation with his best friend, a flirtation which soon developed into a love affair, he threatened to leave her, to divorce her, to lock her up, to kill Tony. She was supremely confident he would do none of these things. She talked to him. Reasonably and gently and lovingly she put it to him that it was he whom she loved and Tony with whom she was amusing herself.

'I *love* you, darling, don't you understand? This thing with Tony is just – fun. We have fun and then we say goodbye till next time and I come home to you, where my real happiness is.'

'You promised to be faithful to me,' he said, 'to forsake all others and keep only to me.'

'But I do keep only to you, darling. You have all my trust and my thoughts – Tony just has this tiny share in a very unimportant aspect of me.'

After Tony there was Philip. And after Philip, for a while, there was no one. Michael believed Norah might have tired of the 'fun' and be settling for the real happiness. He was working hard at the time for his Fellowship of the Royal College of Surgeons.

That Fellowship he got, of course, in 1952. He was surgical registrar at a big London hospital, famous for successes in the field of cardiac surgery, when the first of the Wrexlade murders took place. Wendy Cutforth. Round about the time the account of that murder and of the hunt for the Wrexlade strangler appeared in the papers, Norah met Jan Vandepeer.

Michael wasn't a reader of the popular press and the Lestranges had no television. Television wasn't, in those days, the indispensable adjunct to domestic life it has since become. Michael listened sometimes to the radio, he read *The Times*. He knew of the first of the Wrexlade murders but he wasn't much interested in it. He was busy in his job and he had Jan Vandepeer to worry about too.

The nature of the Dutchman's business in London was never clear to Michael, perhaps because it was never clear to Norah. It seemed to have something to do with commodity markets and Michael was convinced it was shady, not quite above board. Norah used to say that he was a smuggler, and she found the possibility he might be a diamond smuggler exciting. She met him on the boat coming from The Hook to Harwich after spending a week in The Hague with her parents, her father having a diplomatic post there.

'Darling, I absolutely have to have Jan, I'm crazy about him. It's nothing to do with us, though, you do see that, don't you? No one could ever take me away from you.'

He used to come over about once a month with his car and drive down to London through Colchester and Chelmsford, spend the night somewhere, carry out his business the following day and get the evening boat back. Whether he stayed in Chelmsford rather than London because it was cheaper or because Chelmsford, in those days, still kept its pleasant rural aspect, does not seem to be known. It hardly matters. Norah Lestrange was more than willing to drive the forty or so miles to Chelmsford in her Alpine and await the arrival of her dashing, blond smuggler at the Murrey Gryphon Hotel.

Chelmsford is the county town of Essex, standing on the banks of the river Chelmer and in the midst of a pleasant, though featureless, arable countryside. The land is rather flat, the fields wide, and there are many trees and numerous small woods. Wrexlade lies some four miles to the north of the town, Ingleford a little way further west. It was some time before the English reader of newspapers began to think of Wrexlade as anywhere near Chelmsford. It was simply Wrexlade, a place no one had heard of till Wendy Cutforth and then Maureen Hunter died there, a name on a map or maybe a signpost till the stranglings began – and then, gradually, a word synonymous with fascinating horror.

Bismarck Road, Hilldrop Crescent, Rillington Place – who can say now, except the amateur of crime, which of London's murderers lived in those streets? Yet in their day they were names on everyone's lips. Such is the English sense of humour that there were even jokes about them. There were jokes, says Miss Hallam Saul, about Wrexlade, sick jokes for the utterance of one of which a famous comedian was banned by the BBC. Something on the lines of what a good idea it would be to take one's mother-in-law to Wrexlade . . .

Chelmsford, being so close to Wrexlade, became public knowledge when Mrs Daly died. She was last seen locking up her shop in the town centre and getting into her car. It was after this that Norah said to Michael: 'When I'm in Chelmsford, darling, I promise you I won't go out alone after dark.'

It was presumably to be a consolation to him that if she went out after dark it would be in the company of Jan Vandepeer.

Did he passively acquiesce, then, in this infidelity of hers? In not leaving her, in being at the flat when she returned home, in continuing to be seen with her socially, he did acquiesce. In continuing to love her in spire of himself, he acquiesced. But his misery was terrible. He was ill with jealousy. All his time, when he was not at the hospital, when he was not snatching a few hours of sleep, was spent in thrashing out in his mind what he should do. It was impossible to go on like this. If he remained in her company he was afraid he would do her some violence, but the thought of being permanently parted from her was horrible. When he contemplated it he seemed to feel the solid ground sliding away from under his feet, he felt like Othello felt – If I love thee not, chaos is come again.'

In June, on Friday, 19 June, Norah went down to Chelmsford, to the Murrey Gryphon Hotel, to spend the night with Jan Vandepeer.

Michael, who had worked every day without a break at the hospital for two weeks, had two days off, the Friday and the Saturday. He was tired almost to the point of sickness, but those two days he was to have off loomed large and glowing and inviting before him at the end of the week. He got them out of proportion. He told himself that if he could have those two days off to spend alone with Norah, to take Norah somewhere into the country and laze those two days away with her, to walk with her hand in hand down country lanes (that he thought with such maudlin romanticism is evidence of his extreme exhaustion), if he could do that, all would miraculously become well. He would explain and she would explain and they would listen to each other and, in the words of the cliché, make a fresh start. Michael was convinced of all this. He was a little mad with tiredness.

After she was dead, and they came in the morning to tell him of her death, he took time off work. Miss Hallam Saul gives the period as three weeks and she is probably correct. Without those weeks of rest Michael Lestrange would very likely have had a mental breakdown or – even worse to his way of thinking – have killed a patient on the operating table. So when it is said that Norah's death, though so terrible to him, saved his sanity and his career, this is not too far from the truth. And then, when he eventually returned to his work, he threw himself into it with total dedication. He had nothing else, you see, nothing at all but his work for the rest of his life that ended in the North Atlantic last March.

Brannel had nothing either. It is very difficult for the educated middle-class person, the kind of person we really mean when we talk about 'the man in the street', to understand the lives of people like Kenneth Edward Brannel and his father. They had no hobbies, no interests, no skill, no knowledge in their heads, virtually no friends. Old Brannel could read. Tracing along the lines with his finger, he could just about make out the words in a newspaper. Kenneth Brannel could not read at all. These days they would have television, not then. Romantic town-dwellers imagine such as the Brannels tending their cottage gardens, growing vegetables, occupying themselves with a little carpentry or shoemaking in the evenings, cooking country stews and baking bread. The Brannels, who worked all day in another man's fields, would not have dreamt of further tilling the soil in the evenings. Neither of them had ever so much as put up a shelf or stuck a sole on a boot. They lived on tinned food and fish and chips, and when the darkness came down they went to bed. There was no electricity in their cottage, anyway, and no running water or indoor sanitation. It would never have occurred to Mr Stokes of Cross Farm to provide these amenities or to the Brannels to demand them.

Downstairs in the cottage was a living room with a fireplace and a kitchen with a range. Upstairs was old Brannel's room into which the stairs went, and through the door from this room was the bedroom and only private place of Kenneth Edward Brannel. There, in a drawer in the old, wooden-knobbed tallboy, unpolished since Ellen Brannel's death, he kept his souvenirs: Wendy Cutforth's bracelet, a lock of Maureen Hunter's red hair, Ann Daly's green silk scarf, Mary Trenthyde's handkerchief with the lipstick stain and the embroidered M. The small, square handbag mirror was always assumed to have been the property of Norah Lestrange, to be a memento of her, but this was never proved. Certainly, there was no mirror in her handbag when her body was found.

In Miss Hallam Saul's *The Wrexlade Monster* there were several pictures of Brannel, a snapshot taken by his aunt when he was ten, a class group at Ingleford Middle School (which he should properly have never, with his limitations, been allowed to attend), a portrait by a Chelmsford photographer that his mother had had taken the year before her death. He was very tall, a gangling, bony man with a bumpy, tortured-looking forehead and thick, pale, curly hair. The eyes seem to say to you: The trouble is that I am puzzled, I am bewildered, I don't understand the world or you or myself and I live always in a dark mist. But when, for a little, that mist clears, look what I do . . .

His hands, hanging limply at his sides, are turned slightly, the palms half-showing, as if in helplessness and despair.

Miss Hallam Saul includes no picture of Sir Michael Lestrange, MD, FRCS, eminent cardiac specialist, author of *The Heart*, Physician to Her Royal Highness the Duchess of Albany, professor of cardiology at St Joachim's Hospital. He was a thin, dark young man in those days, slight of figure and always rather shabbily dressed. One would not have given him a second glance. Very different he was then from the Sir Michael who was mourned by the medical elite of two continents and whose austere yet tranquil face with its sleek silver hair, calm light eyes and aquiline features appeared on the front pages of the world's newspapers. He had changed more than most men in twenty-seven years. It was a total metamorphosis, not merely an ageing.

At the time of the murder of his wife Norah he was twenty-six. He was ambitious but not inordinately so. The ambition, the vocation one might well call it, came later, after she was dead. He was worn out with work on 19 June 1953, and he was longing to get away to the country with his wife and to rest.

'But, darling, I'm sure I told you. I'm going to meet Jan at the Murrey Gryphon. I did tell you, I never have any secrets from you, you know that. *You* didn't tell me you were going to have two days off. How was I to know? You never seem to take time off these days and I do like to have *some* fun *some*times.'

'Don't go,' he said.

'But, darling, I want to see Jan.'

'It's more than I can bear, the way we live,' he said. 'If you won't stop seeing this man I shall stop you.'

He buried his face in his hands and presently she came and laid a hand on his shoulder. He jumped up and struck her a blow across the face. When she left for Chelmsford to meet Jan Vandepeer she had a bruise on her cheek which she did her best to disguise with make-up.

They had a message for her at the hotel when she got there, from her 'husband' in Holland to say he had been delayed at The Hook. Hotels, in those days, were inclined to be particular that couples who shared bedrooms should at least pretend to be husband and wife. It was insinuated at Brannel's trial that Jan Vandepeer failed to arrive on this occasion because he was growing tired of Norah, but there was no evidence to support this. He was genuinely delayed and unable to leave.

Why didn't she go back to London? Perhaps she was afraid to face Michael. Perhaps she hoped Vandepeer would still come, since the phone message had been received at four-thirty. She dined alone and went out for a walk. To pick up a man, insisted prosecuting counsel, though he was not prosecuting *her* and the Old Bailey is not a court of morals. Nobody saw her go and no one seems to have been sure where she went. Eventually, of course, to Wrexlade.

Brannel also went out for a walk. The long light evenings disquieted him because he could not go to bed and he had nothing to do but sit with his father while the old man puzzled out the words in the evening paper. He went first to his bedroom to look at and handle the secret things he kept there, the scarf and the lock of hair and the bracelet and the handkerchief with M on it for Mary Trenthyde, and then he went out for his walk. Along the narrow lanes, to stop sometimes and stand, to lean over a gate, or to kick a pebble aimlessly ahead of him, dribbling it slowly from side to side of the long, straight, lonely road.

Did Norah Lestrange walk all the way to Wrexlade or did someone give her a lift and for reasons unknown abandon her there? She could have walked, it is no more than two miles from the Murrey Gryphon to the spot where her body was found half an hour before midnight. Miss Hallam Saul suggests that she was friendly with a second man in the Chelmsford neighbourhood and, in the absence of Vandepeer, set off to meet him that evening. Unlikely though that seems, similar suggestions were put forward in court. It was as if they all said, a woman like that, a woman so immoral, so promiscuous, so lacking in all proper feeling, a woman like that will do anything.

Her body was found by two young Wrexlade men going home after an evening spent at the White Swan on the Ladeley-Wrexlade road. They phoned the police from the call box on the opposite side of the lane, and the first place the police went to, because it was the nearest habitation, was the Brannels' cottage. Norah Lestrange's body lay half-hidden in long grass on the verge by the bridge over the river Lade, and the Brannels' home, Lade Cottage, was a hundred yards the other side of the bridge. They went there initially only to ask the occupants if they had seen or heard anything untoward that evening.

Old Brannel came down in his nightshirt with a coat over it. He hadn't been asleep when the police came, he said, he had been awakened a few minutes before by his son coming in. The detective superintendent looked at Kenneth Edward Brannel, at his huge dangling hands, as he stood leaning against the wall, his eyes bewildered, his mouth a little open. No, he couldn't say where he had been, round and about, up and down, he couldn't say more.

They searched the house, although they had no warrant. Much was made of this by the defence at the trial. In Kenneth Brannel's bedroom, in the drawer of the tallboy, they found Wendy Cutforth's bracelet, Maureen Hunter's lock of red hair, Ann Daly's green silk scarf, and the handkerchief with M on it for Mary Trenthyde. The Wrexlade Monster had been caught at last. They cautioned Brannel and charged him and he looked at them in a puzzled way and said: 'I don't think I killed the lady. I don't remember. But maybe I did, I forget things and it's like a mist comes up . . .'

Michael Lestrange was told of the death of his wife in the early hours of the morning. Their purpose in coming to him was to tell him the news and ask him if he would later go with them to Chelmsford formally to identify his wife's body. They asked him no questions and would have expressed their sympathy and left him in peace, had he not declared that it was he who had killed Norah and that he wanted to make a full confession.

They had no choice after that but to drive him at once to Chelmsford and take a statement from him. No one believed it. The detective chief superintendent in charge of the case was very kind to him, very gentle but firm.

'But if I tell you I killed her you must believe me. I can prove it.'

'Can you, Dr Lestrange?'

'My wife was constantly unfaithful to me . . .'

'Yes, so you have told me. And you bore with her treatment of you because of your great affection for her. The truth seems to be, doctor, that you were a devoted husband and your wife – well, a less than ideal wife.'

Michael Lestrange insisted that he had driven to Chelmsford in pursuit of Norah, intending to appeal to Jan Vandepeer to leave her alone. He had not gone into the hotel. By chance he had encountered her walking aimlessly along a Chelmsford street as he was on his way to the Murrey Gryphon.

'Mrs Lestrange was still having her dinner at the time you mention,' said Chief Superintendent Masters.

'What does that matter? It was earlier or later, I can't be precise about times. She got into the car beside me. I drove off, I don't know where, I didn't want a scene in the hotel. She told me she had to get back, she was expecting Vandepeer at any moment.'

'Vandepeer had sent her a message he wasn't coming. She didn't tell you that?'

'Is it important?' He was impatient to get his confession over. 'It doesn't matter what she told me. I can't remember what we said.'

'Can you remember where you went?'

'Of course I can't. I don't know the place. I just drove and parked somewhere, I don't know where, and we got out and walked and she drove me mad, the things she said, and I got hold of her throat and . . .' He put his head in his hands. 'I can't remember what happened next. I don't know where it was or when. I was so tired and I was mad, I think.' He looked up. 'But I killed her. If you'd like to charge me now, I'm quite ready.'

The chief superintendent said very calmly and stolidly, 'That won't be necessary, Dr Lestrange.'

Michael Lestrange shut his eyes momentarily and clenched his fists and said, 'You don't believe me.'

'I quite believe you believe it yourself, doctor.'

'Why would I confess it if it wasn't true?'

'People do, sir, it's not uncommon. Especially people like yourself who have been overworking and worrying and not getting enough sleep. You're a doctor, you know what the psychiatrists would say, that you had a reason for doing violence to your wife so that now she's dead your mind has convinced itself you killed her, and you're feeling guilt for something you had nothing to do with.

'You see, doctor, look at it from our point of view. Is it likely that you, an educated man, a surgeon, would murder anyone? Not very. And if you did, would you do it in Wrexlade? Would you do it a hundred yards from the home of a man who has murdered four other women? Would you do it by strangling with the bare hands which is the method that man always used? Would you do it four weeks after the last strangling which itself was four weeks after the previous one? Coincidences like that don't happen, do they, Dr Lestrange? But people do get overtired and suffer from stress so that they confess to crimes they never committed.'

'I bow to your superior judgement,' said Michael Lestrange.

He went to the mortuary and identified Norah's body and then he made a statement to the effect that Norah had gone to Chelmsford to meet her lover. He had last seen her at four on the previous afternoon.

Brannel was found guilty of Norah's murder, for he was specifically charged only with that, after the jury had been out half an hour. And in spite of the medical evidence as to his mental state he was condemned to death and executed a week before Christmas.

For the short time after that execution that capital punishment remained law, Michael Lestrange was bitterly opposed to it. He used to say that Brannel was a prime example of someone who had been unjustly hanged and that this must never be allowed to happen in England again. Of course there was never any doubt that Brannel had strangled Wendy Cutforth, Maureen Hunter, Ann Daly and Mary Trenthyde. The evidence was there and he repeatedly confessed to these murders. But that was not what Michael Lestrange meant. People took him to mean that a man must not be punished for committing a crime whose seriousness he is too feeble-minded to understand. This is the law, and there can be no exceptions to it merely because society wants its revenge. People took Michael Lestrange to mean that when he spoke of injustice being done to this multiple killer.

And perhaps he did.

Acknowledgements

The Editor and publishers are grateful to the following authors, their agents and publishers for permission to include copyright stories in this collection: Little Brown for 'Down, Satan!' by Clive Barker; Peters, Fraser & Dunlop for 'A Story of Don Juan' by V. S. Pritchett, 'The Cold-Blooded Tigress of London' by Anthony Shaffer, 'Darling Adolf' by Ray Bradbury and 'A Case of Coincidence' by Ruth Rendell; Arkham House for 'The Philosopher's Stone' by August Derleth; HarperCollins for 'The Proof' by J. C. Moore; Mystery Writers of America Inc. for 'The Black Cabinet' by John Dickson Carr; Simon & Schuster for 'A Kind of Madness' by Anthony Boucher; Random House Publishing Group for 'The Fall River Axe Murders' by Angela Carter and 'Was Crippen A Murderer?' by Anthony Berkeley; Davis Publications Inc for 'The Moors Murders' by Miriam Allen deFord; Curtis Brown Ltd for 'The Borgia Heirloom' by Julian Symons and 'Forget-Me-Not' by Bernard Taylor; Mercury Publications Inc for 'The Mirror of Cagliostro' by Robert Arthur; A. M. Heath Ltd for 'The Skull of the Marquis de Sade' by Robert Bloch; Carol Smith Literary Agency for 'Jack's Little Friend' by Ramsey Campbell; and John Farqharson Ltd for 'A Bride in the Bath' by Peter Lovesey. While every care has been taken to establish the copyright holders of all the stories in this book, in case of any accidental infringement the Editor should be contacted in care of the publishers in order to correct this fact in any future edition.

THE FINAL ADVENTURES OF SHERLOCK HOLMES

by Sir Arthur Conan Doyle

Collected and Introduced by PETER HAINING

For many years it has been widely accepted that the complete canon of Sherlock Holmes' adventures by Sir Arthur Conan Doyle consisted of fifty-six stories and four novels. But there have also been persistent rumours of a number of other items that Conan Doyle wrote about his world-famous detective and which, for one reason or another, have never been included in the collected works.

Now, after painstaking research in both Britain and America, the final remaining authentic accounts of the great sleuth are collected here. Stories, plays and poems, complete with fascinating details such as original publication information provide new insight and revelations about the Great Detective. This volume will undoubtedly be welcomed by every Holmes enthusiast and find a place of honour in Sherlockian libraries throughout the world – for in these pages Sherlock Holmes returns from oblivion . . .

A SHERLOCK HOLMES COMPENDIUM

Edited by PETER HAINING

Originally published to commemorate the fiftieth anniversary of the death of Sir Arthur Conan Doyle, the man who created this remarkable saga, the *Sherlock Holmes Compendium* has now been fully revised and updated by Peter Haining to include a wealth of new material. Bringing together some of the best articles, essays and illustrations concerning the Holmes legend since he made his début in 1887, the *Compendium* boasts among its contributors such luminaries as J. M. Barrie, P. G. Wodehouse and Anthony Burgess, as well as the actor who personified Holmes on the cinema screen, Basil Rathbone.

With new essays including an exploration of the character's representation on television, the *Sherlock Holmes Compendium* also contains a generous helping of puzzles and quizzes to test your knowledge, and remains essential reading for any fan of 221b Baker Street's most famous resident.

Warner Books now offers an exciting range of quality titles by both established and new authors. All of the books in this series are available from:

Little, Brown and Company (UK),
P.O. Box 11,
Falmouth,
Cornwall TR10 9EN.

Alternatively you may fax your order to the above address. Fax No. 01326 317444.

Payments can be made as follows: cheque, postal order (payable to Little, Brown and Company) or by credit cards, Visa/Access. Do not send cash or currency. UK customers and B.F.P.O.: please send a cheque or postal order (no currency) and allow £1.00 for postage and packing for the first book, plus 50p for the second book, plus 30p for each additional book up to a maximum charge of £3.00 (7 books plus).

Overseas customers including Ireland please allow £2.00 for postage and packing for the first book, plus £1.00 for the second book, plus 50p for each additional book.

NAME (Block Letters) ....

....

ADDRESS ....

....

....

☐ I enclose my remittance for ....

☐ I wish to pay by Access/Visa Card

Number ☐☐☐☐☐☐☐☐☐☐☐☐☐☐☐☐

Card Expiry Date ☐☐☐☐